TULIPS AND LOST TIME

EMILIA FINN

ISBN: 978 1 922623 84 3 (Paperback)

ISBN: 978 1 922623 85 0 (Hardcover)

Paperback and eCover design: Britt @ Chaotic Creatives

Hardcover design: Britt @ Chaotic Creatives

Editing: Britt @ Bookish B Editing

First printing edition 2024.

Beelieve Publishing, Pty Ltd

PO Box 407,

Woy Woy, NSW, 2256

Australia

www.emiliafinn.com

EMILIA FINN, the ROLLERS logo, the CHECKMATE SECURITY logo, STACKED DECK logo, and INAMORATA are all trade marks of Beelieve Publishing, Pty Ltd

ALSO BY EMILIA FINN

(in reading order)

The Rollin On Series

Finding Home

Finding Victory

Finding Forever

Finding Peace

Finding Redemption

Finding Hope

The Survivor Series

Because of You

Surviving You

Without You

Rewriting You

Always You

Take A Chance On Me

The Checkmate Series

Pawns In The Bishop's Game

Till The Sun Dies

Castling The Rook

Playing For Keeps

Rise Of The King

Sacrifice The Knight

Winner Takes All

Checkmate

Stacked Deck - Rollin On Next Gen

Wildcard

Reshuffle

Game of Hearts

Full House

No Limits

Bluff

Seven Card Stud

Crazy Eights

Eleusis

Dynamite

Busted

Gilded Knights (Rosa Brothers)

Redeeming The Rose

Chasing Fire

Animal Instincts

Pure Chemistry

Battle Scars

Safe Haven

Inamorata

The Fiera Princess

The Fiera Ruins

The Fiera Reign

Mayet Justice

Sinful Justice

Sinful Deed

Sinful Truth

Sinful Desire

Sinful Deceit

Sinful Chaos

Sinful Promise

Sinful Surrender

Sinful Fantasy

Sinful Memory

Sinful Obsession

Sinful Summer

Sinful Sorrow

Sinful Corruption

Lost Boys

MISTAKE

REGRET

Crash & Burn

JUMP

JINXED

Underbelly Enchanted

The Tallest Tower

Diamond In The Rough

Lost Kingdom

Luc and Kari

Tulips and Lost Time

Rollin On Novellas

(Do not read before finishing the Rollin On Series)

Begin Again – A Short Story

Written in the Stars – A Short Story

Full Circle – A Short Story

Worth Fighting For – A Bobby & Kit Novella

AUTHOR'S NOTE

Tulips and Lost Time includes difficult topics such as implied/off page pregnancy loss, off page gun violence, and murder.

Reader discretion is advised.

Note: this book was written for existing fans of Emilia Finn. All attempts were made to ensure the story stands alone, but numerous references exist from earlier books that may be confusing to new readers.

FOREWORD

Dear reader.
Skip chapter 16.
Trust me.
You won't like it.

TULIPS AND LOST TIME
EMILIA FINN

PROLOGUE
LUC

"It's time to go," Jess murmurs. My younger sister. One of two—identical twin girls—both hovering in the NICU and peering over my shoulders as I stare down at a sweet, five-pound, teeny tiny, blonde-haired baby.

Billy.

My daughter.

She's too small, too thin, and way too fucking fragile for me to take home on my own. But our bags are packed. The crib has been built. The car seat is ready, and there are approximately seven hundred pink, and pastel green outfits hung in the closet, in the room we dubbed Billy's, inside the house I bought for my wife.

We did all the things… Dated. Married. Purchased our own real estate. And then styled a nursery.

We followed the steps and obeyed the rules.

Sort of.

But it was all for naught, it seems.

Because if the universe wants to fuck a guy up, it'll do it, whether we stick to the rules or not.

Jess sets her hand on my arm, her glossy, painted fingernails tapping my muscle and drawing my attention. She's the more outspoken of my sisters. The louder one. Though Laine has been known to destroy a man when it was necessary. "They've discharged her, Luc. We've gotta take her home."

1

"But Kari—"

"She would want this." Laine leans around me and picks up the baby—her niece—and presses a gentle, adoring kiss to her brow before turning away and nestling the bundle in her car seat. "She doesn't want you guys hanging around here longer than necessary, Luc. You know that."

"Because she's always the fucking martyr." I turn now that the hospital crib is empty but for rolled blankets and a lost sock.

One tiny sock for one tiny foot.

"This isn't what we planned." I hate that my eyes itch. That my stomach rolls with nerves and the world seems to tip on its axis. "We were gonna take her home together."

"Sometimes plans change." Jess bends to grab Billy's unused diaper bag, overflowing with all the things an expectant mother packs as her ninth month approaches. Bibs. Blankets. Pacifiers. A cute little brush, though fuck knows, we were never gonna use it at the hospital. "You're a dad now, Luc." She hefts the heavy bag up and slips the straps over her forearm. "Your priority is Billy. Everything else needs to be dropped down a peg on your totem pole."

"Not Kari." I look down at my daughter and swallow the painful lump at the base of my throat. "I never agreed to push my wife down a step."

The NICU doors slide open, a humming hallway filled to the brim with nurses and medical staff marching to their own beat as they go about their work. But in the doorway, my best friend in the whole world waits, his sparkling green eyes shimmering. Because he didn't agree to this either. He never accepted a world where Kari wouldn't be number one.

Because Jess and Laine are my sisters.

But Kari is his. She was his to protect first. His sister to raise after their parents died, even though he was still a kid himself.

"Marc...?"

He sets his hands on his hips, his six-foot frame slumping under the pressure of life and loss. To love and grieve and live, when others aren't so lucky. He swallows, so the movement of his Adam's apple is obvious, then he shakes his head and sighs.

Speechless.

Broken.

"It's time to go." Jess picks up the baby car seat in one arm, a woman who clearly knows how to do this stuff, considering she has two of her own. Then she wraps her free arm around mine and forces me to move. "Insurance isn't gonna cover another night, Luc, and sticking around any longer would be like burning money. You can put those funds in Billy's college account instead."

"I don't know how…" I search the bland white walls and the humidicribs that span the room. Other parents exist within a world that terrifies them. Some babies cling to life, half the size of my daughter. Some, even smaller. Machines breathe for some, while others get to graduate to their mother's embrace instead of an uncaring plastic container.

The NICU is a world unlike any other. Where a baby is torn into existence, sooner than they'd intended, and placed inside a contraption like it could somehow simulate the comfort of a womb.

"I'll probably need bottles," I mumble, my mind spinning off in a thousand directions. "Formula, right?"

"I've already taken care of it." Laine moves just two steps ahead of us. "I got you all the bottles and nipples and formula and stuff you need. It's all set up at home."

"And diapers?" I don't know if I'm floating. Or walking. *Am I moving at all?* I can't be sure. "We got diapers?"

"Everything is ready at home," Jess murmurs. "And we'll stay with you till you're comfortable." She leads me through the open NICU doors and into the hall where her husband waits with *their* twin girls—*not* identical. *My* twin sisters are both blonde and blue. But hers are opposites. One blonde and one brunette. One light-skinned, and the other with a year-round olive complexion. They both hold their father's hands, one on each side, but they're still young. Still excited for their brand-new cousin to be here.

Not old enough to understand the circumstances that surround her birth.

"Lenaghan." Kane Bishop—Jess' muscled, mercenary, tatted husband—lifts his chin in greeting. He glances down at the baby that doesn't look a great deal different than his Luna, softening his eyes at the bundle who now expands his family. Then he flattens his lips and brings his focus back up. "She's doubled in size since yesterday, I swear."

"We're taking her home." Jess brushes by him, absorbing the way his nose practically touches her earlobe as we pass, and closing her eyes for a beat as she takes his comfort. Because outside of this, outside of me, her life is amazing. Her marriage, solid. Her daughters, perfect. Her entire reality is the kind you would find in all the great literary pieces.

But now she's in this blip with me. Her loyalty to her big brother ensuring she experiences this horrifying existence where, just weeks ago, we were thrilled for the babies who would soon arrive. With balloons and cake, music and all the people we love, we toasted to new life.

But that excitement is gone, and in its place, worry.

Fear.

Exhaustion.

"Can we come by the house, too?" Kane turns as we continue, his words gentle when, before now, I wasn't sure the guy knew how to be that way. "Luc? Mind if me and the girls drop by? They'd love to see Billy, and you could do with the company."

"Yeah." *I don't care. I don't know. I don't even know what day it is anymore.* "Whatever."

"Angelo's getting the car," Laine inserts, leading us along the hall and toward the elevator at the end. Typically, parents leaving the NICU is a celebrated event. Babies, born too small, or too sickly, growing large enough and strong enough that they get to break out and find freedom. Parents, caged in a room filled with despair, elated at the idea of taking their precious baby home.

I should be high-fiving the nurses we pass for their hard work over the last couple of weeks.

So why does it feel like I'm leaving my heart behind, too?

"Meg went grocery shopping," Laine adds. "And Angelo got a bunch of ready-made dinners stacked up in the freezer for you."

"Not that you'll need them," Jess adds, turning in the elevator and setting the baby on the floor as the door slowly closes. "We'll be by the house every day. I'll cook your dinners, and we'll eat with you, since we like to spend time with you anyway."

"I think I'd like to be alone." The words scrape along my throat, coarse and painful as my brows pinch under the artificial light. I see our trio in the reflection of the silver doors. Siblings, all blonde, all blue-eyed, all quite tall, even the girls. They're moms now, curvier than they were in their teens. And I've filled out over the years, too. No longer a scrawny, too-thin skateboarder who ate nonstop, and still, couldn't maintain his weight.

Finally, I look down at my sleeping daughter, and already, I know she'll take after the Lenaghan side of her family more than she will the Macchio side.

Her mother, of course, possessed glittering green eyes and curly hair she always hated. Kari considered herself plain compared to my sisters. Her freckles, too ordinary. Her eyes, too dull.

And yet, I've spent my whole fucking life staring at her. Half of it, wishing I could call her mine.

"I-I think I'd like a little alone time," I repeat, coughing as the numbers above the doors approach the ground floor. "I know I just told Kane it was…" Okay. *Whatever.* "I don't want to host anyone right now—"

"It's not hosting," Jess growls. "We're not your guests, Luc. We're family."

"Billy is my family." I swallow the sticky, painful lump in my throat that insists on choking me. Then I bend and scoop Billy's car seat up, holding her with one hand while I reach out with the other and snag the diaper bag from Laine. "I want to just sit," I explain. I'm tired. So fucking tired. "I want to sit with her and relax."

"You can relax, even with us there," Jess tries again. "I want to do your dishes, Luc, not run your damn life."

"Maybe come over tomorrow." I move through the doors when they open and find Angelo parked just twenty feet away. He still drives his Charger; the same one he drove in high school. But now he's married to my sister, and instead of making out with girls in the back, he carts their baby around.

Everyone has moved on since school. Married. Made families. They've all found their slice of happiness.

Ironic, considering I'd found mine, too.

I had the girl. The wedding ring. The cute little house, and the completely sensible car after years of riding a motorcycle and copping shit because everyone thought it dangerous.

The joke is on us all, right?

I've never crashed my bike in my life. But that car, with all the airbags and safety ratings…

Fucking useless.

"Hey." I approach my friend and hand off the bag, though he wasn't asking for it. Then I shove the front passenger seat forward with practiced moves, something me and my friends have done a million times over the years. Careful not to jostle the baby, I climb into the back and clip the seat in to the base I guess my sister or someone secured while I sat in the NICU.

"The girls aren't coming?" Curious, Angelo's movements are slow as he dumps the bag and I pull the seat back into place and settle beside the baby. Finally, he closes the door and rests his arms on the frame, staring in at me and furrowing his brows. "Why do I get the feeling you're about to piss a bunch of people off?"

"Because I am." I fix my seatbelt and take Billy's tiny hand in mine, placing my finger in her palm and curling her tiny digits around until her nails, a little too long, become my sole focus. "The twins want to mother me."

"And you're running away?"

"I just need a minute of quiet." I stroke Billy's cheek with the pad of my thumb and exhale. "Would you leave Laine behind?" I gulp and drag my eyes away from the little girl who still has some Macchio features. The shape of her nose is all her mom's. The angle of her jaw. The curve of her eyes. "You waited your whole life to call her yours. Waited nine months for the baby to arrive. Waited through delivery to make sure everyone was safe. And then you just…" I drop my gaze and hate that my eyes burn. That they itch and tempt me to bring my hand up to swipe the irritation away. "Would you leave her behind?"

He shakes his head. Soft, silent, certain. All qualities this man has possessed since we were kids, banging around our friend's garage and pretending we knew how to play musical instruments. "No," he admits quietly. "I wouldn't leave her behind."

"But they're making me leave Kari," I grit out, my vision blurring, though I wish it wouldn't. "After all the promises I made and all the years of swearing to her brother I would keep her safe."

"It wasn't your fault, Luc." He plays with his car keys, dangling the set from the tip of his finger and blocking the rest of the world from looking into his car and witnessing what may be my undoing.

This… right now… today. May be the moment I die.

"That prick ran a red light. You didn't…" He shakes his head. "You couldn't have predicted that. You couldn't avoid it."

"Please take me home." I reach up and wipe beneath my eyes to rid myself of the persistent itch that won't leave me alone. "I can walk," I rasp out. "I will. I don't mind."

"You're not fucking walking." He pushes up straight and turns to study the girls who wait by doors. They hurt for me. I know they do. They love me, just as I love them. And they grieve for me, just as I've grieved for them during their times of need.

But I don't have room for them right now.

I don't have the shoulders to carry their pain on top of my own.

"I'm taking them home," Ang announces. "He wants a few hours alone."

1

LUC

HOMECOMING

"**S**o this is it." I set Billy's car seat on the kitchen counter inside my nineteen-sixties fixer-upper on the very edge of town, unsnapping the straps and freeing the too-small infant from her cushioned safety. Then I pull her to my chest and *hope, pray, beg* for the emptiness I feel to fill with something else.

Something not quite as painful.

I've held a thousand babies in my life. Starting with my twin sisters, six years younger than me, then their kids, our friends' kids, my godson, plus the few I've delivered over the years on the job as a paramedic.

Babies don't scare me, not even the small, slightly early kinds.

But bringing this one home without her mom by our side—*terrifying*.

I study Billy's cheeks, chubby despite her prematurity. Her long lashes and wispy, blonde hair.

"This is home," I murmur, turning a slow circle, though I watch only her. "The kitchen, where Mom makes her coffee and kisses me on the head. Right..." I bring my hand up and tap at the back of my skull, precisely where my spine begins. "Here." She drops those kisses without thinking, a little gift just for me. They're my favorite kind. "And over there," I drag my focus up and glance toward the ratty couch in the living room, still a little messy with unfolded laundry. A tea towel, draped over the arm to dry a spot of water I'd spilled the same day we ended up in the hospital.

Seems like a lifetime ago now.

"That couch is where Mom was sitting just last week." I gently bounce the sleeping baby and wander closer. "You were swimming around in her tummy, kicking her ribs and searching for more space to stretch your legs. So we pointed a flashlight at her belly to make it fun." I lean in and press a kiss to the tip of her button nose. "You chased the light like you were in on the game all along."

Billy is just eleven days old. Still new. So she doesn't open her eyes to hear me chatter.

She doesn't coo or make a lot of noise.

She's just... silent. Unimposing. Exactly like her mom.

I move into the living room and kick a pair of boots to the side, so they don't become a tripping hazard later when the world leaves us alone and it's just me and her and a whole house to navigate on our own.

"Do you wanna see your room?" I wonder. Though I ponder the panic that races along my throat. The ache in the base of my belly, and the grief I feel at the idea of heading upstairs.

Why does it hurt so much?

Because it was Kari's domain. The nursery was her design. Her execution. Her hard work. And in the end, it was supposed to be her prize, where she could bring her babies home and rock in the chair she selected from the store in the city.

"We could see the wall Mom painted for you," I rasp. "The cute little clouds and the tree she sketched with her belly getting in the way. She did it all on her own," I admit, gulping down the dread that attempts to eat me up. "I wasn't around very much," I whisper. "Because I wanted to work extra shifts and save money for you. I thought I was doing the right thing."

I move out of the living room and ignore the shopping bags by the door. The jumbo packs of diapers I never purchased. The wipes, stacked by the box. I pass gifts, some still in wrapping paper, because we didn't get time to open them yet.

And though my heart pains, I place my foot on the first step and start up. Slowly. With an anvil sitting on my chest, and yet, obligation toward my daughter.

She exists, and she deserves a father who is coping, even when it feels like he left his soul inside a hospital.

"I'll put safety gates on these stairs in the next month or two," I mutter, the familiar sirens of a fire truck wailing in the distance. There's no smoke in the air. No flames to be seen outside my windows. Probably a cat in a tree, or a car turned on its head out at Piper's Lane. Neither of which are problems I need to worry about. Not today, and not for another month or so. "Mommy and I already bought them," I tell Billy. "They're packed in a box and ready to go. But we figured there was no point putting them up until you could at least crawl. No need to *create* a tripping hazard until you were on the move."

She dozes. Completely and totally at ease, though I wonder how that could be. She grew in her mother's stomach for eight months. Existed only within Kari's body. Slept to the sound of her heartbeat. Swam in the warmth she won't ever know again.

And now she's on the outside. In the cold. The draft. Where clothes itch and stomachs rumble.

There's no way this world is as comfortable as the place she was before it. But she snoozes in my arms now, none the wiser that the heartbeat she knew is now…

It no longer beats where we can hear.

"You'll let me know when you're hungry, right?" I crest the top of the stairs and spy the gates perched against the wall, in their boxes, just like I said. "You just say so, Billy. Tell me, and Daddy'll get you a bottle."

My phone chirps in my back pocket. A trill I have no desire to listen to. A bleating that grates on my nerves. There's only one person on the planet I want to hear from right now, so I reach back and free the device from my pocket. But I find Kane's name on the screen. My brother-in-law. My family. He's a damn good guy to know. But he's not who I want to talk to right now. So I silence the call, and the device, then I drop it to the carpeted floor and continue toward the nursery.

"Even if you don't like the colors," I whisper, repositioning the baby in my arms and holding her impossibly closer, "don't tell your mom, okay? She worked really hard for months. She didn't even stop working until the day you were born. So everything she did, she did it when she probably should have been resting."

My phone continues to vibrate, humming against the floor as I put more space between it and us. But then I pass the main bedroom. The scent of tulips playing in the air. Kari's perfume, tickling my nose as I wander by the door. The curtains are still drawn; the room, dark. We haven't slept in there in almost two weeks, and as proof, my back still aches, because I chose a shitty recliner chair instead of coming home.

They made me leave Kari.

There was no way in hell I was leaving Billy, too.

"Can you smell that, beautiful?" I lift my nose and inhale the sweet floral scent that shrouds our home. "You would recognize that smell, huh? It's your mommy."

I stop in front of the nursery door, the plain white paint a lie when I know what exists on the other side. We didn't want bright colors in the communal spaces. Pink or blue, clashing with everything else we have. So the door is bland and boring. The secrets it holds, so wonderful in contrast.

But it was a secret Kari and I got to share. A future we got to be excited about.

Licking my dry lips, I wipe my moist palm on the leg of my jeans. Then I reach out and wrap my hand around the knob.

The last person to enter this room was Kari. The last person to exit, Kari.

She dedicated countless hours to transforming what was once a guest bedroom, with an ugly, second-hand bed and a desk with a squeaky chair no one ever used, into a baby wonderland. She tore up the nineteen-sixties carpet, restoring the hard wood beneath. On her hands and knees, she replaced nails and smoothed out imperfections. She donned a mask and re-sealed the wood.

And then she painted the walls to create a garden of peace. With magical trees and mushrooms a fairyland creature could sit upon. She hand drew, then hand painted, fairies whose magic spread from wall to wall. She dabbed on fluffy clouds using a kitchen sponge. Draped fairy lights from the ceiling to simulate a starry night. Hung curtains that created a whimsical look. And when she realized they were too near the crib—dangerous for a baby—she stopped, rearranged, and moved everything around to make sure her vision worked.

She was determined to bring her babies home to a wonderland.

And in the end, she didn't get to come home at all.

Broken, exhausted after weeks in hell, I twist the handle and push the door open, and expose that colorful brainchild of the woman I swore to always protect. I breathe through the pain slicing up through my stomach. The loneliness that eats at my soul. The lost time, already too much, and still more to come.

But Billy sleeps. Comfortable in her daddy's arms. Warm, wrapped in the same pink blanket her mother came home from the hospital in. "This is your room, Bill." I twist to give her the best view, though her eyes remain closed and her sleep, unencumbered. "That's your bed, baby girl. And your bookshelves. Your changing table." My voice catches, the emotion lodging in my esophagus and taking my breath away. "And Mommy's chair."

I head toward the recliner, far and away more comfortable than the one I've slept in for weeks. Suede fabric, soft brown, kind of the same shade as Kari's hair. A little yellow blanket hangs over the back, and pockets in the side hold hidden treasures. Teething rings; though we were aware those won't be required for a while. Rattles; she won't be able to use those yet. Diapers; we'll change those at the table, anyway. Butt creams; table.

Everything this chair holds is useless for now. But we're over-preparers. Both of us. We work in the medical field—me, an EMT, and her, an RN— which means we like to make sure we have a bit of everything, just in case.

It's who we are in our souls. Prepared. Over-thinkers. Worriers. But usually calm in an emergency.

All except that one time.

Billy stirs in my arms, for the first time since before we left the hospital. She scrunches her lips and tenses her belly, and somewhere in the base of her throat, she growls.

"You gotta poop, Bill?" I move closer to the chair and stare down at the suede. At the cushions already molded to Kari's shape. The few strands of hair she's already left behind.

This is her place.

Her domain.

This was her claim, and her dreams, all wrapped up in a rounded belly and a welcome pregnancy. But she's not here. She didn't come home. So I turn at the chair and back up until my calves touch the fabric. Drawing a deep breath and exhaling to rid my body of the anxiety swirling in my blood, I lower onto the cushions and readjust Billy until she's vertical, her cheek on my chest and her feet in my lap.

"Let's let gravity help you out a little, beautiful. Push down on that gas and get rid of it." Reclining back, I reach across to the lever on the side of the chair, and flicking the footrest up, I kick my boots off and snuggle in.

I'm not sure we'll leave this spot for a while.

"Do you miss her too, Bill?" I bury my nose in the warm spot behind my daughter's ear and inhale. "Does it feel like half of you is missing? Because," my voice catches. "Same." I sniffle and count on my willpower alone. To remain whole. To not break down and ruin what is supposed to be a happy day for my baby. "Do you want Daddy to tell you a story? Because I can. I can tell you everything." I press a kiss to her plump cheek. "Why don't I start with the first time I laid eyes on your mom?" Slowly, a shaky grin works its way across my lips. "It was a good day. I met my best friend *and* your mom. I had no clue that would be the day that would change my whole world."

2

LUC

THE BEGINNING OF THE END

"What do you mean you're getting a new brother and sister?" I shove my lunch into my mouth like the world is heading into a depression and this will be my last chance to eat for the foreseeable future. It's not, of course. My parents aren't, like, rich or anything. But we have a decent house. We have clothes and shoes and dinner on the table every night.

Which is a hell of a lot more than Ang gets, that's for sure.

But I'm twelve now, and hell if that doesn't mean my stomach doesn't always feel empty anyway.

"You don't just get new brothers and sisters like they come from a catalog." I roll my eyes. Lounging back on his ratty couch, I side-eye the television while Sam and his brother, Alex, play a racing game on the PlayStation. "They're not even babies. Who adopts a grown ass kid?"

"Swear like that in front of my mom," Alex growls, "and she's gonna shove soap down your throat."

I take another hefty bite and crunch down on the chip sandwich filling my mouth. "Your family already has three kids, dude. Why the hell would they adopt a couple more?"

"Because their parents died." Sam zooms ahead of Alex on the game, his shoulders and arms moving like that somehow makes his turns tighter. His speed, faster. Lowering his voice, he spares a fast glance for the doorway that leads to the kitchen, where all the adults talk adult stuff, and the girls—

Sam and Alex's sister, plus my two—play and squeal somewhere else in the house.

Because the Turners' home is where we all come to hang out.

Chief Turner's is where all the kids come to eat and chill.

Which is probably why the dude is adopting a couple of already-grown kids.

"They had a break in," Sam whispers. His eyes focus completely on the screen again. "Dudes wanted to rob them or something. And they had shotguns."

"You shouldn't have been listening to Mom and Dad talk about that stuff," Alex—aka X—grumbles. "It wasn't information for your ears."

Sam only shrugs. "Their parents got shot. Point blank, buckshot tore them up and made a huge mess. There was blood everywhere, Dad said. All over the kitchen and stuff."

"That's pretty shitty." I take another bite and bide my time until I can race. "The kids didn't get hurt?"

"Nope." His shoulders bounce as his car jumps a ravine and slams back on the road with sparks flying out the back. "The boy, Marcus, he's twelve, too. He grabbed his sister and hid in the closet till they left."

"And the robbers just…" I widen my eyes and picture the scene in my mind. Of course, a pre-teen's imagination, coupled with a Gran Turismo game, makes what I see all the more dramatic. Flying bullets, fighting men. A little ninja karate, maybe. Nunchucks, too. "The robbers left them alone?"

"Didn't even know the kids were there," X inserts. "Or didn't care. Dad reckons they didn't expect anyone to be home at all. Like the Macchios were supposed to be on vacation or something." He hisses in the back of his throat when Sam's car zooms up and smashes him from behind. "So when they got in the house and were busted by the parents, shit was already pretty noisy. They shot and ran. Didn't even go upstairs."

"So it was all over pretty quick, then?" I flop my leg over the side of the couch and kick X's elbow, earning a snarl that turns more severe when I grin. "Walk in, get busted, walk out, and the kids are off to the orphanage?"

"It's not like they're being adopted or anything." Sam cuts left and over-takes his older brother. "And not quick. The parents died at, like, midnight or something. Dad didn't find the kids until the next morning."

"Your dad found them? Like," I shoot forward on my chair and try to catch my friend's blue stare. "Him, personally?"

"Yeah, he was on duty when the call came in, but their house was all the way over on the other side of town. Marcus went to the other school." His tongue comes forward past his lips as he concentrates. It's funny because that's the face he makes when he's writing a song, too. And playing guitar. It's his concentration face. "I heard the cops knew that the Macchios had kids, but thought they'd ran during all the ruckus. Cruisers were all over town for hours trying to find them."

"And they were in the closet the whole time?" I glance back at the door when the girls playfully scream. Laine, Jess, and Sam's baby sister, Britt, are pretty damn inseparable. Just like me, Sam, and Ang... and sometimes X, too. Though he's on the fast track to becoming a cop just like his dad.

He snitches often enough.

"Now they're coming here," I conclude. "Marcus is our age, and the other one, the sister, is Britt's age?"

"Pretty much. I guess that's why Dad volunteered. He already had the same aged kids, and every other kid in town is eating out of our kitchen already."

I look down at my sandwich and smirk. *Yum.*

"Her name is Kari," X inserts, twisting his body to bring his hotted-up car around a tight corner. "And she's apparently kinda small for her age. So just..." He slams his controller to the couch and growls when Sam zooms ahead of him and crosses the finish line. "Goddammit. You cheated."

"I didn't cheat!" Sam tosses his controller into my lap, laughing as X pushes to his feet. "I'm just better than you."

"You're an asshole." Alex shoves past my couch, hitting my leg with his as he goes by and makes a beeline for the front window overlooking the yard. "They're gonna be here in a minute. So you should probably go home, Luc."

"That's rude." I set my half sandwich on my knee and pick up the controller still warm from Sam's palms. He takes Alex's controller and resets a new race. "I'm not leaving because you're feeling bossy." I select my car. My wheels. Paint colors. And when Sam defers to me, I select the track. "Did you ever consider talking to someone, X? You can get a little... ya know... controlling when things aren't going exactly your way."

"Did you ever consider shutting the fuck up?" He releases the blinds, so they snap back into place noisily. Then he turns to me and sneers. "This is my house."

"This is *our* house," Sam counters calmy. If Alex is the tense, grumpy Turner, then Sam is his mellow other half. Calm. Cool. Always kind. Hell, I'm not sure there's anything anyone could do to the dude that would trip his trigger.

Except, maybe, fuck with his family.

"And Luc is my friend," he continues. "Even if he's annoying sometimes."

"Hey." I shoot a look toward *my friend*. "Jackoff."

"He talks a lot," Sam continues, his lips twitching at the corners. "He's not very good at the drums."

"Hell, I'm not. I'm at least as good as Dave Grohl. And I'm still only twelve."

"Dave Grohl would wipe his ass with your play book," Alex growls. "Don't pretend otherwise. What you do is make noise, not music."

"I make damn good noise, considering my inferior instruments. And I have a plan to save up for a better drum kit. It's hard earning money when you're my age. No one trusts you to do the job right."

"That's not age," X grumbles. "That's just you."

"Boys?"

Mrs. Turner stops in the living room doorway, the perfect Mrs. Married Life homemaker. She wears a soft blue checkered dress, with a mini-half apron wrapped around trim hips and her hair styled in a bob I'd swear came straight out of the salon.

Except it didn't.

I know it didn't because I've been here since breakfast time, and salons aren't open that early.

"Dad is on his way back," she murmurs. Her eyes are blue, just like her three kids. Her hair, dark, just like theirs. She smiles, her lips curling with faultless lipstick until her straight white teeth glitter in the daylight flickering through the windows. "It's going to be a pretty big afternoon for us, okay? Marc and Kari are going to be scared and shy. So I thought maybe—"

I set my controller on the couch, unbothered about the race I'm supposed to be competing in, and instead, I shoot my hand into the air. It's like we're in school and she's my teacher.

"I'd like to stay, if that's okay, Mrs. Turner. I know the house is already kinda full, and it's only gonna get worse. And I know X has this *need* to have everyone stacked in their rightful place."

"Shut the hell up!"

"And welcoming new people into his home is gonna take effort and adaptation from him," I tease. "But I feel like Marc is gonna need friends, right? And he's our age." I jab a thumb back at my chest, then away toward Sam. "We're his age, which means he'll come to our school starting Monday. I just figure, he could do with the friendship."

"Luc, honey—"

"I think he needs family, Mrs. Turner. And I know I don't actually live here, but I still consider you my family."

Her eyes shimmer. Target: hit.

"We could take him out to the garage. Get out of your hair."

"We'll give him and Kari a tour of the house, Mom." Sam sets his controller down and rests his elbows on his knees. "Kids want other kids. They don't want adults."

"They're going to want quiet, honey."

"Sam's literally the quietest, calmest dude we know!" I press my hands together as though in prayer. "He's gonna want his people, Mrs. Turner. And he's already spent time with the chief. That's plenty of adult sh—" I choke my word down. Swallow the swear before I get myself booted out on principle. Then I smile. "That's plenty of adult time for now. I'll stick around for an hour or two, then I'll get the girls out of here and you guys can settle in for the night."

"They're here!" Alex practically flaps at the window. Nerves wafting from his pores and presenting as an almost six-foot teenager with ants in his pants. "Mom! They're here."

"Alright." She draws a deep breath and closes her eyes for a long, concentrated moment. Then she exhales and opens them again. She looks to Alex first and lifts a challenging brow. "Relax. Everything's going to be fine." Then to me. "Please don't rile everyone up, Luca. We want quiet." She lifts her voice when I snatch my sandwich and jump up from the couch, striding her way. "We want a peaceful transition." Then she slaps her hand to my chest and stops me when I try to pass. "We don't want drums. Or band practice. Or skating in the street."

I look down at her hand and scowl. "You're taking away all the good stuff, Mrs. Turner."

"Their parents died, honey. Just days ago. They weren't sick. There was no time to prepare, and there was certainly no closure. Imagine losing someone you loved as suddenly as they lost their family." She firms her lips, allowing me time to consider a world where such cruelty exists. "Imagine wanting to hug your mom just one more time, but you don't get to."

"I'm gonna hug my mom just as soon as I get home," I decide solemnly. "And my dad, too."

"And you're very fortunate to still be able to do that. Marc and Kari can't." Dropping her hand, she smiles and pats my shoulder so I can pass. "Calm, Luca. Lock it down."

I stalk straight toward the door as the crunch of gravel outside travels this way. Car doors slamming. One. Two. Three. I look down at my shirt—Tony Hawk, of course—then to my jeans, littered with crumbs I hastily brush to the floor. I fist my half-sandwich, but even with nerves swarming in my stomach, my appetite remains untouched. My need for food, far greater than any other influence. So I bring the meal up and take another bite as Sam walks up on my left, and Alex, on my right.

I glance over my shoulder and spy three little girls at the base of the stairs. Two blondes, the color of their hair so fair, it could almost be white. And their opposite, Britt, with black.

We all have sky-blue eyes, though the Turner family and mine share no DNA.

It's just a coincidence, I guess. One that becomes a little less pronounced when Ang is hanging around and his silver stare breaks up all the blue.

"Are we ready?" Mrs. Turner fusses with her dress. She smooths the already smooth fabric down, patting her mostly flat stomach and presses a hand to her chest.

I bet it's pounding.

Then she shakes her hair back and takes control, opening her front door and smiling for the trio sluggishly moving up the walkway.

A boy and a girl.

And Mr. Turner right behind them.

The boy—Marcus—is damn tall compared to the other guys in our grade, with black hair and eyes like emeralds. He already has a deep wrinkle pounded into the space between his brows, a line that will only grow deeper as he gets older. He carries a backpack slung over his shoulder and wears jeans a little too big for his body. A little slouchy as he digs one hand into the pocket, and the other wraps securely around a little girl's palm.

He studies us the way we study him, I think. Not entirely trusting of the situation. He's tired. Pissed. He's like a cat, I suppose, forcefully removed from his home and shoved into a world he never asked for.

But the girl, Kari… she's his opposite in a lot of ways. She's younger. Smaller. He has broad shoulders, while hers are tiny. His hair is cut short, hers hangs halfway down her back. His is black, hers, brown, and though his is ruler straight, hers comes with curls and frizz I'm not sure she knows what to do with yet.

Maybe that's something her mom did for her.

And now her mom…

I swallow as that thought ricochets through my mind.

Her mom is dead. Just like that. Here one minute and gone the next.

"Uh…" Mr. Turner carries suitcases, one on each side, and sets them on the concrete stoop. Then he clears his throat. "This is everyone." His eyes sweep across our crowd, pausing on me as he shakes his head. Since I don't *technically* live here. And I'm not *technically* part of this family. "Marcus," he murmurs. "And Kari." He doesn't touch the duo. He doesn't dare hold their hands or break the grip Marcus has on his sister.

Already he, and the rest of us, know our place. And it's not holding Kari's hand.

"This is everyone," Mr. Turner repeats. "Alex," he nods to my side, "and Sam. That cutie back there," he points past us, "is Brittany. And her little friends are Jess and Laine." He chuckles. "Since I guess the whole neighborhood has come out for this. We've got Luc too."

He says my name. Not exasperated. Not mad that I'm eating his food again. Just... acceptance. I'm one of them. So I push my chest forward, pride pulsing from my skin like rainbows from a Care Bear.

"Luc and the twins live up the street," Mr. Turner explains. "But they're around a lot. And Luc will be in your grade at school," he says to Marcus. "Sam is a little older."

"I'll be your best friend." I take a bite of my sandwich and grin when a morsel of chip falls to the floor. "You'll live with them, but I'll have your back in the halls at school."

Marc regards me for a long minute, his stare a fiery hot poker that beats at my confidence, if only for a flicker in time. But then he blinks, looking down at the hand he holds, and the little girl who clings to a soft, pink blanket with sweet little bears printed on the edges. "My sister is in second grade." He stands on his toes and studies the girls at my back. "Any of you in second, too?"

"They're in first," Mrs. Turner says gently. "But the school isn't huge, and everyone knows everyone. The girls will get to play together at lunch. And my friend, Betty, will be Kari's teacher this year. So we'll keep a very close eye on things to ensure a smooth transition."

"Will I get to see her?" Marc's jaw ticks. Anger... or maybe worry, pulsing in every breath he takes. "I'm not in elementary school anymore, but I'm gonna want to see—"

"It's a K-through-twelve school," Sam inserts. "We're on the same grounds as the littles, just on opposite sides. So if you wanna see her or whatever, that'll work."

"We could walk you across," I volunteer. "Until you and your sister are comfortable with the new school and stuff." I look at the younger girl and tilt my head to study her glossy eyes. Bright green, just like Marc's. But where his are narrowed and angry, hers are just... round. And scared. And wholly trusting of the guy who holds her hand.

She studies me, starting at my shoes and working her way up my jeans. To my shirt. She examines the chain I wear around my neck. Then she leans a little to the side, as though to get a new view. A new angle.

Finally, she brings her curious eyes to mine and blinks when I lift my chin.

"I'm Luc. And you're little." I look at Marc and break away from our secure line covering the door. "Let's head out to the garage. We got a spare bass you could try." I clap his shoulder and walk down the steps. "We won't be extra loud or anything, Mrs. Turner. And I won't touch the drums. Promise."

3

LUC

NOT THE BEST FIRST IMPRESSION

"**I** hardly even saw her that first day."

Hours after bringing her home, Billy becomes my permanent accessory. Where I once wore a chain around my neck, I now wear a baby. Her hair is wispy soft, her breath, milky sweet. Her bedroom smells of poop after a giant clean up became necessary. And now... the sun droops in the sky outside as I wander to the kitchen to make a fresh bottle.

Kari planned to breastfeed the baby.

She had the pump ready to go, just in case. The pads for leakage. The bras that unsnap and provide the perfect access.

She had all these plans for what she considered the perfect family and circumstances. And yet, those plans came crashing down at the intersection just near Dixie's Ice Cream parlor.

"She was just a kid," I tell Billy. "Seven years old. No way did I think of her in any way except for how I thought of your aunties." I add formula powder to water, then one-handedly put the lid on the bottle. I make fast work of screwing it on, pinching the nipple so I can shake it. "That's not to say that I thought she was a brat the way I sometimes thought of Britt, Laine, and Jess."

I turn and lean against the counter, cradling the baby against my chest and shaking the bottle with my free hand.

"Those girls were little monsters. They were loud and silly and always fussing because they wanted our attention." I drag my bottom lip between my teeth, making it sting, if only to steal my mind away from how my chest aches. "They were beautiful girls who knew they had older, adoring brothers always watching their backs. So they acted the part and made sure they always kept us on our toes. But not your mommy."

I draw a deep breath until my chest grows. Until my lungs stretch and my throat hurts. Then I release it again, securing Billy against my heart. "She was always quiet, Bill. Always watchful. She idolized every move Marc made. Every single thing he did, she was nearby to watch. To catalog. But she never, ever complained. She refused to interfere or whine. She just wanted to be near him, and he..." I sniffle and shake my head. "He didn't mind one bit. They weren't like regular siblings. Daddy loves Aunty Jess and Laine with his whole heart. Always have. But back then, a sister was a sister, and most often, they're annoying. But not Uncle Marc. Not Mommy. They had this whole new family with the Turners. They had security. Food on the table. A bed to sleep in at night. They were never gonna be kicked out or anything, but I swear, they were always on edge anyway. Especially Marc. Acted like it was just him and Kari against the whole world."

"You don't *want* to watch the girls' track team?" I wander by the bleachers and shake my head at an eighth-grade Marc, who stares across the field, past twenty-something babes in tiny shorts and push-up bras. Because he'd rather watch the little-kid side of the school and his sweet baby sister who sits on a log and reads a Babysitters Club book, instead of playing hopscotch with the twins. "Dude. She's fine!"

"She's not fine." He walks with his shoulders hunched. His hands in his pockets and his eyes, dark because of how his brows shadow them from above. "She's having a rough time because some Becky-bitches aren't being nice to her in class."

"She's not with the Becky-bitches right now. She's with the twins. And they're gonna sweep the floor with anyone who wants to disrespect her. You know that."

"Kari's not like the twins." He meanders in her direction. He doesn't storm across and save the day. He doesn't intrude. But he watches the way a hawk watches its babies. "She's not even gonna tell me half the time when something is bothering her. She takes it, like she thinks it's her job to be the world's fucking dumpster, accepting everyone else's trash and carrying it on her own."

"Did you ever stop to think you're a tad… codependent?" I flash a wide grin when he turns, his eyes glacial and cutting. "She's a big girl, Marc. She's okay."

"She's *not* okay. She just won't admit it. Not to me and not to the twins."

"Hey, Marcus." Sassy St James and her *bee-eff-eff foreverrrrrr* strut along the track, their hands on their hips and a rosy, red blush working along their chests after a solid run in the sun. Sassy only has eyes for me. She has since… I don't even know. First or second grade, I guess.

Seems she found her hormones long before my sisters did. *Thank fuck.*

But Lauriana—her name, far more exotic than the person herself— smiles and searches for my best friend's attention. She's a preppy little blonde with big eyes, big lips, and an even bigger chest.

Nevertheless, Marc is the unattainable one. The silent, serious, broody guy all the girls swoon for because of his quiet mystique.

Not really a personality quirk I ever managed.

I'm the louder in our bunch. The one with the mouth and nary a filter. Sam is often introspective. Thoughtful. And Ang is… well, he's abused.

"Are you guys heading out to Piper's Lane this weekend?" Lauriana asks. She knows she has tits. In fact, she knows she was the first in her entire grade to fill out. So she juts her chest forward and searches desperately for Mr. Mystico's attention. "My brother is racing," she simpers. "He said he could get us beer if we wanna come along."

Dun, dun, dun. Wipeout!

"Her brother is out supplying his kid sister with booze," Marc rumbles, turning his back on Sassy and Lauriana and meandering Kari's direction. "Meanwhile, I won't be buying mine alcohol until she's fifty."

"You're a bit overprotective though, Macchio." I leave the girls in our wake and match his steps, my shoulder brushing his as we walk. "It's all fun and games to love your sister, bro. But you've gotta cut the cord and live at some point."

"I will." He slows near the end of the bleachers, tilting his head to get a look at his sister. "When Becky-bitches aren't making her hate herself every time *your* sisters aren't within listening range. Hey, Kari!" He frames his mouth with his hands and shouts loud enough to get both sides of the school's attention. Little kids skip rope on the elementary side. Others play tips, and giggle about… whatever little kids giggle about. But they all skid to

27

a stop when his shout echoes the fifty yards from where we are to where his sister is. "Hey!" He lifts his hand in the air and waves.

I drop mine in my pockets and look over our shoulders to the track girls. Then to the bleachers, to every other person in our school—except Sam and Ang—who watch on.

I'm not a shy guy. Not really. But hell if the back of my neck doesn't warm because my best friend is shouting at a bunch of little kids.

"You okay?" Lifting a thumb in the air, he wiggles it up, for *I'm good*, and down, for *come kick these bitches' asses*. Kari, of course, gives him a thumbs up and looks back down at her book.

"See?" I clap his shoulder and smile when Jess and Laine laugh. At us. At Kari. At this entire spectacle. "She's fine."

"She's *not* fine." But he lowers his hand and digs it into his pocket. Turning on his heels, he meets my slow stride and drops his head. "She says things to make me feel better."

"Because she loves you. She wants you to worry less."

"Telling me she's okay when she's not, doesn't make me worry less. It just means I can't trust her to be honest when something is bothering her. She's a fuckin' martyr who will lie and say whatever she thinks I want to hear."

"She's a good girl. And you both have severe codependency issues after a highly traumatic period in your life." I flash a wicked, playful grin as we approach Sassy and Lauriana again. But Sassy isn't staying back this time. She saunters forward and ducks under my shoulder, wrapping her arm across my back and hitching her thumb in the belt loop of my jeans. "Hey there." I lower my nose to the crown of her head and take a long whiff.

I'm not sure why I do that.

I have never, ever, no matter who snuggles into my side, found a girl whose scent makes me smile. But I continue to try anyway. It's a bit like Cinderella's shoe, maybe. Someday, I'll find the right one. But in the meantime, I'll keep sniffing.

I'm not a creep, I swear.

"Your mom says I'm a creep." I rock in the chair in Billy's nursery and watch as she guzzles milk to the bottom of her stomach. She drinks too fast. Too greedy. Which is why she gets chronic stomach aches and explosive poo. But I'll be damned if I tell her to stop.

My job is to spoil her. To make her happy. To give her anything she wants.

No fucking chance I'm gonna tell her how to eat.

"She laughs about it," I whisper, as the streetlights outside flicker to life. We're on the very edge of town. The outskirts, where there are probably three lights in a three-mile radius. But one of those lights sits near the end of our driveway, providing a beacon for us to come home to.

It was a sign, Kari said, a few years back when I showed her the home we bought—the slightly dilapidated ranch that needed paint before the old coat dissolved and the whole house fell apart.

"But sometimes, Daddy does this creepy, old man laugh," I continue. "I do it to get a rise out of her. And it works." I drop my head back against the chair and study Billy's long, long lashes. "Daddy loves it most when he can make Mommy laugh. She doesn't do it often enough. Like Uncle Marc, she's too serious for her own good. So it's my job, my obligation," I press, "to make Mommy smile."

"Watch this!" I hold my board at the top of the halfpipe on the outdated side of town, where a skate park was once funded by the town council, and kids were given somewhere to hang out that didn't include robbing Jonah's store or racing around in the street and causing accidents.

A one-time infusion of cash was spent here, I guess. But no one factored in a maintenance budget. No one comes out here to check on the facilities. What is probably supposed to be lawn is just dirt. What is supposed to be smooth concrete slopes are now cracked and graffitied.

But they work for a group of kids who have no other options.

Not yet, anyway. But we'll build our own eventually. At the Turners' house, since they have the room and Mrs. Turner isn't likely to strangle us for it.

"Marc!" I cup my mouth and shout to drag his attention from the girls.

Not, like, girls our age who might think to come out here to flirt and play. But *the girls*, as in Kari, Britt, Laine, and Jess. Because wherever we go, they like to follow.

"Hey!" I bend and grab a rock from the top of the pipe, then lob it the thirty feet that separate us, gritting my teeth and thanking the gods when it lands in the dirt and doesn't hit anyone I love.

Maybe I don't want to hang with our sisters *all* the time. But fuck, I wouldn't dump them, I won't hurt them, and I sure as fuck won't let someone else bring them pain.

The rock thuds against the ground, spitting up plumes of dirt and drawing Marcus' focus. Then he turns on his heels, shielding his eyes with the span of his palm as the sun begins to set behind me. "What?"

"I call this the Luca Lenaghan Classic." I drop into the pipe while I've got his attention—not only his, but the girls', too—and zoom across to the coping on the other side. Shifting my feet and grinning as wind blows through hair I've grown out shaggy over the summer, I snap a frontside one-eighty before switching into a nollie. My board slams down onto the steel coping, the noise a ricocheting blow that echoes from here to… well, probably back to town. But I land my move and turn to ride the board's momentum back the way I came. "Fuckin' nailed it!"

"That's not a Luca Classic." Shaking his head, Ang pushes away from an old, splintered wooden bench, the rough lengths of timber snagging his jeans as he steps away. But he's smiling today. His hair, longer than mine, is tied back, and the black eye we all pretend we don't see is fading.

His daddy'll give him a new one before the week is out.

But today… today he's smiling.

He tosses his board onto the pipe and steps on, a smooth transition as he zooms by me and winks for the girls who wander closer to watch. "That was a Nose Blunt Stall, stupid. Stop acting like you're world class."

"Oh!" I laugh. "My bad. You want the *real* Luca Special?"

"I thought it was Luca Classic?" Marcus grumbles. Always too serious. Too cranky. "Your story isn't even lining up, bro."

"Here. Let me show you." I step off my board and jog to the top of the pipe, my shirt flapping as the breeze finally picks up and my skin prickles under the bite of the sun. I set my beloved skateboard on the coping—the board, second only to the drum kit I finally saved up enough for—then I place my foot in the center and send up my prayers.

Because this is gonna hurt.

Reaching up, I swipe the sweat from my brow as another summer day melts us where we stand, and Marc and I stare down the barrel of another school year. The twins watch me like I hung the moon and the stars. Their blonde hair, whipped back in high ponytails. The exact same height on their heads. The same colored elastic. The same wispy bits falling out the back.

They're not the kinds of twins who match their outfits and accessories, so it's not like we can't tell them apart. But fuck, their faces are identical. Their mannerisms. Their smiles.

And the way they think I'm the funniest fucker on this planet.

I draw a deep breath and side-eye a smug Brittany—she knows what's coming. Then a shy Kari, her eyes trained on my feet and her hand clutched around a book.

The others, I think, will give us a run for our money in a few more years. They'll want to party. To talk to boys and dress in such a way that gives the rest of us a coronary.

But not Kari.

She'd sooner spend her Friday and Saturday nights with a book.

"Let's go already!" Britt sets her hands on her head, her black hair a magnet for the summer sun. "Show us the Luca Special, then take us to Dixie's. I want ice cream."

"Yeah!" Laine's eyes widen with hunger. "I want to go to Dixie's, too."

"Don't hurt yourself, Luca." Kari sets her foot on the edge of the halfpipe and inches closer. It's not like she knows what the Luca Classic is. Shit, three minutes ago, it didn't even exist. But she has a brain in her head and more common sense than the other three combined. Her eyes glitter with concern. And warning. Challenge.

Because she has fire beneath the silence she shows her brother.

"No one is filming you, Luca. Hurting yourself for laughs isn't smart."

"Really, though? Laughter is good for us." I send up my prayers and lift my bracing foot from the edge of the coping. And of course, my shitty placement and off-balance footing has the board sprinting away, one leg stretching one way, and the other, another. My stomach drops out my ass, then gravity takes hold and cruelly slams me to the concrete.

I pound the ground with the weight of a one-ton anvil sitting on my shoulders, the back of my head rapping against the ground and the oxygen in my lungs, vacating like, *dickhead, you don't need it anyway!*

The twins squeal out in delight as I roll down the pipe, a lifeless sack of potatoes as my limbs fold, one over the other. My board skitters away,

31

taking its own journey to wherever, while an unimpressed Sam, Marcus, and Angelo stand over me. Their arms folded. Their faces, matching.

Triple the scowls.

Triple the flattened lips.

But my pain is worth it, because Britt, Laine, and Jess cackle, leaning on each other as they laugh and heave for fresh air.

Best of all, Kari smirks. It's just a small upturn of her lips, and when our gazes meet, a roll of her eyes. She's mature beyond her years, and the good old Tom and Jerry humor left her long ago. But when my board rolls back down the pipe, slamming into the base of my spine and reignites the other girls' glee, Kari's smile grows fractionally larger.

"That," I wheeze, reaching around and rubbing my back, "is the Luca Classic."

"You're so dumb." Sam grabs my hand and yanks me to my feet. He keeps hold of me as I sway and search for balance. His laughter, muted, but existent. Then he slaps my back and pretends it's to dislodge the dust from my shirt. "Class clowns rarely turn out to be president, Lenaghan."

"I don't wanna be president anyway." I rub my backside and limp across the pipe, bending to pick up my board before it thinks I don't love it anymore. "I wanna be drummer for the Foo Fighters."

"Foo already have a drummer," Angelo chides. "And he's better than you."

"Then I wanna be drummer for *our* band. Which," I hug the board to my chest and turn back to my friends. My family. "Still needs a name. We got a gig coming up soon, and we still don't have a name for people to talk about."

"We don't need a name." Sam jogs across the width of the pipe and swoops down to scoop up his board, then he turns back, but looks down at the pile of skates that've been dumped. "You girls need to pick these up. We're not carrying them all back for you today."

"But they're too heavy," Jess complains. From laughter to whining, she looks across at me like she thinks I'll save the day. "It's too hot, and we have such a long way to walk. We can't carry them, too."

"I'll carry yours, Kari." Marc snags the purple pair my sisters gifted her last summer, tying the laces together to create a handle that he can swing over his shoulder. Then he strides across and grabs a backpack filled with half-empty water bottles and the trash left behind after we ate the sandwiches and snacks Mrs. Turner packed for our day in the sun. He loads himself up—skates, skateboard, bag—then he turns back and extends his hand for the book she holds, too.

Because Kari is a protected species, and there's no one on this planet, *nothing*, that could get between Marcus Macchio and the duty he has declared for himself as far as his sister is concerned.

"Fine." My ass still smarts, and now I have a mystery ache in the depths of my left elbow. But I follow Marc's lead and tie the laces on the skates so I can carry the damn things and my sisters can remain the passenger princesses they've decided they get to be. I set my board on the ground and roll my eyes, because Jess and Laine know exactly how to get their own way. Jess sits on the very front of the board, folding her long legs up into an impossible pretzel and taking up as little space as possible, then Laine follows, piggybacking her twin so I have two, tiny blondes sitting on a single board and a backache pending.

"Here." Angelo takes the twins' skates and slings them over his shoulder. "Since you gotta push."

"I don't know why we bring you out here," I grumble, bending at Laine's back and using her shoulders as handles. Then I push across the smooth concrete and onto the hard-packed dirt so my friends and I create a convoy of high schoolers and their little sisters.

Well. Except Ang... he doesn't have any sisters.

"It's not cool for us to hang out with little kids, ya know?" I give Laine's shoulder a teasing squeeze until she squeals. "I could be hanging out with Sassy St James right now."

"Sassy St James is nasty," Kari mumbles, drawing a lifted brow of surprise from Marcus as he holds her hand and helps her onto his board. He only has the one freeloader, so Kari gets to stand and take a free ride while Marcus makes gentle, subtle adjustments with his foot. "Sassy's always coming over to our side of the school to pick on Maybel."

Stunned, my nose wrinkles in confusion. "Who the hell is Maybel? And who names their kid Maybel anyway?"

"She's really nice," Kari shrugs. "And shy. She's two years younger than Sassy, and Sassy is a giant jerk who could only win a fight against someone smaller than her."

"Tell us how you really feel," Marcus chuckles. "Anyone else at school bothering you? Because we could slide on over to your side and take care of things."

"Yeah," I laugh. "Nice one, Marcus. Let's beat on a bunch of fourth-grade girls and remain normal, respectable citizens."

"We take care of business," Britt declares. Like the others, she hitches a ride on Sam's board, and while he does all the work, she checks her nails and smirks. "No one comes near us, because we're too scary for the basic girls."

"The basic girls." I snort. Pretty sure they're called basic bitches. But I guess it's not cool to say that at her age. "You girls aren't creating conflict, are you?" I lean around and check my sisters' expressions. One pair of bright blue, then a second pair. Both of whom smile like they're innocent of all wrongdoing. "It's kinda my job to keep you in school. Not getting expelled because you can't stop fighting people."

"That would be so cool, though, right?"

I glance across at Britt's awed expression.

"Cool to get expelled? No! That would be bad."

"No," she snickers. "I mean, it would be cool to fight someone. Like, *pow pow*," she shadow boxes and punches the air. She risks unbalancing her board and slamming onto the road. But she was practically born on a skateboard. Her ability to balance is next level. "I've never punched anyone with my fists before."

"And you won't." Sam nudges the board to the right and leads us back toward town. "Good girls don't get into fistfights, Brat. They don't need to hit people to communicate."

But of course, she cocks her arm back, balls her fist, and smashes her brother's shoulder as snotty laughter escapes the depths of her throat. "Ow!" She giggles and stumbles off the board, almost tripping on her dusty and worn converse high tops. And all the while, Sam continues to walk. "That hurt!"

"Serves you right." He steps onto his board and grins. "Don't hit me, Brat, and you won't hurt yourself."

"Your shoulder is like rock!" She dashes across and jumps onto Ang's board. Uninvited. Without warning. Without permission. She takes his board and sails off ahead of our group, so her laughter echoes in the breeze. "I'm telling Mom you hit me," she calls out. "She won't let you have dessert."

"You all saw what actually happened, right?" Sam skips off his board and flips it up until he catches it in his arms. Then he hugs it to his chest and walks shoulder to shoulder with me. "You saw she hit me?"

"I saw nothing." I push the twins forward and make a show of bringing my hands up to cover my eyes. "Isn't that how things are with these girls? We see nothing. We hear nothing. And we get them out of trouble when shit is going down."

"Not Kari," Marc declares. "She does nothing wrong. Therefore, she doesn't need saving."

"I wanna learn the Nose Blunt trick." She twists on her board and searches first, Marc's eyes, then mine. "I stay out of trouble and give no one any reason to worry. But I want to learn the better tricks on the halfpipe."

"You're doing great with the moves you know, Kar." Marcus spins his sister back, rebalancing the board when her movements throw it off course. "You've got the ollie *and* the nollie."

"I know how to turn a board," she drawls. I hear the exasperation in her voice. But I sure as shit notice the way she *doesn't* show her brother the eye roll. "Good for me."

"You can also kick turn."

"I'm a pro at turning. I'm the next Tony Hawk."

I look down at my shirt and grin because I'm pretty sure ninety-eight percent of all the shirts I own have some variation of Hawk licensing attached to it. The rest of them have Dominic Broadbent on them—*world famous drummer.*

"I can teach you the Luca Special," I offer, bringing my focus back up and feeling absolutely no remorse when sweat dribbles off the tip of my nose and falls onto Laine's ponytail. That's what you get when you're being lazy. "It's super easy. I got it right the first time."

Snickering, Kari turns back and shakes her head. "You're a bit dumb, Luca Lenaghan. Hurting yourself for comedy is immature."

"*Immature.*" I swipe my forehead on the arm of my shirt and ignore the ache brewing deep in my back. "Am I the dummy for falling. Or are you the dummies for thinking it was funny?"

"You," everyone decides at once. Then Marcus shoots me a glare. "You're the idiot. And don't let me catch you teaching my sister the Luca Classic. If you put her in a situation where she breaks her skull, I'll break yours to match."

"So aggressive." Taunting, I chuckle and put more effort into my pushing. "Let's get to Dixie's. It's hot as fuck out here today."

4

LUC

POETRY IN ACTION

"Luc?" Jess' voice echoes from somewhere on the ground floor of my home. Same voice as Laine. Same intonation. Same inflection. Same cussing when something pisses her off. And yet, I can still tell them apart without even looking. "Hey, Luc? Where are you?"

Billy's already asleep, snoozing in my arms and completely relaxed after a bottle and a giant fart. She has a perfectly good crib I could put her in. A blanket I should wrap her in. She has a pacifier I could pop between her lips if she becomes fussy.

But I don't want to put her down yet. And she doesn't seem all that rushed to leave my arms either.

Just like I had an ache brewing in the base of my spine, pushing my sisters along a boiling, almost melting road in the height of that summer, I feel a similar ache in my arm now, holding a baby for hours without moving. Maintaining this exact position even though my bladder reminds me it's almost time to get up.

"Luc?"

"I'm upstairs."

I keep my voice low-ish. Just loud enough for my sister to hear but not so startling that the baby will wake. Then I turn my head on the cushion and study the doorway in silence. Counting down Jess' approach as the fourth stair creaks, then the third one from the top.

I'll fix them someday.

Maybe.

Eventually.

I told Kari I would. But like the floor she ended up doing on her own, this may just be another job I never find at the top of my priority list. Because there's always something more pressing calling upon my time.

I rock in the chair, gentle, slow swoops of the glider that seem to bring the baby comfort. Then I look my sister up and down when she stops in the doorway, her arms so often laden with her own twin girls, now occupied by a foil-covered plate.

She's still as beautiful as ever. As youthful.

Maybe her experience *as* a twin has prepared her for a life of being a mother to two. Because I'll be damned if she looks any older than she did back when we saw her off to college for the degree that would eventually have her sitting the bar exam.

She's got it all; the career, the kids, the husband.

She knows how to make things happen in her life, and even when the world gets a little cruel, she holds on and ensures everything rights itself in the end.

Just another skill I never quite mastered, it seems.

"I brought you dinner," she murmurs. Though she doesn't infringe on Billy's room. She doesn't cross the threshold and invite herself in. "We had baked chicken with all the trimmings."

"Potatoes?"

She grins, her sky-blue eyes twinkling in the overhead light now that the sun has gone down. "Parmesan smashed potatoes. Your favorite. Glazed carrots. And green beans, too." She slides her tongue forward and wets her dry bottom lip. "I ate with Kane and the girls because I knew you wanted to be alone for a while."

"But you couldn't go to bed without feeding me first?"

Her eyes well up, swelling because Kari is her best friend, too. Hurting, because all her life she's idolized the ground I walked upon. And now I'm in pain. "I'm never going to bed and leaving you out in the cold, Luc." She swallows, the bob of her throat visible as she looks down at Billy. "Can I hold her? You could eat," she explains, "and I could have a few minutes with my favorite niece."

"Your favorite?" I force a chuckle through my chest. The sound is tinny and not all that genuine. But it's better than breaking down and giving up on this fucked up world. "You have, like, five nieces, Jess. It's not nice to play favorites."

"We just won't tell the others," she teases. Finally breaking away from her spot by the door, she meanders into the room and carefully sets my dinner on the changing table. "It's still brand new," she snickers. "Still clean enough to eat off of it."

"Not true. Bill shat all over the place an hour ago." My stomach growls anyway. My last meal... I don't even know. Breakfast, maybe. While I sat by Kari's bed and choked down enough sustenance to get me through the day I never wanted to come.

Carefully pushing my legs down, I force the footrest back into its cavity beneath the chair and take extra care not to jostle the baby awake. I hold her with just one arm, numb as it may be, and use the other to push myself up until finally, my feet touch the floor, and pins and needles roll up through my legs to remind me I haven't moved in a while.

"I guess I'm kinda hungry," I admit, rocking Billy out of a habit I never possessed a mere ten days ago. Leaning in and pressing a kiss to her button nose, I wander toward my little sister to hand her off.

But I don't.

I don't offer the baby, and I don't know that I can breathe if she's not in my arms.

"I'll stay right here where you can see me." Jess scoops her hand into the crook of my arm. Her moves, smooth and practiced after a couple of years with her own. Then she backs up toward the recliner. Turning and watching where she's going would be easier. Smarter. But she keeps her word and allows my eyes to stay with my baby. "Eat something, Luc. You have to eat, or you'll make yourself sick."

"I wasn't ready to put her down." I move to the changing table and poke at the foil covering my still-hot meal. "We tried so hard for her, Jess. We put everything we had into this pregnancy. And now it's all just..." I shake my head and peel the foil open to reveal a chicken leg and more potatoes than any man should eat. But it's what Jess does. She feeds me. She takes care of me. "It all fell apart in a way I never could have predicted."

"Because you couldn't have." She settles into the chair and crosses her legs, drawing Billy up to sniff that sweet, new baby smell. "You can't predict an accident, Luc. And you sure as hell can't predict someone else's behavior when they're not following the law or doing the right thing."

"I've been driving since I was a teen." I snag a smashed potato between my fingers and bring it up to my lips. "I've slammed through that set of traffic lights a million times in the ambulance. Red lights and all. And I've never been hit."

"It was horrible luck," she whispers, sniffling as she strokes Billy's chubby cheek. "We can't explain it. We can't understand it. It's…" She sighs. "Sometimes, the world likes to hurt us for no reason at all."

"I can't accept that." Rage burns in my veins, turning my aching stomach to something much darker. Meaner. "I can't accept that there's no reason for this kind of bullshit. There has to be a lesson, right? Or a higher purpose. There has to be something better than *'just because'*."

"Maybe it was a lesson for the rest of us," she tearfully whispers. "A reminder to love our families. To appreciate what we have because a happily ever after isn't always guaranteed."

"I don't want to be the fucking guinea pig in everyone else's lesson!" I drag my hand up and clutch at my hair. Still a little too shaggy for a grown man. A little long, considering I grew up from that stupid *Luc's Classic* bullshit into the man I am today. I'm a professional, educated, responsible adult now. But I'm not so evolved that the universe didn't pick me and my family up and toss us into a blender for the fun of it. "I don't want my daughter to be everyone else's reason to appreciate what they've got," I groan. "That's not fair."

"I know." Jess swallows, an audible, visible movement. "Life is rarely fair. And the universe hardly ever punishes those who truly deserve it."

The universe is a faulty, broken-down machine everyone else considers their fucking be-all and end-all goddess. Ironic, considering nine times out of ten justice comes when a man takes things into his own hands.

"Did I ever tell you what happened to that Maybel chick from school?"

"Maybel?" Confused, curious, Jess's mind spins and swirls back two decades in search of context. A clue. "From school?"

"Yeah. The one Sassy St James was picking on."

"No, she…" She shakes her head. "Jesus. I don't think I've had even a single thought about her since middle school. She got really dark there for a while, right? Sassy was being a bitch, and Kari was sticking up for her for a while." She stops and draws a heaped breath when dots connect in her mind. "Oh geez. She got really dark way back around… like, seventh grade, right?"

"Yeah. Kari was always defending her. Practically throwing hands in the school halls when Marc wasn't watching."

Jess scoffs, soft and tear filled. "She's always had *way* more spine than he ever gave her credit for. But only when it came to standing up for someone else. Kari would take shit all day long and bottle it up to keep her company. She never said a damn thing in school to assert herself when people were picking on her. But the second anyone was throwing shade on someone else, she had her gloves on."

"Get out of my way, you ugly bitch."

I hear her first. Maybel Thompson's nasally, nasty, mean girl voice. But then the echo of the school lockers as a body slams against them comes right after. Setting my temper alight and my pulse scrambling in my throat.

I stop at the corner of the hall, just fifteen feet from the locker I know will now bear a dent the size and shape of Kari Macchio. But I stick to the shadows, narrowing my eyes when I catch sight of Maybel's fist slamming against the steel beside Kari's face.

My temper burns hot, sizzling in my veins and forcing my fists to close in preparation. But Maybel is a girl, and I can't very well go around the school hitting chicks. Not even to defend my best friend's baby sister.

"Why don't you just stay out of my fucking way?" she snarls. "Stay out of my halls."

"I was just putting my books away." Kari's voice shakes. Her breath falters. I know the sound of every inhalation she makes, because I've grown accustomed to listening every time she and Marcus are near.

Which, lucky for me, has been every damn day since I was twelve years old.

"You and I don't need to cross paths," Kari continues. "I never get in your way on purpose."

"Your existence is in my fucking way!" She grabs a handful of Kari's curly brown locks and holds on just tight enough to tilt her head to the side. "The fact you came to this school is *in my way*."

"Let me go." Kari reaches up to grab the girl's wrist. "Mayb—"

"You know what could make all this better?" The bitch leans closer, her braced teeth glittering under shitty fluorescent lights and her straw-like hair, lightened because of the glare off the lockers. "Ya know how my school life could improve, since everyone around here thinks they get to comment about me ever since *you* inserted yourself in my business?" She yanks Kari forward, then slams her back again until the back of her skull raps against the locker. "Is if you killed yourself." She leans closer. Intimate. "Go back in time, stand in front of the gun that killed your mother, and do everyone a favor."

I shove away from the wall and slap my feet against the ground to make it sound like I'm running. Distracted. Not paying complete fucking attention to the bitch whose hand whips away from Kari's hair like she's suddenly grabbed an electrical current. I lope around the corner with a wide smile plastered across my face, almost maniacal considering the rage burning in my blood.

Instantly, Maybel scoots away and loops her hands behind her back, all innocent and sweet like she wasn't just threatening a girl who has never, in her whole life, hurt anyone else.

Marc's at work today, saving cash for his doomsday stash *just in case*. And Ang is putting in a little time at the garage, working with his hands and avoiding home as much as humanly possible. Sam is hanging with his girlfriend, now that he found the love of his life—this month's, anyway—which means Kari-duty is all mine.

And I'm not allowed to hit girls.

So…

"Hey, Care Bear." I stride into their space and bend to snag her discarded backpack from the floor. I swing it onto my arm and ignore the tears welling in her eyes. The pulse I see pounding in her throat. I don't even smack Maybel upside her ugly fucking face, though it would feel good to get it out of my system.

Instead, I give her my back and remind her how utterly unimportant she is, then I drop my free arm over Kari's shoulder—an action Marcus would skin me for—and provide the girl a little of the school cred she so desperately requires.

It's obvious she won't say shit to save her life when the bitches come knocking.

"Marc caught a shift at the club," I murmur by her ear. Her long, mousy brown hair puffs in the humidity drenching the air, tickling my arm and itching my nose when I lean too close.

But I don't sniff.

Sniffing is for the girls I want to bang. Sniffing is most definitely *not* for my best friend's little sister.

"He asked me to walk you home."

"O-okay." She stumbles on her feet as I bring us around the corner and back into the hall I've already walked. She doesn't toss my arm away. Doesn't wrinkle her nose because it's hot and I'm sweaty after PE. She doesn't push me off or show her discomfort even as other kids stop in their tracks to watch us.

But she doesn't hook her arm across my back the way Sassy St James does, either, nor thread her thumb in the loop of my jeans.

She's passive.

And Marc is bound to have something to say about my little show when he hears about it tomorrow.

"Why do you let her push you around, Care Bear?" I loosen my grip on her shoulder as we emerge at the school's front doors and look out at the parking lot buzzing with movement and parents picking their kids up. "You could beat her ass if you wanted to."

"I don't know what you're talking about." She steps out from beneath my arm and starts down the school's front stairs. Then she turns and reaches out to take her bag when I'm close enough. "I can carry—"

"I've got it." I hold the pink and purple backpack like I'm not embarrassed to own it. Then I nudge us both to the right, away from the free-flowing traffic of cars, bikes, and little kids spilling out to find their mommies. "Let's walk this way," I mutter, keeping her in my vision and leading us away from the blacktop and into the trees surrounding our school. This town is essentially sitting in a valley, surrounded by trees and mountains. The best part about that means if you walk in any direction for just a few minutes, you end up in the forest. Where the temperature drops instantly and exponentially, and the noise of town recedes as though we've stepped through a door and closed it at our backs.

"I want you to tell me what the fuck is going on between you and Mad Rat."

"Maybel." She brings a hand up and absentmindedly rubs her scalp where the bitch tugged. "Her name is Maybel."

"Yeah, but she's a nasty bitch bully, and those types don't get the privilege of a respectable name." I fall into step beside Kari, looking down at her too-short four-and-something feet frame, and shake my head. "I heard what she said, Bear. So whether you admit it to me or not, I already know."

"It's not—"

"I'm not Marc." I adjust our direction, knowing this forest like I know the skate park and aim us toward an old, dilapidated house my friends and I know as 'Popcorn Palace'. Because it's shitty and derelict, and the ceilings are made of that ugly popcorn look. "You don't tell him the things that bother you because you never want him to worry. Just like he never tells you the things that bother him because he wants you to be happy and unaffected your whole damn life." I glance down and raise a single, challenging brow when she braves a look my way. "I get what you do for each other, and even if I think it's dumb, I understand it."

"It's not dumb." Cross, she scowls until a deep line forms between her brows. "It's called protecting your family."

"It's called non-communication and a trauma response." I skip to the left, because Kari Macchio has fire and a temper. She proves it when she swings out and attempts to smack me in the ribs.

Too damn bad she doesn't use that same fist to rearrange Mustard's stupid face.

"Someday, Bear, you and Marc will end up at a crossroads, where you're living separate lives. Both protecting each other. Both shielding the other from anything horrible. Until eventually, you realize you know nothing about each other."

"Agree to disagree." She lifts her chin and reaches up to swipe the moisture sitting beneath her eye. "Maybel's behavior is your fault, by the way."

"My fault?" *Kill yourself. Step in front of a gun.* "What the fuck do you mean it's my fault!?" I grab her shirt and pull her to a stop beneath a massive fir tree that blocks us from the sun. "How the hell is Moshpit's bullying my fault?"

"Because *your* bitchy girlfriend bullies Maybel, and now Maybel bullies me. Misery loves company and all that stuff, and you and Sassy are too popular to screw with. So she takes her temper out on me."

"First up." I narrow my eyes and point my finger. *Why?* She's a fucking kid. I don't have to defend myself to her. "Sassy isn't my girlfriend."

Defiant, Kari firms her lips and pops her hip. All attitude.

"She's a girl. And I sometimes hang out with her. But we're not, like, a couple or anything."

"So you're a player," she counters. "Dating a different girl every week, but returning to Sassy because she's easy and good for your ego?"

What the fuck? "No! What do you even know about egos and easy? You're a child."

"You're a child too, dummy." Exasperated, she steps around me and continues. She knows the way we're going. "The point is, Sassy is a bitch. You're a player. Maybel is someone else's victim, but instead of dealing with it the proper way, or," she looks over at me, "ya know, internalizing it like the rest of us, she figures she can pound on me when the other girls aren't around."

"It's because you're a grade up from Jess, Laine, and Britt?"

"Makes me an easy target." Then she grins, though I'm not sure it's a friendly expression. "Kinda like Sassy."

"You're getting kinda mouthy, huh?" I fix her bag on my back and brush a hand over my shoulder. "Jesus, Bear. You're a fuckin' mouse in front of literally everyone on the planet. Cowering in fear and terrified to make a sound, lest someone looks at you sideways. But then you come at me with an Acme rocket and act like your shots aren't pointed and mean."

"I'm not *acting* like anything. School is for learning. It's for going to class, getting an education, then leaving again, and doing it all with as little stress for Marcus as possible." She shakes her head. "I don't care about *your* stress levels, though."

"Great." I look up and study the canopied ceiling just minutes into the forest. "So you let Madge beat on you and you do nothing about it?"

"I don't *let* her do anything. She's bigger than me."

"You throw hands at me, Bear! You're not afraid. You let that bitch say nasty things about killing yourself. Things about your parents. And you just…" I don't understand her logic. I don't get it, and I can't even try to search for the bridge that'll help. "You say nothing. So, what? You don't end up in a fight at school, called into Principal Reeves' office, and Marc doesn't give you the '*I'm disappointed*' eyes?"

"Marc already has so much to worry about." Her eyes remain swollen. Red and hot enough to force her expression into a scowl. "I can handle Maybel on my own."

"Handle her how? By being her punching bag?"

"Handle her maturely. Not something you're capable of."

I laugh, shaking my head and side-step another of her jabs. "If only Marc could see the shit you say and do when he's not around, Bear. He'd be scandalized."

"I suppose it's a good thing you don't tell him, then." She folds her arms and hunches in on herself as the chill of the forest beats out even the filthy summer heat outside these trees. "You don't want him to worry, either." She looks ahead and glares. "Why are we going this way?"

"Because we have nowhere else to be. Marc's working. Ang is working. Sam is macking on Sammy like he's about to be sent off to war. You're crying. And it's too fuckin' hot to skate."

Of every word I speak, she growls and zeroes in on one single point. "I'm not crying."

"You're misty eyed. Got a case of the vapors."

"You're stupid. And I have homework to do. I'm not interested in hanging out with you unless you brought food and music."

"How about…" I snag her bag from my back and tear it open to reveal one of the sack lunches Mrs. Turner packs for her kids each day, regardless of if they intend to eat in the cafeteria. I saw Kari eating meatball subs earlier today with the twins, which means a cheese sandwich, apple, and juice box remain in her bag. "We have the food."

"Give me my bag!" She slaps my arm and tries to pry the purple backpack from my grasp. "Luca!"

"You have the homework." I tug out the pages her teacher assigned her today. "And I have the music." I look down at the girl with kind, green eyes that hide a world of attitude and spine, then I flash a grin that sets her temper alight. "I wanna write a song for the guys anyway. It's my turn to come up with something, especially now that Sam's always writing about Sammy all the damn time."

"It's kinda funny they both have the same name though, right?" Finally, she releases her bag and allows me to stuff the papers and things back inside. "Sam and Sammy. It's a bit silly."

"Sam Turner and Samantha Ricardo." I roll my eyes and slide the zip closed. "Dude swears he's gonna marry her."

"Are you ever getting married, Luc?" Kari glances across and studies the side of my face until her stare feels warm on my skin. She appears angelic for a moment. Sweet. But then she sneers. "You're not gonna marry Sassy St Slut, are you?"

"Slut?" I slap a hand over her mouth and shoot a look in every direction of the forest, like I'm worried a parent—or worse, Marc—will jump out to punish her. "Who taught you that word?! That's a bad word, Kari!"

"We know that word," she giggles. Wrestling my hand away, she slides out of my grip and twirls in the filtered sunlight.

Finally, for the first time today, I see her smile.

"You should hear the stuff Jess and Laine say when you're not around."

"Jess and Laine are pains in my ass." I hitch her bag up and shake my head. "They're gonna give me infinite headaches in the next few years."

"Nah." She swings her hair and speeds her steps. "They're sneaky enough, you won't even notice they've been arrested and posted bail."

"Jesus fucking christ." I mash the heel of my palm into my eye and groan. "You'll tell me, right? If the girls are setting shit on fire, you'll stop them long enough to let me know?"

"Maybe..." She glances across, sly and cunning. "What will you do for me?"

"I'll tell you before Marc is heading your way, so he won't catch you doing shit you really shouldn't be doing. And," I declare, making up my mind and setting my temper to the side for later use. "I'm gonna take care of Mod Podge for you. That way, your problem is solved, Marc never has to worry, and Mucus will stay away from you."

Her smile flatlines and her eyes narrow. "What are you gonna do?"

I flash a grin and replace hers with my own. "I'm gonna deal with it. Now let's get to Popcorn Palace. I'm hungry, and your cheese sandwich is looking kinda tasty right now."

"That's my sandwich! Luc!" she smacks me again. "I was saving that."

Jess rocks in the nursery chair, her eyes wide like saucers as she gently pats Billy's backside. "What did you do?"

"I ate half the sandwich, we shared the juice, Kari did her homework, and I wrote a song."

Frustrated, she snags a burp cloth from the arm of the chair and lobs it my way, though it falls to the floor listlessly long before it comes close to me. "I meant what did you do to Maybel? I didn't even realize until right now that she kinda just... disappeared." Her eyes grow impossibly wider. "Should I turn you in to the chief, Luc?"

I snort. Finally, a soft, almost real laugh rolls through my chest after the world's *second* longest day that ever occurred in history.

The first, of course, was the day Billy was born.

"I kept watch for another week or so." I reach back and take another potato from the plate Jess prepared for me. If I don't eat, I'll feel even shittier tomorrow than I do today. And the bar is already pretty fucking low. "I caught her messing with Kari twice more. I wanted to give Bear a chance to stand up for herself. Ya know, like teaching someone to fish, instead of giving them a fish."

"She never did?" Jess sighs. "She never stepped up?"

"No. She was more worried about protecting Marc's mental health than she was her own, so she took that bitch's shit twice more. The first was another 'kill yourself' bullshit. The second, Mucus Plug popped her in the belly."

"Maybel punched her?" Jess gasps. "With her fists? Kari never told us that!"

"Of course she didn't. She's the martyr, remember? Malarkey got one hit in. One time. She thought she was brave, cornering Bear when no one else was around and slamming her into the lockers when the teachers were looking the other way. But I'd been watching closely."

"Because you were head over heels in love with her already and too scared to admit it?"

I chuckle, shaking my head side to side and chewing my dinner. "Not yet. Not at that point. She was way too young for me back then. And I was way too interested in every *other* female who walked the planet. I was acting in a big brother capacity only."

"Mmhm." She relaxes back into her chair and presses gentle lips to Billy's head. "I think our hearts know, even before our brains admit it. Back then, it wasn't allowed, so you didn't outwardly have those feelings for our sweet Kari. But in the very depths of your soul, I think you knew what was coming. You knew she would eventually hold your heart in her hands. So your instincts were to keep her safe and wait until it was okay."

"Yeah, well..." I shrug and twist to select a green bean. "Maybe. I dunno. I just know, back then, I wasn't looking at her like that. She was my best friend's much younger, and hella protected, little sister. We weren't flirting or anything. Not till way later."

"So what happened to Maybel?" She nuzzles Billy's peach fuzz hair and inhales. "Because now you're telling me you 'took care of her', and I'm remembering I never saw her again. Kinda sounds homicide-y to me."

I roll my eyes. "You spend *way* too much time with Kane Bishop and his crew of murderous thugs."

"Yes, well, considering he's my husband, I suppose it means I enjoy spending time with him. Did you whack Maybel?"

"No."

"Punch her in her stupid face?"

"No."

"Run her down with your car?"

I drop my head and grin. "I actually grabbed Laine that day. Brought her with me."

"Laine?" Jess' eyes pop wide. "You took Laine and not me? What the hell?"

"Pretty sure you were in detention because you rode your blades through the school halls earlier that day. Which," I glance up and meet her eyes, "you knew you weren't allowed to do, considering the detention you sat for the same crime the week before. Laine typically learns from her mistakes the first time, so she was free and clear that day. I pulled her along with me, we stopped in the same hall, on the same corner, at the same time of the afternoon as every other time Malaprop cornered her, and we found her holding Kari by the throat."

Jess growls, dangerous and promising.

"She hit Kari just once, and by that point, I didn't really have to do shit. Laine tore that bitch's shitty hair out, blackened her eye, and punched her in the tit, all before Kari had a chance to realize what the fuck was going on."

"Good." She sneers, and yet, gently pats Billy's rump. "She deserved worse."

"I pulled Laine off and separated the three girls before I became the idiot at the bottom of a pile on. Then I let Maleficence know I would end her fucking life if she came near Kari again." I take a bite of my bean, the crunch audible across the expanse of Billy's bedroom. "Not my proudest moment, considering I'm the nice guy who wanted all the girls to like him."

"Plus," Jess snickers, "you grew up to make a vow to help people, not harm them."

"I didn't harm her," I shrug. "Not technically. I wasn't gonna go down as the guy who beat on girls. But Laine made her point—"

"And never uttered a single word of it to me."

"I told the bitch if she came near Kari again, I'd ram my fist so far down her throat she'd choke on her own lips and shit herself in front of the whole school. Then I suggested she beg her parents for a transfer to the school across town. Probably even change her name. And if she ever saw Kari again, if she so much as spied her from a mile away and they were walking on the same side of the street, then Muu Muu was to switch sides and stay the fuck away."

"You intimidated a little girl." Jess firms her lips. Though I don't miss the sly grin she works to hide. "Big, bad, flirty boy Luca Lenaghan bullied a child."

"I wasn't a bully." I push away from the changing table and turn to grab my chicken. Since Jess went to all the trouble to cook it, I suppose. "Sassy was a bully to Mole Rat. And Megalomania was a bully to Kari. I was merely…"

"The messenger," she finishes. "And Laine was the weapon." She shakes her head. "I can't believe she never told me."

"Kari wanted privacy. And we were sworn to secrecy so Marc would never know. Laine had some pent-up aggression she needed to work through, Kari needed a champion, and Miscreant needed to be put in her place." I take a bite of my chicken leg and groan when the juicy flavors burst on my tongue. "Jesus. This tastes good."

"You're starving. You should have eaten hours ago."

"I'm eating now." I nod toward Billy. "Can I have my baby back yet?"

"Not yet." She shrinks back into her chair and crushes my daughter close. "My girls aren't tiny babies anymore. I miss this."

"You gonna have more?"

"God no." She chokes out a fortifying laugh that brings my lips up. "Having a baby is hard. Having two at the same time, worse. Having Kane Bishop's twins?" She exhales, shaking her head. "I love that man, Luc. I swear I do. And I love my daughters. But hell if I'm getting back on that roller coaster a second time. Especially considering my likelihood of getting another twofer."

"Yeah, well..." My appetite dissolves, like fog on a warming morning. "They say, as a male, I'm no more likely to make twins than anyone else, even though my sisters are twins, and one of them had twins, too."

Jess' cheeks pale. Her throat bobs as she swallows.

"Sometimes these things just happen, huh?"

"Luc..."

"We didn't get identical, though. The universe thought it would be cute to give me a daughter to care for, and a son for Kari to watch over. Was that supposed to be poetic, or...?"

5

LUC

GROWING UP

"**B**oys are so annoying!" Kari stomps through the house, her footsteps echoing all the way out to the garage, followed by a deafening slam of the back door against the side of the house. The *schwoop* of the screen plays in the wind, only to stop again when she grabs it and slams it shut, locking her brother—*the boys*—where he can't reach her.

Kari and Marc have a sick obsession with protecting each other. *Sure.* They want to make each other happy. But sometimes, when lids have been placed on bottles too tight and Kari really wants something to go her way, the siblings have been known to fight.

Especially as Kari moves into her teen years, and in panicked response, Marc becomes more and more controlling.

It's not his fault, really. It's a trauma response he's never really gotten a handle on.

"Guess he told her she can't come to the lake this weekend." Sam—now more commonly known as *Scotch* after an unfortunate drinking incident that ended with stomach regurgitation and dead roses—strums his guitar and lounges back on a ratty bean bag. His hair is longer than mine these days, shaggy enough to dangle in his eyes and curl in the humidity. Like the rest of us, he topped six feet somewhere in ninth grade, and now he has all the girls looking his way with hearts in their eyes.

Though, of course, his love is all for Samantha Ricardo.

His lips angle up as the back door swings open again. But Marc's footsteps are gentler than his sister's. His temper, far calmer than hers.

For now.

"You need to simmer down, Kar." He stops on the back stoop, cupping his mouth to shout across the yard. I don't even have to get up from my perch by my opal drum kit and peek out the back of the garage to know. I've spent every damn day of my life hanging out at this house. "It's not safe out there at night. You know it."

"Are Jess and Laine going?" Mumbling so he's not overheard, Scotch continues to strum his guitar, a quiet melody rolling through the garage. While Ang folds himself over my bike, listening in on two separate conversations and tinkering with the engine to keep his hands busy.

Because he can.

Because he knows how.

And because I thrash the damn thing and enjoy my monthly free service.

"Yeah, they're going." I peek over my shoulder toward the back of the garage and try to see, even through the brick wall, what the sibling duo are doing on the other side. "It's just a party," I shrug. "We'll be there. So they won't be in danger."

"We're playing," Ang rumbles. "You know good and well we'll be busy and won't see half the shit they get up to."

"And *you* know they're gonna go, whether we like it or not. Better we get on their side, so they feel safe to tell us the truth, than piss them off and make them sneaky." I turn back to my drum kit and slide the tips of my fingers over the skins. "They're getting older. They know a party is on. They're gonna be there irregardless. So we—"

"Regardless."

"Re…" I swallow my words and frown. "What?"

"Regardless," Angelo repeats. "Irregardless isn't a real word."

"Whatever, man. *Regardless*, they're gonna do whatever they're gonna do. It's smarter that we get on board now and become their allies." I look to Scotch and raise a brow. "You, too. I know I'd rather party *with* my sisters, than find out they're doing it anyway, unsafe, and hiding from us because they're scared of getting in trouble."

"Don't look at me like I'm some kind of monster." He drops his hand from the guitar's strings and reaches across to scribble something in his notebook. "Britt and I are fine. Alex is the one riding her ass every damn step she takes." He releases his pen and meets my eyes. "He went ballistic when she came home with her second set of ear piercings."

"Wait till she moves on to belly piercings," I chuckle. "Nose." Then I wrinkle my lips. "Worse."

"I stay out of it. I'm not her parent, and I'm not X. He's got all the real estate on the over-protective brother bullshit."

"Kar! You need to stop being so fucking bratty right now and listen to my reasons."

"And Marc seems to have the secret to a great sibling/parent relation-ship," I tease. "Dude needs to calm the hell down before he gives himself a coronary."

"Are you volunteering to tell him?" Ang glances up from my bike and eyes me. "You gonna tell him to cool it with the protective stuff?"

"I might." I set my sticks on the drumhead and push up from my stool. Turning, and careful not to kick things over in our over-full garage, I wander to the door and glimpse outside. "He's gonna make her hate him if he's not careful. She's already keeping secrets."

"What secrets?" Scotch's music stops. His curiosity piqued. "Luca? What secrets is she keeping?"

Maybel.

Death threats.

Stomach aches created because of the anxiety she carries around a school she struggles to fit in to.

She has some of the *best* best friends in this town. Super protective. Super sweet. But when they're in a grade different than your own, things can get kinda lonely, even if they get to reunite in the school cafeteria.

"Just regular stuff," I mumble in response. Vague and unhelpful. Then I drop my hands into my pockets and walk into the backyard where Kari stands on the crappy halfpipe we built ourselves, holding a skateboard and looking down at knees she's already skinned.

While ten feet away Marcus shields his eyes from the sun and glowers.

"It's a friggin' lake, Kar! The depth is inconsistent. The dock is rotting. If you fall in, no one will know until you've already drowned and died. And I won't be able to save you because I'll be busy playing my set."

"Okay." She drops the board to the pipe, letting it roll just two feet before she steps on it to stop its escape. "It's fine."

Confused, Marc's brows furrow as he studies his sister. Then as rocks crackle beneath my steps, he peers over his shoulder and watches my approach. Glancing back, he repeats, "It's fine?"

"Yep." Kari kneels and goes to work tying her laces. She wears little denim shorts today and black high top connies. Her hair is tied in a pony, the curls and waves and frizzy expanse exploding from the elastic, forming a halo around her entire head and tickling her cheeks when the wind blows strands forward. "I'm done arguing about it. I'm done asking about it. It's fine."

"And... and you're not going?" he confirms. "You're gonna stay home and hang out?"

"Mmhm." She switches feet and fakes a small smile for her brother. She's growing up fast, from the little girl she was when she first tiptoed into my life, to the teen she is now, whose eyes are prettier than all the stars put together, and whose brain ticks a thousand times faster than Marcus gives her credit for. "I have a report to write for Ms. Jackson, anyway. So I'll get that done instead." She finishes her second shoe and glances across to meet his eyes. "What time do you expect to get back?"

"Um..." He drops his hands in his pockets and kicks rocks while he thinks. "I dunno. Like midnight, I suppose. We'll stop playing around eleven thirty, I think. Half an hour to pack up. I'll come straight back, and we can catch a movie or something. I don't mind staying up late and hanging out, Kar. I don't have to work Sunday until the afternoon, so I can sleep in."

"Okay." She licks her dry lips and pushes up tall, smoothing her shorts and giving her beloved brother her back. "I'd rather do what makes you comfortable." She places her foot on her board and sighs. "I never want to make you worry."

"Thank you, Kar." He finally breaks away from his spot on the dying grass and steps up onto the halfpipe instead. He walks straight to his sister and wraps her in a single arm hug so tight, part of my soul feels it, too. "You know I don't do anything to hurt you, right? This isn't about control or being a jerk."

"I know." She rests her cheek on his chest and snuggles in. "You just want to keep me safe."

"That's all it's ever been about." He presses a kiss to the crown of her head and hovers. "We already lost everything once. I'm gonna make sure it never happens again."

"I know," she repeats. Closing her eyes, she cinches her arms around his waist and simply breathes. She holds on to the one constant she's decided she has in her life, despite everything else promised to her. "I'm sorry we fought about it."

"It's done now." Pulling back to look down into her eyes, he smiles adoringly. He's gonna be a damn good dad someday. But hell if he won't be carrying a bucket load of obligation and anxiety every step he takes. "Me and the guys have to practice our set in a sec. Then I've gotta head to work." He kisses her temple and squeezes her extra tight. "Wanna come in and watch while we're doing our thing?"

"I'm gonna stay out here." Gently detangling herself, Kari extends her leg and toes the board back into place. "I'm gonna keep working on some stuff to get this energy out. Then I'm going in and getting a start on my report."

"Alright." He winks for his baby sister. She doesn't carry a pink blanket around anymore. Nor is her school bag purple. But in his eyes, I reckon she's still six years old and in need of a night light. Finally, he steps back and turns, grinning at me when he remembers I'm still here. Still listening. "Problem solved." He claps my shoulder as he passes and holds the fabric of my shirt for a moment longer. "Coming in, Luca? We need our drummer."

"Yeah." I smooth my shirt down when he releases me, watching him over my shoulder as he keeps walking. "I'm coming. Give me two seconds."

"Yeah." He turns toward the garage, completely at ease knowing his sister is safe now, locked securely in the Turners' backyard. And yeah, maybe she's gonna skateboard. But a skinned knee is far less terrifying to him now compared to the idea of his sister partying in the dark.

"Why do I get the feeling I'm gonna see you at the lake Saturday night?"

She bends and grabs her board, walking it to the coping and standing on the platform, ready to fly down again. Once she has herself set up, she casts a side-eye my way and smirks. "No clue why you think that, considering I don't intend to be seen."

My heart sinks. The worry she took from Marc, now saddled on my shoulders. "Kari—"

"The twins are going, too. Britt's going. And my report has already been written. I'm gonna be there, Luca. I just won't be where he notices me."

"But now I'll know."

She only shrugs. Zero concern for my moral anguish. "And considering you're cool with the twins going, I'm gonna assume you're cool with me being there, too."

"It's not about me being cool about it! It's about me knowing something my best friend would appreciate being told. You're asking me to keep the secret."

She places her foot on the tail of her board and smirks. "Sounds like a *you* problem. Tell him. Or don't. You're gonna make your own choices and decide where your loyalties lie. I'm gonna go to the lake either way."

"You're a pain in my fuckin' ass." I reach up and scrub a hand through my hair. "If he sees you there Saturday night, I'm staying out of it! I'm not coming to your defense, Bear."

"I'll wear all black," she snickers. "I'll be sneakier than a ninja."

"Great! So when you fall into the lake, wearing black, we won't have to *watch* you die." I turn on my heels and gnash my teeth together. "I wasn't built for this secret keeping stress."

She laughs, just loud enough for the sound to carry on the wind and tickle the back of my neck. "You go about your business, Luca. And I'll go about mine. You never told him about the Maybel stuff either. Seems you're gonna be just fine."

"Swear to god," I turn back and point a threatening finger. "If you drown, I'm gonna be pissed."

"Okay." She drops into the halfpipe, amused when her board spins one way and her body the other. She slams to the wood and skids onto her knees, bringing my heart into my throat and anxiety swelling in my gut. But she giggles anyway. Because Marcus isn't out here to save her, and it's not my job to ride in and do as he would.

"I hope that hurt, Bear." I turn away from the image of Kari Macchio plopping onto her ass. Blood on her knees and a wild smile curling her lips. "I hope you get scabs that ruin whatever outfit you're planning to wear this weekend."

It's hard work playing our set, not only of the songs we're covering from other bands, but originals too, made up of the music Scotch pens, and the few songs I've put together over the years.

It shouldn't be hard.

Fuck knows I'm in my element, smashing away at my drum kit and rocking out under the spotlights we've set up to illuminate the grassy area of the lake while our peers dance and grind.

All the things we don't mind, *typically*.

But the girls are here tonight. Their smiles, too large. Their ability to find trouble, too fucking smooth. And *oh look*, there goes Kari fucking Macchio. Wearing black like she promised, and ducking between trees while Marc's back is to her.

"Dude." Angelo stands over a keyboard, his hair curling from sweat and his shirt sticking to his sculpted chest because of the heat from the bright lights. He scowls when I fuck up the beat. Scotch sings, covering my mistakes and shooting me a glare that says he's gonna smack me upside the head later.

Meanwhile, no one has any damn clue that my brain is currently running between the trees as a guy—Garth Beaterman, junior varsity nobody—follows Kari into the shadows.

"What are you doing?" Angelo growls. He leans over his keyboard to get closer. "Luc?"

"I gotta piss." I set my sticks down and draw ire from both of our guitar players. "Go acoustic for a few minutes," I tell Scotch. Then I look at Marc, my best friend in the whole fucking world, and clear my throat. "Sorry, man. I ate some weird tacos this afternoon. Cover for me."

I clap his back and pray he doesn't follow me, then I step off the edge of our temporary stage and ignore Sassy St James when she places her hand on my chest.

"Where are you going?" She digs her nails into my shirt—into my flesh— and stumbles when I keep walking. "Luca?"

"I've got the runs." I grab her hand and un-peel her fingers from the fabric covering me. But I pull her in when her eyes fire up with what I know will turn to a full fucking tantrum if I brush her off. I set my hand on her hip and bring my lips to her ear. "I'm running to the toilet, then I gotta get back on stage. Are you having fun?"

"Your set is really hot." She pulls back just far enough to search my eyes. Her lips are already naturally full and thick, *sensual*, though I know high schoolers really shouldn't be aiming for that look. But she draws attention to them even more when she runs her tongue over the glossy covering. Humming in the back of her throat so I feel the vibration from where I stand. "You should stay and dance with me for a bit." She tilts her head toward the stage. "They're playing fine without you."

"Just long enough to find a bathroom." I lean in and press a kiss to the very corner of her lips. It's a trade. A placation so she doesn't keep her claws in my skin and follow me to the shadows. Then I pull back and drop my hand. "I'll come find you later. We can probably go for a ride or something after the show."

"On your bike?" Her eyes glow under an almost full moon. "Really?"

"Yeah. Ang just serviced it, so it's running real smooth right now." Fuck knows, if I *really* had the runs, she should be walking the other way and spraying a little Lysol in her wake.

That's what I'd do.

Not climbing onto the back of my bike and snuggling in.

"But I really have to go for now." I catch movement fifty yards away, under the massive weeping willow that sweeps down to touch the grass. So I take a step back, brushing up against kids I go to school with. Some I don't. Faces I recognize from around town, and others, I've literally never seen before in my life.

I have no clue how word travels to let everyone know we're playing a show.

But that's how these things go, I suppose.

I duck through the crowd and make a show of walking one way, so when I glance back and find Marcus' heated gaze following my steps, his fingers strumming the strings of his bass guitar, I can be doing what he expects of me. Finding a toilet. Taking care of business.

But the second he looks down at his instrument and his fingers get busy working through a riff he takes extra pride in performing, I drop my head and cut left, bolting through the stragglers and sprinting toward the willow.

"Kari fucking Macchio!" I race past my sisters and Britt, whose eyes stick to the back of my neck. Their hands coming up. Their triple intakes of air, knowing their fourth is doing something she shouldn't. But I don't stop to chastise them. I don't even comment on their dresses which are way too short for their ages.

I'm not Marc, and I'm not X. I don't involve myself so long as everyone is having a good time.

But fuck, Sassy St James wears clothes like that, and look how she turned out: lusting after a guy who hardly even wants her and licking her lips in a way that we both know she's not verbalizing.

But she's *offering*.

She has in the past. And she will again in the future.

That's not a life for Kari.

"Bear!" I snarl her name and catch a gasp of surprise in the trees. The rustle of a dude moving fast. Then the crunch of bark, dirt, and rocks beneath a girl's high-top shoes.

Because the lake isn't for heels, no matter how short one's skirt is.

"Luca?"

"Kari!" I shove weeping branches aside and stomp into the little getaway beneath, where mosquitoes thrive and sneaking couples come to *sneak*. I zero in on Beaterman first. His wide eyes and panicked stare. He knows whose sister he's fucking with. And he knows if Marc didn't see him do the wrong thing, someone else did.

Furious, I glance at Kari and stop on the spaghetti strap of her top, fallen from her shoulder and draping over her arm, flushed with a blush that stretches up her chest and neck.

Her tank is tiny, the fabric, impossibly thin.

But did I say shit when I saw her earlier?

No.

Did I tell Marc? Or hell, did *I* tell her to go back inside and change?

No.

I mind my own business. It's what I do! I refuse to be the overbearing older brother. But I'll be fucked and stuffed before I stand by and let Beaterman undress Kari Macchio while her brother is too busy to do anything about it.

"What the hell are you doing, Luca?" Kari hurriedly fixes her top and stomps forward. Just one step. It's all she allows herself because she knows if she comes any closer, I'll grab on and take her back to Marcus. Instead, she lifts her chin and puffs her chest forward.

Defiance.

Anger.

"We had a deal!"

"Yeah, the deal was that you'd come out to the lake tonight and I wouldn't snitch. The deal had nothing to do with you, Beaterman, and spaghetti strap tops showing off half your fucking chest. And it sure as shit had nothing to do with you sneaking into the dark with him! He's way too old for you, Kari!"

"What are you even talking about?" Her eyes swing down to study her tank, her hands smoothing over the fabric. "My top is fine! And Garth is—"

"I'm just gonna..." Beaterman steps right. Twice. Three times. Four. Lifting his hand and readying to brush the weeping branches aside. "I'm gonna go."

"Nah, bitch." I stalk forward and grab his shirt, buttons popping under my hold and his face turning an instant, dangerous puce as I twist the collar and tighten the fabric around his throat. "She's too young for you, Dick."

"Luca!"

I stare down into Garth's terrified eyes and sneer. "That's a statutory rape charge if I ever saw one."

"Rape?" He spasms and practically levitates off the ground. His eyes taking up his whole damn face. "What!? I didn't even touch her."

"You're all huddled up out here in the dark." He and I are the same height. Almost the same build. He's got that football broadness I don't have —I prefer to skate and spend my time behind a drum kit—but the fact that he's technically bigger than me seems to count for naught when the dude quivers under my hand. "You're not gonna show her any more attention."

"Luca!"

I ignore Kari. Even when she stomps up behind me and slams a closed fist into my ribs and steals the breath from my lungs.

Instead, I use that frustration and pain to shake Garth fucking Beaterman. "I catch you anywhere near her, ever again, and I'll tear your fucking esophagus out."

"Luc!"

"Do you understand me?"

"I didn't touch her!"

"And you won't get a chance to in the future, either." I give him another shake, his teeth snapping closed and rattling together until the sound carries in the air louder than the band's music. "Turn your ass around," I release his shirt so he stumbles back and half falls through the weeping branches. "And don't come near her again."

"Luc Lenaghan!" Kari growls. "Swear to god, I'm going to kill you!"

"Consider her the fuckin' plague. Touch her, and you die a painful death in six to ten days." I stomp forward and send the pussy football player spilling back until he's through the tree's curtain. He falls on his ass and lands with a muffled thump. But he twists, quick as a snake, and scrambles back to his feet. "Don't let me see you again, Beaterman!"

"You're an asshole!" Kari punches the meaty part of my arm, her bony knuckles digging in and changing the scowl I wore for Beaterman, to a frown as I reach across and rub the stinging pain away. "We were talking, Luca!"

"Uh huh." Finally, I turn from the space Garth occupied a moment ago and glance down to study Kari's furious eyes. Glittering green, even in the dark. "It always starts as talking, Bear. Then our spaghetti strap falls to the side, and next thing we know, a dude's hand is on your shoulder. Then his lips."

Her nostrils flare with rage. "You'd know. You spend tons of time with the female variety. All different kinds. Rarely the same one, two weekends in a row."

"Uh huh. That's exactly how I know!" I blow past the girl and head back to the portion of the weeping branches I stomped through. Slicing my hand through the thick greenery and pushing a few of them aside, I look out to the back of the band. Our music, still playing. Dancers, still dancing. "I know what Beaterman was gonna do with you, Bear, because I do the same shit, same moves, and have the same end goal." I release the tree and turn back to face the girl way too classy to be undressed out at the lake. "Different chicks. Same intentions."

"That makes you a pig."

"Yep. But it also makes me knowledgeable on the matter." I glance out into the dark and find Britt, Laine, and Jess huddled together thirty feet from the stage. Dudes watch them, too. The guys are the lions, and the girls, gazelles. It could be even worse, considering those three are a year younger than Kari. But the one superpower they cling on to is the fact they move as a group.

Sure, they're still gazelles. Sure, they're still targets.

But they stick together, and three beautiful, giggling girls is like kryptonite to any confident dude who wants to make a move. He could try… but the risk, if he fails, is huge.

Kari, on the other hand, is a fucking loner by nature.

That's what makes her a target to the hyena pussy that is Beaterman.

"You and I had a deal, Kari." Bringing my gaze back around, I look her up and down and shake my head. "You said you'd come out and hang with the girls. You swore you'd be careful and do the right thing."

"I wasn't doing—"

"Sneaking under a weeping willow with a football player is dangerous!" I want to grab her. To shake her. I want to knock a little sense into her too-young mind. Because fuck, this is why Marcus worries all the damn time. "This wasn't smart."

"We were just talking!"

"Yeah. And I assure you," I step closer, her gulp audibly hits my ears as I stare down into her eyes, "Sassy St James and I started out talking, too."

Kari's lips instantly wrinkle in disgust.

"It always starts out the same. Guys have a fuckin' playbook."

"The fact that you admit it repulses me."

"Good. *Let* it repulse you. Let *all* guys repulse you. Because you're getting to an age now where they're looking for one thing. And you're still young enough, they know they're gonna be first."

She balls her fists, anger rocking through her too-small frame.

"High school girls have something to give, Bear. And high school boys are in a race to be the one to plant their flag."

"You're despicable."

"I'm telling you the truth. I get you're young, and fuck knows, Marc isn't gonna tell you this shit. He wants to wrap you up in that cute, little pink blanket you still keep near your bed for the nights you have bad dreams, and if it were up to him, he would never give you *the talk*."

"The talk?"

"You're older than the other girls. A whole grade ahead of them. Which doesn't sound like a lot, but it is. You'll be exposed to stuff before the rest of them, and you won't have that mob mentality the others cling to. Because you prefer solitude."

"Oh god." She whirls away and shakes her head. "*The talk*."

"You're getting to the age, Bear! And then we have the added complication of Marcus."

At that, she spins back. "What about Marcus?"

"You're a protected species. Like," I laugh, though the sound holds no humor, "wildly protected. He doesn't let you walk home alone in the middle of the afternoon. He doesn't let you go anywhere unless he's around. He's checking in on you every three seconds of the day."

"Luc—"

"He demanded you stay home tonight and study while your best friends went out to party." I stalk forward another step. "You're protected. Which makes you a sweeter prize."

"You mean, like, compared to Sassy St Slut? She's offering it up every day, which makes her *prize* not all that coveted."

"Bear—"

"Then we consider Britt and the twins," she continues, despite the way my eyes narrow. "Their brother isn't a complete, over-protective, suffocating blanket psycho. Which makes them a little more accessible. But they're still classy and selective with whom they spend their time. So although they appear a little more..." she considers, then settles on, "available, they're not, actually."

"And then there's you," I grit out, taking another step closer. "Like the Mona Lisa."

"So you're saying guys are gonna try to be near me, purely because they're not supposed to be?"

"Yes." The music changes outside the tree's branches. Marcus' bass disappearing from the air. The difference, like a red-hot fire poker branded against my chest. "They're gonna try to take something from you, Bear. They're not gonna be around because they like your personality."

"Oh, well..." She throws a hand up in frustration. "Great. That surely rebuilds my confidence."

"This isn't about you! This has nothing to do with who you are or the fun qualities you might bring to a relationship. This isn't about the fact you're getting really fucking pretty. Or smart. Or that you have a nasty right hook."

In response, she looks down at her hand and flexes her fingers.

"This is about conquering something no one else has."

"That is absolutely disgusting."

"Yep," I quip. "It is. Boys are disgusting. But seeing how Marcus is never gonna tell you this shit, I figure, as his best friend, it's on me. If it's not Beaterman, it's gonna be someone else. The whole fucking team probably talks about you. And I bet my left nut they're gonna be tripping over themselves to invite you to prom when the time comes. Guys are gonna say and do whatever you need to hear, Bear, just to get you to trust them. And by the time they have you in the dark, hiding under a weeping willow, and your fucking spaghetti strap coming down, it's all over."

"So you're saying my free will is a non-consideration in all this? What I want doesn't matter?"

"Not to the wrong guy, it won't! Some dudes are out here, and they're gonna take what they want, whether you're offering or not. It's best you stop assuming every guy is protective of you the way Marcus is. You're lunch, Macchio, and they're hungry."

"You're a pig." She stalks forward and slams her hand to my chest as she passes. Bursting through the tree's overhanging branches, she emerges outside. Right where Marcus will see if she's not careful. "Seems only a guy with bad intentions would know what other guys with bad intentions are thinking."

"I don't need to *take*, Bear!" I follow her through the tree's curtain. "Not when Sassy is offering it up every damn time I blink. Stay the hell away from Beaterman!" I call at her back. "Grow a brain and scrounge up a little common sense. He wasn't coming out here to color rainbows with you." I look at the twins and jerk a finger to the right. "Pack your shit up and go home. All of you. The party's over."

"Aww man." Jess drops her gaze and kicks rocks as Kari wanders closer. "We were behaving."

"And now it's done." I stomp closer to the group, brushing past so only a hairs breadth separates me and Kari fucking Macchio. "Stick together. Call

X if you have to. But you go straight home and don't stay in the street." I meet Laine's stare. "Understood?"

"Straight home." She rolls her eyes. "Fine."

"Promise?"

She drops her chin in agreement. "Yeah. Come on." She takes Jess' hand, who takes Britt's, who swings around and grabs on to Kari's. They create a chain of little, angry girls who will bitch and moan about me the whole way home.

They'll marvel at the fact that I'm supposed to be the cool older brother. But tonight, I became their warden.

That's not my role, dammit. But when X isn't here, and I'm keeping Marcus deliberately in the dark, my options become severely limited.

And considering I've been gone from the stage for an easy five minutes already—maybe even ten—I know I'm on the clock. I watch the girls disappear into the dark, the lion's den. But I can't follow them home. I can't leave the lake and not expect shit to go bad when I get back.

So I trust them to stick together. I trust my sisters to steer the ship and keep everyone safe. And when they're out of my sight, I spin on my heels and dash toward the stage before Marcus comes looking for me.

6

LUC

REVENGE IS OFTEN COLD AND UNCALLED FOR

"I didn't see Beaterman for ages after that night at the lake."

Sated, as warm chicken and delicious potatoes settle in the base of my stomach, I kick one foot over the other and lean back against the baby changing table. Billy sleeps peacefully, and Jess rocks herself into an almost comatose state.

But her lips curl as she remembers that night, too. Maybe she didn't hear the shit Kari and I said under the willow tree. Perhaps she didn't catch all the details of how a high school boy's brain works. But she saw the aftermath. And no doubt, they bitched about me after.

"We didn't go straight home that night." Snickering when my brows shoot high in surprise, Jess pats Billy's backside and nuzzles the side of her head. "Kari was *so* mad at you. We knew we couldn't take her back to the Turners' house and leave her there when she was spitting fire."

My heart gives a heavy thump, almost like she's a kid again and admitting to something naughty. "You told me you went home."

"We told, and still tell, our brothers all sorts of things." She shrugs. "It's a game of keeping the peace, Luca. Not telling the truth. Even now, there's a lot you don't need to know about my relationship with Kane. A lot you don't need to know about Laine and Ang. It's called privacy."

"It's called being a pain in my ass." I fold my arms and drop my head back to study the ceiling. "If I'd known you girls would fuck around that night, I'd have followed the four of you home and marched you straight to your bedrooms."

"Yeah, well..." She snickers. "We got back before you guys did, and we lied through our teeth to make sure we got away with it."

"Where'd you go?"

She stops rocking. Stops patting. Stops breathing, even. Then she laughs. "We circled back, went to the other side of the lake, sat our asses on the dock, put our feet in the water, and watched our brothers play their set." She goes back to rocking again, content in her comfortable position with the baby sleeping on her chest. "We didn't want to miss out, and as long as Marc didn't know, we didn't feel the need to follow your orders."

"That was dangerous, Jess. Any one of you could have fallen in, and we wouldn't have known to come looking. Anyone could have followed you, and we wouldn't have known you were in trouble until you'd already been victimized."

Her eyes flicker for a beat. A memory, perhaps. A response of some sort. But she covers it with a gentle shrug and continues to pat the baby's backside. "It worked out in the end. No one followed us across the lake. You thought we'd left, so you stopped looking. And once you finished, we got up and ran all the way home."

"As soon as we finished our set?"

Her stare glitters with deviousness. "As soon as the set ended, and the guys started packing up. That was the point *you* got lazy, letting them do all the work while you sucked face with Sassy instead. I didn't realize back then that you and Kari would end up," she gestures to the baby, "ya know. I had no clue a romance was blossoming."

"It wasn't." Defensive, I scowl and look down at my shoes. "Not yet. She was still too young."

"Well..." she scoffs. "Then I guess Kari had some especially harsh feelings about her *friend* swallowing Sassy St Slut's tongue. Because the second you grabbed her boobs and forgot to help clean up the stage, Kari went on a rampage. We went to the other side of the lake to calm her down. Ya know, after your big sex talk fight. She was angrier than ever and ready to tear the skin off your face."

"Guess that explains her icy mood the next morning." I remember back to her snarling temper. Her *'does anyone want a soda?'*, only for her to get something for everyone else... but not me. Kari Macchio knew how to throw a tantrum just as violently as Marcus did—it's in the blood, I guess—

but I suppose I had assumed it was because I'd chastised her the night before.

Not because I spent time with Sassy after our set.

"Everything made so much sense after you and Kari came out as a couple," Jess sniggers. "There were so many holes in my memories. So many missed details over the years. Turns out my brother and my best friend were hip deep in a scandalous love affair the rest of us didn't know about."

"We weren't a couple yet," I argue, our age difference still a sticking point for me. I fought my attraction for the longest time out of a moral and loyal code.

Rule one: You don't hit on your best friend's sister.

Rule two: You especially don't hit on your best friend's *much younger* sister.

Not until she's eighteen, at least.

"Not way back then," I continue. "Not even close."

She shrugs, her smile curling up playfully. "Like I said: I think the heart knows. Even before things become romantic, your future rides on you taking care of that other person. You were protecting her from guys like Beaterman. And she was pitching an epic fit because you were kissing the wrong girl."

"And maybe you're stretching," I counter. "You're looking to add a starry-eyed twist to a story that's already happened. You can't go back and rewrite history to further your narrative."

"Uh huh. So Beaterman?" She firms her twitching lips. "What happened with that situation?"

Ugh. I groan, remembering. "He beat the shit out of me."

"Hey, Lenaghan?" Garth Beaterman might have eggbeaters for brains, but he has the brawn that comes with a football education, and the guts to come for a guy in the middle of the day when there's no one around to defend him.

There's a difference between a guy who bangs on a drum for sport, and a guy who tackles other dudes on a football field.

I'm not, and I never have been, insecure about my choices in life. But fuck, I'm realistic enough to know I can't go toe to toe with the linebacker.

I glance up at his voice, the splintered wood on the park bench grabbing onto my shirt so the crackle becomes audible even above the din of traffic and a regular week in this town. A couple of blocks one way, garage employees bang away with their work, the impact wrenches buzzing into the air, and the clatter of tools hitting the floor, a racket we hear even from our house. A couple of blocks the other way, Main Street hums with cars puttering by and businesses doing... *business.*

Whatever it is they do to get through a day.

And here I am, with a notebook balancing on my knee. A pen clasped between my fingers. And a fucking douchebag meandering closer with fire in his eyes.

I don't get up. Don't even feign to respect him or his approach. I merely firm my lips and wait.

"You're all alone today, Lenaghan." He rubs his palms together; *he's a regular Dr. Heinz Doofenshmirtz.* "Your friends aren't around to make you brave, huh?"

A long, drawn-out sigh rolls through my chest. It's not like I didn't know this day was coming. His stare downs in the hall were becoming tedious. His shoulder-checks, constant. His bullshit on school grounds was becoming less subtle and more noticed. So I knew things were escalating. Though I figured in the middle of the park, in the middle of the afternoon, was a low risk kinda place to be. "Pretty sure I was alone that night at the lake, too." I lower my pen and scan his ugly face. "I mean, Kari was there. But I don't consider her muscle, so to speak."

He whistles, loud and blistering in my ear. But of course, that's not even the worse shit that'll happen to me today. Because the rest of the football team steps out of their hiding places and surrounds my place on the bench.

Maybe not the *whole* team. But six guys. Seven. Could be eight, though I don't intend to look over my shoulder to confirm.

"Ah..." I click my tongue, though my heart thunders in my chest. I can throw hands with enthusiasm more than finesse, and usually, that keeps me out of trouble. But me versus our high school JV team? "I see what's going on here."

"You see now?" Beaterman stops a few feet from where I sit, his eyes hooded and hideous, leering down at me. "Feeling brave today, Drummer Boy?"

"Dunno." I carefully close my book and place it on the bench to my right. Then I drop my leg and set both feet on the ground. "Feeling kinda rapey today, Beaterman?"

His face burns red, anger making his fists ball tight. "I was just talking to her!"

"At night, hidden behind low hanging branches, with her top coming down at the side… annnnnnd, she's just a kid." I glance to my right, to a dude I know to be the quarterback and *leader* of his friends. "He had no business taking Kari Macchio anywhere alone. Especially at night."

"Says you?" Packer growls. "Luca fucking Lenaghan. The dude who has run through half the team's sisters already?"

I gulp and cast my gaze over to Manny Paige—his sister is Julie. Then to Carter Day—his sister is Tara. Hernandez—his sister is Gloria. By the time I reach Tyler St James, I know I'm fucked.

"Every moment I have ever spent with a girl has come with consent." I drag my focus back to Beaterman and glower. "Always my own age or older. You have no reason to even go near Kari Macchio."

"And you probably shouldn't have come to the park alone." A flat palm slaps the back of my head until bells ring in my ears and a deep buzzing saws in the base of my skull.

I swing forward with my attacker's momentum, slamming my knee to the ground in front of the bench and twisting to find whoever the fuck is throwing hands.

"You don't get to bang every other chick in the school, then lay claim to the one you haven't, bitch."

Shoes scraping against loose gravel draws my focus back around. My neck swivels faster than is probably safe, but then a heavy boot slams against my ribs, lifting me from the ground a couple of inches and moving my bones until I think they might puncture my lungs.

But anything that goes up—according to Miss Caine in third period science—must come down.

I drop back to the ground with a thud, my knees hitting the edge of the concrete platform the bench was built upon and my lungs heaving for fresh air. But Beaterman lays his foot into my gut again, stealing whatever oxygen I thought I'd scraped together.

Then more join in.

Motherfuckers kick me in the back. In the kidneys. Thighs. My brain vibrates in my skull, and a deafening bell rings in my ears. Dust and dirt stirs under shuffling feet, filling my mouth and nostrils so it becomes damn near impossible to breathe.

I peel my eyes open, just in time to catch Beaterman's size ten Nike flying at my face.

Fuck.

"Hey!"

Beaterman's foot catches the side of my jaw when I turn, the solid kick cracking my neck and leaving my brain swirling as I consider a life in a wheelchair. But then feet start moving again. Half a dozen sets, thundering against the patchy grass as the football team runs away and others, friendlies, sprint in my direction.

"Shit. Shit. Shit. Shit. Shit!" Marcus' voice is first. The panic in his tone. The fear that grips him as his trauma takes over and the thought of losing people is, literally, his one and only fear. He skids onto the dirt, his knees slamming into my stomach cause more damage when his momentum is simply too fast.

His hands are rough. His intentions, pure, but fuck, he's not careful as he grabs my shoulders and flips me to my back. "Luca!" He presses his hands to my chest, like he's gonna do compressions or some shit. I dunno. We didn't listen that day in class.

"Stop." I cough, which hurts my injured ribs, which steals the breath from my lungs and ends with a groan rolling along my throat. "Shit, Marcus, stop."

"Are you okay?" He swats my cheek—to clean the dirt away, I'm sure, though it feels like he's slapping for the fun of it. "Luca! Are you alright?"

"Dude." I groan and turn away, spying a larger than us, older than us, Alex Turner pounding Beaterman into the grass. He rests his knee on Beaterman's chest and just... hits. And hits. And hits. "Someone probably should stop him."

"Give him a sec," Angelo growls. He stands over us, his hands on his knees and a long grease stain marking his face. "He knows how to do it without killing the guy. And none of us are gonna snitch."

"What the fuck is going on between you and Beaterman?" Marcus growls. "He's been on your case for weeks. What'd you do? Screw his sister?"

"He doesn't have a sister." I draw a breath into my lungs and pray it doesn't spill out into my chest à la punctured organs. Then I turn on the dirt, placing my hands on the ground and grunting when my body rejects the idea of moving. "Jesus, that stings. Where did you guys even come from?" I glance to my right to find Sam half watching me, half watching his brother lay Beaterman into the ground. "Scotch? I thought you were hanging with Sammy this afternoon?"

"We were at the garage first," Marcus rumbles. "A dude just brought a

Charger in that he wants to sell. And Sammy is with Meg. What the hell are you doing getting beat up in the park?"

I choke out a laugh and plop back to my ass, sending plumes of dust up and glancing at my knee——denim scraped away and blood trickling along my skin. "Bastard. These were my favorite jeans."

"Get the fuck up!" Alex yanks Beaterman to his feet and holds him steady when the guy wants to sway.

"He's going to prison if your dad finds out he did that." Breathing through the nausea rolling in my gut, I rest my aching back against the park bench and drop my head. "That shit hurts."

"What is going on between you and Beaterman?" Marcus grabs my jaw and forces my eyes to come to his. "If you have a problem with him, then *I* have a problem with him."

"It's not—"

"But you're not even telling us! You haven't said shit about your beef with him. So we're going about our business, no fucking clue we're supposed to be watching your back. And you're out here getting pounded on by the entire JV team."

"It was the whole team, right?" I drag my gaze across to Ang. "Felt like the whole team."

"Eight of 'em," he smirks. His eyes burn with rage, but he makes a conscious effort to relax. To smile. He knows what it is to have your guts kicked in. He knows how much it hurts.

Most of all, he knows how annoying it is for your friends to fuss about it.

"Can you get up?" He steps closer, nudging Marcus to the side. Then he takes my hands, linking us together and wrapping his palms around my wrists. Hooking us securely, he tugs just hard enough to start the momentum. Then he becomes my leaning post as my head swims and my ribs smart. "Hospital or home?" he grumbles. "You need a doctor or just a little rest?"

"Doctor," Marcus snarls. "Then a baseball bat. We're gonna take care of business."

"Business has been taken care of," Scotch inserts. He steps closer, and Marcus pushes to his feet, so my friends become my wall. A shield. But we all still look over at Alex, who says something to a glassy eyed Beaterman. He doesn't shout. Doesn't swear. The most terrifying part of his actions are that he's entirely too calm and collected. And like a good, obedient boy, Beaterman nods.

His friends, though, are long gone.

"Come on." Ang claps my shoulder, dislodging a plume of dust so it wafts into the air. "The sooner you walk it off, the better it'll feel."

"What the fuck was that all about?" Marcus repeats. While Scotch leans in and grabs my notebook and pen from the bench, Marcus pushes in front of us, giving his back to the rest of the park and staring at my face. His glare is like a warm touch on a hot day. His concern, the reason we love him. The reason we're best friends: now and forever.

But thirty feet back, at the edge of the park, with one foot on the grass and the other still on the road, Kari stands with her hands pressed to her mouth. Tears, glittering in her eyes. Her chest heaves in silent panic, and worst of all, no one is there to comfort her. Not my sisters. Not Britt. None of the guys. She's all on her own.

And she knows what Marcus doesn't.

She knows what neither of us have verbalized in all the time since that night at the lake.

"Luca?"

"I hit on his cousin or something." I shrug my friends off and step-shuffle away from the park bench. The sooner I walk, the better I'll feel. "And maybe I told him to fuck himself over it. He didn't like it."

"**Y**ou never told me that." Marcus wanders into Billy's bedroom, surprising me so I jerk to my right and feel those phantom pains from forever ago in my ribs. My shoes scuff against the floor and startle sweet Billy, but she settles again just as soon as Jess pats her butt. "You protected my sister from Garth, told no one, then took his beating all alone?"

"How the hell did you get into my house?" I press a dramatic hand to my chest and laugh. Because if I don't, I might fall apart. I've lost too much today already. Fighting with my best friend, *my brother-in-law*, isn't something I intend to do. "Dammit, Marcus. You couldn't even make the stairs creak to give me warning?"

"I was listening to your story." He stops on the threshold and leans against the doorframe. "Beaterman wanted to take advantage of Kari, you stepped in and dealt with it, and told no one?"

"Well…" I drag my eyes across to a grinning Jess. "I was protecting the girls, mostly. Though if you heard the part about them staying at the lake that night, that's not on me. I thought they'd left."

He casts a judgmental, impatient gaze toward Jess. Though fuck knows marriage and parenthood has mellowed the guy out. "You were a bad influence on my baby sister."

Jess snickers. "And just so we have it on record, Kari was older than the rest of us. So were we the bad influences, or…?"

"Yes." Marcus and I both answer at the same time. Then he adds, "You, Laine, and Britt were always the crazies. Even now. You married a fuckin' thug. Laine married Ang—"

"Hang on." I feel the need to stand up for my friend. "What did Ang ever do to you?"

Marcus snorts. "If you don't know what he gets up to with Bishop, then that's on you. If you hadn't spent so much time and effort sneaking around with *my* sister, you might've noticed how unhinged the dude actually is, especially now that he's one of *them*."

"One of them, what?" I point a finger at my sister. "Jess married Bishop! Laine got hitched to Angelo. If you have any information for me, Marcus, feel free to share."

Chuckling, he moves further into the room and sweeps in to steal Billy from Jess with smooth movements. He's a dad now, too. He knows how to cradle a baby and keep her safe.

Jess scowls at her loss, but when Marcus sits on the arm of the recliner and holds Billy close, Jess only presses her cheek to his arm and sighs.

"Nah." He smiles at a sleeping Billy, stroking the bridge of her nose with fingers callused from work. But gentle enough, they wouldn't pop a soap bubble. "I went through hell figuring things out about you and Kari."

"*You* went through hell? Dude. I was the one who got his ass beat, day after day, by my best friend. All because you wanted to avenge her honor, and I was too in love to walk away."

"Seems Beaterman's flogging wasn't the last you would take for Kari." Jess pulls back and smacks Marc's arm. "You were a jerk back then!"

"Oh sure," Marc rolls his eyes. "Blame me for being mad my best friend was sneaking around with the one and only person on this planet I lived to keep safe."

"Funny," I drawl, looking down at a completely content Billy. "I felt the same way."

7

LUC

SWEET... AND STILL TOO YOUNG

No one expected *me*—slutty, goofy, rarely-serious Luca Lenaghan—to graduate high school among some of the top in his grade. Nor, enter a medical technology program through the college an hour from home, graduate long before he could even drink—that's not to say we didn't, just that, legally, we weren't supposed to—and go on to complete a paramedic program... all of which, on my first attempt.

But here I am, working the bus and juggling two earlies, two lates, and an overnight shift until I end up with my four-day weekend. It's a routine I've come to enjoy. A way to see every hour of the day and feel productive, and yet, still get to play in the band with the guys.

Scotch is a full-fledged friggin' lawyer these days. I mean, he has the documentation to say so, though he spends most of his time in a *big brother role* for disadvantaged youth. Ang bought the garage and is now someone else's boss. Alex is a cop—*a fuckin' cop*! After he beat Garth Beaterman so good, he was missing a few teeth, but had gained enough common sense to never come near me or my friends again.

Marcus makes furniture for a living. Like, the good stuff. The hand-crafted, only rich folks can afford it, kind of furniture.

And the girls... well, they're racing toward graduation. Though Kari, of course, remains a year ahead of them.

"What the hell do you mean you're going *away* to college?" Marcus

79

stomps across the Turners' backyard, the same as he's done a million times over the last decade, and watches his sister crash her board on the halfpipe.

Because he never wanted to teach her properly—god forbid she skin her knees—and no way was any other dude gonna step into this yard to help her. She's a study in willpower. In stubbornness. Because she can't do it. She doesn't have the same natural ability the other girls have.

Or maybe they're just better, because they've been on boards since they were able to walk.

Kari got a late start, and even then, a handicap named Marcus Macchio, holding her down.

"You can stay here, Kar! Get an online degree."

Save me the heartache and mental anguish, is what he meant to finish with.

"I was accepted into the school I wanted, Marcus." *Thud!* The wheels of her board slam against the aging wood. "I got accepted into four schools, but this is the one I want."

"Kari—"

"I could have gone to the University of Texas."

I walk to the back door of the garage and peek out into the dark yard. The moon is already out. The stars, shining above. It's not late—a little after seven, I suppose—but the sun has abandoned us, so now the brother-sister duo are lit up by the light screwed to the back of the Turners' house. The spotlight we begged for years and years ago, so nighttime wouldn't mean we had to go inside.

And call me crazy, but I get the feeling Mrs. Turner was happy everyone was outside as much as humanly possible.

Kari stands in the bowl of the halfpipe, close-fitting jeans wrapped around her thighs and squeezing her tight enough, they may as well be leggings.

Which is cool and all; I'm not gonna judge a girl for what she wears. But seriously... they're leggings, right? Leggings, made to look like jeans, so women could go to the store and pretend they weren't, in fact, wearing leggings.

"I could go to New York," she presses, pleading with the brother who has not, in all the years since the pair walked up the Turners' stairs, given up on protecting her.

"I could go all the way to Phoenix. I have options, Marcus. And I'm choosing to stay near home."

"You're choosing to go to college and live somewhere else!"

"It's an hour away! Stop being so dramatic."

"Exactly! It's an *hour* away. So when you're there all alone—because the twins and Britt are still a year behind—and you have no one nearby to watch your back, an hour is a fuck-of-a long time until I can get to you."

"You're catastrophizing." She turns on her heels and bends to sweep up her board. Speeding from a walk to a light jog, she makes her way up the incline and sets the deck down on the coping.

She's going to smash herself to the bottom, all because she's feeling defiant.

"It's college, Marcus. A lot of people go to college once they're done with high school. And guess what? Most people are my age when they go. They sure as hell don't bring their big brothers along to keep an eye on things."

"Maybe I *should* come." He's a stubborn mule, too. Dropping his hands into his pockets and stepping up onto the pipe to block her way down. I mean, she could still go, and if she hits him with her board just right, she might break his ankles.

But she wouldn't dare.

She idolizes him, even when he infantilizes her.

"I didn't do the college thing. Could be time I educate myself."

"Oh, please." She rolls her eyes and gives up on her stance at the top of the platform. Instead, she drops to her ass and dangles her legs over the side. "You're doing your thing here, Marcus. You're making really beautiful, special stuff. What would you do in college, anyway? An accounting degree?"

"I would be with you." He gentles his voice and takes a step closer, staring up at the one and only person he's tasked himself with protecting. He's dated over the years. He's watched his friends do the same. He would run someone down with his truck if they were giving Mrs. Turner, or, hell, any of us, trouble in the street. But Kari is where he starts and ends.

His life as he knows it began when he tossed a seven-year-old into a closet and listened while his parents were murdered, and his mother's screams turned to a gurgle.

A gurgle to a pained gasp.

That gasp to complete silence.

And however long later, silence turned to sirens.

He doesn't know how else to *be*. It's hardly even his fault for loving her the way he does.

"An hour away, all on your own," he groans, "is too far. It's not safe. Especially in *that* city."

"I'll be living on campus the first year. In the dorms with all the other people my age. I'll make friends I can actually attend class with."

"And guys," he groans. "Lots and lots of guys."

"So is this about safety? Or sex? Because I'm gonna tell you, Marcus. One makes you overprotective. The other, overbearing."

Why the fuck does thinking of Kari Macchio heading off to college and staying in the dorms where other guys will be make me sick to my stomach?

Why? It's not like Jess and Laine aren't right behind her.

Jess wants to be a lawyer someday. Laine, an elementary school teacher. The irony isn't lost on me that the girls who are possibly the least mature females I know, will someday hold positions of respect and power. One of them will work with, and sometimes, against, the legal system. The other will teach young minds. The opportunities both will be given boggle my mind.

But they both require a degree.

And not once have I sat down and thought, *well, gee, I hope they're not going over there to fuck.*

"Well?" Kari demands when Marcus remains silent. The word sex on her lips, I bet, was what did it. "Speak, Marcus! Is this about my safety or my personal life?"

"It's about the fact your personal life is bound to lead you into unsafe situations. College isn't like high school, Kar! Here, the oldest dude who is gonna scam on you is, what, eighteen? There? They can be damn near thirty and still bumming around on campus. And that doesn't even include the TAs. Fuck," he groans. "That doesn't include the professors! Next thing we know, you're bringing a middle-aged guy home, and he has his claws so deep into your skin, you won't know which way is out."

"Good lord." She drops backward and lies on the platform of the half-pipe. Her legs continue to dangle, which means her spine arches at an awkward angle.

And still, I eavesdrop on someone else's conversation.

"You're hypothesizing these wildly ridiculous scenarios, Marcus. I'm not going there to hook up with some middle-aged creepo. I'm not even going there to hook up with someone my own age. I want to learn. I want to help people. And in a few years I'll come home with a shiny new degree, and I'll work out of our local hospital, if I'm extra, extra lucky."

"And if you're not? If they ship you to Phoenix?"

"I'll be a grown woman, making grown decisions when the time comes.

Luca works for our hospital," she thrusts her hand straight toward me, sitting up and meeting my eyes like she knew I was listening all along.

Of course, Marcus turns as well.

"He got the placement he wanted," she insists. "He can probably talk to someone once I have my accreditation that'll give me a step up when the time comes. I could work from the same hospital! Then you'd have a guard dog on duty all day long."

Marcus rolls his eyes, turning back to his sister and firming his lips. "He's not my guard dog."

"No?" she challenges. "Could've fooled me. When you're not around to watch every step I take, he is. *Don't walk on the road, Kari, you might die. Don't go to the lake, Kari, you might die. Don't spend time with any boys, Kari, you might be taken advantage of. And then you might die.*" She drops her hand and scoffs. "It would be your dream come true, right? For me to work somewhere that not only has doctors on staff, security cameras in every hall, and medicine nearby in case I *nearly die*. But your best friend will be able to report back about every person I spoke to on shift."

"I would be working too," I grumble, just loud enough to prick her ears. "No time to watch your steps when I'm out on the bus."

"So I suppose those moments of peace will be the ones I cling to the most." She drags her focus back to her brother and glares. "I'm going to school, Marcus. And I'm going to learn how to help people."

"Kar—"

"So next time a man and his wife are shot in their own homes for no reason except some asshole wanted something that didn't belong to him, maybe I could be part of the team that saves them."

Finally, Marc's tone softens. "Kar..."

"I won't be able to help everyone. Just like you can't protect me from every single person, every single minute of my life. But I can try. I can do my very best to ensure a little boy, only twelve years old, doesn't have to become his sister's keeper. I can do my part to keep a family intact, and a child's trauma as minimal as possible."

"You're hitting me with logic, Kar. And emotions." Marc climbs the timber with ease, dropping down to sit on her left, blocking my view of the girl whose eyes search for mine every time we're in the same room.

It's not proper. And I'm not sure she'd admit it even if she was asked.

But love it or hate it, she searches for me every time.

Maybe it's to know where her guard dog is, and thus, where not to be.

But maybe it's something else. Maybe it's for the same reasons I look for her, too.

"You're growing up on me," Marcus moans. He wraps his arm over her shoulder and pulls her in till her mousy brown hair cascades over his shoulder and her cheek rests on his chest. "You were six the last time I checked. Now you're not. And you said that thing about sex."

She chokes out a watery, shaky laugh that cuts straight down the middle of my stomach.

"I was lashing out."

"Ya think? You took my kryptonite, and shoved it up my ass. No mercy."

"It's because you're so annoying." She squeezes in extra tight and happily sighs. "This isn't how things are supposed to be, Marcus. I should be arguing with the Turners about growing up. I should be discussing college with them. Not my brother."

"It's my business."

"It shouldn't *have* to be. You're supposed to just be my brother. The way Luca is just a brother to the twins."

"Fat load of good that does. His sisters have been voted three years in a row as most likely to go to prison for egging the police station." He pulls back and looks down into her eyes. "They're not pillars of society, Kar. They're the future of America's Most Wanted billboards."

"I'm still here, you know?" Pushing away from the garage door, I wander across the yard and approach the base of the halfpipe. "Pretty sure you guys are bitching about my family."

"It's okay," Kari sniffles, pulling back from her brother and wiping her sleeve across her top lip. "They're my family too. So I'm allowed."

8

LUC

ALONE NEVER FELT SO PAINFUL

"I take offense to that entire conversation I never even knew existed before this minute." Amused, Jess leans against Marcus' arm and plays with Billy's hair. "America's Most Wanted, my ass."

"I dunno." Marc grins. "You married Kane Bishop."

"Stop using my husband as some kind of criminal underworld symbol. He's former law enforcement! He's a respectable human being."

"*Former* being the operative word. Now he's the kind of guy the cops come looking for. He's a thug, Jess. You know that. I know that." Marc looks over at me. "Luc knows it. That's why you kept him a secret."

"I kept him a secret because the sex was good, and I wasn't ready to share him with my friends yet."

"Ugh!" I plug my ears, childish and stupid, and look up at the ceiling. "I don't want to know about my sister's sex life!"

"Welcome to my fuckin' world." Marcus rises from his perch on the chair, drawing my eyes back down as I feel, in my soul, the way Billy is shuffled from one set of arms to another.

I want her back. I want to hold my daughter and return to it just being me and her.

Daddy and his little girl.

Alone, in a world we were never supposed to be alone in.

Marcus hands her off to Jess, but he doesn't bolt right away. He leans over his niece and places a long, slow kiss to the crown of her head. "Her entire existence is built upon the fact my sister has a sex life." Shaking his head, he rises and shoots a heated glare my way. "With my best friend. That's on you, Luca. And I'll never truly forgive you for it."

"Yeah, well..." I give up on my dinner. On my generosity of allowing someone else to hold my daughter. I give up on standing so far away. And instead, I push away from the changing table and scoop Billy up before Jess even gets the chance to settle back comfortably. "I don't know that I'll ever forgive myself, either. If not for me, we wouldn't have been in that intersection eleven days ago, and if not for the pregnancy, Kari's injuries and treatment wouldn't have been so complicated." I turn on my heels and stalk toward the door. "That's all on me."

"Luca—"

"I'm going to bed," I call back. Outside Billy's bedroom door, I bend and scoop up my phone before continuing to the main bedroom. Fuck the crib. Fuck sleeping apart. Fuck the rules and the pamphlet the hospital foisted into my hands about safety and the dangers of co-sleeping.

Fuck it all.

No one will protect Billy the way I will.

"Let yourselves out," I tell Jess and Marc. "Lock up as you go. I'll call you tomorrow sometime."

I kick my shoes off as I walk, exhaustion beating down on my shoulders as though a one-ton anvil literally rests on my back, buckling my spine and making me weak. I close my bedroom door, locking the rest of the world out. Then I wander to my side of the bed, freshly made, though I know Kari and I didn't make it before heading out that last day. We were in a rush to get somewhere. Bickering, because I'd been working too much and Kari only wanted to spend the weekend locked up together. Curtains drawn. TV on. Just the two of us, the way it's been for so long.

But no.

"Daddy is an asshole, Bill." I drag the covers back and place the baby on the mattress. No pillow. No blankets. Nothing that'll harm her. Then I toss my phone down too, and step back and unsnap my jeans to reveal plain black shorts beneath. "Daddy was so focused on making money and *going-going-going*, using up every spare second because you and your brother were coming soon. And in the end, I screwed it all up."

I shuck my jeans away and peel my socks off. Outside the bedroom door, I hear shuffling feet. Hesitant steps. The *do-I-or-don't-I leave Luc here to bathe in his grief alone?*

But I don't go out to discuss it with them.

Not now.

Not tonight.

"Daddy wanted to save every penny for you, Bill. For our family. Because I didn't want that to be a stressor that would later make me a shitty dad. But in the end..." I draw a long, filling breath that expands my lungs and stretches them to their limit. Then I exhale again and edge my way onto the bed, careful not to compress the mattress too suddenly and have the baby roll toward me. "In the end, my stupid need to control it all was the reason we ended up in this mess."

Carefully, I lie on my side, my back to the massive picture window that overlooks our front yard, and scooping my hand under Billy's too-small body, I drag her closer until she nestles against my chest.

"Now it's just me and you, beautiful. Not so long ago, you would have been sleeping with your back against your brother's. Your little limbs, almost tangled. I bet you miss them, huh?" A heavy lump of nerves stops in my throat, balling in my windpipe and making it hard to breathe. "You've known a life of being inside your mom. Sleeping beside your brother. And now you're out here, in this crappy world where it's never really the right temperature and clothes itch our skin."

Swallowing, I reach over the baby and snag my phone.

The battery is already in the red. My screen, littered with messages from Ang. From Laine. Scotch and Sammy. Meg. Alex and Jules. Mitch and Nadia. Everyone who exists within this world Kari and I built together reaches out, hoping to bring me comfort. To ease the guilt that washes through my stomach every time I have a single second to think.

They're my friends. My family.

But they're outsiders.

And they're not who I want tonight while I snuggle in beside my sweet baby girl.

Ignoring the countless texts and missed calls, I jump to my messages and find Kari's name instead. I stare at our conversation history; the, *I love yous.*

The, *I miss yous.*

The, *what time will you be homes?* And, *can you pick up Ben and Jerry's on the way?*

There's a lifetime of *us* in these messages, decades of history already lived.

And there are way too fucking many, *are you picking up another shift, Luc? Again? Please come home.*

I failed my wife.

I failed my family.

With shaking fingers, I tap out a pathetic, *Billy and I miss you, Mommy. Sleep well.*

9

LUC

PLAYING WITH FIRE NEVER FELT SO FORBIDDEN

"Hey, Luca!"

I glance up from my focus on my shoes, my eyes on my feet only. My entire soul refusing me the chance to screw with the friendship I have with Marcus Macchio. But Kari's tinkling, playful voice is becoming a daily occurrence that haunts me. Her tormenting smile, a constant black mark on my life.

Not because I don't love seeing it.

But because I think she gets off on tempting me with it.

I grit my teeth and tilt my head up to catch sight of Kari at the bowl of the halfpipe, her knees already scuffed, her cheeks rosy and bright. Her hair is a frizzed mess, exploding from a single, struggling hair elastic.

Worst of all, she wears itty bitty shorts and an oversized Van Halen T-shirt.

"Marcus is working at the club this evening," she calls out. Her lips curl higher, taunting and devious, as my eyes scan her bare legs. "Scotch isn't here. Ang is at the garage. The twins and Britt are somewhere else." She places her foot on the tail of her board and smirks. "Guess that just leaves me and you."

Hence, my eyes on my fucking feet!

"Luuuuuca?" she teases. "Did you hear me?"

"Yeah…" I turn from the garage, my destination because I came here searching for my notebook, and instead point my body toward her. But I'll be damned if I take a step closer. I don't even lift my eyes beyond her knees. "It's getting dark, Bear. You should probably head inside or something."

"Or..." She kicks her board and flips it up. Most of us catch it after that. Too lazy to bend and collect it, we send it spiraling into the air and grab on with our fingers. But Kari was never skilled in this department. So instead, the board smacks her shin and elicits a stunned gasp from deep inside her chest. But she covers her reaction fast, swallowing down her squeak of pain and giggling, when I'm certain, the alternative would be to whimper.

The board rolls away and discreetly—but really, it's impossible to do so —she rubs her leg with her left hand.

"I'm staying out for a little while longer." She hobbles forward a step. "You should join me."

Yeah? Well I think that's a really bad fucking idea.

Because she's not a kid anymore. She's spent months manufacturing moments just like this one, where Marcus isn't around, and my sisters are off causing trouble somewhere else.

My willpower is crumbling faster than a sandcastle during high tide.

"I wanted to talk to you about some stuff anyway." Another hobbling step. "I've had some things on my mind. And I definitely can't talk to my brother about them."

"Maybe you could ask Britt, then. Or maybe Alex. He'd be great at whatever sensitive issue you want to discuss."

She chokes out a laugh. Her knowledge of Alex's *subtlety*, giving me away like a spotlight in the dark. Then she steps off the halfpipe, but lowers to sit on the edge. And still, she angles her head as though to force herself into my peripherals. "Luca?" Gently, she pats the wooden structure beside her thigh. "Please sit with me."

"Actually... I'd rather stand over here." I dig my hands into my pockets, fussing with the lint buried deep inside. Finding a guitar pick. A piece of string. An old pencil, used, sharpened, and used again until only an inch remains. "I'm good where I am."

"You used to hang out with me more." She rests her arms on her heightened knees, then her chin on her arms. "You used to walk me home a lot. Take me to Popcorn Palace. You'd even spend time with me out here in the yard, even when Marcus wasn't around."

Yeah. Back when you were a kid.

Now you're eighteen, and fuck, but that's messing with me.

"I've been busy."

"You've been avoiding me."

"I've been working." Fuck, but I want to look up and meet her beautiful eyes. "I've got this new partner on the rig, and he can be kinda prickly sometimes. He's a bit like Marcus," I scoff. "Super protective big brothers whose tempers trigger kinda fast."

"So you have tons of experience handling him." She rubs the spot beside her leg again. "Sit with me."

"I don't want to."

"Is it because you want me, too?"

Instantly, my head jerks up against my wishes, and my eyes lock on to hers. "What?"

"I mean…" She hugs her legs and smirks. "I spend time with Scotch. And Ang. And of course, Marcus, too. I hang out with Alex. And Oz. I have all these guys in my life, brothers I never really asked for." Her cheeks warm. "And I'm not as pretty as Jess and Laine and Britt. Sammy might be the most beautiful person I ever met. And Meg, too. So much confidence oozing from her pores."

"You're comparing yourself to your friends?" Scowling, I take another step forward. I swear I don't instruct my feet to move. I don't even recognize the moment my brain allows the action. But if she's comparing, then she's hurting herself. And hell, but I've lived a life where my role was to keep her safe.

For Marcus. For her own good.

For my own selfish needs.

"You can't compare yourself to them, Bear. They're people. You're a different person."

"Laine is so confident," she sighs. "And Jess is just a single step behind her. They rule the school, Luca. It's not like it was when you were there. It's not even a jock's school anymore. It's Jess and Laine's. They run the place, and it's gonna get worse now that they're about to start their senior year."

"Jess and Laine are pretty, tall, blonde chicks. They're literally what basic white dudes like to look at. Doesn't make you any less…" *Beautiful.*

But shit, I can't finish my sentence without giving too much away.

"Comparison is the thief of joy… or something like that," I mumble. "Don't do that to yourself."

"Why not? You have no problem sitting next to the twins."

"They're my sisters."

"And Britt?" she challenges. Firming her lips, she raises a single, demanding brow. "You hang out with her all the time."

"She's just…" Frustration sizzles in my blood. "She's my friend's sister. It's always been this way."

"And you've always been happy to spend time with me." She lies back on the halfpipe, her feet still on the ground, and her back arching against the wood. Smiling, she stares up at the stars and exhales. "Something changed, Luca. And I think that thing is that you're attracted to me."

Fuckkkkk her. Fuck her age. Fuck her brother. And fuck the stars, too.

"I think I'm not nearly confident enough to have this conversation with you, eye to eye," she snickers. "But I've been sitting on it since my birthday. Trying to talk to you. Trying to understand the change. But you've made it impossible. It's like I turned eighteen and developed a rash you really don't want to catch."

"That's not true, Bear." I move closer, slowing when ten feet separate me and her. Seven feet. Six. Already, her sweet perfume wafts through my nostrils and stops in the base of my lungs. "I've been working. We aren't teenagers anymore. School isn't my life. I have to work, and those shifts aren't always conducive to hanging out with my friends."

She tilts her head and glares, fearlessly calling me out on my shit. "You hang out with Marcus every single day."

"He's my best friend. I like to get a beer with him sometimes. So what?"

"You leave your beer half consumed and walk home when I turn up to hang out."

Damn. It's not like she's wrong.

I look down at my feet and bite my lips together before she manages to squeeze a smile from me. "I have to be on shift early the next morning. Drinking a whole beer and staying out late would be irresponsible."

"Liar." She drops her hand to the side and pats the splintered, wooden platform. "Sit with me. Study the stars for a minute. No one else will come out here tonight."

"Bear—"

"No one will see you. I won't tell anyone." She exhales a heavy, contented sigh and grins. "I love to stare up at the stars. It's my absolute favorite thing to do. And I'd really, really like to share that with you."

Fuck. Fuck. Fuckity, fuck.

Loyalties can sometimes blur when a man is being asked by the love of his life to spend time with her. Jesus, lines cease to exist when his heart shatters open and something unexpected dives in.

Some*one* unexpected.

And no matter how hard he fights against it, no matter how strongly he clings to what is right, what is fair, and what will, eventually, hurt like hell when Marcus smashes his face in for looking at his sister, there's only so much one can do to stop the inevitable.

So I force down the nerves in my throat and wander the rest of the way to the halfpipe. I stare at a watchful, grinning Kari, and hold my jaw firmly. I don't open my mouth to speak. I don't smile. I don't even roll my eyes when she makes a double chin and a silly face.

But I turn and press my calves to the base of the halfpipe, lowering my ass to the shitty, bowing wood and know, months of hard work, of being where she's not, and yet, watching over her to keep her safe anyway, will all be for naught if she gets her way.

"I can think you're pretty, Bear." Hesitant, I glance to my right and rest my chin on my own shoulder. "I can think you're smart and funny and amazing. And I can even grieve the fact you're heading off to college in a few weeks, leaving us behind and starting a life that doesn't include me in it. Doesn't mean I can step across a line set down more than a decade ago."

"And that line is… what? Don't mess around with your friend's sister?"

I nod, ever so gently and firm my lips. "Amongst others. Messing around with your friend's sister is a big one. But there's also the friendship you and I share."

"A friendship you've abandoned for most of this year. You dumped me faster than Sassy St Slut dumps hair colors."

"I have a history," I groan. I study her slender neck. The million freckles smattering her cheeks that kind of look like stars in the nighttime sky. "I'm not exactly known around town as a dude who takes relationships seriously."

"I believe the word they use is slut." Her plump lips curl playfully. "You're known as a dirty, filthy, nasty fun-time, Luca. It's okay; we know what they say."

"Well… yeah," I sigh. "That's what they say. Because I'm the guy who dates for fun and spends time with women because I enjoy them."

Her eyes darken. Dangerously. Threatening.

"I don't take relationships seriously. I rarely revisit the same person more than a time or two. And I'm okay with what people say about it. I am who I am."

"And perhaps you're you, because you haven't found a woman to take seriously yet." She grabs my shoulder, digging her nails into my flesh until I feel her threat, then she drags me back until I lie flat on the halfpipe and my head tilts her way.

But now our eyes meet.

Her sweet breath on my tongue.

Her soft exhalations, a tickle on my lips.

"You're a chauvinistic pig who tries women out like they're a 'trial before you buy' kind of situation. It's an icky personality trait to have."

"Exactly, so—"

"But I have a theory." She glances down at my lips. It's brief. Fleeting. So fucking inappropriate, I already hurt from the punishment Marcus is going to slam into my body. "My theory," she whispers, "is that you've been waiting."

"Waiting?"

She nods, just a tiny movement that somehow packs as much punch as if she'd swung her head around. "Waiting. Your heart knew those women weren't right. But you were so caught up in loyalty and family and what was *proper*, you never stopped to examine the why and the who."

"Kari—"

"Are you attracted to me, too, Luca?" Her green eyes glitter under a million stars. Her cheeks, warming because she's just not *this* person. She's not forward. Not confident. She doesn't solicit a man and put her feelings on the table first. "I need you to answer me with just a yes or a no. There are no justifications allowed here. No qualifiers. It's really simple. Are you attracted to me too?"

A long, pained groan works along my throat. "Bear... I can't—"

"Yes," she growls. "Or no?"

"Yes." I bring my head back around and my eyes up to the half-moon shining bright in the darkened sky. "Yes, I am. But it's not gonna happen."

She turns on the platform, resting on her side and cupping her face with her hand. I see her in my peripherals. But I refuse to drop my gaze and look her way again. "What's not gonna happen?"

"You and me."

"A relationship? Why not?"

"Because you're a fucking child. Because you're way too young to be thinking about *anything* with a guy like me."

"I'm not a child." And just to fuck with me, she hovers her free hand over my chest and traces the pattern of my shirt with the tip of her finger. "In fact, I haven't been a child in quite some time."

"You're my best friend's baby sister."

"A topic that has been discussed ad nauseum. Men hit on your sisters every single day of their existence. Do you think it's something you, as their brother, get to control?"

"No. But I'm not Marcus, and Marcus has made his wishes clear on the matter."

"You mean, his wishes that I live a very long, very boring life with my girlfriends, seven cats, and absolutely no interaction with danger, excitement, or men?"

"Pretty much." I reach up and take her hand. It's short lived, and still, her eyes alight in my peripherals. But then I push it away and release her before I forget how.

Now her eyes darken. Narrow.

"You're heading off to college." I swallow and glance to the side. It's a mistake. A weakness I swore not to give in to. But she's so pretty. So sweet. And so close, I'm not sure in all my life I've been this near to her. "You're leaving, Bear. And you're gonna be gone for years."

"School is an hour away, not the other side of the world. I could come home every single night if I wanted to. Every weekend if I was feeling lazy."

"Being on the freeway every damn day is dangerous. And you'll need weekends to catch up on your schoolwork."

"So you don't *want* me around?"

"I don't want you to plan your life around a fucking relationship that can't happen. You're gonna be free, Bear!" Giving up on my distance, I flip onto my side and set my hand beneath my ear to cushion it from the splinters. "Our town has, like..." I wrack my brain and think of the welcome sign on the outskirts. "I dunno. Six thousand people. Max. Everyone knows everyone. There's no such thing as career advancement unless the person above you retires or dies. There are no guys around here nearly good enough to date you. And if you sit your NCLEX and come back here to work, you'll spend your life helping idiots who flip their cars at Piper's Lane, and kids who screw around down at the steel mill. You have a chance to get away, Bear. A chance to escape Marc's protective suffocation."

Her eyes widen, scandalized and a little horrified. "You *want* me to move away from my brother?"

"I want you to have the choice. To be whoever you want to be. To do whatever you want to do. I love your brother, Kari, like he's my brother, too. But I also know a trauma case when I see one. He needs help to understand what the fuck happened to him, and you need help to understand your life doesn't have to be controlled by a man."

"And so..." Her lips curl higher. "In your attempt to piss Marcus off and set me free from his dictatorial regime, you're telling me what to do? And on top of that, you're especially certain you *won't* cross the best friend picket line and kiss me on the halfpipe we all helped build and repair over the years?"

I drop my gaze to her lips. My hunger to taste her, almost jumping from my throat like a wildcat.

"Luca?"

"I didn't say he was a dictator. Or that he should be escaped." I force my eyes up, like a physical, torturous climb my soul rejects. But I stop on her eyes instead and enjoy that balm one feels after a burn. "I said I want you to have choices. Whatever they might be. Wherever. With whomever."

"And if my choice is... you?"

Yes. Please. Fuck. For the love of god, let her be mine.

"Staying in this town and choosing me is not a choice at all, Bear. It's a *lack* of choices. You have a crush, just like every other schoolgirl does over time. It's a natural phenomenon for little sisters to flirt with their older brother's friends. You think Britt isn't hitting on Ang half the time? You think Jess and Laine don't give me a heart attack daily, checking out Alex's *much older* friends? It's the way of the world. So of course, me walking you home when Marc was too busy to be there, and us hanging out at Popcorn Palace was gonna leave a mark on your soul."

"We wrote songs together."

"Yes." I gulp so the ball of nerves lodged in my throat fights its way into my stomach. "And we've skated together. We've had secrets."

"You took a beating from Garth Beaterman and his friends for me."

"Because I'm here to protect you. I'm here to make sure you're okay. But of course, all that history is gonna cloud your judgement. You think there's something here, when in reality, all it is is a lack of choices."

"So you won't kiss me tonight?" She breaks our eye contact, stealing her soul away from me, and looks up at the sky instead. "Under the stars. While it's just the two of us."

"Bear..."

"You'd prefer I go off to college and screw around with those guys instead. To understand my options."

The very thought is like a hot poker to my stomach. But I do the right thing. The selfless thing, and nod. "Yes. I want you to experience college life the right way."

"So if I do that," she drags her eyes back down, her long lashes, like wings framing the windows to her soul. "If I sleep around a little bit, kiss a few frogs, get that experience on my bedpost, so to speak…"

Filthy, disgusting, burning acid creeps along my throat.

"You'll kiss me next summer? Since, by then, I'll have all this worldly experience?"

"The theory stands," I grit out, "that once you've made out with those frogs, you'll have forgotten about your silly little crush."

"You offend me." She licks her dry lips and brings her arm back behind her head. Then she gives up on me, resting on her back instead, and stares up at the moon. "Invalidating my feelings. Calling them silly." She looks to her left, just a movement of her eyes. "That hurts. Are you dating anyone else right now?"

"Am I…" I push up to my elbow and set my chin in my palm. "Why are you asking about my dating life?"

"Because I wanted to. You in a relationship I don't know about?"

"No."

"Bringing any women home that you haven't told us about?"

"No."

"When was the last time you went out on a date?"

"Kari, I don't—"

"Answer the question, Luca!" She shoves up to rest on her elbow, her chin folding in a wholly unflattering way, and yet, she's totally, impossibly beautiful. "When was the last time you went on a date?"

"May. Why?"

Her eyes dance with something I haven't yet figured out. "Interesting. And more weight added to my theory. How does it feel here," she presses her palm to my chest, her fingers like fire against my skin that speeds my heart to a thudding roar, "to hear me plan out a year of casual fuckery with random men you'll never know the names or faces of?"

Homicidal, mostly. Sick, definitely. "Hopeful," I choke out, "that it'll be the start of a very happy, fulfilling life that you won't eventually regret."

"You think I might regret staying?"

"Yes!" I take her hand and move it away. *Second time. Second sin.* "You stay in this podunk town in the middle of nowhere, hook up with a guy you've known your whole life, and see *nothing* of the world? Yes, you'll regret it, Bear. What are your plans for this?" I look down between us, loathing the three inches that separate her body from mine. "We make out a few times. Break the news to Marc. I propose or risk his bullet in my back. We get hitched, make a few babies, destroy the career you're about to build. And then… what? Die old, but together?"

"I don't think Marcus would demand a proposal." She's entirely too fucking flippant about things, lying back and grinning up at the sky. "I think he'd sooner kill and bury you in the woods out by Popcorn Palace. I don't intend to destroy my career. In fact, women have married and made babies for a long time, and they've still maintained outside employment. Oh, and," she glances across to meet my stare. "I feel you're jumping way ahead here. I'm not asking for marriage tonight. I'm asking for a kiss. Ya know… to test things out."

"To test what out? How long I can live with Marcus's fist planted squarely in the side of my face?"

She sniggers, full of fun and tempting. So fucking tempting.

"You're exceptionally dramatic, considering the vocation you chose. Your job is literally to remain calm in high-stress situations. And yet, you're here throwing out marriage proposals, best friend blow ups, and the sex talk, all before we've even kissed."

"You're trying to wear me down." I drop to my back and close everything up. My eyes. My lips. My ears, if I could. My entire fucking soul, if only I hadn't already given it to someone else. "You think you can be cute and consistent, and my baser instincts will give you anything you want."

"It's working, right?"

I feel her weight on my chest. The stab of her elbow against my sternum. Instantly, my eyes fling open and stop on hers, just two inches away. Her large halo of hair, blocking my view of the sky. Her gentle breath, coating my lips and tongue. And worst of all, her smile, swearing that everything is already agreed and sorted. "It's just a kiss, Luca. You've done it a million times, I'm certain."

Yeah. That's the fuckin' problem.

"I'm eighteen," she insists. "I'm grown. And soon, I'll be kissing someone else anyway."

That's a fuckin' problem, too.

"Don't let me go to college without knowing what it could be like."

"Bear…" I groan. "Stop."

"You love me," she pleads. "Whether it's familial, or friendship, or something more, something deeper, we can both acknowledge out loud that we have love." She searches my eyes. "Right?"

Say no. Say no. Say no! But I can't. It's impossible. So I dip my chin just a fraction of an inch. "Yes, Bear. There's love."

"And we both know this isn't me." She looks down at my chest. At my lips. Then up to my eyes. "I don't put myself forward like this, ever. I'm terrified of rejection. And here you are, saying no, time and time again."

Pain lances through my gut and up to stab at my heart. "I'm not trying to reject you, I swear. I'm not trying to hurt you."

"No. You're trying to do the right thing. But that right thing is Marcus' version of right. And yours." She searches my eyes. "But what about mine?"

"What do *you* consider the right thing? Me having a one-night stand with my best friend's sister, all because she was feeling bratty and wanted a quick fuck before college?"

"I said kiss," she smirks. "I didn't mention fucking. And yes, my version of right is experiencing some of the big things with someone who loves me. Someone I love in return. Would you have me trust some douchey Chad when he says, *'it's okay, baby. Sex isn't supposed to be pleasurable for you. Just for me.'*" She deepens her tone, setting my temper on fire. "Or, *'it's okay, babe. Kissing includes me grabbing your tit, even if you didn't say I could.'*"

"If someone grabs you without your permission, you cut his nuts out and call me so I can help clean up. If he fucks you and it doesn't feel good, then he didn't do it right."

"Should I cut *his* nuts out, too? For being a dud."

"Yep. Then you aim for better. Because the one you chose was useless. You're not the first inexperienced girl to go off to college, Kari. It's okay to not know everything right away."

"It's just a kiss, Luc." She drags her bottom lip between her teeth and searches my eyes. She readjusts her weight on my chest, pressing down on my ribs and reminding me of the beating I took for her years ago. "Just one time," she implores. "I'll never tell Marcus. And for the rest of our lives, even after I head off to college and marry someone else who'll impregnate me and ruin my life, we can continue to sit across from each other at family dinner and know, we have our secrets."

She walks her fingers over my chest and around to stroke my neck. It's like fire and ice in one, a nirvana-like touch that sets me ablaze, and yet, soothes my soul.

"I want to have that secret with you." She pauses for a moment, smirking when my eyes flicker between hers. "I've thought about it since I was fifteen years old and you stopped being that annoying guard dog I was trying to hide from, and instead, you turned exceptionally handsome in my eyes."

"You're asking for trouble." *And I'm running out of excuses.* "Kari…"

She inches forward. Closer, closer, until I think my heart might stop completely. Her lips are just a hair's breadth from mine. Her lashes, almost near enough to touch my cheeks. Best and worst of all, her heart pounds against mine.

Her intentions, clear as day and as unavoidable as a collision on the freeway.

"I'm going to kiss you," she whispers. "So if you're ever asked, you can deny being the instigator." Closer, until her moving lips brush against mine. "If you love me at all, in any way or form, at any point in our lives, then I'd like for you to kiss me back. Because if I'm being completely and totally honest," she pulls back to search my expression, "rejection might break my heart."

I slide my hand into her hair. I don't mean to. My fingers combing into her locks. I swear to god, I don't make the decision to move my arm. But I still find myself cupping the side of her head. My heart, thundering in my chest until I'm certain it'll burst free and fly away.

"Just one time," I groan. "Because I'm not gonna be the guy who breaks your heart."

"Thank god." Her breath comes out on an emotional shudder that claws at my soul. But then she folds in closer, keeping up her end of the deal and being the one who starts us.

Because when the day comes and Marcus finds out what I've done, I have to be able to say I fought it.

She presses her lips to mine, hesitant at first. Shaky, like she thinks I could actually reject her at this point.

But then she gets brave, moving her lips, opening them fractionally. Stroking my bottom lip with the very tip of her tongue.

She undoes me.

Her vulnerability destroys me.

But her fear… it shatters my willpower.

I fist my hand in her hair and tighten until a devastating whimper rockets along her throat and out to bathe my tongue. But then I smile. Her eyes turn to molten lava. And I ruin all the *I didn't start it* bullshit when I push up to my elbow and cushion her head until she's lying on her back, her heart thundering and her breath racing. Lowering over her, I press my lips over hers and taste her tongue on mine. I squeeze my eyes shut and lock down on every muscle in my body, refusing myself the opportunity to touch her the way I want to. To have her the way my body craves.

I slide my tongue along her bottom lip and groan when she whimpers. Suckling on her lips and tasting her right down into my soul. I release the fist-hold I have on her hair, only to growl when she reaches up and forces my hand back into place.

She wants me to hold on. She wants me to be in charge.

I fight against everything I am when my hips would have me climbing over her delicate body. Pinning her down. Separating her legs and finding comfort in her warmest places.

Because fuck, if I could, I would.

If I knew for sure we wouldn't regret it tomorrow, I'd take her out here and satisfy the million questions firing through my mind.

"We have to stop." I break our kiss with a gasp, pulling back and pressing my lips to her shoulder instead. A poor second choice. A mirage to a starving man. "Fuck, Bear." I bury my face in the warm curve of her neck and work to collect my wits.

My common sense.

Marcus could be standing over us right now, clutching a meat cleaver and ready to lop my head off, and I wouldn't even know it.

"That wasn't so bad." Humming with satisfaction, she releases my hand and allows me to place it on the halfpipe instead. To push myself off her chest and create space, though we both know it's too late for that.

I've crossed the line I said I wouldn't. I've tasted her.

I sampled Kari Macchio, and now I'm a man addicted.

"Tulips."

Stunned, reeling, I turn and lower to my back beside her. My shoulder touching hers, and her long, wild hair, tickling the bare flesh of my arm. My breath continues to heave. To search for fresh air, and yet, it scrambles to keep *her* inside me.

"Luca?"

"Hmm?" I just turn my head and search her eyes. "What?"

"Tulips."

"The flowers? What about them?"

"I don't want roses. I don't want diamonds. When you want to show me affection, or apologize for something you did, or maybe even *just because*, I like tulips."

"Oh...kay?"

"I like chocolate. White chocolate is better than milk chocolate. Milk chocolate is better than dark chocolate. I prefer my steak cooked until it's still just a little pink. I don't want it to bleed, but I also don't want it to be all brown."

"Alright..."

"I like to read. All the time. All the books. I like the kissy kind. The ones where the hero would do anything for his heroine. Where he will *be* anything she needs." She rises to her elbow and looks down at me. "I like staring up at the stars more than anything else. And quality time spent with those I love. I don't want diamonds or chocolate or even tulips if I can have time instead. Oh, and I've been waiting for years for you to invite me onto the back of your motorcycle."

"Onto my bike?" I choke out. "Marc would kill me!"

"He'll wanna kill you for kissing me anyway." She leans in and drops a fast, sneaky kiss to the center of my lips. "We won't tell him. I like coffee first thing in the morning. It's not an addiction, it's a routine. I could quit any time."

I narrow my eyes and question her honesty.

"I'm going to be an RN. Ultimately, I'd like to work trauma in the ER. So comfortable shoes and a nice watch are probably right up there for yearly Christmas gifts. I want children someday. Lots of them."

"Children?" I scramble onto my elbows and pull back to place space between me and her. "Kari, hold on—"

"I don't necessarily mean with you. I don't even need you to get me steak or shoes or books. But I'm sharing the things you don't know about me. So eventually, someday, when you're not afraid of my brother and *if* we continue kissing some more, you'll have a head start. And if not, then I'll tell these things to the next guy I kiss. And the guy after that. Eventually, one of them will be the right one, and at that point, he'll order my steak exactly right, and maybe he'll have a motorcycle too."

"I'm not taking you on my bike." Hard stop. No way. Not happening. "It's too dangerous."

"Then maybe a guy in college will." Satisfied, she flops back down and brings her hand up to touch her plump bottom lip. "I liked kissing you, Luca. It was better than I expected."

"Kari—"

"And you gave in way faster than I expected."

"For fuck's sake." I slam my eyes shut and groan. *I'm a dead man.*

10

LUC

IT'S CALLED BONDING

I wake in the dark to Billy stirring, her little body twisting in her wrap and her face readying to screw up. I've spent enough time with infants to know she's hungry.

And she's about to be pissed about it.

"I got you, Beautiful." A long, drawn-out yawn wracks my frame and holds me captive, while remnants of a dream fade into the back of my mind. A first kiss. A challenge. Kari Macchio's first ever attempt at being seductive.

And me, the idiot who could never say no, even when we both knew we shouldn't be playing with fire.

I think of what came after that kiss. The hours we spent on the halfpipe. Talking. Skating. Laughing. She was able to relax because she'd gotten her way, and her nerves had subsided. But in exchange, my stress levels were at an all-time high.

Because I kissed my best friend's, completely, totally, off limits, *don't touch or you'll die*, little sister.

And I was certain the next time Marc looked me in the eye, surely he'd know what I'd done.

You need to relax, she'd laugh, taunting me. *It was just a kiss.*

But it was never just a kiss between us. Ever. Not then, and not now.

I scan my bedroom in the dark, the streetlights outside casting just enough muted light through to make it possible to see where the bed starts and ends. Where the dressers are. Where the catch-all chair is, still, with Kari's shirt draped over the arm. I search the bedroom for a bottle of formula and a chance to not have to leave the bed.

Though it's futile. I haven't made any bottles up, and doing so and leaving the mixed formula out all night would make my baby sick.

I know this.

But a tired brain needs a few extra seconds to click back into gear.

"We need milk, Bill." I yawn again, my face aching and my jaw clicking from how wide I open my mouth. I toss my sheet aside and place my feet on the throw rug Kari and I had bickered over for hours.

She wanted a shag, so the long threads would be the first thing we touched in the mornings.

I wanted something lower cut. Something more sophisticated.

I dig my toes into the lush shag now and try to smile, knowing she won that argument. She won the argument we had about pillows. The one about live plants in our bedroom. The one about getting a dog—I wanted one, and she was entirely too sensible, citing our ridiculous shifts and the fact that the pup would be home alone a little too much.

Things have changed now, of course. Billy has arrived, and no matter the plans Kari and I made that led us here, my work commitments are going to have to change.

Because bad things happen to good people.

Assholes run red lights.

And best laid plans are always a magnet for utter devastation.

"Come on, baby." I push up to stand and turn to scoop Billy into my arms. She doesn't smell yet, so I have time on the diaper change situation. Instead, I hold her close and rest her ear over my heart. It's what she'd find comfort in, right? She had her mom, and now… she has me.

A heartbeat is surely the next best thing in an otherwise fucked up situation.

Stepping away from the bed and using the streetlight outside to guide my way, I wander toward the bedroom door and into the dimly lit hall outside.

Tomorrow, I'll sort out a solution to make bottles upstairs. Maybe boil and prep water, then divvy up the powder and ready it to be dropped into the bottle at the last second.

It could all be done without me getting up and wandering downstairs. Waking us both all the way up when sleep is where we could be visiting the woman we love.

The one our entire existences revolve around.

"Does it feel like you're missing half of you, too, Bill?" I move down the stairs, one slow step at a time as the world outside is just... silent. Cool. Calm. "Does everything feel too quiet for you, too?"

"I'm down here," a male voice rumbles through my home. Instantly, my head snaps up and my heart gives a painful knock. "Just be cool," Kane murmurs. Slowly, he steps into view at the bottom of my stairs, the six and a half feet of tatted thuggery skulking around in the shadows. "I didn't want you to get down here and panic."

Anger beats in my blood, though it's fleeting. Worry follows after, but Kane is a safe person for me and my family. Despite his criminal enterprises. Despite the danger his very existence poses. "Jesus, Bishop. Why the hell are you in my home?"

"Jess wanted to stay." His eyes are on Billy, his almost-black stare seemingly threatening. But I know better. I know differently. He drops his tattooed hands into his jeans pockets and tilts his head as I come to a stop. Then he grins, boyish and playful when I push the baby toward his chest. He cradles her instantly. Protects her as I move off the bottom step and head toward the kitchen. "Your sister wanted to stay," he repeats and rocks the baby, following me toward the kitchen. "But the girls wanted her at home, too. No way was I letting her or them sleep here on the couch, so I traded off. Jess is with the twins, Jay and Soph are staying with them, too. I'm here keeping an eye on you, since you're clearly about to light this town up with your rage and an automatic weapon."

"I don't even own one of those." I roll my eyes and snag an already half-filled bottle of water. My sisters have intervened. They've taken some of the work out of my hands, like they said they would. Then I turn to find the tubs of formula, just two feet away. "I'm too busy with Billy to embrace my anger just yet."

"Seems I'm an overachiever then." Kane wanders in and leans against the counter. "Because I can be pissed, productive, *and* get revenge on a guy, all at the same time. Sometimes, that's what makes it extra fun."

"Yes. But you're a fuckin' psycho whose rap sheet has not yet been shared with me." I firm my lips and get to work mixing formula and water. "I'm starting to hear things about you, Bish. Concerning things."

"Yeah?" His lips curl in my peripherals. His mischievousness, the very reason my sister fell in love with a thug in the first place. "The ink dried on my marriage certificate a while back, Lenaghan. Seems the return policy has ended." He chuckles, his chest cushioning my daughter and bouncing while she half dozes. "What have you heard about me?"

"Illegal things. Marc said something about you."

"Then Marc and I will talk tomorrow." He lifts Billy and presses a kiss to her pert nose. "She looks just like Luna did when she was brand new."

"Lenaghan genes were strong." A lance of pain works across my stomach and almost takes my breath away. "Seems like a lot of work for a woman to carry a baby as long as they do, only for them to give birth and have it to come out as a copy/paste of their daddy. Doesn't really seem fair."

He strokes a tattooed finger along the bridge of Billy's nose, providing a contrast most others would panic at. The hardened, dangerous, machine-like mercenary, and the sweet, innocent, days old infant. I should be worried. I should snatch my baby back and keep him away... according to society. But there's this thing they say about judging books by their covers.

And Kane Bishop is nothing if not the epitome of a mismatched cover not representing the heart inside.

"She's her own human being, Lenaghan. This is who she is, and this is what she looks like. Are you gonna look her in the eye and tell her she's doing it wrong?"

"No." I tip powder into the water and re-fasten the lid. "She's beautiful exactly the way she is."

"Would you change her, then?" He's biased because he married a Lenaghan, then he created one that looks just like mine. "Would you swap her out for something else?"

I pinch the bottle nipple closed to avoid liquid spraying the counter and cupboards, then I turn and study my sweet baby, shaking my hand to mix her meal. "No. I'm not giving her up for anything."

"So there you have it. Maybe you think it's unfair, because Kari did all the hard work. But I assure you, if she heard you questioning this, she'd smack you upside the head for it." He holds her in one arm and reaches out with the other hand. "Can I give her the bottle? I've missed her."

"Sure." I place it in his palm and head over to the dining table instead, a long yawn wracking my frame and bringing tears to the corners of my eyes. Pulling out a wooden chair and gritting my teeth when the legs scrape along the floor, I flop down and set my elbows on the tabletop, my face in my hands. "She's supposed to be here with us, Bish." I force my eyes open and my head around until I catch him swaying with a tiny baby in his arms. "This wasn't the plan."

"Sometimes plans change." He places the nipple between Billy's lips and grins when she guzzles instantly. "It's not fair. It wasn't what she wanted. And it sure as shit wasn't nice that the universe wanted to punish you. None of that is your fault, though."

"I feel like a shit dad on top of it all," I groan, "because Billy's here. She's safe. Strong. Beautiful. She was allowed to come home, but instead of celebrating how amazing she is, I'm being a dick and thinking about all the things I don't have."

"Makes you human. You love someone enough to marry them, Lenaghan, you're gonna miss them when they're not here with you."

"What would you have done if it was Jess?" Emotion balls in my throat, strangling me until I'm not sure I have the strength to stand again. "You're married to the love of your life. She's pregnant. Glowing and beautiful. Approaching full term with your babies. And then you just…" I exhale the welling, venomous poison bubbling along my esophagus. "Some asshole runs a red light and destroys every happy plan you ever made."

"Well, personally, I would destroy *his* every happy plan." Deadly serious, he glances across in the shadows and meets my eyes with a black stare. "He didn't run it because he was momentarily distracted, Luc. He wasn't tired from working hard. It wasn't even a cellphone that had his attention, though that would *also* be a fucking crime. This asshole was drunk. Plain and simple. And it wasn't his first rodeo. He's been in and out of prison his whole life for far worse crimes. He gets out after the last stint, moves back into his trailer and drives around drunk every few days on his way to the liquor store to stock up on more. Sometimes the cops see him. Sometimes they don't."

"You have a lot of information about these people that I don't."

"Because Kari is my family. Because these babies are my family." He taps Billy's nose with the tip of his pinky finger. "I make it my business to research this stuff. And then I watch. When the time is right and you're feeling up to it, I'd be happy to drive you over there and show you how I take care of my family."

My eyes narrow, my brows pinching in suspicion. "Take care of them, how?"

He smirks. "Until you're ready to ride with me, you don't get the details. That's just smart business."

11

LUC

TIME TO PAY THE PIPER

"Luca!" A door slams, startling me from my sleep as I shove up in bed and process Marcus' enraged voice tearing through my house. Remembering Kari on my lips, her hand on my chest, and my fingers in her hair, my soul shrivels up.

The end is here.

"Luc!" Marcus calls again. I don't know where the rest of my family is. Why is no one intervening? Why do they so willingly step aside and allow me to be murdered by my own best friend? "Hey! Are you in bed?"

Yes. Fuck. Alone.

Thank god.

I look to my right to make a hundred percent certain I haven't had a stroke over night and brought Kari to my bed. But there's no one else here with me. No one whose presence would make my inevitable death exponentially more painful.

"Luc!"

"I'm up here." I pull my sheet up and shuffle back on the bed until I can rest against the headboard. Then I rub my eyes and spy the clock on my bedside table. It's barely seven in the damn morning. "What the hell, Marcus? I'm on night shift tonight."

He stomps through the door, swinging it open without knocking and skidding to a stop on the threshold to look me up and down. He hasn't changed a lot from when he was twelve. His hair is still midnight black, his eyes, green. The chiseled lines of his cheekbones and jaw have become more angular. *And his right hook... more powerful.* But all in all, he's still mostly the same tall, broad-shouldered soldier who stands in front of Kari every second of every day.

"What?"

He doesn't speak. Doesn't dive over my bed and pound my face in for kissing his sister. He doesn't even appear to be overly angry, which is a welcome relief.

"Why are you stomping into my house at this godawful hour and waking my family?"

"Your parents are at work, and the twins are already at Turner's place." He wanders into my room, digging his hands into his pockets and scanning my walls. He's like a fucking cop, and I'm his suspect.

Or maybe that's just guilt eating me up.

"Kari called a girl's meeting or some shit. Had something exciting to share with everyone."

"Oh?" *Calm down, dickhead. Calm the hell down.* "W-what exciting thing?"

"I don't know. That's why I'm here." He stops by my old drum kit in the corner of my room and runs his finger across the layer of dust that has collected since I replaced it with a newer, better set a while back. "Do you have any clue what's going on?" Suspicious, like Mulder and Scully—I have no fucking clue which one is which—he glances over his shoulder and pins me with a knowing stare. "Have you heard anything from the twins?"

"No." Jesus christ. Kari swore she wouldn't tell Marcus about our kiss. But did she swear not to tell the girls?

No!

"I don't know..." I swallow to lubricate my painfully dry throat. "Um... what do you think it could be?"

He shrugs and turns, setting his hands on his hips. "She's going to college in a few weeks. She's pretty fuckin' thrilled about it," he adds bitterly. "Got her dorm assignment already. We're in the middle of ordering textbooks. Nothing new is going on with all that." He kicks one ankle over the other and sneers. "It's a guy."

My stomach lurches, threatening to make a fool of me and mess up my bed. "What?"

"She must be seeing someone, right? Girls don't get squealy and weird except about men. Then they lose their absolute fucking minds and regress back to the school-girl giggles."

"Um…" Push it down. Push all the vomit down. "I dunno, man. They're not in seventh grade anymore. I'm not sure *these* girls do that stuff."

"Maybe not the twins."

His instant dismissal has my brows shooting high in question. *Excuse, the fuck, me?*

"Jess and Laine, and even Britt, are constantly talking to guys," he continues. "It's like you and Scotch don't give a single fuck about their dating lives."

"It's not that we don't care. It's that we don't feel the need to control everything."

"It's not control." He brushes me off again. "It's precaution. Kari is the quiet one in that group of girls. She's not out there chatting up guys every damn day. She's not as outgoing or as confident. So if one caught her eye, then that would be *exciting news* to share, no? And considering what we know about her being shy and all that, chances are *the guy* is some opportunistic prick we need to protect her from."

Fuck. Me. Sideways.

"I think you're jumping way ahead of yourself." I slump back into bed and flop my arm over my eyes, blinding myself and pressing down until stars float in my vision. "Your sister wants to hang with her girlfriends. And you're catastrophizing that until it's a situation where she's being taken advantage of by some fuckin' Chad you don't even know."

"Exactly." He grabs my sheet and yanks it off my legs until I'm completely exposed in the middle of my bed. The cool morning air, prickling my skin. "Let's go for a drive and see what we see."

"You're insane. And I have a shift tonight. If I'm tired and someone dies on my watch, who do you think the board will hold accountable? Me?" I lift my arm and eye him across the room. "Or my best friend who wants to sneak around and make sure his *adult* sister isn't having any fun?"

"She's allowed to have fun. In fact, she's allowed to have as much fun as she wants." He snatches up a pair of my jeans and tosses them at my legs. "It's the guy we're keeping on a leash. Get dressed. We're heading out for a bit."

K ane's lips curl high, a taunting smirk like daggers straight to the center of my gut. "You were banging his sister and playing sleuth with him on the side?" He sets Billy's empty bottle on the counter and lifts her until her cheek rests on his chest. "You're a fuckin' clown, Lenaghan. You should have just told him you were the exciting news."

"Dude! You don't understand the beat down he had planned for *any* guy who looked at her. No way was I volunteering that information."

"Makes you a pussy," he snickers. "I knew Jess had a brother. I had even crossed paths with you in my former thug life."

"Current," I grumble. "You've yet to leave that life."

"Can't say I gave you a single fuckin' thought when I was getting to know her." Like a pro, he pats Billy's back and grins when she releases small bubbles of air. "I knew you existed. But you didn't get even a second of consideration within my relationship."

"Makes you disrespectful."

"Funny, Jess held the same sentiments. Still," he shakes his head. "Didn't care. When a man loves a woman, it's about him and her. It's between them, and only them, and once they've got their shit figured out, then the rest of the world *may* be invited in. But they don't get a say on what happens."

"My daughter is eleven days old and already knows seventeen different cuss words because of you. Wanna cool it?"

Thoughtful, he pulls back and looks down to study my sleepy baby. Then he chuckles and brings her in again. "I think she's gonna be okay. Her cousins will teach her whatever we don't. And when the time comes, I bet none of them will care about your opinion on whoever she's dating."

"She doesn't get to date." I push up from my chair, the legs scraping on the floor until the baby startles in Kane's arms. But she settles again. Closing her eyes and snuggling into his chest.

I could leave them alone. I could allow her to rest on her uncle where she's completely safe and unequivocally loved.

But it's my turn now. It's my time. And it's still the middle of the damn night.

So I move closer and take the tiny bundle from his arms. Unphased by his scowl of disapproval. Unbothered by the danger he represents.

It's funny. Kane Bishop might literally be the deadliest motherfucker I have ever, or will ever, meet. His military training is so rarely acknowledged verbally, and yet, unavoidable when simply looking at him. The weapons he carries daily, never mentioned. But the threat he poses, and the protection he promises, is absolute.

He, himself, is a weapon created and set free by the US Government, yet somehow, he calls our tiny town home, and my sister, his reason for everything.

But it's Marcus whose opinion always mattered the most.

Even now, all these years later, his approval helps me sleep at night.

"She wanted to sneak around and have this torrid affair, Bish. The rest of the world saw this quiet, mousy, and shy Kari Macchio. But the woman she showed me…" I continue patting Billy's rump, wandering across my kitchen with a gentle shake of my head. "The woman she was beneath all that was not the same."

"Probably not something you wanna tell Marcus," Kane sniggers. "I don't have a sister, but I bet if I did, I wouldn't wanna know who she is behind closed doors. Even Twink—"

"Laine?"

He nods. "She's *your* sister, but I have this sense of kinship, too. I trust Angelo with my life. He and I are blood in. But he doesn't give me the details of what they do in private."

My nose wrinkles with disgust. "Yeah, we don't need that information."

"That's what I'm saying. So Kari's a viper behind closed doors?" He flashes a wicked grin. "Not that I couldn't tell. She's stitched me up a time or two now. I know she's no simp."

"She was rebelling," I sigh. "Eighteen years of being under Marcus' reign. She had spent her whole life doing what he wanted, when he wanted. Previously, she would go out of her way to make sure he was comfortable. She refused to be the source of his stress. So by the time she was eighteen, she was ready to fuck some shit up."

"My favorite way of handling things," he smirks. "And just in case we're keeping tally, *you* just said *fuck* in front of an eleven-day-old baby. So don't come for me when she's talking in a couple of years and saying some things that kinda sound like they came from Uncle Bish's mouth."

I roll my eyes, but I close them, too, so the action is invisible to everyone except me. Then I tuck my face into the crook of Billy's neck and inhale. She smells like baby. Like hospital. She even smells a bit like sour milk. Though beneath all that is the faint scent of flowers.

She got that from her momma.

"She didn't even want a relationship that everyone else could know about. It would bring stress to Marcus, she said. It would complicate every-thing. So she was completely and hopelessly okay with sneaking around."

"Luca?"

Kari wanders into Marcus' living room, the wood paneling an overwhelming feature in the old A-frame home Marc bought not so long ago. It's a loft-studio set up, with one bedroom exposed to anyone sitting downstairs. A kitchen. A teeny, tiny little laundry off the side of the house, and a giant barn out back.

We're not the only people here: Angelo takes up the single recliner, and Scotch sits on the floor in front of the three-seater couch. His shaggy hair dangles in his eyes. His entire body, bowed over a guitar, and his mind, swirling in a depression he's yet to escape from.

Because Sammy, that girl he swore he would marry and love forever… left.

She got the wedding certificate. She got his heart. But she skipped town the second she could and stomped on his soul on the way out.

Jess and Laine lounge on the couch, and Marcus sits on the end, his feet on the cushions and his hand wrapped around a PlayStation controller. Because this is what we do on the rare, rare nights where the band isn't playing at the club, Marcus isn't bussing tables, I'm not on night-shift, and the rest of us have nothing else to do.

We come to Marc's house and chill the fuck out.

In fact, this is so completely normal, no one even looks up at Kari's seductive summons.

Though, of course, I doubt anyone else considers it seductive.

I swallow the painful lump of nerves settled in my throat and drag my gaze around. Away from the shoot-'em-up game on Marc's flat screen and across to an impossibly beautiful Kari in little shorts and a slouchy sweater.

"Can you help me in the barn for a sec?" Her lips curl high, forcing her cheeks up until they squish beneath her dancing eyes. "Please?"

"I can help you, Kar." Marcus pauses the game and looks over. "What do you need?"

"It's okay." She saunters into the living room and presses her hand to the top of his head. It's a pat of sorts, but also a caress. An, *I love you* ruffle of his hair. Then she leans over him and un-pauses the game. "I just need to get something down in the barn, and Luc is the only one not doing anything." She glances across and stares into my eyes.

How is it possible no one else sees what she is?

How can they not know what she's doing?

As far as I'm concerned, she walks around with a giant, fucking neon sign flashing over her head.

"Luca?"

"Yeah." I *want* to go out there with her. And yet, guilt eats at my soul. But above all else, my body moves. Without my brain openly acknowledging the actions, my feet touch the floor, and my ass leaves the chair. My back crackles as I straighten out and turn in her direction, then my cock hardens when she smiles.

That's it.

A fucking smile.

But it screams a million naughty things her brother would kill me for.

She licks her bottom lip and grins like the she-devil herself. And when I'm close enough, she turns on her heels and walks by my side, close enough our shoulders touch and her long locks tickle my arms. "Thank you, Luca."

I want to groan. I want to shout my innocence in all this. But fuck, most of all, I want to sneak out to the barn with her, too. Because she goes to college in a week, and I haven't had my fill yet.

"You *sounded* like Mrs. Robinson when you said my name in there, ya know?"

The second we're outside and the door closes us out, Kari's lips swing higher, visible even under the bright moonlight.

"You're trying to get me killed."

"I'm trying to assert myself." She ducks around the side of the house, out of my sight for just a single second. But in the dark, in my current frame of mind, it's a lifetime.

What if she disappears? What if she gets hurt?

I quickly follow her around and step into the shadows, only for my back to hit the external wall of the house, my breath exploding from my lungs as Kari's arms slide around my neck and her chest crushes against mine.

Shit. Shit. Shit. Shit. Shit.

"Bear—"

"You're allowed to touch me." She stands on her toes, nibbling on my bottom lip and stealing from me whatever pitiful willpower I might pretend

121

to cling to. She grabs my hand and slides it down to cup her ass. And fuck, but we both moan when my fingers squeeze and pull her closer. "You're too hard on yourself, Luca. Always staying away when you should stalk forward."

"I'm saving you from yourself." But hell if my resistance doesn't snap and have our lips clashing. I slide my tongue across hers and moan when she pushes closer. Her body, draped over mine and just feet away, on the other side of this wall, my death lingers. "You're on a path to destruction right now, Bear. You're playing with fire and don't care about the consequences."

"You're being overly and annoyingly cautious." She bites my bottom lip, hard enough to elicit a hiss of pain from the depths of my throat. "I'm leaving soon."

"I know." I bring my free hand up and hold her neck. My fingers curl around to touch the top of her spine and my thumb stretches to the front until I feel her pulse and mine racing for superiority. "I know it down to the fucking minute, Bear. The seconds."

"Because you're gonna miss me?"

"The way I'd miss my arm if I no longer had it." I swoop in and taste her neck. No biting allowed. No suckling. No fucking marks left behind. "But I'm so happy you're going. You deserve this chance to stand on your own two feet. To know what it feels like to be free."

"I'm gonna come home every weekend." She twists and drags us around, so her back hits the wall and my body pins her close. I swear, I don't mean to do it. I don't mean to hold her up.

But my hands drop to her thighs without thinking, and her feet simply… cease to hold her weight. She wraps her legs around my hips, squeezing until I feel the pinch. Her tongue seduces me. Her lips, playing with mine. She slips her hands into my hair, grabbing fistfuls and tugging until I hiss.

"I'm gonna come back every single weekend," she repeats. "And we can still see each other. We can text and call and stuff."

"You're supposed to be going there single," I groan. "Independent. Not tethered to Marcus. And sure as shit not tied to me."

"You don't want me?"

"With my whole fucking soul." I bruise her thighs and *know* she'll have to wear long pants for the next week, or two, so no one sees. But I don't stop. And try as I might, I can't quiet the way my breath races. "I want you, Bear. Like I've wanted no one else in my life. But you're not just a random girl I get to fuck around with and toss aside when I'm done."

"So don't toss me aside."

"Don't limit yourself to just *this*." I drag her bottom lip between my teeth, tempting fate when I know her plump lip will only swell. Soon, she'll have to go back inside. "Go to college, Beautiful. Get out of this fucking town and meet some people who aren't *us*. See the world. Travel! Do something that doesn't consider Marcus' codependence and trauma. I want to see that version of you."

"Kari?" Marcus' voice booms from inside his house, but from the back door. "Hey, Kar? You okay out there?"

"Shit." I practically throw her off. Slamming her to the wall in a wholly ungentlemanlike way and instantly regretting it when she stumbles to her feet and frantically searches for air. "I'm sorry!" I whisper my words, pressing my hand to her lips, though she's not the one talking. "Shit, Bear! I'm sorry."

She bites my palm and snickers when I tear it back on a hiss. Then she reaches up and brushes loose tendrils of hair behind her ear. Her chest heaving for air, her lips, way too fucking swollen for me to still live beyond the next five minutes. But she's smooth. Innocent. She clears her throat and sweetens her tone, "Around the side, Marc." She steps out from between me and the wall and fixes her top, so the slouchy fabric sits exactly right on her shoulder. Then she beams when Marc steps around the corner, his expression not nearly as suspicious as I expected.

"We got caught up checking out this crack in your foundation."

"What?" Instantly panicked, Marc grabs his phone from his pocket and switches the flashlight on. Then he stalks closer, illuminating the concrete footings hidden neatly under the wood siding. "What crack, Kar?"

"Here." She crouches, her long, long legs like that of a praying mantis. *And everyone knows what happens to the male mantis after he gets his rocks off.* Leaning in and pointing, her long hair dangling over her bare shoulder, she draws her brother in and hoodwinks him like she's been practicing her whole life. "Do you see that crack?"

"That one?" Frowning, he reaches out and touches a hair-line mark on the concrete. Then he drags his thumb across it and grins when the line moves. "It's mud, Kar." Exhaling a long, relieved sigh, he pushes up straight and drags his sister up. "Scared the shit out of me, though."

"I was getting to the touching." She giggles, *so, fucking, innocent,* and slides under her brother's arm. "Swear I was. But then you came outside."

"I'm glad you told me. It could have been really bad if the foundation

123

was actually cracked." He presses a noisy kiss to her temple and turns away. Leaving me, *his best friend*, behind like I don't even exist. "Did you get what you wanted from the barn?"

"Yeah. I put it in my car. That's when I noticed the crack. Luc and I were heading back to the house when I looked over and noticed it." She wraps her arm across his hip and snuggles in. "Did you win your game?"

"No. Jess was a total shit and kicked my ass. It's your turn now, if you want it."

"Sure." Kari glances back as they approach the corner of the house. She meets my eyes, her smile, way too fucking devious to not be pure evil. Then she snickers and continues on. "We should order pizza for dinner. I'm starving."

"I'll do you one better," Marcus counters. "I have bases and toppings in the fridge already. I'll make you pizza. Way nicer, and a fraction of the price."

"Marcus often talk shit about my wife?" Kane pulls out a chair at my kitchen table and sits, lazing back so the frame groans, and digging his hands into his pockets. "Does he need a little talking to?"

I cough out a gentle laugh and turn away. "Marcus will talk shit about anyone who doesn't fit into his life exactly right. He's not a dick," I amend. "He's just wildly unhealed from childhood trauma, and as a result, likes for square pegs to fit into square holes. Jess," I happily sigh, "has always been a round peg trying to fit into a square hole. And you…" I turn at the counter and meet his fiery eyes. "You're the grenade, tossed into the room and fucking everything up beyond recognition. It's just good, I suppose, you fell in love with *my* sister and not his."

"You think he'd be a threat to me?"

"I think he'd destroy himself and everyone around him trying to protect her from the unknown."

"Meanwhile," he smirks. "You're out here macking on Kari and fucking her against his house." He lifts his chin, offering his extended hand and a closed fist. For *bumping*. "Badass, Lenaghan. I'm proud of you."

"I wasn't fucking her." I leave his hand hanging, and instead, look down at a sleeping Billy. "And this conversation is entirely inappropriate. Don't listen to the things he says, Sweet Girl. In fact," I glance up from beneath my brows and eye my brother-in-law. "Don't listen to anything he says, ever. It's not safe."

"Hell it's not."

12

LUC

DOING WHAT IS RIGHT... EVEN IF IT'S WRONG

Kari: *Why haven't I seen you since Thursday, Luca?*

Kari: *It's been days! And it's not like we haven't been in the same space.*

Kari: *I saw you walk out the back door when I arrived at the Turners' yesterday, Luc! You got on your bike and left because I arrived.*

Kari: *Luca fucking Lenaghan! You're a coward.*

"You keep staring at your phone like that," Mitch mumbles, kneeling in the back of our ambulance and counting supplies while we have a quiet moment on shift, "and the glass might shatter."

"Leave me alone." I sit on the bucket seat bolted into the back, my knees higher than my hips and my elbows perched on top. "I'm approaching a mid-life crisis, Rosa. I need a minute to deal with it in silence."

"You're hardly mid-life." He shoves fresh gauze into the tub secured to the side of the bus and makes a note in his book. "And you're normally a pretty fuckin' chill dude. Annoyingly so," he grumbles. Because he, too, has a baby sister *and* childhood trauma. It's like I attract the same kind of friends. "So whatever this is, it's kinda big, huh? It's got you twisted up."

"It's kinda private." I nibble on my bottom lip and groan when another text pops through.

Kari: *I know you're reading these messages, jackass. You have read receipts on.*

Then another: *You're avoiding me, and that's not cool. You're hurting my feelings, and you promised you wouldn't be that guy. I'm leaving tomorrow, Luc! You know my plans, and you're going out of your way to not be where I am. That makes you an asshole.*

"I wanna ask if you have girl problems," Mitch wonders. "But you're Luc Lenaghan. The only girl problem you have is how many you want in your bed at one time."

He speaks with humor. A lighthearted jab. But his words are a direct fucking shot to my stomach. Because he's not entirely wrong. I have a certain reputation around town for being slightly... *friendly* with the female variety. They were my attempts to focus on something else. Anything else. They have always, and only, been a distraction from an addiction I wasn't allowed to explore.

But now my Kari-flavored cocaine is knocking on my door. Blowing up my phone. She's offering herself to me freely. And I'm terrified that if I try just once, if I claim her as my own, we won't ever come back from that.

If I claim her, then she won't get to see the world. She won't get to explore kissing other men. She won't get to experience sex except with me. And if that's the case, then she won't have lived a life where even for a minute, a single second, she didn't belong to *someone*.

She was Marc's, and then she would be mine. And it's taking all of my fucking willpower to let her go.

Once we've crossed the line and I've had all of her, there's no changing my mind.

So yeah, I'm ignoring you, Kari! I'm avoiding you! I'm tearing my fucking soul out every time we're near and I force myself to walk away.

"I can't talk about my girl problems unless they remain completely private." I lower my phone, lock the screen, and glance up, meeting Mitch's light eyes. "Like, take it to the grave kind of private. There's no room for fucking around on this one, Mitch. It's a big fuckin' deal."

"Okay, well..." Frowning, he remains crouched, but lowers his pen and gives me all of his attention. "I can keep a secret."

"Even if it flies in the face of what *you* consider right?"

A single, questioning brow shoots high on his forehead. "Did you kill someone? Hurt someone? Fuck someone without their permission?"

I roll my eyes. "No."

"Rob a bank? Commit a crime?"

"No. Jesus. *Fuck someone without their permission?* Who the hell do you think you're working with?"

"Just checking." He casts a fast glance out the back of the open ambulance to ensure we're alone, then he drops to his ass and takes a break from work. "When you say I consider it right or wrong, and you're not talking about the law... what do you mean?"

"I mean... you're an overprotective older brother of someone you think *needs* your constant and unwavering attention and protection."

Abigail Rosa. The town's sweetest, smallest, loveliest cancer survivor ever.

Of course, bringing her up tweaks Mitch's temper. "What about her?"

"Not about her." I drop my face into my hands. "But you're the type to take the side of the protective brother."

"And you're having girl problems with... someone's sister?"

"Yes."

"Not my sister?"

"No! Fuck." I release a pent-up breath of frustration. "This has nothing to do with Abby. But yes, I'm having a moral dilemma surrounding *some-one's* sister. She's..." I consider for a beat. Wrack my brain for the appropriate description without giving myself away. This town is small, and sisters aren't in massive supply. "She's protected. By someone I'm very close with."

"You're messing around with your friend's sister." He scoffs, shaking his head. "Makes you an asshole."

"Makes this conversation over." I push up to stand but remain hunched under the low roof. "Forget it. I'll go somewhere else and—"

"Wait." He grabs the pocket on the side of my pants before I can pass, yanking me to a hard stop so I almost overbalance and pitch straight onto the concrete bay outside the double doors. I grab the walls of the bus before I fall and glance down with a snarl when he chuckles. "That was my bad. Automatic reaction." He releases me, but he looks up, burning me with a stare that has me pausing. "Sit down. Talk it out."

"You're not an unbiased audience."

"I'm shedding a lifetime of hard training here, Lenaghan. It's like discussing racism or genocide, and you're Hitler. You're asking me to set my own emotions aside for a second to remain unbiased. And, by the way, you're still an asshole."

"This is gonna be a fuckin' disaster." I bring a hand up and scrub it over my face. A long, pained grunt rolls along my throat and out to echo within our limited space. But I back up, tugging my pants from his grasp and sitting so the seat bolted to the wall groans. "I'm gonna regret this."

"Perhaps." He sits back, lazy as a lizard in the sun, and grins. "So you're scamming on someone's sister?"

"That's such a lovely, impartial question to ask."

"Oh, I'm sorry," he chuckles. "You have wonderful, beautiful, completely honorable thoughts and feelings about a woman. And this woman just so happens to have a brother. This brother is someone you're fond of."

"Yes."

"Dick," he sniggers. "So what's your problem? She doesn't want you back?"

"She does. She's quite eager, actually, for the idea of something happening between us."

"And the friend?"

"Has no clue. If he did, I'd expect to have my face rearranged, and my brains smeared on the wall."

"Sounds like the kind of guy I could be friends with," he teases. "You're sneaking around with her behind his back?"

"Sorta." I shrug. "Not completely. We've made out a couple times, and it seems she wants more. But my friend matters to me. And *her* age and life experience matters."

"She's young?" His brow slowly comes up. I'm not sure he even realizes. "Too young?"

"She's a legal adult. But yes, she's young. And similarly to Abby, she's spent a lifetime inside a bubble her brother guards. She has no clue what dating other people would be like. She hasn't kissed anyone else. She hasn't had sex with me or anyone else. She doesn't know the things the world is offering, but she thinks being with me is what she wants."

"And you don't feel the same?"

"Of course I do! She's my end game. But not yet. Not now when she doesn't know what the other options are. If a starving man walks into the room and there's a can of beans on the table, he's gonna eat the beans and be thankful for them. But if he walks into a room filled to the brim with a selection of steak, dessert, pasta, and pizza. All the good things. Then he gets to pick and choose. Maybe there are beans at the buffet too. But who the fuck wants beans where there's a steak sitting right there?"

"So... you're the beans?"

"No! I'm the steak, I hope. But she can't know what I am if she's not out experiencing the rest."

He draws a long, noisy breath until his lungs fill and his chest expands, then releases it again with a quick nod. "Alright. So... we're working with food analogies. You have this woman who you consider end game, which implies this shit is serious. Perhaps, even love."

He peers across and waits for my nod of acknowledgement.

"And in honor of this love, you want her to... sample other plates? Are you fucking crazy?"

"I want her to know there are other plates out there. I want the other plates to tempt her. I want her to know these other plates want her, too. And then when she's seen it all and she knows her options, *then* I want her to choose me."

"An ego boost?" he challenges. "You want to know you're the best?"

"No." I drop my head and jam my thumbs against my eyelids. "I just don't want to be the beans she's forced to appreciate. She's worth so much more, Mitch." I peel my thumbs away and wait for the stars to clear from my vision. "She's everyone's end game. And I want her to be confident knowing that. I want her to know I want her, too. She's not my beans. She's my steak. But if she doesn't leave this town and experience men outside of me, how can she know what she is?"

"You're twisting yourself up over this." He tosses his notebook and scratches his stubbled chin. "Believe it or not, but I'm following you. You love her, you want her. But she's quality, grass fed steak, and you want her confidence to be built up before you claim her for yourself."

"Yes. Mostly." I shake my head. "Sure. Whatever."

"You want her to know this is a choice you both make, and not a '*well, that person will do*' kind of thing. Have you considered the consequences that may come if she explores the world and finds steak somewhere else?"

"Yes." My stomach rebels at the thought. My heart aches at the threat. "And if that was to happen, then I would need to find understanding. Whatever is best for her, is best for us."

"Jesus." He scoffs, the sound mocking me from the back of his throat. "Magnanimous of you, Lenaghan. So if she finds her steak elsewhere, you're just gonna go to her wedding? Cool as a cucumber? You're okay with that?"

"As long as she's happy," I bite out. "She has the right to choose, Mitch. And if I claim her as mine now, she's too loyal to sneak off and look at the other plates in the meantime. This is a risk I *have* to take. For her own well-being."

"Selfless of you," he breathes, puffing his cheeks and widening his eyes. "As the brother of a protected woman, I suppose I can respect that."

"Great." I crush my eyes closed. "So that's my dilemma. She's heading out of town soon, and although she can come back regularly, she'll technically have four years to... explore."

"But she wants a commitment from you?"

"Kinda." I drop my hands and shrug. "She's calling me a coward because I'm avoiding her as much as I can."

"Out of loyalty to her future *and* to your friend?"

"Basically. If I see her before she goes, I'm gonna fuck everything up. Either I'll chicken out on the sampler thing and demand she be mine. Short-term gain. Or I'll hurt her feelings and screw everything up. Long-term loss."

"And you think ignoring her is the best solution to this?"

"What the fuck other solution do you have?"

"Luca?" Marcus' voice echoes throughout the garage we're parked in. His boots thumping against the concrete floor. Color drains from my face—*I feel it*—and in response, Mitch's brow shoots up in question.

He glances over his shoulder and grins when Marc stops outside the bus.

"Oh, hey Mitch." Marc extends his hand and shakes when Mitch reciprocates. "How's it going?"

"Aww, ya know. Drama, drama, drama." He chuckles, pulling back and picking up his notebook. "You need an ambulance, or...?"

"No." Marc's eyes jump to mine. "We're grabbing pizza at my place tonight. It's Kari's sendoff."

"Yeah?" My throat aches as that single, painful word rolls along it. "That's cool."

"She's invited all the family. But she mentioned getting RSVPs from everyone except you. She was gonna head down here on her way home, but I was already near, so I told her I'd drop in."

"I probably can't come," I rasp. "Mitch and I are on shift. So—"

"We're off at six," Mitch, oh-so-fucking helpfully, adds. Fuck him. Fuck his sister. I hope whoever she falls in love with fucks him up. "I'll make sure we're clear on the dot."

"Dude—"

"Excellent." Marc claps his knuckles on the shell of the rig and turns away. "I'll see you there then. I've still got a few errands to run before everyone arrives."

"You're a dog." I shove up from my seat and slam my palm to the side of Mitchell's face as I pass. "I hope your sister falls in love with your worst enemy."

"He's your best friend, bro! Why wouldn't you go to your best friend's younger sister's farewell dinner?" He turns at the back of the bus as I step to the concrete. "Make it make sense, Lenaghan!"

"I'm gonna drive our bus straight off Lookout Hill." I spy Marc climbing into his truck on the street, then I look back at my partner and sneer. "You brought this on yourself."

"This is karma," he quips. "For scamming on your friend's little sister." He picks up his pen and chuckles, making notes in his book again. "Dick."

K ane pulls up a chair to my dining room table, his chest bouncing with the knowledge of Mitchell's sister's current husband.

Not only did Abigail Rosa marry up.

But she married one of the baddest dudes around.

"Pretty sure that's called karma," he snickers. "He screwed you over. Now Spence—"

"Screws her. Yep, I got it. Mitch learned his lesson and never works a shift now without complaining about it."

His shoulders bounce, and under the dim lighting, his eyes shadow and almost look bruised and dangerous. But his lips curl into a smirk, playful and taunting. "So we know you and Kari end up together. We even know you screw, at least once. Considering the crotch trophy you're currently snuggling. So you went to that farewell dinner and claimed her as yours?"

I scoff and look down at my *crotch trophy*. "I went to dinner. But I achieved nothing positive while there."

13

LUC

FAREWELLS FUCKING SUCK

"I think someone should make a toast." Alex is already three beers in to his evening and half a pizza down. So while I do my utmost fucking best to sit in the corner of Marc's kitchen and take up as little room as possible, X is out here, standing on the coffee table Marc carved by hand from a single tree stump. "Kari." He lifts his beer and grins, foolish as he always gets after a couple of drinks. "You became my little sister way back in..." He blinks once. Twice. "Shit. Forever ago. Long time. And though I already had a sister, I was happy to make room for another one."

"Aw shucks," Britt drawls. "So glad you had that room in your heart, X."

"Shush!" He smacks a silencing finger to his lips. Though he smiles for his actual, biological sister and winks. "Brat was enough for us. And we didn't even know we'd need more kids in our family. But then you and Marc came along. You slipped in and just... became part of the family."

Kari's eyes mist. Her cheeks warm. She's embarrassed, and yet, completely enamored by the love Alex pours her way.

"I'm really sad about how things happened," he continues. "About the things that hurt your family and led you to ours. But I'm thrilled I got to have you in my life. And I assure you, I'm driving over to the city five nights a week to make sure you're behaving yourself."

"She's gonna be fine." Jess jumps up from her chair, extending a long flute of soda water. Since drinking, *in front of the older brothers*, isn't gonna go down well.

Even though, deep down, we know the girls enjoy a sneaky beverage here and there.

"Kari is our trailblazer," Britt announces, long black hair dangling from a high ponytail and tickling the middle of her back. "She's always been ahead of the rest of us. The bravest. The smartest. The nicest." She looks at Kari and smiles, though it's shaky. "I'm counting down the seconds from now until the rest of us get to join you next year. You take this year to be a badass. We'll do our best to turn up to class and get our diploma. Then it's on."

"Or!" Marc declares, drawing everyone's eyes. "Kari can study remotely for this year. Stay here. Be with us." He presses his hands together, pleading. "Wait for the others, so you can be with your squad and not all alone in the fucking city with no one to have your back."

"I have my own back." Finally, Kari speaks up. Her voice trembles, but her shoulders broaden. They hold the weight of the world and show no weakness. "I will take care of myself, and in the moments that I feel like I need home, I'll come back here." She meets Marcus' eyes. "I know where you live. I know how to get here. And I know it would only take a phone call to have you in your truck and coming to me." She looks at Alex. "Get off the table before you fall. I'm not a nurse yet." Then to the cluster of girls in the middle. "Jess. Britt. Laine. I love you all, and I'm excited for you to join me. But in the meantime, I'm going to enjoy being alone. I'm going to thrill in my independence because this will be the only year in my entire life I get to just... *be*. Alone. I had my family, and then I had your family."

She casts a glance at the rest of us. Angelo. Scotch. Oz. Then she stops on me and narrows her gaze. "I'm immensely appreciative of the family Marc and I were swallowed into when we needed somewhere to call home. It was never a *them* and *us* situation. There was never a moment I felt excluded or *other*." She drags her eyes to Scotch and smiles. "You guys were already a family. Completely and totally whole without us. But when these kids turned up on your doorstep with nothing to their names except a fluffy blanket and a metric ton of trauma, you didn't hesitate to step up and welcome us in."

"You were too cute," Scotch smirks. "Too little to send to the forest." Then he peers Marc's way. "And we needed a fourth member for the band."

"Which has still not been named," Marc chuckles. "I mean... not officially. Not really."

"We love you," Scotch finishes. "You were never *other* in my eyes. And even though you're leaving, you're still ours. You'll always have a home with me. With Oz."

Oz nods.

"With Alex."

Alex grins.

"With Luc."

I gulp.

Because Kari's blazing eyes swing back to mine.

"Is there anything you'd like to say, Luca?" She lifts a challenging brow the way an archer prepares his bow. "Alex has spoken. Marc. Britt and Jess. Scotch, too." She flattens her lips and takes a step closer. Then another. "Anything you'd like to declare in front of all our favorite people?"

Oh god. Oh fuck.

Swallowing, I look at Marcus and shake my head, instant, jerky, and cowardly.

"Um..." I bring my focus back to Bear and clear my throat. "Just I'm gonna miss you. With my whole soul. I hope you visit us often, and I pray the next four years fly."

She takes another step closer, somehow closing the walls in with each movement she makes. "That's it? After all these years?"

Marc's stare is like a red-hot poker on the side of my face. So I gulp again and nod. "Hurry back to us. Things won't be the same while you're gone."

She stops and firms her lips. Her eyes blaze with a million questions and demands. But I can't say shit without ruining everything. I can't ask her to stay without destroying her future. And I can't announce how I really feel in front of our family without, well... chaos.

So I reaffirm my stance and nod. "That's it."

Disappointed, she turns on her heels, sighing but faking a smile. "I'm so thankful you guys wanted to do this tonight. You've humbled me."

"Anything for you, Kar." Alex stumbles off the coffee table and snickers when he sticks the landing. "Who wants to watch the fights on TV tonight? They got some title bout going on."

"Sounds good to me." Kari bends by the television and snatches up the remote, then flicking it on, she flops onto the single recliner and drapes her legs over the arm. "Watching guys beat the shit out of each other in high definition is exactly what I want to see right now. *Allegedly.*"

"It's a bit like a textbook for you." Oblivious, Britt snatches up half a slice of pizza and drops on the other arm of Kari's chair. "You get to see all their cuts and shit." She points toward the fighter on the screen and nods. "Why do you think they put the goopy stuff on their face?"

"To stop their skin from tearing." Kari stares at the television and does a fan-fucking-tastic job of ignoring me. "They're there for sport. Not to disfigure each other."

"Fighters are kinda sexy, right?" Britt tilts her head, smirking as she watches the ones on the screen. "They've got that primitive, gonna protect the women-folk with my fists kind of energy."

"You're not allowed." Alex saunters across and steals his sister's slice. "No fighters for you, Brat. They're not even in the same fuckin' stratosphere as you."

"You think I should date a banker?"

"I think you should join a nunnery. But if you insist on living in the outside world, then yeah, date a banker. You're gonna be a teacher. Teachers don't date fighters. Silly women date fighters, and then they become a victim behind closed doors."

"Wow." Britt pushes forward and swings out to smack her brother's thigh. "*Wildly* inappropriate and judgmental comment. People are people, X. Pretty sure the statistics say cops are at the top of the charts as far as domestic violence goes." She purses her lips in dare. "Wanna make a comment on that?" Then she leans around him and looks to Oz. "Deputy? Have something to say?"

Oz lifts his hands in instant surrender. "I'm just gonna watch TV and mind my business if that's cool with you." He reaches around and grabs his beer. "The chick fighters are hot, and so, I'm just gonna appreciate them in silence."

I'm done. I push off my stool and leave my singular, barely touched beer behind. Making a beeline for the backdoor, I move in complete silence. I'm not here to make an announcement. I'm not looking for a goodbye. And I sure as fuck don't want Kari to notice and follow me.

Slipping through the doorway and onto the wooden porch out back, I close the glass door behind me and look up at the stars above. The moon is out and almost completely full. The summer breeze, cooling despite today's filthy temperatures.

I wear jeans tonight, and a shirt that hugs my chest. But nothing sticks uncomfortably, because the humidity, for today at least, has backed off.

"You're such a coward, you know that?"

I spin to the back door, my hand pressed to my heart and my brain sputtering when I find the glass still closed. Then I turn again and find Kari at the corner of her brother's house. Her eyes drawn and sad. Her shoulders slumped in a way she wouldn't allow them to be inside.

"You couldn't even say anything nice about me?" She wanders closer, her hands in her pockets. Though she remains in the shadows. Forcing me to go to her... or stay away. "After all these years of being family. Of being friends. It all comes undone now and right before I leave, you can't even set aside the new stuff for the old?"

"You want us to be together, Bear." I stalk off the back of the porch and meet her in the dark. Fuck knows, no one else has to hear this conversation. Worse, they shouldn't see it. So I grab her hand as I pass and continue toward the barn at the back of the yard.

"Luc!"

"You're asking me for something I *want* to give you." I drag her around the side of the barn and shove her against the splintered wooden wall. Instantly, her eyes pop wide and her pulse thunders in her throat. "I *want* you, Kari. I want to give you the things you're asking for."

"So what's the pr—"

"Sometimes, people don't realize the thing they're asking for isn't in their best interest. You're still so young! You need to experience college and everything that comes with that. Sending you away, but tethering you to me back here, is unfair."

"Unfair to me?" she snarls. "Or to you?"

"To you! You're not seeing the bigger picture here! You're not seeing the long-term gain because you're so fuckin' focused on the *now*. You want what you want, and it's entirely in character for someone your age to not consider anything outside of that thing."

"Oh good! So you're like Marcus, then? Another quasi-dad to tell me what I should think and feel?"

"Dammit, Kari! You're not—" But I stop. I shake my head and cast a look over at the house bursting with people who love us both. We're one family. And falling in love with someone in that tight knit group of friends is not what someone who cares about the collective should do.

It's selfish and wrong.

Shortsighted and stupid.

"Luca," she groans. Dragging her hand along my chest and up to rest over my heart, Kari stands on her toes and waits for me to bring my gaze back around. "You're sending yourself crazy over this. And it doesn't have to be so complicated."

"It was wrong."

"Wh—" She frowns and drops her head back to stare up at the sky. "They say the stars already know. They're millions of years old, so they've already seen our past. They've seen our future. Whatever is coming, they already know about it."

"We shouldn't have kissed." My words are like acid on my tongue. Like razor-blades in my throat. Because she's not going to listen to the *I'm trying to protect you* spiel. She's heard it her whole life from a brother who took his duties too far, smothering her in love until that love felt like a straitjacket.

Kari Macchio is not looking for a guard at her door.

She wants a white knight to slay the dragon and take her on an adventure.

A role I would *love* to fulfill for her. If that's all I got to do with my life, then it would be a life well lived.

But it's not my time yet. The knight still has to wait. Because she's eighteen years old and still so naïve to the world.

"Luca—"

"What we did was bad, Kari." I swallow the poison in my throat and study her lips instead of her eyes. The way the former tremble and not how the latter glitter. "It was wrong."

"It wasn't wrong! It *can't* be wrong when there's love."

"It was a mistake." *Lie. Lie. Lie!* "I was opportunistic and took what you were offering because it was right there for me to grab on to, and I'm the asshole who will take advantage of a girl throwing herself at me."

"Stop it!"

"I wanted your first kiss," I sneer. "Fuck, Kari, I'm a greedy man who likes to collect that sort of stuff."

"You're being a dick. You're doing this on purpose."

"Go to school." I pull back and drop my hands. Because if I don't create space between us, I'm not sure I'll ever let go. "Go find some other dude to lust over. Because this isn't how things are gonna end up for us."

"You're setting things on fire," she moans. "You're overreacting because you think it's the noble thing to do. I'm not asking for a friggin' marriage proposal! I'm not even asking for a boyfriend. I just…" She reaches up and swipes beneath her eyes. "I'm asking you to admit you want this, too."

"No—"

"Luc!"

"I. Don't. Want. You." I take a step back, looking down at the woman who was a girl too few months ago. The child I practically helped raise. I try to place her back in that *little sister* column she's been in for well over a decade. But she insists on jumping out. She demands to be treated the way I treat the others. "I got my taste. And now I'm done." I bring my hand up and wipe my lips, as though I got to taste her tonight. As though I could handle this goodbye differently—better—and enjoy another before she climbs into her car and leaves.

Because that's how things *could* have gone. If I was more of a man and better with my words, and if she was less interested in something more.

But I'm not. And she's too brave for her own good.

"Be safe while you're away, Bear." I pause and swallow the ache in my throat, then I glance across the yard to Marc's A-frame, lit up on the inside and illuminating all the people I'll hurt by hurting Kari. It's inevitable, really. She has to feel the pain; better today, when so little is on the line, than ten years down the track, twenty years, when she realizes she rushed to claim the only can of beans she ever knew. "I hope to see you when you come back for break."

"Screw you." She shivers against the barn wall, her hands balling into fists and her chest heaving for fresh air. "You're making a horrible mistake, Luc. The stars already know."

I cast a look up to the sky and curse every single star that dares give a beautiful woman false hope. Then I look down again and shrug. "There's a saying, isn't there? About loving somebody and setting them free."

"There's also a saying," she snaps right back, "about being careful with the hearts you break. Because you may not have time to make it right again."

"So, go." I turn on my heels, though I'm the one telling her to leave. Then I dig my hands into my jeans pockets and find the keys to my bike. "Live your life, Bear. Get out of this town and do something amazing. If you come back, I'll be the first one here waiting for you."

"And if I don't?"

I skid to a stop on the gravel path laid between the house and the barn. Shoots of grass try to grow through, and little, incessant weeds pop up like pimples on a teenager's chin. Then I peer over my shoulder and take one last look. One last study of the most beautiful woman I have ever known. "Then I hope you're happy. Truly, with all my soul, I hope whoever you give your heart to treats you the way you deserve."

Forcing myself to turn again, I continue toward my bike and take out my phone to toss together a fast text to Marc. Something about being called in to work. An excuse for my sudden departure from the evening that honors the most important person in his life.

Because despite what I've done behind his back, falling in love with his sister and touching, when I should never have touched in the first place, I love my friend, too. He's as much my brother as Scotch and Ang. And if I can't have Kari in my life, I'd like to keep, at the very minimum, Marcus.

He can be my connection to her.

Yeah. I'm an asshole.

I hit send on my text and drop my phone into my pocket. Then climbing onto my beat up dirt bike, I kick the old thing to life, revving the engine and pretending like I don't hear the devastated sniffles of a heart I've fractured.

Tulips, *I remember.* The flowers I hope to someday hand over, to begin mending what I broke.

But until then… time.

Time is what we need.

"You know, nobody ever liked a fuckin' martyr." Kane leans back in his chair, kicking one foot over the other and digging his hands into his pockets. He shakes his head, completely and totally disappointed in the things I've done in my past. "You were pretending to be some kind of saint, allowing the naïve little damsel to run off and live a life of fucking around. Like that somehow made you… what? Superior?"

"I wasn't trying to be superior." I exhale until my lungs ache and press a gentle kiss to Billy's sweet head. "I was trying to do the right thing."

"By making her feel like she meant nothing to you?"

"I don't think you realize the situation we were in, Bish! She's my wife now. The mother of my children. And Marc's eye *still* twitches when he looks at us."

"So you sabotage your relationship with her, for the friendship you had with him?"

"No! I…" I roll my eyes and swear I thought I was done explaining all this years ago. I thought I'd told this story for the final time when all our friends became aware of what me and Kari were. But I guess Kane wasn't around back then. He didn't get the details when they were fresh.

And now that I'm explaining it all to new ears, I realize how utterly close I came to complete devastation.

"You heard the thing about beans and steak, right?"

"Yeah," he scoffs. "You explained it like seven different ways."

"And you heard my intentions. How I didn't want her to settle in this tiny town and not even *see* what exists on the other side of the train tracks? I wanted her, Kane, and I intended to keep her. But she deserved a chance to see what else was out there."

"And to achieve that, you told her she meant nothing to you." He brushes his hands together in an almost silent, mocking clap. "Bravo, dipshit. That would have left a scar."

"Shut up." I rock my sweet baby and work to swallow down the stomach acid rolling along my throat. "I don't know if you realize it, but right now, I'm feeling a little fuckin' sensitive about my wife and the ways I've hurt her in the past. So if you could gentle the f—"

"Nah." He sits forward at the table and rests his elbows on top. "Tell me she went off to college and ate *all* the steak, dickhead. And then tell me you stayed here and cried about it."

"Well—"

"No tears?"

I roll my eyes and consider, briefly, taking Billy back upstairs and putting her in her crib. That's what good, responsible parents do, right? They put their infant to bed when it's—I look to the clock on the microwave and groan—two fifty-five a.m. But I'm not ready to let her go yet. And I'm not ready to sleep now that I'm up.

So I snuggle her in closer and take comfort in knowing she'd rather be right here with me, pressed to my chest, than upstairs alone, flat out on a brand new crib mattress that would no doubt feel like concrete.

"Kari went off to college that next morning. Everyone was out for the goodbye. The street was basically packed, and Marc was losing his mind about it all."

"And you?"

"Sat on the Turners' front porch in their swing chair and watched."

"Like a pussy," he coughs out. "Total fucking pussy."

"She saw me there," I sigh. I remember sitting forward in the chair, my elbows on my knees and my chin in my hands. My heart pounded until it felt like I might die. And my brain swung violently from side to side. Let her go and live a life of freedom. Or keep her for myself and trick her into thinking I was the best steak on offer. "Our eyes met a couple times," I murmur. "But she was furious by that point. Even if I wanted to change my mind and beg her to stay, she was way beyond the point of discussing it."

Slowly, I bring my eyes up and stop on Kane's. "I don't know what you think you know about her, Bish. But Kari is the sweet and quiet kind, until she's not. Then she's gonna set shit on fire and watch the world burn."

His lips quiver with the shadow of a smile. "My kind of girl. I always liked her."

"Yeah, well…" I shrug. "She was at the setting things on fire phase in her life. And I was the idiot who refused to step out of the flames."

14

LUC

THANKSGIVING

"So she's just…" I follow Marcus across his yard, my boots hitting the rocks and dirt below as he makes his way to the barn. "It's Thanksgiving, Marc! She's not coming home?"

"Nope." He yanks the barn open with a grunt and shuffle, moving out of the way before the solid wood slams into his leg and breaks it clean in half. "I'm not happy about it, but she's not coming. She says she wants to stay on campus and catch up on her course work and stuff."

"And you're just letting her?" My words come out in a boom of anger, but when Marc glances over his shoulder, curiosity burning in his eyes, I swallow the rage down and calm myself before I make the mess I've worked so hard for months to avoid. "I just meant…" I draw a long breath and fill my lungs until bursting. Then I release it again and find my calm. "She doesn't come back for weekends, even though she said she would. Now she's skipping Thanksgiving. And you're okay with that?"

"I thought you said I should stop smothering her so much?" He wanders into the barn and flips a switch that has massive overhead lights flickering to life. "You've spent the last ten years boasting about how cool you are with the twins, and how I could take a leaf out of that book. Now I'm finally letting Kari have a little slack on the leash and you're calling me out on it?"

"You're suddenly listening to my advice? Since when? And why now?"

He chuckles, heading to the north-facing wall and releases a shelf that holds tools all nestled comfortably in slots, so his workshop is entirely organized. "She calls me damn near every day, Luc. And she told me she probably wouldn't make Thanksgiving. I'm not happy about it. But there's not really a lot I can do about it. She's a grownup now, and I have to trust her to make the right decisions for her."

"Jesus christ." I bring my hand up and scrub at my face before I scream. After *all* these years of him being her prison warden, I expected to be able to rely on that same watchfulness while she was away. I intended to monitor her through him, since she's too fucking busy and stubborn to communicate with me herself.

But no… because Marc has had a sudden fucking stroke that has led him to relax where she's concerned.

"You seem overly concerned about this." He takes down a hand-held lathe and turns to face me. He could split my skull in a single second if he knew the things circling my mind. "You've spent all these years telling me to cool it. Now you're acting like I've tossed her to the wolves and smothered her in barbecue sauce. She's fine." He pushes away from the shelf and heads toward his current project. "She calls me all the time to tell me how things are."

"Well…" I turn and follow him to the half-complete headboard he's making for someone who can afford to spend money on handmade stuff. "How *is* she doing? Is she enjoying college?"

"Yeah." He shrugs. "She's going to class and trudging through all the book work. Said she's excited for when she gets to do more of the practical stuff. Which is…" He runs his tool across the crown of the bed. "I dunno. Probably next year or the year after, I guess."

"Is she doing okay in the dorms?"

"Seems to be. She got paired up with some other chick for this year. Though I know the other three are already scoping out apartments for next year. Britt, Jess, and Laine are pretty noisy about their plans for after high school." He pauses his work and glances over his shoulder at me. "You know you could text Kari, right? Ask her yourself. I know I've always been pretty tense about guys and my sister. But you're not just a guy, Luc. You're my best friend. I wouldn't be mad if you texted her on the side."

Fuck. Me.

"I trust you," he continues. "And I bet she'd be happy to hear from you. She said she talks to the girls a lot. And Scotch and X."

"She said that?"

"That she talks to the others?"

"No. That she'd..." I drop my hands into my pockets and study my feet. "That she'd like to hear from me?"

"I mean... she didn't say you couldn't message her. So..." Clueless to the torment slinging around my brain, he goes back to work, sliding the heavy steel tool along the top of his project, his arms firing with muscles that come specifically after countless hours doing the same damn thing, day after day. "She's had you in her life since forever. I bet she's feeling out of sorts with all the changing this year."

I inhale until my lungs ache. Then exhale again until there's nothing left. "I suppose I could drop a text or something sometime. I didn't wanna step on toes or anything."

"No toes to be stepped on. You're my best friend. You have just as much right to worry about her as I do."

"**O**uch." Kane chuckles, his chest bouncing and eyes dancing. "You were a snake in the grass, and then you complain that he hits you sometimes?"

"You're jumping the fence on this. Over and over again." I study my brother-in-law. "You wanted me to claim her for my own, but then you sympathize with Marc and call me a snake."

"I'm allowed to play both sides," he smirks. "I know how this story ends. You get together. You say *I do*. You have sex sometimes, and you do the extra thrust thing, so now you got twins."

But of course, the giant elephant that wanders my home comes to sit square on the center of my chest. Because Kari's not here with us. And neither is Billy's brother.

We came home without them. And now my family won't leave me alone, terrified of how I'll unravel once I've taken a moment to breathe and think.

"She went off to college and left me behind," I admit. "Just like I told her to. And though I was the one who said she should check out everything else the world had to offer, it seems I wasn't quite ready to accept the consequences that came with that."

"She fell in love with someone else?" he guesses. "She found steak elsewhere?"

"Pretty fucking much."

15

LUC

WHAT WAS THAT THING ABOUT LOST TIME?

Christmas comes and goes. And then Kari's nineteenth birthday. The twins and Britt age up. They graduate high school, and my work keeps me busy.

And all the fucking while, I'm left on the outside looking in.

Even with my sisters. They grow and mature. They date and break up. They attend their prom, and they sure as shit didn't sleep in their own beds once the dance was over.

Because they're women now, and not children.

Colleges are applied for. Not just the one in the city Kari attends, but others, too. There's no point placing all of one's eggs in a single basket, so Jess and Laine applied all over the country. They would have gone to New York if that's how things turned out for them. They'd have gone to Boston if the acceptance letters came in that way. California would have suited their beach bum personalities. And Seattle would have served their wanderlust. But of course, the trio—four, including Kari—made a pact that if they could all attend the same school, they would.

All for one, and one for all... or some such thing.

So when those letters started arriving and things were getting real, the trio sat down and considered their options.

Kari was in school for nursing.

Jess was heading toward law.

While Britt and Laine had similar aspirations—teaching was where their hearts laid.

And in the end, matching letters were laid out on the Turners' kitchen counter for the rest of us to inspect and dissect.

The girls would reunite in the next school year, and an apartment would be secured. Not only were my sisters heading away, out of my day-to-day life, but Kari would be leaving the security of a school dorm. Leaving where she has guards on the grounds, a meal plan to ensure she ate each day, and a roommate to keep an eye on things. Instead, she would move in with the wild three, forced to shop for their own food or starve, and experience freedoms she's never had before in her life.

Fuck. This. Shit.

For two and a half years, my texts remain unanswered. Unopened. Unacknowledged.

For two Christmases. Two Thanksgivings. Birthdays: hers and mine. The guys and I continue to hold on to our day jobs, because that's what we *like* doing. But our band gains notoriety, too. Permanent gigs at a local club. Real life rock stars commissioning our words, our songs. Life just trudges forward callously, like my whole soul isn't someplace else. In someone else's hands. And as the time passes with no word from Kari, I'm forced to accept that I fucked us up.

I broke a heart I swore I would not. And now I have to live with the consequences of knowing Kari is safe and fine just an hour from where I lay my head each night. She's happy and learning, getting that college life I wanted her to experience.

I told her to go away. And she's listening.

"We're all back together again," Alex announces at family dinner, Thanksgiving, in Kari's third year away. She's a full-fledged, grown ass woman now. One who can legally drink and smoke—not that she does either. She can party and have sex. She can practice her learned skills on real life humans, and when the situation arises, she can probably save a life, too.

"Well…" Alex amends. "Almost all back together." He sits at the head of the table, a beer in one hand, and an eye scanning the occupants who sit with us. Jess and Laine on either side of me. Britt across, so when she looks up, it's me she sees first. Marc and Ang. Scotch. Oz. The Turner parents are off on vacation now that the kiddies are all grown, and my parents are doing their own thing tonight too.

But one seat remains empty. Desolate.

Kari's place has been set. Her plate, laid out. A knife and fork await her hands to use them. But she's not here.

The one person I've waited years for remains firm in her stance against letting me back in. She robs herself of the chance to come home because she knows I'll be here. She starves herself of the opportunity to be with her family because she knows that family includes me.

All she ever wanted was to be wanted.

I'm an asshole.

"It's a fuckin' tragedy," Alex grunts, giving her empty chair one last glance. Then he brings his focus back to those of us here. "She's been gone for too long. And though I know I saw her just two weeks ago in the city—"

Wait. What?

"It doesn't feel the same when she's not *here*. She's my baby sister too," he laments, casting a look to Marc. "I know she's yours first and foremost, but fuck, we were all kids when you and Kar came along. So I'm allowed to call her my sister, too. And I'm allowed to grieve the fact she's choosing her life over there instead of being here with us."

"It's because of Ten," Jess announces with a smile. She reaches across the table and snags a baked potato from the massive bowl in the center. "Ten has her attention right now, and since she's the shy one of our group, the rest of us are supporting that."

"Ten?" I lean forward so I can turn back and study my sister. Then I do the same on the other side, catching Laine's eyes. "What's a Ten?"

"Blake," Britt declares. She, too, is done waiting for our dinner to be officially started. So she reaches across and steals a green bean. "Blake is also in the RN program, so he and Kari have had a few study sessions this year."

"He's pretty cute," Laine smirks. "And he's a total gentleman. He stays at the apartment sometimes and—"

"Wait." Finally, I speak up. "He stays at the apartment?"

Britt scoffs. "Yeah, but we're adults now. So getting your panties twisted over this is like asking the *Titanic* to stop sinking. What's done is done."

"I don't want to hear about it." Marc plugs his ears with two fingers and groans. "Don't talk to me about the *Titanic*. And don't tell me about this dude who sleeps over in the same apartment as my sister."

"He stays, like…" I swallow the painful lump in my throat. "All night?"

"Yeah," Jess inserts. "But he's a total sweetheart. Like, me and Laine are careful to be dressed appropriately. But he's also thoughtful enough not to wander the apartment for no reason. He arrives, but only after letting Kari know he's coming. And she tells us before he gets there, so we're aware of what's happening. He goes straight to her room, and he doesn't really come out again till the morning. So there are never any awkward hallway dramas, and we never feel like we have to do that weird dash from bedroom to kitchen or whatever."

"He just…" My stomach heaves with disgust, vomit sprinting to the base of my throat. "He just hangs in her bedroom all day and night." I look at Marc. "That's so fucking *thoughtful* of him."

"I'm not listening." He closes his eyes and drops his head. "I refuse to get obsessed about this."

"Get obsessed!" I shove my plate away and stare straight across the table at Britt. "That's your apartment, Brat. You have a right to privacy there. So unless Blake—"

"Ten," she counters with a grin. "We call him Ten."

"Unless *Ten* is paying a portion of the rent, then he shouldn't be staying the night."

"I mean…" Laine shrugs. "It's not a big deal to us. We all…" she clears her throat. "Ya know, we all have a guest over sometimes. And Ten is pretty damn cool. He's cute, and he has that star QB energy, but he has a brain on his shoulders, too. He and Kari are bonding on needles and medicine and stuff. So intellectually—"

"He's perfect!" I throw my hands up. "Great! He sounds like a fuckin' peach."

"What's with the Ten thing?" Alex demands. He eyes the twins. Then Britt. "Ten, like how we say someone is a ten out of ten or something?"

"Uh… No." Britt sniggers. Then she lifts her hands and slowly parts them to create space between. "Ten, like…"

"I'm done." I shove up from the table before I toss my last three years of my lunch all over the turkey. Spinning away, I throw my chair back in until wood slams against wood and silverware clatters. "Eat," I call back, stalking across the dining room and into the kitchen. "My phone is ringing," I lie. "It's the station."

"But you—"

I take out my phone and stupidly bring the damn thing to my ear, and loudly, I growl, "Hey Mitch, it's Thanksgiving, bro. I'm off shift."

I don't stop once I hit the other side of the kitchen. No, I have a sudden fucking urge to make like Forrest Gump and keep going, so I stalk into the mudroom at the back of the house, then out the door until I'm on the porch that overlooks a not particularly well-kept yard. The grass is thin and patchy. The garden beds… accidental. The skate ramp is still the most prominent feature, yet I don't remember the last time we, as a group, came out here to spend time on it.

I ignore the very bottom of the bowl, where Kari and I laid that one time, kissing, and me, swearing I shouldn't. If I stop and really concentrate, I can still feel her elbows bruising my chest. I can taste her breath on my tongue. And when I flex my hands, I feel her hip in my palm. Her flesh under my fingertips.

"Fuck!" I crush the phone in my hand and thrust the other into my hair, pulling until it stings and scratching until I feel something other than the vicious ache pulsing in the depths of my gut. Then I stride to the side of the house and along the narrow pathway until I reach the gate that separates the back yard from the front.

Flipping the latch and shoving the gate open, I make a beeline for my bike, anger pulsing in my veins like mud after a long storm.

"Luc?" Alex steps out onto the porch and folds his arms as I throw my leg over the bike. "Something happening at the station that I should know about?"

"Nah. I'm just heading in for a bit, but you're good to have your dinner." I jam my phone into my pocket and the bike's key into the ignition barrel, and starting the engine, I rev loud enough to piss off every neighbor between here and the other side of town.

I don't bother with a helmet, though I know I should.

I don't wear a coat appropriate for the road, or lined jeans.

If I crash my bike on the freeway, I'm pretty well fucked. But that's cool, because a little road rash and losing half my face might be a welcome distraction from Kari Macchio spending the night with Mr. Ten Inch Cock, the quarterback dreamboat.

K ane laughs, his shoulders bouncing and his jaw quivering. So fucking entertained by my horror. So thrilled with the idea of my wife going to town with the local stallion.

"Ten inches!" he chokes out. "Like, ten when it's soft, or ten when it's hard?"

"None! Fuck you." I bring my free hand up and rub my eye. Because mentally, maybe I'm in hell and not nearly tired enough to drift off. But physically, I don't remember the last time I slept a full night. "Worst Thanksgiving of my entire life," I groan. "Ten! They called him Ten!"

"My wife called him Ten," Kane snickers. "I assure you, we'll discuss it when I get home. Now please tell me you didn't ride that bike home and hide in the bathtub and cry about your woes. For the love of fuckery," he giggles. "Tell me you went to her and cut his 'ten' off?"

"I went to her." I drop my head back and simply... breathe. "I'd reached my limit. *Ten* was where I drew the line. No more buffet for her."

"Halle-fuckin'-lujah. You went there, tossed her over your shoulder, smacked her ass, and impregnated her, right? Like a man."

I bring my gaze down again, scoffing deep in the back of my throat. "I went there. But I didn't get to smack her ass *or* impregnate her. Not yet, anyway."

"Pussy."

My lips curl. My ability to smile about this bullshit, finally, slowly, leaking through. "This is still a long while ago, Bish. The twins were conceived nine months ago. Your math ain't mathing."

"And your enthusiasm for practicing the twin thing is lacking." This motherfucker looks me straight in the eye and grins. "Practice is the best part."

"That's my sister you're talking about, asshole! Watch yourself."

"Or what? You gonna be mean and send me away? How will I live?" He brings a hand up and dangles it by his brow. "Luca Lenaghan will say unkind things to me and break my heart."

"You could go, you know?" I firm my lips and wait for him to lower his tatted hand. "It's three in the damn morning. You could go back to your house and leave me alone."

"Fuck I will." He pushes up from the table and makes a line for the coffeepot. "I'm invested in this story now. I had no clue Jess' family was a whole subplot in *The Bold and the Beautiful*. Go on," he teases. "Tell me what happened when you went to surprise your Care Bear and her ten-inch cock."

"You're such an asshole." I shake my head and pray to hell and back newborn babies don't understand the bullshit they hear in the first weeks of their life. "I have no clue what my sister sees in you."

"Ten inches," he smirks. Opening his hands, he cackles when my nostrils flare. "When it's soft."

16

LUC

NOT ALL SURPRISES ARE GOOD

I ride my bike to the city and take solace in the fact that I didn't drink at the dinner table with everyone else. No one in our family drinks to excess. Not since Scotch killed his mom's roses back in high school and earned himself a new nickname. But just one beer, even half, would be dangerous as I cruise faster than the speed limit all the way to the city.

The November air is like razor blades on my nose. The icy breeze, like knives against my ears.

But the ride is short, mercifully. The roads, all but empty until I hit the outskirts of the city, and two lanes turn to six. Even then, I zoom through traffic on my bike, choosing the shoulder and mid lanes instead of sitting with everyone else.

Horns honk at my back, and my brain cruelly forces me to reminisce from one part of my life to another. I should've put music on. Headphones in my ears and something other than Kari's voice playing on repeat. But no. I didn't do that. So instead, while staring at the road and crossing a city I hardly know toward the apartment the girls share, I think back on fifteen years of memories. From a little girl who clutched her pink blanket to a grown woman who demanded I notice her.

From that child I ignored, even when my heart gave an odd tug, to the woman I sent away... even when it felt like shoving a dagger between my ribs.

I think of the kisses we shared. The secreted moments spent in the dark.

I think of the things she asked for—not even a relationship. Just… truth—and then of my final words to her.

I. Don't. Want. You.

The nastiest, most villainous words I've ever muttered in my life.

I blow through a yellow light just before it turns red and zoom across the intersection filled with pedestrians waiting to cross. Then I cut left and close the final few blocks until I find her building.

What am I planning to do when I see her?

Fucked if I know.

What will I say?

No clue.

Will I demand she send Ten *home?*

Hell knows.

She's doing *literally* the very thing I told her to do. She's seeing the world and meeting new people. She's honoring my wishes and living her life.

And I'm… throwing a fit about it. Because all along, I wanted her to choose me.

I pull up outside Kari's apartment building and back my bike up until the rear wheel touches the curb. Then killing the engine, I merely sit and shiver. Because it's November! And I'm cold and stupid.

What are you gonna do, Luc?

Huh!?

What are you gonna do?

My phone vibrates in my pocket, an incoming call that buzzes against my leg and reminds me I left the table back home in a ridiculously conspicuous way. Everyone will have noticed. And several of them will have questions.

But not Marc. Hopefully not him.

Digging my freezing hand into tight denim, I pull the device out and bring it up. Only to frown when I spy Britt's name flashing on my screen.

Curious, I accept the call and press the phone to my ear. "Brat?"

"Hey." She's often the person who matches my energy when we all hang out as a group. She's one of the wild ones. One of the loud, brave ones. So even though I don't see her right now, I still see in my mind the way her lips curl. "You okay? Where'd you go?"

"Out." I sit back on my bike and study the street surrounding me, my breath coming out in white puffs that remind me how miserable I'm going to be tomorrow. "I got a call from work, so I'm dealing with that."

"I'm worried about you." She cuts through my shit and silences whatever rebuttal I might've thought to spout off. "You haven't been yourself in a long time, Luc. You think you're slick, but when people care about people, they notice."

"Um..." Nerves lodge in the center of my throat and damn near strangle me. "What?"

"I don't know the *who*. And I don't know the *why*. But my brother is a broken man because of a girl. Sam is..." She shakes her head, sighing. "She destroyed him, Luc. So I know what a man hurting looks like."

"And I...?"

"Am a man whose heart hurts because of a woman. You're ridiculously discreet about it all, and I haven't seen you with a woman in a while. I swear, I've been watching, trying to figure you out." She softens her voice, gentling it for my benefit. "You can tell me, Luc. And then we can hang out and bitch about her until you feel better."

"I'd rather we didn't." I glance across the street when moving shadows catch my gaze. A Thai restaurant, lit up with colored lights and a line that stretches out the door and along the block. It's obviously a good restaurant, or perhaps there are simply too many lonely people tonight with nowhere else to be on Thanksgiving. "I don't want to talk about girls right now, considering I'm busy working. And I especially don't want to talk about girls with my friend's little sister."

"Why not?"

Yeah, Luc? Why not?

"I've known you my whole life," she presses. "I've grown up watching you and the guys. I observed you across the school every damn day we were there, and every night the band played a set, I watched. You're Luc," she groans. "You date women. You have fun with them. Then you walk away. So who is this person who has you all messed up? And why the hell does she get that kind of power over you? Have you learned nothing from Sam?"

I study the long trail of people across the street. Those on a date, wrapped in each other's arms, and the women, most of them, huddled in their man's jackets. I run my eyes across the families. Young parents with small children, who, for whatever reason, don't have anywhere else to go tonight.

"Luc?"

I spy the front of the line, and the hostess waiting to seat those who stand there. "What?"

"Sam is broken! Destroyed! That bitch waltzed in, threw his heart in a blender, and sashayed her ass back out of town again. I'm not gonna sit here and watch someone else do that to you. So tell me the who, and I'll take care of it for you."

I choke out a soft chuckle, the first real moment of levity I've felt in… a while. But then my eyes stop on a perfect green set. A beautiful, round face framed in wild brown hair made worse by the breeze in the air. Most fucked up of all, is the man draped over her. He's about six-and-a-half feet of football muscle and math club nerdy, all wrapped up in one dude.

Kari's face drains of color. Terror burning in her gaze.

She's not scared of *me*. But she's scared… of something.

"Luc?" Britt grumbles. "You still there?"

"Yeah." I peel my gaze from Kari's, like tearing tape off sensitive skin, and look down instead at the fuel tank of my bike. "You wanna get drunk tonight?"

"You wanna drink?" she sniggers, confused and yet, as always, willing to match my energy. "Like, two beers chill, or like, Scotch got a new nickname?"

"The second one." I try not to do it. I swear, I don't want to look. But my eyes move anyway, peeking up from beneath my lashes until I find *Ten* pressing a noisy, juicy, homicide enticing kiss to the side of Kari's face. "Give me forty-five minutes," I growl. "Find some liquor and meet me at Popcorn Palace."

"Oh geez. Really? You wanna drink at that dusty old place?"

"I don't want to drink at your house. And I sure as shit don't wanna do it at mine. I'm gonna hang up, because I've got a little work to do. But have the shot glasses ready. I don't want to remember this shit."

She snorts. "I got you. You want me to invite the others? Marc is wandering around bored, since Kari isn't in town. And—"

"Nope. Definitely fucking not. Catch you in a bit."

"And that's when you accidentally slept with Britt," Kane guesses on a gusting exhale. "Liquor. Shot glasses. Heart ache. It's a recipe for disaster, dude."

"It was a mistake," I sigh. "One I literally possess no memories of today. But I know it happened, because I sure as shit remember waking up the next morning, crusty mouthed and puking." I drag my bottom lip between my teeth and study Billy. "Britt's a good girl, and luckily for us both, we had, and continue to have, respect for one another. What was done was just… It was a thing we did. There were no emotions involved. We weren't in love with each other, nor were we mad at each other once it was done. It was just…"

"A thing," Kane nods. "I get it. I made out with your sister one time."

It's like he gets off on annoying me. "You're married to her, Bish. I don't need to know the details."

"Nah, I meant the other sister." His lips twitch with a smug grin. "Picked the wrong one that one time," he chuckles. "It happens. Jess forgave me. And evidently," he extends his hand and gestures toward Billy, "Kari forgave you."

"You're comparing mixing up identical twins and kissing the wrong one, one time, to me having sex with the best friend of the woman I loved, and the sister of my friend?"

"Yes. I am," he sniggers. "So long as you didn't fuck Jess, I'm here for it."

I drop my head back and roll my eyes. "Yes. So glad I didn't fuck my own sister, Bish. Close call."

"Word on the street is Britt announced what you did at the dinner table a few years later. That's how Jess tells it. Would've been rough for Kari to find out that way."

"Yeah? Except Jess doesn't know everything all the time." I bring my focus down and study the sweet baby that came only after years of heartache. Of forgiveness. Of thinking about a prick known as *Ten*.

I wake to the sun's rays filtering through broken panes of glass. The shards of light hitting my eyes like lasers on steroids, their only purpose in life, to irritate me when my head already pounds. My mouth tastes of dirt and vomit. My lips, dry and crusty.

And when I peel my eyes open, narrowing them again in defense of the brutal daylight, I groan as my body aches and rejects… life. It rejects the living.

"Fuckkkk." My stomach rebels, acid rolling along my throat and threatening to make a mess of the already filthy floor. "Kill me."

"Shh…" Britt moans, lying on her belly so her bare back and plenty of ink I know her family doesn't know about, flashes back at me. Like the universe wants to remind me exactly who the hell is here with me.

Like it's not done punishing me.

"I want to die." I slam my eyes shut again and wait for the reaper to take me. "Make it painful. I don't even care. Nothing is as bad as this moment."

"You're being exceptionally dramatic." Slowly, she clings to the paltry blankets we've left here over the years and turns over, gripping the fabric to retain her modesty. Though I'm not sure it matters at this point. "You're not dying, Luc. And this never happened."

"You fucking think?" I force my eyes open and stare up at the popcorn ceilings of the old, dilapidated house. "I slept with my friend's little sister."

"No, you didn't." She drags the blanket all the way up and covers her face with it. "I don't remember it. Therefore, nothing happened."

Vomit teases the base of my throat. The burn of acid, the first layer of punishment coming my way. "You don't remember because we drank enough brandy to have your stomach pumped. Jesus," I grunt. "I'm probably going to prison."

"You're not going to prison." She fusses under the blanket, pulling clothes on and making sounds akin to a dying boar. "It happened, Luc. It was Hennessy's fault. We never speak of it again."

"Yeah? Real mature." I drag my hands to my eyes and press down until I see stars. "I slept with my best friend's sister."

She laughs. Actual, out loud, barking laughter as she pushes the blanket off her face. "You slept with Sam and Alex's sister. I assure you, you didn't sleep with Marc's sister. That would be *way* worse."

Way worse.

Nausea rolls through my belly as I snag my boxers and hurriedly slide them on. Then scrambling from my uncomfortable, make-do bed on the floor of a derelict home, I stumble toward the door that hangs off one hinge and into the yard out back. The instant my feet touch dirt, I toss a gut-full of brown liquor onto the ground, the dirt so hard-packed, it's almost like spewing onto concrete. It doesn't absorb. It merely splashes back and coats my feet.

"Ugh. That's nasty." Britt stumbles through the door behind me. Her black hair, wild, and the black makeup she wears around her eyes, smudged. She's still in her emo phase, punk rocker, and pretty enough to tempt a guy.

All guys.

But not me. "It's like I woke up beside my sister."

I throw up again, groaning as my chest retches and my stomach empties. "Fuck." And again. "Britt…"

"Don't say my name." She plops her ass onto the wooden step, risking splinters in her thighs and frostbite on her toes. "Just…" She drops her face in her hands. "Don't say my name. Ever."

"We fucked up."

"We hung out." She keeps her face in one hand but uses the other to stop-sign me. "We are grown-ups who drank way too much alcohol. Then we did some stuff." She heaves, but locks it in and whimpers. "We are consenting adults. And we used protection."

She pauses and looks up with her panda-smudged eyes. "We used protection?"

I rest my hands on my knees and simply… wish for death. But I nod. "Yes, we used protection. Condom wrapper on the floor inside. I saw it."

"Thank god." She dangles her hand and breathes, heavy and noisy. "We're not in a relationship now, are we?"

"Fuck no." But of course, my harsh words have guilt rearing up and eating at my soul. "I mean… not that you're not worth a relationship, Brat. You're a good, nice girl and I—"

"There's no shotgun pointed at your back. Don't worry. My feelings aren't gonna be hurt, and your obligatory marriage proposal is unnecessary." She rolls her face in her hand and whimpers. "People have sex. You've done it. I've done it."

"Wait…" I lift my head and study the woman who shouldn't be *that* experienced in all this. "You've had sex before?"

"You did *not* take my virginity. We're okay."

"And you're…" Am I her one-night stand? Or am I her quasi-big brother? Fuck. "You're being safe and stuff, right? These guys are treating you right?"

"Better than my current experience," she jokes. But that turns into a growl of anguish. "Why am I smelling purple? What the fuck is that?"

"Inebriation and bad choices." I bring my hand up and swipe my chin and mouth, wiping the unsavory leftovers on my shorts and mentally begging for a shower. Clean clothes.

A different life.

"Are you okay?" I stagger toward the steps and drop down so I'm not sure if I'm sitting or collapsing. But I set my head in my hands and try with all my might to push away my own troubles. My own disgust. "I'm sorry this happened." I turn my face and meet her eyes. "I took advantage... maybe," I burp. "Probably."

She angles away from the stench of my breath and screws up her face. "You're taking responsibility for something we *both* did... while drunk."

"I'm the adult," I moan. "It's my responsibility to carry."

"We're both adults. And you were clearly working through some stuff. It's..." She rolls her head side to side. "It's fine."

"It's not fine!"

"It was sex," she growls. "People have sex. Good, healthy, mature people are able to still be friends with someone they've had sex with."

"You want to stay my friend?"

"I sure as hell don't want to be your girlfriend! I don't want to be your wife. And I don't want to cast you out of my life. So yeah..." She dangles her head back and points her face toward the sky. Eyes closed. Cheeks warming under the morning sun. "It was a thing, Luc. And now that thing is done. It won't be repeated."

"You reject me so easily?"

She snickers, soft and playful. "I've got the ick, like I slept with my brother."

My stomach lurches again, regret rushing along with the acids burning the base of my throat. "That's how it feels for me, too."

"I think, if not for Hennessy, that would have never happened."

"No shit?" I rub my eyes and search for a way back. For a rewind button. For a reset. "Fuck. That was never supposed to happen."

"As far as I'm concerned," she lowers her face and exhales a noisy, liquor infused breath. "It didn't. I won't tell anyone. And you won't tell anyone. It'll go to the grave with me, I swear." She lifts her hand between us, presenting me with the side of her fist. "Silence. Forever."

"Yeah." I bump her fist and whimper when last night's paltry dinner swirls in my stomach. "Forever."

"Thank god." She pushes up to stand, swaying in place until I reach out and set my hand on the side of her hip. But of course, she slaps me away and lopes back up into the house. "You don't get to touch me there. That's intimate. And people who aren't intimate don't do that."

"I should just kill myself." I jam my thumbs against my eyes and pray for a fast death. "Put us both out of our misery."

"You could, I suppose." She bangs around inside the house. Stumbling as she pulls the rest of her clothes on and stomps into a pair of platform boots. "Or you could just... ya know. Move on with your life."

"Wait." I push up to my feet and heave when my stomach and head aren't quite in sync with each other just yet. Then I turn on my heels and trudge into the house. "You're being way too cool about this, Brat. Girls don't often react this way the morning after."

"You'd know." She drops to her ass and works on her laces. "You've left a string of broken hearts in your wake." She shakes her head and glances up. "Don't worry, my heart is fine."

"You're way too comfortable right now. How many *morning afters* have you walked away from?"

Her lips quiver with the ghost of a smile. "You're not my boyfriend, so you don't get that information. And you're not actually my brother. So again..."

"I don't get that information." I lean against the wall, because I'm not sure I can stand all on my own for much longer. Then I drop my head back until it hits the plaster with a dull thud. "You're being safe, right? I don't just mean condoms. I mean everything."

"Always. And except for *this* one time, the girls and I have a safety system in place. We're always careful."

My sisters. And the woman I love.

Fucking awesome!

"I think I have to tell someone about us." I peel my eyes open and search for Britt's. "I have to tell her."

"The one who has you all messed up and heart broken and drinking with another woman? Fuck that bitch. Anyone who hurts you like that doesn't deserve you."

"It's not her fault my heart hurts." Sliding down the wall, I lower to my ass and wrap my arms around my legs. "It's completely my fault. And what you and I did last night makes it so much worse."

She finishes with one shoe and moves to the other with a shrug. "So don't tell her. Did you miss that part where I said it's to never be spoken of again?"

"You can't build a relationship with a lie like that." I press my chin to my knees and groan. "I can't not tell her. Not if I want us to be together eventually."

"Are you together now? Like... in a relationship?"

"No."

"So is this a bit like Ross and Rachel? Are you on a break?"

"No. We're... we've never *actually* been together. And I'm pretty fucking sure she's dating someone else right now."

"So you're in the clear. That's like me worrying about some future, potential boyfriend I don't even know yet. We're not together, so it's none of his business who I've spent time with. And if *your* chick is with someone else right now, do you think she's waking up each morning wondering if she should tell you she slept with someone?"

No. Fuck. It's not like she called to tell me about *Ten*.

And I can't even be mad about it. *I told her to go!*

"No."

"Exactly." She finishes her second shoe and pops up to stand, swaying on her feet and pressing a hand to her stomach. "I'm never drinking again."

"No shit." I pinch the bridge of my nose and exhale until my lungs ache. "Fucking hell. I've made a mess."

"No mess." She wanders to the makeshift bed and bends to grab her phone. Keys. Chapstick. "We're both single—even if you're heartsick for someone else. We're both legal, consenting adults. We have mutual respect for one another. And neither of us will leave this shitty house today with bad feelings toward the other." She straightens out again and pushes long, raven hair behind her ear. "And thank god, I'm heading back to the city tomorrow. I won't have to see you again until Christmas, and by then, we'll both be sober enough to not want to puke on the floor. This is gonna be fine. You just need a shower and a breath mint."

"I can't take you home." My head pounds, like heavy bass drums in the back of my skull, and just to be extra annoying, my heart thunders to the same beat. Painful in my chest. Throbbing, because I screwed up. "I drank way too much to ride right now. It's not safe."

"It's okay. I'm still too drunk to sit on the back and hold on." She grins, like maybe she really is still a little on the tipsy side. "I'm gonna walk. The fresh air will be good for me. But I'm going to the bathroom first."

She sways as she walks, making her way to the toilet we've used a million times over the years while pseudo squatting in this house. The girls and the band have supplied the place with toilet paper and hand soap. There's no electricity here, but there's a flushing toilet and a tap that still, somehow, has water supply.

"I need to clean my face before I go anywhere," she calls back. "And I suggest you wash yours before you step outside. You're still in your underwear and you have vomit on your chin."

"Fuck." I look down, though I know I'm still in my boxers. Because the November air bites at my skin and yet, I don't shiver the way I should. I think it's shock. Perhaps trauma. "If I tell this person what we did, I'm gonna have to use your name." Grunting, I push along the wall until I'm standing tall once more. But I continue to lean for a beat. To find my bearings. "I have to tell her, Brat. Keeping the secret wouldn't be right."

"Suits me. But ask her to keep it between you two. My brothers *don't* need to know about this. In fact, Jess and Laine don't need to know, either. It will make life *so* awkward."

"Britt—"

"Is she likely to kick my ass?" She pokes her head back through the door, half her makeup gone as she clutches to a wad of moist toilet paper in lieu of a face wipe. "Will she try? I'm not afraid, but I'd like a warning, so I know to watch my back."

"No." I draw a heaped breath and work to replace the fumes of liquor with fresh air. "She won't hurt you, but she'll probably kill me. And even then, she won't forgive me."

"Sounds like you're making the wrong move, then. The secret is safe." She steps back into the bathroom to continue cleaning up. So while she's gone, I dress. Pulling on my jeans. Shrugging into my shirt. "There's no rule that says you *have* to confess to this. Especially considering you and I are the only people on the planet who know, and I'm not saying shit to anyone."

"But it's about integrity, right?" I reach up and run a hand through my hair, then down over my face until the stubble on my chin crackles. "If I want to be an honorable man, she deserves the truth."

"If you say so." She comes out of the bathroom, looking like her usual beautiful and innocent self. Gone is the dark makeup. The panda smudge under her eyes. Even the lipstick I hadn't really noticed she was wearing, since it was only a shade or two off her natural color. "I think it's important to remember that you and her are *not* together. And that she's dating someone else. This isn't Ross and Rachel, Luc. This is…" She wracks her brain for a moment, only to bring her shoulders up in a shrug. "This is Claire, Jamie, and Randall. When she was married to Randall, she didn't know Jamie. And when she was with Jamie, she thought Randall was gone from her life forever. Claire shouldn't feel guilty for the things she did in those situations."

"I don't even know who the fuck you're talking about." I fasten the button on my jeans and draw the zipper up. "And this isn't about me searching for a loophole. If I tell her, it'll be because I chose to. Not because I got caught out."

"Okay, well…" She turns toward the door. "As long as you're not expecting her to return the sentiment and tell you about who she's dating. If you're not together, then you're not together. You don't get to get pissy about her dating someone else."

"Do I look pissy to you, Brittany!?" I stomp across the room and grab my shoes, proving to us both that I am, in fact, pissy. "I know she's dating, okay?" *It was the fucking deal I made when I broke her heart and sent her away.* "I'm trying to be the better man," I sigh. "She deserves better than me. Which is why we're not dating in the first place."

"So..." She stops by the front door and turns back to wait for me to fix my shoes. "She wants to date you, but you don't want to date her? But she's dating someone else, and now you've slept with someone you probably shouldn't have, so as a result, you feel guilty enough to consider confessing what we did to the someone you're not dating?"

"Yes." I hate that she makes me feel stupid. That she simplifies a lifetime of heartache and makes me feel like a fucking idiot. "I was trying to be noble," I admit, switching feet and tying my second boot, "sending her out into the real world to date other people, even though she was in love with me."

"And what did that achieve in the end?" She flashes a taunting, beautiful grin that'll be the end of some other guy.

She's smart. Witty. Bratty. Crazy. She's going to make someone very happy someday. But I'm not that someone. Not when my heart belongs elsewhere.

"Luc?"

"It ended with her dating someone else, and me tossing my Thanksgiving dinner onto the ground outside this shitty house." Done with my shoes, I push up to stand and pat my pockets to make sure I have everything I need.

Liquor bottles litter the floor, and blankets remain strewn in the middle of what I suppose was probably the living room at one point in this house's lifetime. Random things we've left over the years lie around. Hair ties. Socks. Clothes. Pillows. The mess we leave behind today will be no different to the mess we've left behind before, so I don't bother cleaning up.

Instead, I dig my hands into my pockets and skulk toward the door. "Let's walk. I'll come back later and get my bike."

"Sounds to me like you're bitter and jealous."

"Yeah, smartass?" I hold the broken door and draw it shut as Britt steps out ahead of me. "How do you suppose that is?"

"Well... did you *actually* expect her to go out and date, like you told her to? Or were you hoping she'd wait for you, to prove you're the one?"

I trudge down the front steps and onto the hard packed driveway someone will clear out someday. Maybe. They might even concrete it, before bringing this old house back to its former glory.

"Luca...?" Britt saunters, swinging her hips and glancing over her shoulder to search my eyes. "Bitter? Jealous?"

"Sad," I clarify. "Because I've only ever tried to do the right thing by her. But every step I take pushes us further apart."

17

LUC

WHAT WAS THAT THING I SAID ABOUT SURPRISES?

"You're a whole Doctor Phil mess," Kane rumbles. Though his lips curl high with playfulness. "Your entire family is chaos. And that includes the woman I coerced into saying '*I do*'."

"Yep." I glance out the windows as the early morning sun finally, barely tickles the horizon and teases the start of a new day. Billy has slept damn near the whole way through, and yet, I'm not sure she spent any of it not touching me or Bish. "This is what happens when a group of dudes all have sisters, and all those guys and girls grow up together. Relationships get blurry and sibling protectiveness feels weird when people cross the line."

"Can't say I've ever had that problem," he chuckles. "I only have one brother. And I sure as shit have no sisters."

"Two."

He frowns, a deep line etched into the middle of his forehead. "What?"

"You have two brothers." I feel, for a moment at least, a little humor flittering into my heart. "You forgot Griff."

"Oh, well..." He shrugs. "I guess. Though we didn't meet till we were adults. So it kinda doesn't feel like it counts."

"It would count if he was a chick, and you slept together."

At that, Kane throws his head back and laughs. "This is true. Though thank Christ, neither you and Britt, nor you and Kari, share parents. Shit gets messy real fast in small towns."

"Yeah. It does. Especially when you and your entire friend group stay in the same town forever. We're forced to watch our sisters date. We're limited in who we can date. And shit, in this town, sometimes we end up dating people our friends have dated, simply because the pickings are slim."

"Which is precisely why you sent Kari away." He picks up his coffee mug and glances inside, though I know the contents will be cold. "You wanted her to see what existed outside of this place."

"Fat load of good that did me. She ended up with a dude with a ten-inch wiener, and I had another giant secret to keep from a different friend. That's two." I bring my free hand up and present two fingers. "Four guys in the band, Kane. Three of us had sisters. I crossed the line twice, with two different friends' sisters."

"Which is precisely why I'm thrilled I don't have a sister." He flashes a playful smile. "Luca Lenaghan can't be trusted, evidently."

"The secrets were kept, for quite a few years. And Britt held her tongue for a long time. Until she didn't, anyway." I bring my hand up and run my fingers over my forehead in remembrance. "Everything was mostly calm after that night."

"So you didn't tell Kari?"

"I didn't have to."

"We just go home and act normal," Britt presses. She walks with her hands in the pockets of her jacket. Kicking her feet out to send a rock rolling along the road. "We eat at the dinner table, and we say nothing. Sam isn't really gonna care. But Alex will probably have a complete meltdown. So it's best if he doesn't know." Then she glances across to me. "And if you decide to tell your lady friend, then that's cool. Though it would be appreciated if you could ask her to be discreet. The last thing either of us needs right now is to have Alex coming after you with his police issued gun." She raises a single, pointed brow. "We know he can get kinda heated sometimes."

"Britt!" Laine's playful voice carries along the street. Her excited yelp echoing as Britt and I come around the corner. But I groan as I bring my focus up and find Jess, too. "She's returned!"

"Oh god." Britt presses a hand to her stomach and silently burps, her cheeks filling with air in the world's least attractive way. "Not a word,

Lenaghan. Your sisters and I always talk sex. Like…" She widens her eyes. "Always. I do not want to discuss the size of your dick with them."

"Please don't." I look up at the sky and shake my head as Britt's footsteps speed up. "Not a damn word."

"We have a surprise for you!" Laine calls out. We're still a block away, which means everyone in our street gets a front-row seat to the girls' reunion. Anyone would think they'd been apart for years. Potentially a whole world war, too.

"Kari?" Britt squeals. Jump-skipping as her fast trot turns to a scream and sprint. "Kari!"

I swing my head back down, my stomach hurdling when our eyes meet and her cheeks turn a pale, pale white. The three others all run toward Kari, crushing her in a group hug that brings Marc and Sam out of the house. But no matter the noise they make, no matter the strength they hug with, Kari's eyes stay on mine.

Fuck. My. Life.

"I didn't think you were coming home!" Britt wraps her arms around Kari's neck and squeezes. "You said you were staying to spend time with Ten."

Kari's eyes trail over my face. Does she know what I did? Or is she more concerned about me knowing about *Ten*? Does she love him? Does she *not* love me anymore?

"I changed my mind," she gulps, pulling back from her friends and fixing her hair. "I missed you guys, so I drove over late last night."

"Oh man!" Britt grumbles. "If I knew, I'd have been home."

"Where were you, anyway?" Jess grabs Britt around the neck and turns, so the foursome gives me their backs. Then they head toward the Turners' house. "You sure as hell didn't sleep in your own bed," Jess continues. "And I tried calling your phone."

"I was out with friends." She lifts her chin for Marc as they pass. "Women are allowed to have fun without constant brotherly supervision."

"Yeah?" He smiles at least, too fucking happy to have Kari home to care that someone else's sister was out all night. And he's so blind to the possibility it was *me* she was with, he doesn't even give me a second thought. "You wanna go tell X where you were, Brat? He's on duty down at the station. Bet he'd love to know where you slept."

She scoffs and trudges up the porch steps with her girlfriends. "No thanks. I'm not really interested in that right now." She turns and presses a noisy kiss to Kari's cheek. "Welcome home, Kar! We've missed you."

"I saw you yesterday," Kari drawls. "Literally, less than twenty-four hours ago."

"Yeah, but I haven't seen you *here* in forever."

"**Y**ou pussed out." Kane pushes away from the table, the legs of his chair scraping along the tile floor and makes his way to the coffeepot. He passes me and Billy by, unable to help himself as he drapes his fingers over her cheek and strokes as he goes. "She came home to check up on you, huh? Because she saw you the night before in the city. She knew you saw her with Biff, so she came running home to ask for forgiveness. Which could have been a cute romance movie thing, where she runs into your arms and three years of heart ache washes away with happy music and noisy kisses."

I firm my lips and let him waffle on with his version of my story.

"She never wanted Biff. She just wanted companionship. So when she saw you'd come for her, she tossed him on his ass and chased you home. Except." He places his mug under the coffee spout and hits the button to get the machine started. "You weren't home when she came looking. Her romantic movie montage came tumbling down because you weren't where you were supposed to be."

I turn in my chair, twisting my neck to search his eyes. "You finished embellishing my life story yet?"

He only shrugs. "Does your version get interesting soon? Because apart from Biff's ten-inch cock, I can't say anything has been entertaining so far."

I turn back and look down at Billy's sweet face. "I hope to god you can't hear or understand what he's saying, Bill. This is completely inappropriate for baby ears."

"She's fine. We had two girls to test inappropriate discussions in front of. Chicken and Nugget are totally normal."

"Says you. The rest of town knows to steer clear of the Bishop babies." I bring my hand up and stroke the bridge of Billy's nose, while outside, the sun rises in the sky until the world turns less black and more pink. "So I guess she came home looking for me," I agree. "Maybe it's because she knew I saw her with Biff."

"Ten?"

"Yeah, we're not calling him that anymore."

Kane chuckles and heads to the fridge for creamer. "But *Ten* is just so… descriptive. And to the point."

G uilt slashes through my stomach, burning me up and tearing at my heart as I sit in the Turners' backyard and all my friends hang out. It's like we're in high school again. The skateboards are out. Jess is zooming along the halfpipe in her blades. Britt, no worse for wear after our night together, laughs and plays and ollies on the halfpipe, barely avoiding a collision with Jess every time they pass one another.

Scotch sits with his guitar, plucking away at the strings, and Ang tinkers with his car. Marc watches his sister, and Kari watches everyone else.

It's like the old days where we had nothing to worry about except school on Monday and whatever fears Marc was working through in his mind.

But while everyone else is chill, I keep Kari in my peripherals and sit in my pool of shame. My horror and guilt. I baste in the hatred I hold for myself. And every now and then, I get caught staring because she cuts a look through the corner of her eyes and catches me.

How the fuck am I supposed to tell her I spent the night with her best friend? With her foster sister! How am I supposed to admit to what I did, when my spiel all along was for *her* to get out of this town and experience what everyone has to offer?

She did.

She literally did what I told her to do, and when I found out about it, I drank and made horrible choices.

"You look like you're gonna be sick." Scotch comes to a stop on my left, his frayed jeans in my peripherals and the myriad of leather bands he keeps on his wrists stop by his thighs when he drops his hands. He sets an old acoustic guitar on the concrete beside the porch, leaning it against the house. Then he drops down to sit beside me, his shoulder touching mine, and his feet coming up to perch on the porch step. "Wanna talk about it?"

"Are you still in love with Sammy?" I peel my eyes away from Kari and look at my friend instead. Though my question was cruel and uncalled for, Scotch's eyes darken the moment my words register in his mind. "She was it for you, right? She was your everything."

"So you're going through an existential crisis of some sort, and instead of dealing with that in a healthy way, you thought it would be fun to toss me under the bus? Did it make you feel better?"

"No. Shit." I lower my head and press the heels of my hands to my eyes. "I'm sorry. I wasn't trying to hurt you. I just…"

"You're having a crisis," he repeats. "Fucked if I know what it is, Luca. Or who it's about. But I see it in your eyes. You're hurting."

"Sammy's been gone a few years now." I turn my head and study the side of his angular face. "You married her, dude. You were expecting a baby. And then she just…"

"Left," he nods. Then he sighs. "Yep."

"I haven't seen you with another woman since." I swallow the ache in my throat and probe my temple with the pad of my thumb. Anything to combat the headache pulsing just below the skin. "I haven't made it a mission to keep tabs on you or anything, but I've noticed. You aren't bringing anyone else around."

He places his hands together, twining his fingers and studying them like they hold the world's secrets. "I suppose it's one of those things. When you've loved the very best…"

"No one else will do." I sigh. "Yeah. That's what I figured."

"I try. When we're playing a set or whatever, and girls are looking up at us. It's not so hard to pick up women when you're the lead singer in a band," he chuckles, though the sound is sad and weak at best. "I try to see them for who they are. I try to look into their eyes and not see Sammy."

"But it doesn't work? You can't see past her?"

"I wish I could." He glances down at his hands again and massages the center of his palm with the opposite thumb. "I seriously fucking wish I could."

"Would you tell her?" I cast a look out at our friends, though I'm careful not to stop on Kari. Hell. I'm careful not to stop on Britt, too. "You're not, like, together right now. It's been years. So if you went to bed with someone else, would you feel you needed to tell her?"

He considers me for a long beat. Rolling his bottom lip between his teeth and humming something in the back of his throat. "I'm actually not sure. Assuming I knew where she was, and assuming we had a way to communicate, then… sure, I guess. I wouldn't hide it from her. She left me, Luc. She ran away. So I don't know that I'd feel guilty about it, if that's what you mean." Finally, he drags his gaze away from his hands and studies me. "Have you done something you probably shouldn't have?"

"I mean…" I shrug. "Sort of. And not really. There's this woman I've had feelings for, for a really long time."

At that, his brow pops high on his forehead. "You?"

I choke out a soft, almost silent laugh. "Me. But this person and I aren't really suited for each other. She has a life elsewhere. She even has a boyfriend, and that guy isn't me."

"I see." He goes back to studying his hands. "Your heart wants what your heart wants. But your body, sometimes, does something else."

"In a way. I guess."

"So you hooked up with someone, and this someone isn't the same someone your heart hurts for. And now you're feeling guilty, even though, technically, you and the chick you have feelings for aren't together."

"In a nutshell." I drag my head up and make a point of watching my sisters. Totally safe. Totally normal, protective, older brother stuff. "There's a whole lot more between the lines. But that's the gist of things."

"Well…" He gives my situation more thought, rolling his bottom lip. "I don't know if there's a right or a wrong answer here. You're not together, so neither of you are betraying the other by dating other people."

"But in the spirit of honesty and integrity? Would you tell?"

"Would telling her help *her*? Or would it help you? Her hurt feelings, in exchange for you offloading your guilt?"

"You make it sound like being honest, in this case, would be the wrong choice."

He scoffs, low and subtle. "I don't have any fucking clue what the wrong choice is. Clearly, I'm not the guy to ask. I got married when I was eighteen. And she left me before the ink was dry. I've been a fucking eunuch since, and I'm the frontman of a band. Pretty sure that makes me pathetic."

"Makes you loyal." I bring my hand up and clap his shoulder. "Makes you a good man, and her, not who we thought she was back in high school. The Sammy we thought we knew wouldn't have done what she did."

"I'm still loyal to the Sammy we thought we knew." He shrugs my hand off, but he looks my way and meets my eyes. "I try every day to convince myself she doesn't exist. That she was a liar. But hearts can be nasty, finicky fucking things. Which…" he turns to survey the yard, "it seems, you know about. Considering your current predicament."

He stands, but luckily for me, he's a discreet man. Softly spoken. So he turns his back on our friends and murmurs, "Do whatever you think is best for you and the other person. You have to be able to live with your choices.

But you should also be mindful of what the truth will do to the woman who is currently squeezing your heart. You didn't technically do anything wrong, since you and her are not together. So just… I dunno, man. It's on you to decide your next move. I'm around if you ever want to talk about it. Or, ya know, if you get married and she leaves you anyway. I can relate to that."

"Sammy's back now though." Kane drops into his chair, setting his coffee down and frowning as he studies my eyes. "I know she is. I fucking own this town, so I know Sam Turner and Sam Turner remain married now. They even have a kid."

"They sure do. And he deserves every single second of happiness he has with his girls. Took her thirteen years to come back. Thirteen," I repeat, shaking my head when I think of Kari. I've been without her for approximately fifteen hours, and already, it feels like my skin is on fire. "Sammy eventually came home. And in all those thirteen years, he didn't touch another woman."

I mean. He kissed one, one time. Literally the same night Sammy came back to him.

The universe's timing was cruel, as is often the case.

"So Kari had come back for the first time in, what?" Kane mentally tracks back through my stories. "Like, three years? And you'd just spent the night with Britt."

A long, pained groan works along my throat. "Nice reminder, jackass."

"*Jackass?*" He laughs. "Dude! Tell the fucking story. Did you tell her, or did you keep the Britt thing to yourself? Did you choose *her* feelings, or *your* guilt?"

18

LUC

SINCE WHEN IS TELLING THE TRUTH THE SELFISH THING?

"Luc?" Kari steps up behind me later that night, when bodies ache from skating, and throats tickle from a day of laughter. Today was the first in years that *everyone* has been back together. And not for a single second was anyone going to pass up the opportunity to bathe in the familiar.

It could be years before we get this again.

Or maybe never, depending on the things I tell Kari tonight.

Her sweet scent filters into my lungs, though I don't mean to inhale quite so deep. Her soft, curly hair tickles my arm, since the Turners have good heating, which means I don't have to wear a jacket inside. Her soft voice, though, that's what undoes me as I turn from the television, a show I have no clue of the details, however anyone watching me from the outside would swear I was an avid fan.

I swallow and meet Kari's eyes, her perfect green stare like aloe on a sunburn, and her hand, when it presses to my shoulder, like popping candy on a man's tongue.

"I've caught up with everyone, I think." Her nose twitches, oh so subtly. "Everyone except you. I was wondering if you'd like to go for a walk with me?"

"A walk?" I shoot a glance across the room. To Jess and Laine. To Marc. Scotch. Ang. Even Alex, and at the kitchen counter, Oz. Everyone is here, but no one pays a great deal of attention to anyone else.

Bringing my focus back to Kari, I repeat, as though her words don't quite make sense, "You want to go for a walk? With me?"

Her lips curl, sweet and kind and just big enough to make my stomach jump. "If you would like to. It's been a while since we've been in the same place. So I just…" The longer she talks, the less confident she becomes with her words. "I just thought—"

"Yeah." I bound up from the couch, too fast to be subtle. Too noisy not to draw eyes. But I'm Luc, and she's Kari. This group of people have co-mingled since the dawn of time. "Sure. I'll come for a walk." I stride toward the door before she has a chance to change her mind. And swinging my coat on, I grab hers and head out until she's forced to follow. "Here." I wait for her on the porch, as she steps through the door and into the dark outside. Then I move in behind her and offer her coat.

She smells like home.

Like flowery shampoo.

She hasn't changed a lot in the last three years. Still the same height. Same build. Her hair is still wild and long, and her eyes are still shrewd. But her face is a little leaner than I'm used to. Her freckles, less pronounced, as though college has kept her busy and out of the sun.

"Thank you." She slips her arms into the sleeves of her coat and turns when I release the fabric, fixing her buttons and dropping her hands into her pockets. Then she glances up and holds my stare for a long, long minute.

The longest of my life.

"It's been forever," she breathes, her sweet breath like candy on my tongue. Her cheeks still warm when she's embarrassed. And her eyes still dance. She's as easy to read as a book laid out and open. "I've missed seeing you every day, Luca."

"I mean…" I was the one who sent her away. I know. She knows. "No one said you couldn't come home every weekend, Bear."

"*Bear.*" She sighs, happily and yet, in a way I know translates to heartache at the same time. Breaking away from where we are on the porch, she starts down the steps and moves slowly until I catch up. "I forgot you used to call me that."

"It's the only name that comes to mind when I think of you." I dig my hands into my pockets and pace my steps to match hers, so together, we move out of the Turners' yard and onto the street instead. "I haven't stopped thinking about you since you left."

"You told me you didn't want me." She cuts straight to the chase, slicing me off at the knees and peering up until our gazes meet. "You looked right into my eyes and told me that."

"I looked right into your eyes and said what I thought was the right thing to say."

"To make me leave," she surmises, dropping her head back and wandering with her focus on the stars instead. "You dismissed me, so I would leave, and you wouldn't have to deal with me anymore."

"So you would leave and see what life is like outside of this town," I clarify. "So you wouldn't marry the only option you thought you had, settle down, and live a bored life."

"Presumptuous of you." She slides her tongue along her lips to moisten them in the cold air. "You just assumed my whole life, based on a high school crush? I asked to kiss you, Luca. I didn't ask to be your date to our wedding."

"I was trying to do the right thing."

She scoffs, lowering her eyes and shaking her head gently from side to side. "I don't remember ever living a moment where some guy wasn't making choices *for* me, all in the name of doing the right thing. Marcus. You. Blake."

Instantly, like my jaw is controlled by a fucking lasso, I turn and stare down at the side of her face. "Blake is your boyfriend?"

"I know you saw us last night." She swallows, the sound audible as she exhales again and white fog races ahead of her. "I thought I was seeing a ghost, to be honest. You were completely out of context, so it made no sense to me. But I saw you, Luc. And you saw me."

"I saw Blake." *Ten.* The RN. "H-have you been dating long?"

"A few months." She watches her feet as we walk. "He's good to me. He's a gentleman." She tilts her head and eyes me. "But he considers himself the authority on what's right for me, too. Seems I have a type, jumping from my brother, to you, to him. Everyone wants to take care of me, no matter if I have an opinion of my own."

"Does he..." I frown and try, so fucking hard, not to assume the worst. "When you say he considers himself your authority, do you mean that in a cute, boyfriendy way. Or are we talking about Marc and I heading to the city to kill a man?"

She snorts, shaking her head and huddling into her coat. "Case in point. I'm a full-grown adult now, Luca. But you assume I'm in a controlling relationship, and the only way I can leave it is if you and Marc come and rescue me."

"So stop with the vague bullshit and just tell me what's up." I grab her elbow and pull us both to a stop, then tugging her around, I swallow when our chests clash and her breath races into my lungs. "Are you happy, Bear? Is this a good relationship for you? Is he…" I swallow the ache in the base of my throat. "Is this an *I'm experiencing college* kind of relationship, or are you marrying him and staying away forever?"

"Once again," she murmurs, meeting my stare and firming her jaw, "you presume to have a right to that information. But that's not how things work anymore."

"So that's it, then?" Anger surges in my blood. Pain. The regret of what I sent away, and the guilt for what I did last night. "All this history, and now I'm locked out? I don't even get the benefit of being your friend? Because friends are allowed to make sure their friends are happy and okay."

"Friends don't tell their friends they're not wanted." She turns on her heels and stomps along the road. "Friends don't show up unannounced, after *three* years, then disappear for the night, so that friend is left wondering where the hell they went to, and if they're okay. Because for all I knew, you, my friend, saw me with Blake, then you left again and rode your bike off a friggin' cliff. I had no clue why you were in the city in the first place, and I sure as hell didn't know if you made it home safe, considering *no one* knew where you were all night." She slows her steps and peers back over her shoulder. "Seems you're not a good friend to any of the people who care about you."

"I didn't know anyone was waiting on me." I grit words past my teeth and keep walking to catch up to her. "I don't make a habit of sending good morning and good night texts to my pals, Bear. So I didn't think doing so last night was required."

"And yet, I sat up all night wondering where you were. *Who* you were with."

"So we're doing that, then? Comparing notes of who we spend time with?"

"No, I—"

"Let's start with Blake," I bite out. "Because dating a dude for a few months kinda implies monogamy and feelings." I grab her arm and swing her around again. "You're in a relationship, Kari. Can't say that doesn't make me bleed."

"And you had a one-night stand last night." She smirks, though it's not playful or sweet. "I can't find it in my heart to feel bad for you. You think I'm stupid? That I don't see you for who you are?"

"What?"

"You're still you, Luc! It's like we're still in high school. You have Sassy and Belle and Katie and whoever the hell else rotating on your roster. But you feel the need to comment on me dating *one* guy? One, consistent, trust-worthy person."

"I feel the need to comment on him because according to you, he controls you, and according to my fucking sisters, his nickname is *Ten*."

Shut up! Shut up. Shut up!

"Ten?" I press. "*Really?* You sure as hell took my *go see the world* for every-thing it was, huh?"

She shoves my hand off and turns away with a scoff. "Jealousy is not a valid reason to throw a fit, Luca. You didn't want me, remember? You *chose* this life."

"I didn't choose this dude! I sacrificed my own fucking happiness in favor of what I thought was best for you! I sent you away, so you could experience something other than small town life, so you could open your eyes and see what's available. So *when* you came home, you could see me and still know I'm the best man for you."

"Oh, sure!" she laughs, maniacal and mean. "So I was to toddle off and do as you asked. And in the meantime, you could still see your roster and have the time of your life."

"I haven't been sleeping around!" I lose my temper and shout too fucking loud. Brutally aware an audience is the last thing we need, I firm my jaw and bite down on my words, leaning in and grabbing her hip to keep her close. "I haven't been with a single person since you left, Bear. Not one, single, fucking, person. Because I love *you*. I was waiting for *you*."

"Not one?" Her eyes soften, flickering between mine as she searches for truth. "Three years, Luca. And you're telling me you haven't been with a single person?"

"That's what I'm telling you. Until yesterday, I—"

"Until yesterday." She nods, accepting my words with pain slashing through her eyes. "Until yesterday, when you decided you were done proving a point you didn't even tell me to pay attention to. Until yesterday, when you snuck into the city, spied on me out on a date with my boyfriend, then you... what? Raced back to town, picked up the closest, loosest chick you knew, and went crazy working through three years of frustration? Because poor you, Luca. You're so fucking hard done by."

"It wasn't like that! It was—"

"And then, what? This morning, you're walking home from your hookup. And Britt is walking home from hers. And like a totally normal, healthy family, the two of you decide to—"

But then her eyes widen. Her cheeks pale.

She gets it now. Her brain smashing her with the realization that makes her skin green. "Britt?"

"Bear, stop—"

"Britt!" She presses a hand to her stomach and heaves. "Holy shit. Holy shit, Luc, you… and Britt?"

"Please, Kari." I cup her cheek and try to bring her eyes up to mine. "Please just take a second to—"

She slaps my arm away with a ferociousness that has the sound reverberating along the street, then she shoves me back when I try to charge forward. To stop her. To keep her here.

"You slept with Britt!" She snarls, low and poisonous in the back of her throat. "Are you fucking serious, Luca!?"

"Please, just stop and listen for a minute."

"I can't believe she would do that." She brings her hands up and scrubs at her face until I'm sure she'll leave marks. "She went to bed with you *willingly*?"

"Kari—"

"Does she know about us?" She steps around me, angling toward the house. But she doesn't start that way. She doesn't take off and leave me behind just yet. "Did you tell her about our history?"

"No, I—"

"Don't." She turns back and looks me up and down. For the first time ever, she regards me the way she would the gum on the bottom of her shoe. "I never mentioned us. And you never mentioned us. Britt was seduced by the man who has the power to ruin lives. It's hardly even her fault."

"Kari—"

She slaps my hand away again, spinning toward the house. "I have to live with her, Luc. Whether in the city, or back here. There's no need for this to ever be mentioned."

"Kari!"

"I'm going back to school in the morning. Please don't come looking for me again."

19

LUC
OUCH

"Jesus." Kane rubs his palms over his cheeks, much the same way Kari did all those years ago. "Fucking brutal, man."

"Ya think?" Shaking my head, I look down at Billy and scoff. "Kinda hope to never experience a discussion like that ever again."

"Why'd she come back to town, though?" He sits forward at the table, resting his elbows on top and linking his tatted fingers together. "Like, I get that she saw you the night before. And that probably spooked her. But she told you point blank you don't get to ask about her relationship. She said you don't get to ask about her life. So she wasn't there to explain Biff."

"She was, actually." I sit back in my chair and revisit some of the darkest days of my life.

Darkest... until now.

"It took a lot of years for the truth to come out, but Kari admitted she was coming home to explain that he was just a friend."

"A friend?" he snorts. "Yeah, no. Blake was not a friend. He was a ten-inch dick she liked to spend time with. But then she got caught."

"No." Chuckling—because it's not like I didn't believe the girls at first, too—I play with Billy's peach hair and wrinkle my nose. "Setting what you think you know aside, it eventually came out that Kari and Blake were friends. Buddies in class. They became kinda close, but they were never intimate."

"Dude! The girls call him *Ten!*"

"And if you asked Jess today, she'd laugh and tell you how they called him that because it was funny. These are the same girls who snuck a butt plug into Jess' bag and let you assume it was hers. The same girls who snuck around the club and scoped out the one blind spot that existed, so they could dance and drink and flirt without their brothers supervising them. Blake got that nickname because he's tall. But none of them, especially not Kari, knows what size cock he has. And last I heard, he and his boyfriend, Clint, are quite happy together."

"You lie." Kane narrows his eyes. "You're more gullible than a puppy if you believe that."

"Kari and I went to his wedding two years ago, but okay. You believe whichever version you want. You asked why Kari rushed home to see me, and I'm telling you: she wanted to explain Blake."

"But she didn't! She told you to mind your business."

"She's stubborn. And she'd seen me stumble home from a one-night stand. Her plans went out the window the second I screwed up. We fought that night, and so, instead of explaining, she tossed lighter fluid and a match on anything we had left. Because of what I did."

"Years?" He tilts his head to the side to study me. "Took her years to fess up?"

I exhale a long, tired sigh and look down as Billy finally begins to fuss. Her little body wriggles, her chapped lips wrinkle. She's not quite awake yet, but she will be. Soon. "She went back inside the house after our argument and kept her word on not telling Britt she knew. All four of them returned to school the next morning. And I…" I groan. "I didn't see Kari again for another three years."

"Another three!" His black eyes, and the permanent lines etched into his cheeks below, lift in surprise. "Three years! Lenaghan. That's six, gone. For no good reason at all."

"Six," I agree. "Gone. And though the first three were spent alone and sad and working, the latter three were not quite the same."

"You slutted it up," he guesses. "Which was the reputation I heard around town. Before you eventually settled down with Kari, word was you were nothing but a filthy whore."

I bring Billy up to rest her cheek on my chest and let her legs dangle. She's working through a gas bubble that gravity might help. "As far as I knew, Kari was heading back to Ten. I thought I'd lost her, so I…" I grit my teeth and pat Billy's backside. "I spiraled a little bit. I'm not proud of it. But I'm man enough to admit my mistakes."

"Brave of you," he smirks. Then pushing up from his place at the table, he steps around and extends his hands for the baby. "She's about to drop a giant deuce, and then she'll want a bottle."

"So you're volunteering to clean her diaper?"

"I want more babies, Luca." He takes Billy and holds her close. "I want a dozen more the way I used to want to make bad decisions."

"So..."

"Jess doesn't want a dozen more. I figure changing a massive, smelly shit might bring me back to earth on the baby front." He chuckles and turns away, swaying and almost dancing with my daughter across the kitchen. "So Kari was sneak-dating a gay man who may, or may not, have had a giant dick, and you were sorry for sleeping with Britt, so in apology, you went out and slept with every other single female in the state." He glances back with a grin. "That's where we're up to in the story?"

"Seems that way." I don't get up. I don't think my legs could carry me if I tried. But I meet his eyes before he disappears around the corner and out of sight. "I fucked everything up to a point of no return. I broke Kari's heart... *again*. I drunk-slept with my friend's little sister, and I sure as shit never told him about it. In fact, I considered myself a *saint* for not sharing that information, since Britt didn't want anyone to know, Kari didn't want anyone to know, and Scotch was still dealing with the *wife who left his heart shattered on the side of the road* thing. I was the martyr for shutting my mouth."

"Bet you were," Kane snorts. "Total martyr. Make the bottle, I'll change the diaper. Then you're cooking me breakfast. Jess and the girls are gonna drop by in a little bit. And I don't know about you, but listening to your heartbreak and six wasted years makes me yearn for my family."

"Glad I could be of assistance," I drawl. I slump in my chair and drop my head back until I study the ceiling above. There's no popcorn texture in this house. No water stains in the paint. There aren't even spiderwebs taking up residence in the corners.

While he's gone, I try not to think of those lost six years. The massive chunk of my life wasted on all the wrong things.

Most importantly, I try not to think of this past year of us being together. The ways I didn't hold up my end of every deal we made. The pregnancy Kari carried, not alone, but certainly not with the partner she deserved. The house she worked for, once again, not alone, but not with the husband she was promised.

I try not to think of the car accident that ended everything.

Or that Billy and I are home again… alone. Not with the wife and mom we wished for.

"Shhh…" Jess' soft, sweet voice carries across my house and into the kitchen. "We have to be quiet," she whispers. "Uncle Luc and Baby Billy might still be asleep."

"They're not." Kane traipses down our stairs, squeaking on the third from the top, and again on the fourth from the bottom. Then he stops by the front door when a bevy of little girl squeals surround him and, I'm certain, Billy. "The baby just dropped a *giant* turd, girls." He animates his voice and makes his twins giggle. "Swear, it was bigger than my whole arm."

"Eww!" Luna—a.k.a. Nugget—cackles and stomps her little feet. "That's gross!"

"She's your cousin, Nug. That poop was your family."

"And now it's down the toilet." Rosalie—a.k.a. Chicken—giggles. "Billy's butt isn't even the size of your arm, Daddy. Her whole body isn't the size of your arm."

"That's because Daddy is super strong." I hear the peck of a kiss. The familiar sound of a husband and wife greeting each other after being apart. "Blondie. I missed the shit out of you."

"We missed you." I catch a glimpse of her sweeping Billy from Kane's hold, then as she sets bags on the floor and wanders this way. "Uncle Jay and Aunty Soph hardly ever sleep. Like," she presses a noisy kiss to Billy's cheek. "Barely at all! Which is something I guess they've taught their girls. Who then felt the need to keep our girls awake. So now Aunty Jess needs coffee and a long vacation." She steps into the kitchen and flashes a smile for me. "Hey there, handsome. You look like you haven't slept in a thousand years."

"Kinda feels that way." A long yawn wracks my frame and stretches my mouth wide. My jaw clicks, and my eyes water as I squeeze them shut. But I pull it all back in. Forcing my mouth shut and my body to relax. "We've been up since two, I think."

Surprised, Jess peeks over her shoulder at Kane. "Billy give you guys a hard time?"

"Not at all." He holds his girls, one on each hip, and makes it look easy. "Baby woke at two for something to eat. But then Luca got lonely, I suppose, because he came downstairs and sat at that table to tell me a story about a dude known only as *Ten*."

"Ten?" Jess' cheeks flame bright red. Her eyes widen as she glances back around to me. Then she barks out a laugh loud enough to have her girls stare. "Oh my gosh! Ten! I forgot all about that name."

"How much of *Ten* did you know, Blondie?" Kane wanders up behind her. And since his hands are full, he leans in and bites the back of her neck.

He bites. My sister's. Neck.

Gag.

"Did you see proof of this appendage you and your girly pop friends declared a ten?"

She cackles, her chest and shoulders bouncing with humor. "He's such a fun guy."

"He slept over at your apartment! Luc is over here telling me the dude was gay, but the first part of his story had Blake sleeping with Kari." His eyes widen, faux shock. "Did she turn him?"

Jess drops her elbow back and nails her husband in the middle of his stomach. "Blake was gay. Blake also stayed at our apartment every now and then. Ya know," she firms her lips and looks over her shoulder to him, "people can be friends, platonically. Even if one is a guy and the other is a girl."

"I'm calling shenanigans."

"You would." She meets my eyes. "He doesn't think anyone of the opposite sex can be friends without at least testing the tip."

"Not completely true," Kane grumbles. "I'm friends with the Twink."

"Laine?" She rolls her eyes. "She's married. She's a mom. Ang would kill you. And that's even if you survive me. Since I don't accept sleeping with someone's sister."

"Ironic." Midnight black eyes swing across and pin me to my chair. "Considering where we're up to in Lenaghan's story. He bedded Britt."

Jess grits her teeth, her lips thinning and her eyes dancing. "Admittedly, that was a bad move."

"So Kari knew from day one," Kane surmises. "And Britt obviously knew. And neither of them said a word?"

"Nope." I sit back and run my fingers through my hair. "They both kept their word. Britt wasn't saying shit, and she had no clue Kari knew. And she sure as hell had no clue the woman I was pining for was her best friend. So it wasn't weird on Britt's part. And Kari wasn't saying anything, because she hated me, and she didn't want to fracture the relationship she had with her foster sister. She understood Britt had no clue, so it wasn't a crime on Britt's part."

"Just yours," Jess acknowledges. "Kari was mad *only* at you."

"I have no clue what life was like for her for the next few years," I admit. "She didn't come home to hang out. No Christmases. No birthdays. Not even when Mr. and Mrs. Turner set off for their world trip. Nothing." I glance down at the table and spy my empty coffee mug. Yearning for more but not quite ready to get up and make it. "She was gone, and as far as I knew, she was dating Blake. I was locked out, and no one even thought to give me intel, since I couldn't tell them what was going on between us. I especially couldn't tell them *why* she was mad at me."

"But you snuck information from Marcus." Jess wanders to the kitchen counter, holding Billy in one experienced arm and pulling the fridge open with her free hand, while Kane sets the twins on their feet and allows them to explore.

Our home is already kid proofed. Toys abound, and soft edges ensure everyone is safe.

Thanks to Kari.

"You and Marcus were always pretty tight," Jess continues. "Same age. Same grade. Ang and Scotch were in the band as well, but they were close, and you and Marcus were close. It's just the way things were."

"Right," I agree. "So I caught updates from Marc, mostly. That Kari was doing well in school. That she was graduating. That she was preparing for her NCLEX." I look at Kane. "She had to sit those final exams before she could practice and take a placement in the hospital."

"Why didn't she stay in the city and work there? Earlier, I get she wanted to come home and be with everyone else. She wanted to be with you," he clarifies. "But by the end of her degree, she was pissed and wanted nothing to do with you. Whether Ten was gay or straight, she'd clearly created a special relationship with him. So why not stay there and work at whatever hospital he ended up at?"

"She did," Jess answers. "Sort of." Closing the fridge, she turns with a bottle of regular cow's milk and sets it on the counter. Reaching up, she grabs a couple of small, plastic cups, and prepares to pour a little for the girls. "Blake failed his NCLEX the first time they sat it. He's good at his job. And he's a good guy. But I guess things just weren't working in his favor that year because he bombed."

Kane studies his wife expectantly. "Did Kari bomb?"

I snort. "No chance. She graduated top of her class, since *clearly* she had all that rage to fuel her education, and a secret gay best friend to keep her mind off guys. She tests well. But Blake on the other hand—"

"Failed his NCLEX," Jess adds. "Then he re-sat them at the next opportunity a few months later. Bombed those, too."

Kane grits his teeth that way people do when they're thinking *'eek'*.

"Kari wasn't having it," Jess finishes. "So she studied with him for the third attempt. It was one of those *no man left behind* missions. So while Blake was freaking out about his future, Kari was sitting on a nursing degree and able to practice. She refused to bail on the poor guy, so she signed a twelve-month contract with the hospital in the city."

"Which isn't common," I clarify since Kane wouldn't know. "Typically, a nurse just gets his or her job and… that's it. They stay. Or they don't. When they're leaving, they give two weeks notice. Kari, being the clever one she is, was headhunted for a clinic in the city, and in exchange, she got some kind of grant that essentially wiped out her college debt."

"Money," Kane acknowledges, "in exchange for a year of her life."

"Right. And since Blake was spiraling, it worked out anyway. Laine and Britt were in their final year of college too, and Jess was spreading shit out, since she likes to be difficult."

Jess, our lawyer, only grins. "Difficult? Or thorough?"

"Difficult," Kane decides. But he winks when she flattens her lips. "So everyone was still in the city."

"Yep, for that extra year," I clarify. "I learned that through Marcus, too. I learned about Blake's NCLEX failures. And Kari's contract that would keep her away. I learned about the clinic she was helping build. And the relationship I thought she was having with Blake was seemingly flourishing."

"Since she decided to stay back and be with him," Kane sniggers. "Makes sense."

"So by the time the girls graduated and were preparing to come home, I was on the edge of my fucking seat, dying for information on what Kari would be doing. They were giving up their apartment since the others were coming back. The question I was screaming in my mind was, *what about Kari?* Was she moving in with the ten-inch dick, or was she coming back to town and settling in at our hospital, which was the plan all along?"

"And let's not forget your gentle manipulations," Jess giggles. "The, *'Oh gosh, Marc, didn't she promise to come back and work at our hospital?'* and the, *'Oh gee, don't you miss her, Macchio? You should visit the city this weekend and remind her of the job she could have if she came back.'*" Snickering, she fills the plastic cups halfway and offers them as each twin marches through the kitchen. "*Wow, the crime rates sure are getting a little high in the city these days, Marc. How do you feel about that?*"

"I did what I had to do," I grumble. Though my lips curl with smug satisfaction. "You three were coming home, and the options, as far as I saw them, were between forcing her home, even if she didn't like it, or letting her shack up with the dick." I firm my lips and lift a single, challenging brow. "I knew which route I was taking."

"Though god forbid you pick up the phone and just…" Jess rolls her eyes. "Call her."

I shrug and look down at sweet Billy. Her eyes are open, which isn't a super common occurrence for her yet. She's still in the calm new-newborn phase. The one where I'm not sure she's aware she was even born yet. "I was getting desperate. She left as a teenager. She was, at that point, a beautiful, intelligent, and dangerously stubborn mulish woman who needed to be reminded of the promises she made years before. I wanted her back here, and I was willing to annoy Marc to make it happen."

"Pretty sure the courts call that coercion." She brings her free hand up and studies her nails. "Controlling, even."

"I call it a gentle nudge for the greater good." I smile when she drops her hand and looks across. "From where I stood, she'd been in a long-term relationship, and Marc wasn't setting the city on fire. She was grown. She was sexually active—or so I thought—and she had graduated from school."

"Pretty sure we call that open season," Kane sniggers. "She was a giant, red bullseye, and you, Luca, were done being the martyr. Game on."

20

LUC

A LITTLE HOPE

"Luc?" Marc wanders onto the dock down at the hospital one day, deep in the later parts of the summer. September evenings are finally, desperately clawing toward dusk before nine p.m. But even with the hottest part of the season behind us, sweat still dribbles along my spine as I count stock in the back of my bus after pulling a kid out of the lake.

She was seven and had no business swimming on her own.

Luckily, she lived, and if Alex gets his way, he's about to put a scare on her parents they won't ever forget.

"Luc?"

"I'm in the bus." I bring my arm up and swipe at the sweat beading on my brow. It pebbles along my skin, dripping from the tip of my nose when I don't catch it in time. The heat is frying my brain anyway, so I set my clipboard down and swap my pen for a bottle of water as Marc comes to a stop at the back doors and grins uncharacteristically wide.

His giddiness sets me on alert. "What?"

"The girls asked for help."

Maybe the temperature has already boiled my brain because my thoughts swing around, Tweety Bird on a swing, singing a song and not doing much else. "You're happy because the girls need help?"

"They need help moving." His eyes grow impossibly wide. Very non-Marc-like as they dance. "They're coming home! *Kari* is coming home."

"No shit." *Be cool. BE COOL!* "When?"

"This weekend. They asked me to drive the truck over Saturday morning and load their shit up. Ang said he can't help because he's got some big job coming in he has to do. But he offered his car, so you need to drive that over and haul some shit back."

"So you're just planning my weekend, huh?" *Bullllllllshit. I'm coming with bells on.* "What if I'm busy?"

"Cancel." He practically fucking tap dances on the smooth concrete. "Kari said she's finishing up her contract with the clinic and her boss is writing a glowing recommendation for her. The administrators here are already making offers since she's so fuckin' smart."

"Is that, like... a formal recognition?" I tease. *"Fuckin' smart.* Or are you being a weird big brother, gloating about his little pet?"

"I don't give a shit. She's coming home!" If he was a woman, and, or, holding a bouquet of flowers, I get the feeling he'd hug them to his chest and twirl in circles.

There are so few things on this planet that make Marcus Macchio happy.

The first, last, and every one in between, revolves around his baby sister.

"You'll be here too," he sighs. "You're at the hospital damn near twenty-four seven. So I know, as my friend, you'll keep an eye on her. And even though she's getting an apartment in town, I'll have her at my place as much as I can get away with. The twins are officially unofficially moving in, too, which means you'll have a green light to visit as much as you want. So basically—"

"So basically, you're setting up your network of spies." I nod, faux impressed with his deviousness. "You know she'll skin you, right?"

He laughs, completely unphased by a very real threat. "She loves me. Even if I frustrate her sometimes. And the times that she's angry at me, just means when she forgives, she spends even more time with me to make up for what we lost."

"Pretty sure you're still grossly codependent, bruh." I open my bottle of water and tip it back to fill my mouth. I don't mind the extra that dribbles onto my cheeks. I don't care about the droplets on my chin. My skin is sizzling hot, and the water is blissfully cold.

Hell, I get why a curious seven-year-old thought going for a swim today was a good idea.

"What about her boyfriend?" *Be cool. Casual. Non-obsessive.* "You know about them, right?"

He knows. I know he knows. But I want to gauge how he feels about it now that Kari is twenty-four years old and all grown up.

"They've been together a while, huh? Is that, like… weird for you?"

He shrugs. "Guy seems nice. And she hasn't complained about him once since they met."

"So you just… you're cool with her dating?"

He scoffs. "Have I ever had a say in the matter? She's an adult, and she made a point to go away for college to somewhere I wouldn't be able to stand over her shoulder and watch every move she makes. I'd say my opinion is no longer relevant. And even if I tried, she'd tell me to mind my business."

"So you…" Stunned, my stomach whooshes with nerves. Opportunity. Hope. "You're gonna let her date. Whoever. Whenever. And you're not gonna freak?"

"Well… no." He drops his hands into his pockets and smirks. "I'm gonna mind my business on the Blake thing, since the dude is more feminine than any chick I know. He's with her because she's sweet, not because he's attracted to women."

"You…" My heart gives a single, painful knock. "What?"

"He's gay."

"No, he's not!"

Marcus beams, giddy with the knowledge that his baby is coming home. "Yes, Lenaghan. I assure you, he likes dudes. It's not like I've asked Kari, and she hasn't mentioned it. And I don't have any problem with guys liking guys, or girls liking girls. Love is love and all that. But I'd bet my entire house he isn't into women the way we've been led to believe."

"What the fuck?" I set my water down on the ambulance floor, liquid splashing over the lip and onto my hand for a blissful, cooling second. Then I shove up from my makeshift seat and hobble into the mildly fresher air outside the bus. "She's dating a gay guy? Bullshit."

"I mean… has she *actually* said she's dating him? Or have we made assumptions?"

"I…" I don't know! "The girls call him *Ten*."

Marc's cheeks turn a sickly green, but he shakes his head, rejecting the idea. "The girls—as in, *your* sisters—are the biggest troublemakers I've ever met. They'd call him Gandhi if they thought it'd get a reaction out of someone."

"No, she's—"

"Blake is not my sister's boyfriend. Not in an intimate way. I'll eat my hat if I'm proven otherwise."

"Saturday?" My heart thunders in my chest. My pulse, physically notice-able in my wrists and throat. *Could it be?* Is it possible we've assumed shit, the girls have stirred the pot, and Kari is stubborn enough to play along?

Yes.

Is it wishful thinking on my part?

Also yes.

"This Saturday?" I clarify. "Two days from now?"

"Bright and early. I wanna leave here around six, so we can get over there and pack their shit up. It's time to bring my sister home. I'm not wasting a second."

After Marcus walks away, a tune on his breath and a skip in his step, Mitch wanders closer. Like they're playing tag team. Though the latter approaches with a brow raised in curiosity and a long slick of sweat running along his shirt from the boiling heat. "You look like you ingested a couple of funky mushrooms." He stops in front of what I suppose is my vacant stare and waves his hand in my face. "You okay?"

"Kari's coming home." I press a hand to my stomach, nerves battering until I can almost feel the wings of anxiety brushing my palm. "In two days."

"Kari... Macchio? Marc's sister?"

"Yeah." I break my focus on nothing and turn back to the bus to continue working. "Her."

"The one you sent away all those years ago because she was steak. and you were tofu or some shit?"

"I was steak. She needed to experience the buffet."

"And did she?" He follows me to the back of the bus, but though I climb in, he presses his hands on the doorframe and remains outside. "Did she glut herself at the all-you-can-eat buffet?"

"Well... no. I don't think she did. But she saw what was offered." I turn and grin, woozy with happiness as I meet Mitch's stare. "She got to sample the buffet. Met thousands of other dudes in her age bracket. She had the freedom to do what she wanted, go wherever she pleased, and do it with whomever she fancied. And now she's coming home."

He looks at the ceiling and smirks. "So now you can present your steak on her plate and declare *home sweet home?*"

"You're messing with my analogy. But yes. Sort of." I glance at the back wall of the ambulance and get back to counting supplies. "I'm gonna help Marcus pick her and the others up on Saturday. We're gonna bring them home and settle them in at their new apartment. And soon, whenever she starts work, I get to bring Kari to the hospital and be that one person she knows in a big, new, scary place."

"Oh cool!" he drawls. "You get to pretend to be her white knight. That's so noble of you, Lenaghan. I'm thrilled for you now that your morals have slipped. I mean… it doesn't matter that she's still younger than you, or that her brother is still your best friend. So long as *you've* decided to make a move, then I suppose all is well."

"You're thinking like an older brother of a girl you never want to have a dating life." I nibble on my bottom lip and write notes in our files so we can re-stock the bus before our next call out. "Try coming at this from the point of view of your friend. The one who has been in love with a girl ever since he could remember, but he was honorable and refused to accept her offerings because she was too young to make an informed choice, and he didn't want to take advantage of a girl too inexperienced to know better. *Now* she's a full-grown adult, and Marcus himself admits he doesn't get a say in who she dates."

"Cool." He claps the door of the bus and smirks. "Let me know how that discussion goes when you tell him you wanna bang his little sister. In fact," he adds playfully. "Let me know before you tell him, so I can pull up a lawn chair and pop some popcorn."

"You're being dramatic." I pull a drawer open and count the contents inside. "You're making it sound way worse than it is."

"Alright." His soft chuckle echoes throughout the bus and into the free air outside. "If you say so. I'm just happy I get a front-row seat to the drama."

"There's no drama." *Please, for the love of love, let there be no drama.* "It's under control."

"There was definitely drama," Kane snickers, allowing sweet Luna to circle his finger with her fist and twist beneath his hand so she becomes a spinning ballerina. "No way there wasn't drama once she came home. Kari's too stubborn to just fall into your arms and pretend all the shit that came before never happened."

"I'm honestly surprised Kari knew about you and Britt," Jess murmurs.

"She didn't say anything to anyone else. She didn't side-eye Britt once in all the years I lived with them. And Britt didn't know about you and Kari, because if she did, girl code would have had her throwing herself on a sword searching for mercy."

"Which is why Kari never said anything, I suppose. No point punishing Britt for a crime she didn't know she committed."

"Fuckin' martyrs," Kane grumbles. "You make the perfect pair."

"I agree." I reach out for Billy and smile when Jess hands her over. No delay. No disappointment. Family is family, but a man's child is a whole other level no one would dare mess with. "We're perfect together now. Or at least," I look up when Billy stirs in my arms. Already, Jess turns to prepare a bottle. "Kari is perfect for me. She's perfect, full stop. Can't say she got the same kind of luck though, considering she was always carrying us."

"Stop it." Jess drops a lump of powder into the bottle and screws the lid on. "She was happy in her marriage, Luc. Stop acting otherwise."

"She was *tolerant* of her marriage and accepting of my shortcomings because I loved her, and she was loyal."

"Bullshit." She turns from the counter and vigorously shakes the bottle to mix the water and powder. "Stop acting like you made your lives miserable. She adored you, and you adored her."

"We fought nonstop for the last six months! Because she was begging for me to be home and spend time with her."

"And you were picking up extra shifts at work, to help pay the utilities and support the babies that were on their way. This isn't a friggin' fairytale, Luc. The bills have to be paid, no matter how much you wanted to stay home and snuggle up together. The hospital bills were coming, no matter what, considering you had two on the way and insurance only covers so much."

"She asked me to help her build the crib." My words come out harsh, but my hands are gentle as I accept the bottle and bring it to Billy's plump lips. "She asked me to paint the nursery. Instead, it was her taking care of shit while I was nowhere to be found."

"You were at work! Sure, maybe hindsight would have you making different choices. Tragedy will make anyone sit back and obsess over the details, desperately searching for a way to change things. But you weren't screwing off, drinking at the club, and gambling your house away. You were at work, saving every penny so you and Kari could bring the babies home and have one less thing to worry about."

"Fat load of good that did." My jaw aches as I clench it tight. As my eyes sting and my nose burns. "I did the work, saved the money, and look at us." Slowly, I bring my focus up and meet my sister's eyes. "Billy and I are here all alone. While Kari is..." I draw a shuddering breath and shake my head. "I fucked up, Jess. It's okay to admit it."

"You made the best choices you could, using the information you had at the time. No one could have predicted this." She drags out a chair and brings it closer until the wood hits my knee. But then she sits, blind to the way her daughters cling to her every move. Her every word. "You love your wife, Luc. And you love your children. You were handed a shitty set of cards because someone else chose to drive drunk that day. That's not your fault."

"We can deal with that," Kane adds solemnly. "Ya know... when you're ready. I'll ride with you."

I drop my gaze and exhale a long, weakening breath until my chest caves and practically wraps around the baby. "If I knew then what I know now, I would've painted the walls and built the crib."

"And you would still be here." Jess sets her hand on my arm and gently squeezes. "Painting the walls wouldn't have stopped that asshole from getting in his car that day."

"No." I study Billy's long, dark lashes. The curl of her hair, and the smooth sheen of her skin. "But it would have reinforced to Kari that I love and care about her wants."

"She knew," Jess groans. "She knows."

"She shouldn't have lived a single moment where she questioned it. And being six months pregnant, with twins, and tearing up carpet on your own while the husband you begged to be home by a certain time, wasn't, was surely one of those moments."

"You were showing your love in a different way." She reaches up and swipes a hand over her cheek. "She wanted help with a few chores, you wanted to financially support your family. They're both acts of love, Luc. They're just not the same acts."

"Yeah, well..." I roll my bottom lip between my teeth and lock my feelings back up inside my heart. The way I've secured them behind a wall for most of the night. I don't have time for self-loathing right now. I don't even have time for regret. My priorities right this moment are to care for Billy and make sure her needs are met. And when it's time, head back to the hospital to see my wife and son.

"Hindsight," I finally settle on. "Hindsight can be a nasty, nasty bitch who keeps a man awake at night." I look down again and watch as Billy glugs her breakfast, swallowing so her throat visibly bobs. "If I knew then what I know now, I would have done things differently."

21

LUC

DECLARATIONS AND DELULU

I follow Marcus all the way into the city on Saturday morning, driving toward the sun and squinting for every minute of the trip until we move from a single-lane highway onto six lanes of traffic already chugging and thick despite the hour.

Marc's truck is large and old, squeaking every time it hits a stone on the road. While Angelo's Charger is in showroom condition. Her age, not defining her beauty. The roar of the engine, forcing the whole frame into a soothing vibration that settles in my veins and leaves me a little jumpy as we cross the city.

Anyone who wasn't awake before stirs to the rumble of a perfectly kept motor when I pass.

Pulling around one corner, then another as my smile grows a little larger, nerves batter at the back of my stomach as we come within a block of the girls' soon-to-be former apartment.

I wonder what I'll do when I see her for the first time in three years... again.

Will she look different? Will she be different? Will she still hate me? And beneath that hate, will she still love me?

Fuck knows. But a lot can change in a single second. Six years is a lifetime to some.

I follow Marcus all the way to the front of the girls' building, double parking in the space I stopped on my bike three years ago. Curious, I glance

211

across to the Thai restaurant I saw her lined up in front of, huddled with another man and snuggling in like they knew intimacy with one another. Then I think of the cold, miserable ride home, and the liquor I chugged until I felt warm again.

I think of the black spot in my memory, the night I know I did something bad, but the act, mercifully, wiped from my memory banks, either a result of alcohol poisoning, or pure, sheer will.

The second, probably. But I have no room in my consciousness to know what Brittany Turner looks like beneath her clothes. I have no *desire* to remember. And I have no intention to ever repeat the experience.

Once was more than enough.

"Kari Macchio!" Marc climbs out of his truck, banging the roof with the side of his fist and making a racket so unlike any he would usually make. But he's still excited, and so I guess he's living his own Lloyd Dobler moment. "Wake up, kiddo. It's time to come home."

"Jesus christ." I cut the Charger's engine and tug the key from the ignition, pushing the door open, I step onto the street outside and pray no one will scratch up Ang's pride to spite my inconsiderate parking. "The sun has barely come up, stupid. You want the whole neighborhood to strangle you?"

He laughs and slams his door shut. "I figure if we're noisy enough, they might be inclined to come out and help her load up and leave. Remove the troublemakers, so to speak."

"Mmhm." I move around to the front of the car and lean against the hood. A crime, should anyone take a photo and share it with Angelo Alesi. "And if the girls aren't even awake yet?"

"Then they're about to be woken up." He looks up when the girls' street-facing apartment window slides open in a shitty, ill-fitting frame. Then as Laine pokes her head out the window and her eyes zoom straight to me. Maybe it's a familial bond thing, her instinctually knowing where her brother is. Or maybe it's the shiny red hood I rest my ass against. But her eyes stop on mine and her lips flatten into dangerous lines. "Shout like that again, and I'm gonna stab you both." She casts her eyes along the street. "Angelo here too?"

"Nope." Marcus cups his mouth and shouts again, "Kari! Move your ass, little girl. I've waited six years to bring you home."

"Shut up already." Kari stomps through the front door of the building, her body wrapped in itty bitty sleep shorts and an oversized T-shirt that dwarfs her frame and makes her appear a little... short and round. She looks at Marc first, snarling as he drags his focus down. Then she scans across and finds me.

From anger to shock.

Shock to disbelief.

Finally, she transitions from disbelief back to rage and aloofness. How someone can be both pissed and unphased, puzzles me. But when I flash a wide grin, big enough to compete with a clown on coke, her eyes only narrow. "What the hell?"

"We're your ride home, Bear. Get your shit and pick a car." I glance to Marcus and pray he means it when he says he's cool with her dating. It's not like I'm gonna grab a poster and markers and declare our history for the world to know. But I'm also done treating her like she's five years old.

Our cards have been dealt and the game is underway. It's time to play like I mean it.

"Cute shorts." I bring my gaze back and stop on hers. "A little under dressed for moving day, aren't you?"

Her nostrils flare. Her cheeks warm. And then her chest puffs forward. She wants to deck me—in fact, I think she'd *love* nothing more than to grind me into the concrete—but she spins on her heels instead and slams back into the building with a shouted "UGH!"

"She's not great with mornings," Marcus ponders. "I guess. I dunno. She used to be."

"Sometimes people change as they age and mature." I drop Ang's keys into my pocket and push away from the car. "Come on. The sooner we load them up, the sooner we can be on the road. Do you know what day Bear starts at the hospital?"

"Yep!" He's way too fucking happy. It's weird to see Marcus Macchio so... *flamboyant*. "Tuesday in ten days. She's on afternoon shift, two days in a row. Then nights."

"Excellent." I whistle under my breath and grab the door to the building before my friend can. "I'm on afternoons on Tuesdays, too."

"I know." He steps in ahead of me, smiling like he thinks he's funny. "I talked to X, who talked to the scheduling person at the hospital, who spoke with Kari's supervisor. Somehow, I managed to slide her in so her first month of shifts correspond with yours. Familiar faces and all that." He moves onto the stairs and starts up on my right. "If I can't be there with her, then I figure my best friend is the next best thing."

"Mmhm." I'm a dead man. Dead, dead, painful dead. But I'll be long gone and buried before I can take the smile off my face.

"How are you, Bear?" I sidle closer when everyone else is carrying boxes downstairs. It took a shit ton of maneuvering to time myself with Kari, but also with the other four, so my loitering doesn't come across as strange and their brains would be busy with their tasks. There are six of us here today, and I'm having to manage them all just to get a single second alone with the one I want. "You look pretty today."

"I look like a sweaty ape you visit at the zoo." But she peers across the top of her box, hugging it to her chest, and smiles the smile of... well, someone who wants to hurt me. "Isn't your type more along the lines of brunette, pierced, and skateboards?"

Okay. So she's still *pissed* about that. Noted.

"We can talk it out calmly," I offer. "Maturely. We're adults now, and we've had years to process this clusterfuck since everything that happened back in the day. Or we can take potshots at each other until someone's feelings get hurt."

"I choose the second." She bounces to readjust her box and starts toward the door. "I'm coming home to be with my brother and friends. You and I don't need to co-exist, Luca. If you insist that we do, then I insist on cheap shots and general nastiness."

"You want me to be mean because that's the only way you can manage your grudge." I move toward the door too, faster than her, so I block her exit before she can escape. "You're a sweet girl, Bear, and your biggest flaw is your inability to *stay* mad at someone. You're afraid of being my friend because you know you still want me."

"Is that what we're doing?" She looks at the ceiling and laughs. "You sent me away, Luc! You. Sent me. Away. Don't act like I was the one who chose this."

"I sent you away because you were a teenager who needed college life to see something, *anything*, outside those train tracks back home. You needed time to mature. You needed life experience. So that when you came back, you would know what the world had to offer. And only then would I allow you to still choose me."

She scoffs, deep and piggish, and shoves through the door until the corner of her box scrapes my ribs as she passes. "An argument you might have had a right to… *years* ago. But time has gone on, Luc. How on earth do you expect me to still harbor those same feelings all this time later?"

She's so fucking pretty.

So sweaty and dirty from the dust floating around the girls' apartment. Her shorts, though she's changed them, aren't much better than the pair she wore to bed. The only difference now is that they're made of denim and support the globes of her ass in a way the soft cotton never could.

"You're delusional," she adds. "Completely and ridiculously insane."

"I'm a man who knows what he wants." I match her steps, so we descend the stairs shoulder to shoulder. "I knew back then, too. But you were too young, and I wasn't the man who was gonna tie an eighteen-year-old to the feelings she thought she had at the time."

"And yet, you expect me to still have them now that I'm twenty-four." She shakes her head, smiling to herself in the way some folks do when they think their companion is stupid *and* crazy. "I'm not even sure how you connect the dots in your brain to make your delusion work. My feelings back in high school were invalid, but now they're to be honored? I was too young for you back then, but now I'm not?"

"Age doesn't matter so much as maturity and responsibility."

"Cute." She stops at the landing of the third floor and meets my eyes. "I've been more mature than you since I was seven years old."

She spins on her heels, hair flip and all, and continues down. "Let's not pretend you've ever been anything but self-centered, egotistical, and self-serving."

"Uh huh. But even as the less mature one, I was older." I follow her down. She's playing a game of Russian Roulette, walking toward her brother and spouting off at the mouth. Guess that's a game she's willing to play. "The fact that I was older, regardless of maturity, meant it was my responsibility to keep us both safe and emotionally undamaged. I was not going to date an eighteen-year-old, no matter how fucking mature you were. And I wasn't gonna tie you down to a town with nothing in it."

"But you will now? Since, obviously, my college degree somehow fixes everything."

"Now." I grab her arm at the next landing and swing her back until she crashes against the exposed brick wall, her breath coming out on a loud gasp, and her box, the only barrier standing between us. "Now, you're grown. You're fucking beautiful. And you still want me."

She lifts a single, dangerous brow. "Presumptuous of you."

"Is it?" I look down at her body, grinning because her pulse thunders in her throat and her lips firm into thin, unimpressed lines. "If you didn't still want me, you wouldn't carry so much anger. If you had no lingering feelings for what we could be, then you wouldn't want to deck me right now."

"You're reaching," she seethes. "I want to deck a lot of people in life. Doesn't mean I want to date them, too."

"Love and hate are a part of the same spectrum, aren't they?" I lean in closer, folding myself over the box and crushing her against the wall. "You think you hate me, Bear. I'm patient enough to wait you out and see what happens."

"Kari?" Marc's voice floats up the stairs and echoes from wall to wall. God forbid the guy *doesn't* see his sister for more than a minute. "You coming down or what?"

"Think about it." I study her perfect green eyes and the freckles littering her cheeks. "Carry your anger, Bear. But when you wake up in the middle of the night, throbbing and curious, I promise I'll take your calls. I'm not saying you have to choose commitment today and fall into line. But I'm saying we have unfinished business, and I think it's high time we lay it out."

"And Marcus?" Her nostrils flare, drawing my gaze down and my smile up. "My age wasn't always our only red flag. You so easily dismiss your worries about my brother, all because I'm older?"

"I don't dismiss them, but I allocate priority. And right now, they do not trump your needs and wants. And they sure as shit don't trump what I want."

"Kari?"

"I'm coming!" She glances past me and down the stairwell that turns onto the next landing. "I'm coming, Marcus."

"Perhaps." I lean in and press a gentle, barely there kiss to the corner of her lips. "I don't know what the fuck we're gonna do about this, Bear. But I know we're gonna figure it out. I know I'm ready to make up for my mistakes."

"As in, your mistake of sending me away? Or the mistake where you slept with Britt? Oh! Or the seventy-three thousand other mistakes I've heard about, parading through your door every Friday and Saturday night for the last several years?"

"You're exaggerating." But my smile grows larger. "And the fact that you've checked in on my weekend companionship proves you're still interested."

"The fact you had female companionship proves you're an opportunistic pig." She shoves off the wall, using the brick as a launching pad and the box as a shield, jamming the corner into my stomach. "You don't know loyalty or commitment, Luca. You just know you would've gotten in trouble if we went to bed together six years ago. Now you see the green light—no prison time for you—and so you figure you want to add me to the tally marks scratched into your headboard."

"And I figure you know better than that. Which brings me right back around to the fact that your feelings are hurt, so you're gonna swipe at me until your heart feels better."

"And I figure, seeing as how I've been out of town for the last little while, you must've run out of vaginas to stomp through. It's a small town, after all, and you're known to be quite the lady's man. You want to try something you haven't had before, and history has proven you don't like being de-prioritized."

"Blake?" My lips curl into a long grin. "You're talking about him?"

"You mean... *my boyfriend?*" She turns toward the stairs and wanders down. "Who is also moving to town, by the way."

Boyfriend, my ass.

"The second you found out he existed, you ran off and fucked Britt." Mercifully, she lowers her voice and meets my eyes. "History doesn't lie."

"And six years helps us all mature in new, and beautiful, ways."

"Uh huh."

"I'm gonna fix what I broke." I allow her to go. To traverse the stairs without me. Because I'm not sure I can reach the bottom and look into Marc's eyes and not share all that history Kari mentions. "Watch your back, Bear. I'm gonna fix this."

22

LUC

CHALLENGE ACCEPTED

"You're such an ass," Jess sniggers. She plops a fresh coffee on the table by my hand and claps the back of my head. Barely. Gently. But it's a statement, regardless. "You screwed up. She was trying to live her life with her fake boyfriend. And you're aggressively accosting her in the stairwell! What the hell is the matter with you?"

Kane sits forward at the table, fist extended, and a goofy grin on his face. "Aggressively accosting my girl is my favorite thing to do."

"Your girl is my sister. Shut up." I slap his hand away and shake my head. "I don't want to hear about you and her, ever."

"We had no clue any of that was going on." Jess drops onto Kane's lap and wraps her arm around his neck. "No clue! She never even hinted about you and Britt. And she sure as hell didn't mention the stairwell stuff once she got down to the truck."

"She's too private for her own good. She could have taken back her power that day by snitching on me." I pick my coffee up and carefully, so fucking carefully, hover it over Billy's head so I can take a sip. "If she had screamed at the top of her lungs and threw me into the fire, Marcus would have beat my ass that day and tossed my body into the lake."

"But she doesn't like to make a scene," Jess concludes. "Instead of speaking up, she locked everything down and dealt with it in private."

"Which is what I knew she would do." I set my coffee back on the table and grin. "I knew she'd rather deal with this situation in silence, when she could have just blown the lid off and had me whacked in three seconds flat."

"And by *this situation*," Kane sniggers, "you mean you and your dick?"

Jess wrinkles her nose in disgust.

"Me and my heart," I amend. Though we're all aware my dick was totally invested, too. "She said she didn't want anything to do with me. But the fact that she stopped to argue implied she was lying. She could have simply ignored me. That would have hurt so much more than a little verbal sparring."

"So your plan was to annoy the shit out of her." Kane rolls his eyes. But then he looks up and studies Jess with a smile. "No, I see the legitimacy in that plan. It works for me."

"I'm heading to Jonah's store," Kari announces a couple of days after moving back home. She wanders through the little apartment she shares with the girls, ignoring my existence completely, and heads toward the door. It's not even like she can demand I leave. Jess and Laine are allowed to have guests. And until Kari announces to the world *why* she wants me gone, she's stuck.

Make a scene, or tolerate the things that irritate you? Those are her options.

"I'm gonna grab some things for dinner, too." She slips into a pair of sneakers, bending at the doorway in a pair of cutoffs I've come to appreciate this past week. "Any requests?"

"Steak." Britt flops onto the long, secondhand couch we procured from someone's online post, draping her legs in every direction simply to get respite from the summer heat. "I wanna grill outside tonight. No way we're turning the oven on and heating this place up any more than it already is."

"We should go to X's place," Jess announces. "He has air conditioning and an incessant need to spend time with us. It's win-win."

"You guys call him and ask." Kari pushes up straight and slips her phone into her tight back pocket. "I'll get supplies. Someone text me if he asks for anything specific."

"I'll call him," Britt drones. Too hot. Too uncomfortable. But she half-rolls on the couch and snags the device crushed between cushion and chair frame. "He's been texting me non-stop anyway."

"God forbid your big brother miss you, Brat." I grunt and peel my back from the couch cushion. But of course, the fact that I even speak to Britt has Kari's emerald eyes flashing with rage. "I'm heading back to my place. I've got some shit to do before we head to X's."

"You don't have to come." Kari, oh so sweetly, smiles from the front door. "I bet he'd just like to see the girls, since we've been away."

"Yeah, but I miss him." I dig a hand into my pocket and fish out the key for my bike. Dangling the set off my finger, I pass my sisters and drop a kiss on the top of their blonde heads as they go. "I'll head over to X's in a few hours."

"Yep." Laine pores over application forms. She has a teaching degree now, and a plan to get a job. "See ya. Don't melt into the road. It's stifling out there."

"I'm leaving." Kari grabs a wide-brimmed hat from a stack of boxes not yet unpacked or put away, and plops it on her head. "We should also pool our money and consider air conditioning for this place. Otherwise, I'm considering sleeping in the lake."

"We should call someone." Listlessly, Britt sighs. "Like... one of the someones we know. Bet one of them has an air conditioner they'd loan us."

As triple clones, Britt, Jess, and Laine all turn their heads and look at me in expectation.

"I don't have an air conditioner to give you." I lift my hands in surrender and back up. "But I'll ask around and find something. Promise."

"Maybe ask Marc," Jess suggests lazily. "He has that whole barn filled with stuff. Maybe he'll have a spare. And he's obsessed with Kari. He would be devastated to learn she's in any way uncomfortable."

Kari rolls her eyes and heads outside. "Stop using my brother to get what you want. He worked hard for the things he has. He didn't do it to buy us things, too."

"Yes, he did!" Laine calls out. "He did it purely to make us happy. Make the call, Macchio!"

"I'm melting..." Jess runs her hands over her face. "Melting!"

"You're being really fucking dramatic." But my heart just walked out the door, so I spin on my heels and follow. All nonchalant and shit. Kari is fast —she knows I'm on her trail, so somehow, she's already down the steps and across the shitty yard made up of dirt and weeds. She doesn't have a car yet, and though Marc is doing okay for himself, he doesn't have a spare to give her, so she's already on the road, heading toward town using the shoes express.

I'll give her a minute. Enough time to work through her anger and feel a little of the summer breeze on her skin. And in the meantime, I wander down the steps in front of the girls' place and move toward my bike.

I'm still a little lazy on the helmet situation. Since our town is so small, speed limits are insanely monitored, and X is the new chief. So I grab my bike by the handles and drape my leg over the seat. Kicking the stand up and slipping the key into the ignition, I cast a glance along the road to a too-pale Kari wandering into the heat. Her long hair, smooshed under a wide hat. Her Irish skin, reddening under the sun, whereas mine and the twins' tends toward brown after a long summer.

I start the bike, the loud engine roaring into the street so Kari's shoulders come up in defense—*she knows I'm coming. She knows!*—but she doesn't turn. Doesn't dare peek over her shoulder and meet my eyes. Using my feet, I walk the bike across the girls' lawn and onto the road, then I set my boots on the pegs and slowly potter along behind the girl who wants nothing more than to be left the hell alone.

I keep pace with her for a minute or two. Walking my feet along the road more often than not or risk tipping over. Then I creep a little closer. Closer as we leave her street and enter another.

"Leave me alone, Luca."

Grinning, I speed up a little more until I come up on her right, sandwiching her body between my bike and the curb. Then I simply... roll. "I'd rather offer you a ride, Bear." I twist and tap the leather seat behind me. "You asked for this once upon a time. You told me you wanted me to take you for a ride."

"I was eighteen and immature back then." She folds her arms, despite the oppressive heat, and lifts her stubborn chin. "I've changed my mind."

"When does Blake move to town?"

Snarling, she wrinkles her nose and looks across to meet my stare. "On the third day of *Mind Your Business*. Why are you following me?"

"Because I'm in love with you." Fuck it. I waited six years for her. I'm done wasting time. "Because I'd like to spend time with you."

"I heard we're rostered on for the same shifts next week. Surely that's plenty of time spent together."

"Fun coincidence." I cut the engine, so we don't have to speak louder than necessary, but I remain on my bike and continue to roll it. "The fact is, you'll be working the ER floor, and I'll be in the bus. So even if we get to flirt during handover, our time will be limited."

"Such tragic news." She cuts across in front of my bike, so I brake, or risk running her down. Then she crosses the street and forces me to do the same. "I don't want to do this with you, Luc. I don't want the push and pull drama. This isn't my attempt to convince you to chase me. Hell," she glances back and seethes when she finds me on her heels again, my bike positioned so she's sandwiched between it and the curb. "I'm not playing a game. I'm not asking for attention. I just want to be left alone."

"I believe you when you say you're not playing a game." I press my feet to the ground and roll the bike a little faster, then cutting her off and turning my front wheel to trap her, I grab her arm and bring her around until our eyes meet. "I understand that I hurt you, Bear. More than once."

"Too much time has passed." Her eyes glitter and dance, not with glee, but with the kind of heartache that makes my stomach hurt. "We're completely different people now."

"Which makes this better." I tug her closer, her knee hitting my thigh and her breath bathing my lips. "We're different now, Bear. We're older. Wiser. Braver."

"I'm not braver. I used up all my bravery when I was eighteen and begged my brother's best friend to kiss me. Then I scraped a little more together over the next three years and followed you back to town that one Thanksgiving. All I got for my time was the realization that you didn't love me at all."

"Bear, I—"

"A man who loves a woman doesn't sleep with someone else."

"I thought you were dating that other fucker!" I squeeze her arm and feel that mild stab of guilt because I know I hurt her. "I hadn't seen you in three fucking years, Kari! Three. I didn't touch a single woman in all that time. Then I *do* see you, and from where I was sitting, it looked like you were cozied up with that other dude."

"So you slept with my best friend!? Who does that, Luc? Who the hell acts that way and calls it love?"

"It was a mistake." I swap hands, taking hers in my left, and bringing my right up to cup her delicate neck. "It was something that happened after a fuck ton of liquor and a heart filled with pain. It doesn't make it better," I push on when she opens her mouth to speak, "I know it doesn't excuse it. I feel like shit, and there isn't a single second of any day I don't wish I could go back and make different choices. But you *have* to allow us room for the fact you and I were *not* together. We had *not* been in the same fucking room for three years. And I was under the impression you were in a relationship with someone else. You can consider me a bastard, Bear. But you don't get to call me a cheat or a liar."

"You broke my heart." She brings her free hand up, sliding her palm over my arm until goosebumps sprint along my skin and pebble my flesh. "Twice."

"I know."

"You sent me away. And then you went to bed with my sister."

I nod in acknowledgment. "I know."

"There's nothing left for me and you," she whimpers, her voice crackling with pain. "Even if I want there to be. Even if I wish things could be different. Even if," she drags my hand off her neck, bringing it down to rest over her pounding chest. "Even if my heart still beats for yours. There's nothing left. Because there isn't a single moment where I can look into your eyes and not think of you and Britt together." She drops my hands and takes a step back. "It takes everything I have to not let Britt know that I know. By the time I'm done salvaging that relationship, there's nothing left for you."

"Kari—"

"Please don't make things worse. I'm seeing Blake now, and it's taken me *years* to reach a point where I don't feel like I'll fold over and die when I think of you."

"I know you're not actually dating him, Bear. I know it's a front, so you can protect yourself."

"So let me." She moves onto a corner block, to cut around and shave off a minute from her walk. "Let me protect myself. It's the least you could do."

"Hey Kari?" I sit tall on my bike, swallowing as I watch her back and wait for her to decide: stop and turn, or walk away and leave me behind. "Babe? Look at me."

She pauses in the dirt, shaking her head. But she doesn't turn. She doesn't give me that gift.

"Then look at the ground beneath your feet. It's September, so the season is wrong, and the summer is too damn hot. But come back here in May, and you'll be standing in a field of tulips."

Stunned, her head comes up again and around, her glistening green eyes destroying my heart and yet, restoring hope. Slowly. Painfully.

"What?"

"Maybe what we need is more time." I gulp the dust from my mouth, swallowing my spit and lubricating my dry throat. "And tulips."

"What we need is a time machine," she sighs. "We need to go back and choose differently. Because we picked wrong back then. And now we can't fix this."

23

LUC

TOO MUCH DAMAGE

"It hurts!" Jess presses her palm to her chest and swipes beneath her eye with the other hand. "Oh my gosh, Luc! I asked for an air conditioner that day. Not a broken heart."

"Lucky for you," I chuckle, soft and sad and still, so filled with regret all these years later. "You didn't know about all this back then. Your biggest concern at the time was getting a job, getting your degree, and not melting into the carpet."

"It was bad carpet," she snickers. "Pretty sure we all caught fleas from that place."

Surprised, Kane pulls back and re-examines the high maintenance, Louboutin wearing, Lawyer-Barbie he married through fresh eyes. "Fleas, Blondie? Really?"

"You made gross assumptions about me," she giggles. "Horrible, judgy assumptions about my economic stance. And you wouldn't have believed the flea thing even if I told you."

"No shit, Ms. Fancy! You were white girl broke, huh?"

She curls back into his chest and laughs. "Rich with personality."

"And sass," he adds. "Then you went ahead and birthed two more sass-butts who cost me a fortune."

"Can we talk about me and Kari now?" I firm my lips and wait for the pair to focus on me once more. "This is my story, not yours."

"Yours hurts," Jess grumbles. "And it's taking a really long time."

I look straight past her to Kane, eyeing him in that, '*see the shit I have to deal with?*' kind of way. In response, he wraps his arm around her neck and presses his tatted hand over her mouth.

It would be kind of funny, if not for the way she grunts and the lance of *ick* that races through my stomach.

"So Kari was still in love with you?" he prompts. "She basically admitted it. But she was hurt because of what you and Britt did."

"In a nutshell, yeah. That's about everything."

"And setting the obvious aside," he drops his gaze to the sleeping baby in my arms, "since we know you *eventually* end up together, where did you go next? What did you do to convince her to give you guys a go?"

"I annoyed her until she cracked."

"Oh, hey there, Bear." I wander along the rotting dock stretching across the lake, making sure to lift my feet, since dragging them would result with a splinter the size of a tree branch and tetanus threatening the future of my limb... and my life.

I beam when Kari's mind registers my voice. And thrill when she sits up from her lounging posture in an itty bitty orange bikini. Her skin is reddening, and her freckles are on fire. But who am I to preach sun safety when it's a hundred degrees out?

"You could give yourself melanoma, dummy."

Oops. Nope. There it goes.

"You're gonna hate your life when you go home tonight, lobster-red and in pain."

"I've been out here about thirty-three seconds." She flops back again with a huff, dropping to her towel with a grunt and draping her arm over her face to shield it from the sun. With her free hand, she blindly searches, searches, searches until she finds a tube of sun lotion. "And I'm wearing SPF 50. You can leave now."

"I would," I tsk in the side of my mouth, "but it's hot out, and I could really do with a swim. I only have today and tomorrow off work, then I'm on afternoon shift, and after that, nights. Which is never all that much fun. As a result," I chuckle when she lowers her shielding arm and glares at me through the gap, "I really value my downtime. It's a happy coincidence that you're here, too. And in such a..." I purse my lips, "lovely outfit."

"Good to see you value consent and general decency." She drags the end of her towel up and over the top of her head, using the fabric to cover her eyes. "I asked you to leave me alone, and yet, here you are, not only bothering me, but you're commenting on my clothes as though the fabric I wear somehow invites a man into my personal space. I feel as though I was exceptionally prodigious in recent conversations in convincing you that your presence was not desired."

"Cute." I set my hands on my hips and stand over her lithe body, shielding her from the sun. "Did you study the entire thesaurus while you were at school, or do you receive word of the day emails like the rest of us?"

She purses her lips. Pissed, and trying with every scrap of willpower she possesses to *not* cause a scene. She's good at what she does. Gifted and practiced in shutting her mouth and locking shit down. So I toss my towel and keys to the dock, the latter landing with a racket. Then I kick my flip-flops off and drag my shirt up.

Because I guess I'm okay with the world burning if Marcus finds us out here together, hardly dressed.

"I feel like you forget I'm the kid who practically adopted the Turners and had two homes. It's almost as though your *extensive* absence these past few years has meddled with your memories. I assure you, Bear, I'm gonna squat until you pay attention to me. Then I'll eat your bread and chips too. Just show me the kitchen."

"No thanks." She exhales a heady sigh, her chest shrinking and her stomach emptying until the waistband of her bathing suit lifts off her hipbones. But then she inhales again, her chest and belly growing. "Are you seriously insisting on being here, Luc?" She shifts her towel and peeks up at me. "You're refusing to leave?"

"Yep." I lower to the edge of the dock, dangling my feet over the side until my toes touch the water, and setting my hands behind my back so they act as a leaning post. "I'm refusing to leave. This is a public place, I feel like I can't breathe when I can't see you, and you can't control who is here."

"I guess that's where you're wrong." She tosses the fabric off her face, angry as she sits up again, and completely hurdling my middle statement. "Because I can control me. That's actually a lesson you taught me years ago."

"I did?" I tilt my head and watch as she flips to her hands and knees and hurriedly begins packing her things. "Care to elaborate?"

"Sure." She lobs her lotion to the middle of her towel, then her sunglasses and keys. It's like she's preparing to make a knapsack. "You taught me, way back when I was younger and less *worldly*, that no matter how much I wished for something to be true, no matter how much I wished that you would come for me, I can't control you. I can't control anyone except myself." She folds her towel, tucking things in so they remain secure. "You taught me that even if I loved you, and even if you *not* sleeping with my sister was, like, the *bare minimum* thing to do, you were still going to do whatever you were going to do. It was outside of my control. But—" She pushes to her feet, practically downward-dogging the lake and me for a split second before she straightens, "I *can* control how *I* deal with it. The Britt thing, I handled by pretending you no longer existed. This lake thing," she turns and folds her arms, staring down at me like I'm nothing more than a bug on the bottom of her shoe, "I can control by removing myself."

"So you're leaving?" I laze back, moving my hands and taking up entirely too much space. "That's it for us, Bear? You're never going to speak to me again?"

"If I can help it." She nestles her things in her arms and creates a double chin as she glares down at me. "Please move."

"Can't." I lie back, taking up the whole width of the dock so she'll have to step over me if she wants to pass. "I'm feeling a little lazy. And I don't want to move. Fortunately, we've just established you can't control me. So..." I squint my eyes most of the way closed to shield them from the sun, then I listlessly wave a hand toward the water. "Go over me. Or swim around. Control you."

"You're being an asshole." She would stomp her foot, if only her too-mature self would dare allow it. "I don't want to step over you. It's no secret you're a pervert."

"Oh sure," I chuckle. "I'm also the asshole who wouldn't mack on you when you were begging for it. I'm the asshole who had a beautiful woman resting on his chest, pleading for me to put my tongue down her throat. But I'm the pervert."

"Move!"

I open my eyes and cast a glance along the lake's edge. *Is anyone watching her throw a tantrum?* "What would you say if Marcus drove out here right now and saw this little orange bikini show you were putting on?"

"I'd say he has poor taste in friends. Then I'd help him kick you to the curb and find someone better." She spies the other side of the dock, gauging how far she has to step to clear my broad frame. "I'd also tell him not to comment on my clothes. Since he's clearly a more evolved man and knows better than to shame a woman for what she wears."

I snort, and braver than I thought I could be, I wrap my hand around her ankle and stroke her creamy flesh with the pad of my thumb. "I don't recall shaming you." I look up into her terrified eyes and swallow. "I merely commented on it. What I *didn't* say out loud was that you look absolutely fucking delicious in that tiny scrap of nothing."

"Luc—"

"I didn't say the bit about wishing you would forgive me. Or the part where I'm desperate to just be near you. We don't have to be touching. Or dating. Or even best friends. But nearness…" I draw a long breath and hate how her eyes shimmer with unshed tears. "I would die to be near you again, Kari. Breathing the same air."

"Please let me go." Her voice crackles, an ache so deep, it makes my heart tug. "Please let me live my life without worrying about your happiness."

"I worry about yours." Slowly, I push up to sit and drag my hand along her calf, hovering at the back of her knee and gulping because her leg breaks out in goosebumps. "I worry about you every fucking minute I'm awake. And when I sleep—"

"Luc…"

"I dream of you." Carefully, I bring my free hand up and gently tug her things from her tight grasp. Thankfully, the towel doesn't unravel and the phone and keys she hid in the center remain secure. Then I set everything down before I bring my eyes back up. "There wasn't a moment I didn't want you, Kari. There was just right and wrong. I was doing the best I could to get us through a period of our lives where it was simply not okay for us to be together."

"You hurt me. You sent me away. And then you continued to hurt me, even while I was gone."

"You pretended to date a dude twice your size, allowing him to sleep over so much the girls created a nickname based around the size of his cock." I draw my hand along the back of her thigh. But I don't go so far as to cup her ass. I don't violate her completely… until she's ready. "I made bad choices over the years, Bear. I admitted to them. And I *never* hid them from you. But when I tell you it took *everything* I had to not drive over to your place and put a scalpel in Blake's heart—"

"So your self-control is to be celebrated," she drawls. "You didn't kill a man, and so, you're a hero?"

"I didn't take you when you were eighteen, even though I wanted to. That makes me the fuckin' messiah."

"You're a pig."

"And you still want me. You've *always* wanted me, and I've always wanted you. We know how this ends, Bear. So how about you stop fighting it and just sit in my lap?"

I'm such an asshole.

"Marcus would kill you if I told him the things you're saying to me."

"Uh huh." I flash a wide grin and thrill in the way her eyes drop to my lips. "You're not ready to give in to me yet?"

"No! I—"

So I do what any man in my position would do. Noble or not. I grab her hip and shove her to the side, physically yeeting her off the dock until she floats in free air for an impossibly long second. Her wild hair flipping around her head, and her eyes, wide like saucers.

"I love you, Kari. But it's time you cool off."

"You ass—"

She hits the lake with an undignified splash, water sloshing in her wake, lapping onto the rotted dock and wetting my ass until my skin prickles and a laugh crackles along my throat. She stays under for what seems like forever. Her arms and legs spinning out of control. Her orange-covered backside, presented straight up as she fights with her hair and searches for the surface.

I could dive in and save her, I suppose. I could swim around with her. Perhaps even touch her a little. Hold her. But that's not for me. And I suspect if I tried, I'd end up with her knee crushing my nuts.

So instead, I sit back and smirk, waiting for her to find her bearings and locate the surface.

Then I bite my lips shut when she breaks free of the water, her hair draped over her face and covering one eye completely. Her chest and shoulders heave, her arms calmer now as she treads water.

"You're a complete jerk, Luca!"

"You were getting a little heated. And seeing as how you're at the lake, I figured you'd come prepared to swim."

"I hate you."

"No, you don't." I angle forward, dangling perilously close to where my balance could be overthrown and my ass would end up in the water. But I cup Kari's cheek instead, holding her up with my thumb on her chin and my fingers wrapped around the back of her neck. Then I bring her closer,

closer, until her tongue comes out to wet her already wet lip. Her eyes, widening in fear. "You hate vulnerability," I murmur. "And you hate that I hurt you. You hate that I have that power."

"Free me," she grits out. *Her heart?* I wonder. *Or her face?* "You've had me on the hook for too long, Luca. Let me go."

"I can't." I lean in and press my forehead to hers. It's brief. It's way too fucking forward. Too intimate. But it's what I need. And I've spent six years depriving myself of that. "I want to keep you," I whisper. "For the rest of my life."

24

LUC

GUNKLES

"**O**h my god!" Jess melts into Kane's lap. "You guys hid all of this from the rest of us! What the hell, Luc!"

"Well… Kari wasn't wrong about the *dead-Luca-when-Marc-finds-out* thing." I look down at a sweet, sleeping Billy and grin. "So I was in her face. Making a scene and working to force her hand. But I knew I had to be discreet, too. I wasn't ready to spill my shit to Marcus before I even had Kari on side."

"Did she kiss you then and there?" Jess wraps her arm around Kane's neck and smooshes her cheek to his. "Was that where things turned around for you?"

I snort and remember back to that day. The sunburn I went home with. The stomachache I walked around with for days after. And then I remember her hand in my face, her knuckles bruising my skin. "I'm not saying she punched me," I chuckle. "But I am saying she pressed her fist to my cheek and pushed me back."

Kane snorts. "She decked you, bro."

"More like…" I bring my free hand up and touch my cheek, right where she did that one time. "Shoved me. Forcefully. She didn't kiss me. And she sure as shit didn't fall into my arms and declare her love."

"You bombed out," Kane sniggers. "You gotta get slicker than that. Declaring your love was the wrong move. Instead, you trick her into bed. Once they figure *that* out, it's all over."

I look at my sister, cuddled into his chest, and sneer. "Gross."

"Tried and true," he taunts. "Tried. And. True."

"Stop talking now." Jess plants her elbow into his stomach until he lets out a muffled grunt. Then she looks at me expectantly. "She left you at the lake, longing for her to love you back?"

"That was the problem. She *did* love me. And that inability to turn it off is what hurt her."

Jess, Laine, and Britt are at Alex's place tonight. Making a mess. Making noise. They let him cook for them, because they long ago perfected that princess energy, and he's nothing if not a simp for the girls.

He sourced an air conditioner for their apartment about twenty-three seconds after he found out they wanted one. Then he and Oz sweated their way through installing the machine and securing the apartment so the girls would still be safe and the window, lockable.

But while he and the girls are busy watching the *Titanic*—extended edition—and eating enough ice cream to make them all fat, I get myself across town.

Because apparently Kari forfeited dinner in favor of date night with *Blake*.

Because he's in town now, ready to set up his life and hopefully—if he can manage it—work out of the same hospital Kari does.

Too bad for him, he doesn't know X, and X isn't inclined to open doors for some dude whose nickname is *Ten*.

I pull up outside the girls' apartment, the lights inside switched on and the blinds closed. Though the summer is still clinging to our side of the world, which means the sun is still up.

But Kari's apartment is closed up, which means the air conditioner is on and the inside will be blissfully cool.

Fuck knows who the girls think will pay their electricity bill.

But that's a problem for next month.

I kick the stand down on my bike and lean the machine to the side until it's steady, then bringing my leg across the tattered leather seat, I stand tall on the hard packed dirt and turn to study the apartment that smells of flowers already. Perfume. Cookies.

Shacking four girly women up in one building and expecting them not to *girl* all over the place is like filling a room with shit and not expecting it to stink.

It's impossible.

But I can't find a single slice of my soul that minds the perfumes and flowers and the all-encompassing fragrance that hits a man in the face, even all the way back on the street.

I like how it smells.

Dropping my hands into my pockets, and with them, my keys, I lower my head and start toward the concrete stairs at the front. A beat-up Camry sits in the driveway. A car I haven't seen except one other time in my life, parked on the street in front of a packed Thai restaurant.

I didn't know then that Blake owned it. But now, the evidence is clear.

Worse, he's here, and Marc's certainty that he's as straight as a pretzel quivers in the back of my mind. What if Blake is *actually* into women? What if he's *actually* into Kari? And what if, right now, they're up there doing what couples *actually* do when they have time alone after a few days apart?

My palms slick with sweat, and the closer I come to the front door, the harder my heart pounds with hesitation. Could I see her with him again and not lose my mind? Will my memory be branded with a new trauma and my soul, shredded just a little more?

My phone vibrates in my back pocket. A call demanding my attention. A chance, possibly, for me to turn around and walk away before I make things worse. The universe may be offering me this out before I kill a man and destroy the future I want so badly with Kari.

But I ignore the olive branch offered.

I cast aside the mercies the universe might be trying to shove in my way. And instead, I clamp my lips shut and stomp up the front stairs to the door Kari hides behind.

Maybe he's there. And maybe they're fucking around. My heavy foot-steps, at least, will alert them to put some clothes on.

It's the least I can ask for.

"What the—" Kari's voice dances on the gentle breeze. Her question beats out even the drone of the air conditioner that spits boiling air from a motor working triple time to cool an apartment. I don't even have to knock once I arrive at the top of the stairs because my steps are as loud as a fist banging on the door, and because they are, Kari shoves her blinds aside and stares out the window.

She searches for only a second. A single, tiny beat of my heart. Then her eyes lock on to mine and narrow.

"Luca! Go away."

"Let me in, Bear." She's dressed. She's decent. And she's still pissed. *I can work with that.* "I want to come in and hang out."

"You are clearly delusional!" She glances over her shoulder, reacting when a deep male voice questions my presence. Gay, straight or something else, the dude would surely know who the fuck I am. No way he's sleeping over in an apartment with Kari, Britt, and the twins, and they haven't mentioned me. "If you don't leave," she brings her focus back, "I'm gonna call the cops!"

"Do it." I come to a stop by the door and rest on my heels. "X is cooking dinner for the twins right now. Bet he'd love to take your call."

"I'll call the station, stupid! X is not on duty, which means I'll get one of the others. Bet they'd love to arrest you."

"So make the call." I lift my shoulders and shrug, smiling when her eyes narrow to dangerous slits. "Libby's on duty, I think. She and I have always been pals." *Ish.* Mostly, I think, she tolerates me, and when I'm riding my bike across town, she gives my un-helmeted head a beady stare. "Call the cops, Bear. Or open the door and let me in. I wanna talk."

"I'm not letting you in! I have guests right now!"

"Your guest is Blake, and I assure you, he won't mind that I'm here."

"You're incredibly rude!" she snarls. "I get an hour alone. One hour! Before the girls are back and this apartment is overflowing with estrogen again. I have no desire to spend that hour with anyone except my boyfriend."

Alright. Fine. *Now you've done it.*

I bring my hands out of my pockets and jangle the keys connected to a keyring I've had since my first bike. I spy the shiny, newest addition and look past it to Kari. "I can let myself in, Bear. Or you can open the door. Don't make me be that guy." I peek over my shoulder at the street and pray no one overhears this shit. "Don't make me let myself in."

"How the hell did you get keys?" She pushes away from the window, tossing the blinds back in place so they hit the glass with a hollow clatter. Then she stomps her ass across the apartment and yanks the front door open. *Thank the good lord because the air conditioner motor is practically melting the skin from my bones.* Shooting her hand forward, palm side up, she sneers. "Give me every single key you have to my apartment."

"No thanks." But I stalk forward, forcing her to get handsy if she wants to stop me. I slip through the gap between her supple body and the door-frame, then I step into air-conditioned bliss, stopping in the middle of the living room and coming eye to eye with a dude way taller than me.

It's not that I'm small. I stand at a few inches over six feet, and my broad shoulders mean I weigh in at a healthy hundred and ninety ish pounds. But Blake is *large*. The dude is closing in on seven feet, with long, spindly arms and legs. He, too, would weigh in under two hundred pounds. He's just leaner than your average monster.

"Luc Lenaghan." His voice is deep, gritty, almost like he smokes a pack a day and chews glass for dessert. Of all the men, on the entire planet, he's not the type I would expect Kari to aim for when she's dating. But he offers his hand, and for that, I suppose, I can respect him. "Blake."

"You've heard of me." I ignore Kari and step closer until our hands clap together in a slow, firm shake. "She tell you she's gonna marry me someday?"

Kari gasps by the door, slamming it shut in anger. "Luc!"

"She told me you broke her heart." He squeezes me, risking my career and my limb, when he tightens his grip and refuses to let go. "She said you did some pretty gnarly shit, and so, if I happen to be holding a shotgun when I see you…"

"She'd be sad if I died." I pull my hand free of his grip, wiping my palm on the leg of my jeans. Then I grin. Because he's protective of her. Like a brother is of his baby sister. He's not banging her. "I've made it a mission, actually, Blake, to win her back now that she's in town again. It'd be a lie if I said you being here wasn't a wrench in my plans."

"Perhaps that's why I'm here, then." He sets his hands on his hips and studies me. "Maybe she doesn't want to be won back."

"She's still really mad at me." I peek over my shoulder and find a seething Kari, practically billowing steam from her ears. Then I bring my focus back to Blake. "*Really* mad. Because she's a proud woman, and I'm an asshole who messed up. But," I interject when Kari scoffs. It's not a friendly scoff. But rather, one that precedes a steak knife in my back. "I was just a boy back then. Older than her, certainly, but with minimal life experience. I was doing the best I could with the tools I'd been given. I—"

"You sent me away!" Kari sneers. "Cruelly."

"You were a child!" Fuck it. I turn my back on Blake and duke it out with the one who needs to hear it most. "You need to stop with the victim mentality and take a little responsibility for yourself, Bear! Yes, I sent you away. But had I not, then I would have been consenting to a grown ass man dating a girl who was, just a month or two prior, a child."

"I was eighteen!"

"And before that, you were seventeen. And before that, sixteen, fifteen, and stretching all the way back to six. Whine all you want, but the fact that I knew you when you were seven, and kissing you when you were three minutes past eighteen, screams grooming to me."

"Grooming?" Her nose wrinkles with anger. "What the hell is wrong with you?"

"Maybe *I* know the truth. And maybe *you* knew the situation differently. But if you'd stayed and we were together, all anyone in this town would have seen was a grown man and a girl who was once young and vulnerable."

"You're insane!"

"I was being sensible. I was saving you from the choices you were making. I was saving me from having a shotgun shoved up my asshole. And I was saving us both from the teenage bullshit relationships go through." I stalk toward her, staring down into her moist eyes. "I was not gonna spend a year with you, Bear, then have us fizzle out because the spark had worn off and suddenly, you're wondering if maybe you chose wrong."

"You continue to think you get to make the choices for us both!" She presses her palms to my chest and shoves me back. Except, I'm heavier than her, so it's she who moves. "Dammit, Luc! You don't get to plan my life out and expect me to be your little puppet, moving where and when you tell me to move."

"Seems I do. Because you were so fucking focused on the *now* of everything, you never once stopped to think about the *later*."

"There is no later! There's nothing. Because you sent me away and life moved on."

"Kari—"

"This wasn't something that happened last month. Or even last year. It's not like we had a huge fight a week ago, and now you're here in my home, begging for another chance. This is all ancient history!"

My heart splinters in my chest, aching and bleeding.

"It's been six years," she groans. "An entire quarter of my life. I've changed since then."

"Kari—"

"You've changed," she whimpers. "Our lives have changed. It's like you thought everything could be paused and I would go away for a few years. Age up a little. And when I reached a certain number of birthdays that would please you, then you could *un*-pause and we'd continue on. But that's not how life goes. You don't get to mess with people like that."

"Give me a chance! Meet me, now, as an adult. Spend time with me. I dare you to do that and still deny loving me."

"I do love you." Her eyes spill over, fat, heartbreaking tears dribbling onto her cheeks and down to the edge of her jaw. "That's the problem, Luc. But that doesn't mean you get a free pass to break me, time and time again. I already gave you my heart, but you didn't take care of it."

"I was doing the best I could," I groan. "But saving you from yourself, and caring for your heart, were two separate missions. Sometimes, they required opposite actions."

"And now I'm dating someone else." She gestures toward Blake, who just... hovers. Listens. Watches. "Six years, Luc. And he hasn't made me cry once."

Six years, I internally sigh. *And I continue to make her cry.*

"Are you dating him because you love him?"

"Am I..." Her eyes glisten with pain. "What?"

"Are you in love with him? Or is he safe? Is he protective and harmless and kind, and now you're clinging to him the same way you clung to a soft, pink blanket that first day you walked into my life?"

Her jaw quivers. "Stop it."

"Answer my fucking question!" But I step to the left so I can see him, too. "Are you dating Kari because you're a man attracted to women, and you genuinely see a future with her? Or is she a cute little lamb you like to protect? She's so fucking sweet, so friendly and undemanding, considering she's in love with me, anyway, that she becomes the perfect side piece for you to keep around. She's witty and silly, so it's not like it's hard to spend time with her. And she's so beautiful, any man would be thrilled to have her around."

"Luc!"

I stare into Blake's eyes and already know the truth. "If you think I don't already know the answer, then you're kidding yourself." I look back at Kari. "He can be your second best friend for the rest of your life, Bear. Bring him to our home for dinner every single Sunday night. He can be the godfather to our child and the fun uncle. I don't even mind. I'm not in competition with him, and I won't cast him aside because I want to call you mine." I grab her jaw and hold her still when she tries to turn away. "But he will always only ever be your *second* best friend. Because I'm first. I refuse to accept anything less."

"You refuse to listen to me when I tell you I'm not interested."

"Babe…" I stare into her dancing, devastated eyes, and shake my head. "You admit you still love me. That's not *not interested.*"

"It's a trauma bond. It's PTSD. It's not affection."

"Liar." I lean closer, guilt stabbing at my heart when her lungs stumble and her breath comes out on choppy exhales. But I don't kiss her. I don't even rest my forehead on hers like I did last time I saw her. "I'm gonna make it right, Bear. Because you have my heart and I have yours. We're both a little bruised and battered right now. We're both hurting. But I swear, I'll make it right."

"I'd rather you just stopped. Give me mercy and leave me alone."

"I can't." I press my cheek to hers and just… hug. Sort of. I close my eyes and breathe her in. "I can't let you go. So I'm gonna convince you to be brave instead."

"I'm gonna keep arguing with you."

I choke out a small, soft laugh. "I like it when you argue. It's way better than seeing you hurt." Slowly, I pull back. "Will you invite me to stay for dinner? I don't even mind if Blake is our third."

She shakes her head, her cheeks warming and her eyes dancing. "I'm not inviting you to dinner with me and my boyfriend."

"It was worth a shot." Turning, I meet his stare and offer my hand once more. "It was nice to officially meet you, bro. Thanks for being her friend these last few years. I appreciate that she was able to find someone who made her feel safe."

"And you just…" he takes my hand, less *squeezy* this time, "assume we haven't had a wild, heated love affair these last few years?"

"If you had, you'd have picked my ass up and tossed me onto the street ten minutes ago. Additionally, I don't think heterosexual men call it a *heated love affair* unironically." I release his hand and smirk. "You're gonna be a great uncle to my kids someday."

"You just…" He puffs his cheeks wide. "You leapfrog all the way to the finish line, and she's still back near the start, stalled out and hoping for an ambo evac."

"Good thing I know how to get me an ambulance, huh?" I clap his shoulder and turn to a silent, boiling Kari. "He's cool. We can keep him around. I don't mind."

"You're an ass. Dismissive and rude."

"Dismissive? I just invited him to dinner every Sunday for the rest of our lives! Do you want me to name our son after him, too?"

25

LUC
CLEO

"So your plan was to…" Just like Blake did back then, Jess inhales and fills her cheeks, shaking her head in surprised exasperation. "You were just walking in and setting up camp, no matter that no one wanted you there?"

"She wanted me there. She just wouldn't admit it yet because she was in pain and her stubborn streak made it impossible. But I'd known her for more than half my life at that point. I knew who she was beneath the words she spoke."

"Also known as disrespecting a woman's clearly spoken boundaries," Kane chuckles. "Smooth and effective, like a battering ram and ten men breaching a door."

"I'm typically a fierce advocate for boundaries and respect. I was raised with too many women around for me not to be. But Kari was saying no to what I knew would be our entire lives together. And she was saying no because she was scared."

"So you considered it your job to talk her around?" Kane's lips curl a little higher on the left. "Gentle encouragement."

"Battering ram style."

I wait in the hall just outside the emergency department on Kari's first day. Her first shift. The first hour of what she worked so hard to achieve. And with my radio pinned to my shirt, my hands in my pockets, I kick one ankle over the other and grin as doctors and nurses and patients wander by.

Yes, I have a job to do.

Yes, I should be on the bus with Mitch.

No, we don't have any active call-outs right now.

Yes, I have my radio turned up and my ears pricked. If I need to go, I'm only ten seconds away. But until then...

"You're a stage three creep at this point." Mitch comes around the corridor corner and looks me up and down with a smile. He's in a uniform just like mine. Cargo pants with more pockets than we can count, and a navy button-up shirt with a patch on the shoulder, his name sewn above the breast pocket. In the winter, we would have high-vis jackets, and hats that cover our ears. But this summer is still holding on, so even in just shirts, we still sweat. "She's working, Lenaghan. She doesn't need you hovering around and throwing her off her game."

"I haven't let her see me yet." I fold my arms and grin. "I can hear her, though. I know she's doing the job. Janey's giving her the tour."

"They have time." *If you can't beat 'em, join 'em.* Mitch comes to stand on my left, his shoulder almost touching mine and his fresh aftershave hitting my senses. Then he presses his back to the wall and settles in. "Things are pretty chill around town right now. So until we get busy, she won't be busy."

"I like that she gets a minute to breathe. She's worked her ass off for this, so she deserves to be *eased in*, so to speak."

"What about that other guy she's supposedly dating? He here?"

"He doesn't have a job yet." I angle my head forward and glance along the hall when the ED doors swing open. A fleet of doctors finishing their rounds stream out, but Kari doesn't move with them. And she doesn't hover by the door where I can get a glimpse.

Which is both good and bad.

"Kari got her job because she has a history in this town, she graduated at the top of her class, and she aced her NCLEX. Blake is an implant from the city, doesn't have a foster brother as chief of police, and the dude failed his exams... twice."

"Doesn't make him bad at his job," Mitch mediates. "Maybe he just doesn't test well."

"Maybe. But the data is the data, and for right now, he's unemployed. He'll probably land one soon. It's not like folks are flocking to this town and locking themselves down."

"Yay us," he chuckles. "We get the cast offs and flunkies because no one else wants the job."

"Nah." I peer across and grin. "We get Kari, the cream of the crop who could work in any hospital in the country, but she *chooses* to be here with us. Come on." I tap his arm and push away from the wall. "Rounds are complete, which means she's likely to come out that door soon. I don't wanna be here when she does."

"Afraid she'll kick your ass back outside where you belong?"

I scoff. "Afraid I'll pick a fight on her first day and land her with a lecture from Nurse Janey. Kari and I aren't... getting along right now."

He laughs. "Ya think?"

"She and I tend to shout at each other when we're in the same space." Then she cries. And fuck, but I don't want more of her tears on my conscience. "I don't want to get her in trouble."

"Ambulance three," a voice crackles over the radio. "This is dispatch. Motor vehicle accident on Third and Grey."

"Shit." I grab my radio and take off toward the ambulance bays out back. Pressing the button on the side, I respond, "Ambulance three responding. ETA four minutes."

"Ambulance three, acknowledged." Dispatch crackles and calls in trucks. Police. They create their fleet of first responders while Mitch and I scramble onto the dock, and I make a beeline for the back of the bus. Mitch runs for the driver's seat. "Victim is reported as a six-year-old female," dispatch continues as I yank the doors shut. "Hit by a motor vehicle."

"Dammit." I hold the walls of the ambulance when Mitch starts the engine and zips across smooth concrete. "Just a kid!"

"She's alive," he responds. "Alive is good. Alive is wonderful."

"Alive is a temporary fucking existence, especially when you're six years old and have been mown down by a one-and-a-half ton vehicle."

"Two minutes out." Mitch brings us around a tight corner, racing other sirens toward Third. "We're gonna be looking for internal injuries. Lots of little bones, Luca."

"Yep." I don't even have time to sit. I don't bother with my seatbelt, though official protocol says I'm supposed to. I balance in the back, my hands on the ceiling and wall, and the moment we come to a screeching stop, I burst through the doors and unsnap the stretcher to bring it out with me.

Mitch slams his door and bolts toward a woman screaming and covered in blood.

"Shit, shit, shit, shit, shit." I toss a med bag on top of the stretcher, and the straps atop that, so they don't get caught up in the wheels. Then I start toward the sweet baby girl plastered to the road. Her leg bent unnaturally to the left, and her arm folded the opposite way. Gashes on her forehead practically spray blood and make the scene so much more disturbing.

But for me, the absolute worst fucking horror in my eyes, is the torn and bloodied blanket clutched in her hand.

"This one's gonna sting." I set the brakes on the stretcher and snag the med bag, then I kneel by the girl while Mitch deals with the woman. "Hey there, Sweet pea." I release a shaking breath when her lashes flutter and her eyes crack open. She's too calm. Too broken. But she clings to me with glittering, silver eyes. "You're awake. That makes me so happy, baby girl. Can you tell me your name?"

Her eyes swell in an instant, filling with tears as her face screws up. "I want my mommy."

"Oh god." Jess looks at her girls and breathes too heavy. Too wounded. "I know this case. I know what story you're about to tell us."

"It became the talk of the town," I acknowledge with a dip of my chin, holding Billy just that little bit more closely. We have to get up soon. Get dressed. Consume something other than coffee—me, not her—then head over to the hospital. But it's still early, and I'm not quite ready to move yet. "It definitely became the talk of our family, since that was Kari's first day on the job."

"The similarities were too much," Jess murmurs. "It was too close."

"But it was handled." I firm my jaw and refuse to allow anyone else to question that day. Kari already questions too much. "It was handled really fucking well."

Mitch and I burst through the emergency department doors, little Cleo strapped to our stretcher and my heart thundering in my throat. But instantly, like she knew I was coming, and like I knew she'd be the first thing I see, my eyes stop on Kari's as her cheeks turn sheet white.

But we're working now. We have too much responsibility sitting on our shoulders for me to do anything except the job.

"Six-year-old female with a sustained head injury and loss of consciousness for less than one minute, according to witnesses. Alert and oriented now, though she complains of a headache." I release the stretcher as Mitch steers the girl into an emergency bay, then I stop in front of Kari and block her view. For just a second. Just long enough to prepare her. "No nausea or vomiting. Two-inch laceration above her left eyebrow. Suspected fractured left leg. Suspected fractured right arm. Not open."

"Why are you standing in my way?" She doesn't spit her words at me like she so often does lately. She doesn't shoulder barge and try to get past me. She stays with me, studying my eyes. "What's wrong?"

"Home invasion." Mitch steps up and hurries through his report. "Mother was home with her daughter. Father was at work. Perps helped themselves to the family home and attacked the mother." He waves over my shoulder as the next ambulance and set of paramedics roll in. "GSW to the stomach, but that's not your case."

"H-home invasion?" Kari's eyes widen and search mine. "But she was hit by a car, right?"

"She ran out of the house to get help." I step to my left when Kari glances that way. "She's okay. And Mom will be fine, too. But now you gotta do the job."

"I don't…" Instead of moving toward the little girl, she looks at the mother, wailing and filling the ED with her cries of anguish. "Luc, I don't—"

"Bear." I grab her chin—*wildly inappropriate inside this building*—and force her eyes back to mine. "Do the job. The girl is yours. The mother is someone else's. What are your next steps?"

"I want my mom," Cleo sobs. She attempts to move on her stretcher, leaning toward her mother's screams. "I want my mommy!"

"Kari!" I catch her eyes and snarl, "What's the fucking job?"

"Move her." She takes a long, heady breath and releases it with a shudder. Then she nods and turns toward the girl. "Let's transfer her across to our stretcher, then hook her up. I want to hear her heart, then I want all her vitals." She waves to another nurse. "Let's get started." She stalks toward her patient and leans over the little girl, a kind smile on her lips, though her eyes scream a thousand traumas. "Hey there, cutie." She flashes a penlight in the girl's eyes and checks for dilation. "Can you tell me your name?"

"C-Cleo." Cleo's chin and cheeks quiver, smattered in blood and smudged with tears. "I want my mommy."

"I know, honey." Kari had wanted her mommy, too. Way back when she was almost the exact same age and terrified, I bet she'd have done anything to see her mommy one more time. "My name is Kari." She stows her penlight away and goes to work inspecting the deepest gash on the girl's forehead. "And I would be so lucky if you agreed to be my friend. My other friend told me you were six."

"Let's go." Mitch comes up on my left, tapping my arm. "We gotta go, Lenaghan. We've handed her off."

"I want five minutes." I back up to stay out of the way. But I watch with my heart in my throat and pride swelling in my chest. "I just wanna watch."

"She was the same, right?" He keeps his voice low, tilting his head when Kari commands a doctor like she's a fucking drill sergeant and rattles off orders for x-rays. "Home invasion?"

"When she was seven. She wasn't harmed, though. No broken bones." I draw a long breath and reach up to silence my radio as it crackles by my ear. "She had Marcus there to protect her."

"Lucky." Mitch brings a hand up and scratches the stubble on his jaw. "Good thing she had him."

"All a matter of perspective, right? Lucky, she had Marcus. Lucky for Cleo, her mom and dad will live." I firm my lips and fall head over heels, irreversibly fucking stupid when Kari looks across and meets my eyes. She's insane if she thinks I can walk away from us. Delusional if she thinks I'll even consider it. "I met her just a few days after her parents were murdered. And it was just... It was our normal. I didn't even stop to pat her on the head or tell her to be brave the way I want to with Cleo."

"Because you're grown now." He leans back and folds his arms. "Cleo's a little girl you wanna protect. Kari, back then and always, was your equal."

"I probably could have been nicer to her. Even a gentle, 'sorry your parents died' would've been better than she got."

"You were a kid, too. And hindsight is always around to make us feel like a dick. Come on." He claps my chest and drops his hands. "We have to keep moving. Let her do her job. We've gotta do ours."

"But she's so beautiful." I turn and walk, my head swiveling on my neck and following the girl I vow to marry. Obsessed with the woman she grew to become. "She's so powerful."

"Let's get her up for an all over CT!" she commands. "We need a look inside. Right now."

"Dude." Chuckling, I spin and speed my steps to follow Mitch. "She's ordering Dr. Eastgate around on her first fucking day."

"He'll eat her for breakfast unless she cools it."

"Or he'll worship at her feet because she's so fucking incredible." I cast one last glance back before the door closes, grinning when Eastgate nods and does as he's told. "She's queen of the ED, Mitchy. She's gonna be amazing."

26

LUC

ANYONE UP FOR A RIDE... ON A CARGO SHIP HEADED FOR GREECE?

The best part of living and working in a small town is that our first responders don't typically work the same as big city first responders.

Elsewhere, cops and paramedics and nurses are on wildly different shifts. They're not connected, and they're not reliant on one another. But here, most of our team comes in at the same time, and like clockwork, we tend to leave at the same time.

It's nice, really, since that means I get to hang with the same crowd more often than not. Nicer yet, because as the end of my shift approaches and the town surrounding us slumbers, I wait out on the ambulance dock with a can of Pepsi and get a chance to finally breathe. Because with the loss of the sun, comes a little reprieve from the heat.

And with the end of my shift comes the end of *hers*.

I sit on a tiny, raised wall, only two feet high and two layers thick. I'm not even sure of its purpose, except, perhaps, to discourage cars from driving over here.

But it makes for a good seat, and it comes with the perfect view of the back of the ED, where the double doors swing wide and anyone coming off shift wanders out. Usually, I take my time. Head to the locker rooms, have a shower, and chill the fuck out before I go home. But tonight, I didn't even change. I have someone's femoral blood on my pants. And someone else's tears on my shirt. But I also have a little girl inside that building, trauma-tized and broken, but she's alive.

And better yet, for her, her mother is alive, too.

She'll always carry trauma from today. But it won't be quite as heavy as the burden Marcus carries with him. Or as hidden as the load Kari walks around with daily.

"Why are you staring at the doors?"

I startle and twist in my seat, grinning when I find Mitch in fresh jeans and a shirt that is surely lighter than the uniform I wear. He's showered and his short hair has been combed clean; I guess I had time to change after all, though I didn't want to risk it. Shaking my head as my thundering heart slows, I turn back to study the hospital and bring my soda up. "You scared me."

"You're skulking outside a safe place, hiding in the dark with your hand in your pants."

I sip and snicker, flexing my hand as though to prove where it is. "Maybe I *really* like sick people."

"Or maybe you're on a fast track to being slapped with a protection order." He comes around and sits on the wall, too. Dropping his duffel so it lands on the concrete with a thud, "What's your plan if she doesn't want you, Luc?"

Aching, I turn and study the side of his face.

"There has to be a plan that doesn't involve prison and stalking, right?"

I roll the Pepsi between my palms and enjoy the cold metal on my skin. "You think I should move on?"

"I think you should consider the possibility." He reaches up and swipes his hand through his hair. "It's been six years, bro. People change. Wants change. The world changes. She's been gone a long time, and you're counting on the word of an eighteen-year-old to ride in and save the day."

"I'm not counting on her word." I glance back to the ED doors and drag my bottom lip between my teeth. "She didn't promise me anything back then."

"So what are you—"

"I'm counting on her heart. Because it's pure and perfect, even when wrapped in pigheadedness."

"She's dating someone else."

"She's *friends* with someone else." I push to my feet when the doors swing open and three women step out. Two of them are old enough to be my mother. But the one in the middle... her eyes shoot across the wide driveway and stop on mine. "He's actually pretty nice," I finish. "She chose well." I couldn't peel my gaze away from Kari even if I wanted to. I can't look away from the color in her cheeks or the flex of her jaw. But I stay put. I give her that hundred feet and allow her the chance to make a choice. She can turn and go with the older nurses. Or she can cross the concrete and be brave. "You should leave now, Mitch. I'm done talking."

He scoffs. "First of all: that was rude. And second: it might be best I stay. When you end up in handcuffs, the cops are gonna want a witness statement. Considering you'll scream that you're innocent, my respected word will carry weight."

"Respected? Your brother is a firefighter. He's the chief's enemy. What makes you think X wants anything to do with you?"

"You're just being hurtful." Mitch stands in my peripherals, ducking to grab his bag and straightening out on my left. Then he claps my shoulder. "Be safe. Do whatever it is you're gonna do. But I'd really like for you not to get arrested. I've spent years training you to be a reasonably non-annoying partner on the job. If you make me start again with some other asshole, I'm gonna pay a prisoner to shank you in the showers."

"You've put too much thought into this." I hate that Kari only stares. That she freezes in place by the doors, clutching to a backpack and watching me warily.

Like I'm the enemy.

Like I'm dangerous.

"Good luck." Mitch taps my shoulder one last time, then he continues forward, filling in the space that separates me and the pair of green eyes that stare. He approaches her, unafraid, smiling and throwing his bag over his shoulder. "Hey, Kar." Friendly, he wraps her in a one-armed hug. "You rocked today. I saw you bossing Dr. Eastgate around."

"Got a little ahead of myself," she blushes. "But I didn't get written up for it."

"It was a damn good shift." He steps back and follows her gaze when she looks across to me. Then he shakes his head, chuckling. "You're as bad as each other. Take it easy on him, okay? Whatever choice you make about this, be gentle. His intentions were always to do the right thing by you."

"Don't be that guy." She peels her eyes from mine and meets his stare. "Don't become the messenger and make me hurt you."

He lifts his hands in faux-surrender and backs away, amused. It's easy for him, considering his whole world isn't on fire. "I'll catch you tomorrow for your second shift. Maybe I'll see what kind of roadkill I can scrape off the pavement. Make you fix a raccoon or something."

"Raccoons?" Sly, she looks him up and down. "Isn't that your brother's job?"

He snorts and turns on his heels. Lifting a single hand in the air to say goodbye, he wanders to the other nurses. The older ones. And hustles them away. Since I suppose they've taken it upon themselves to protect Kari from the big, bad jerk who breaks hearts.

Taking a fortifying breath, I set my Pepsi can on the small brick wall and turn back to meet Kari's terrified eyes. It's midnight. The cicadas scream, while the rest of town slumbers. We're outside the emergency room of a hospital, but all is silent around us except for the sound of my heart thundering in my ears.

"You need to stop staring at me." Kari swallows the nerves in her throat and plays with her fingers. Fussing. Nervous. But she doesn't run away. So I take that as a decent sign, at least. Promising.

I start forward, empty-handed, since my bag and clothes are still inside the hospital, still in my locker. "You're asking me to do the impossible."

"You need to move on," she rasps. "Find someone else to harass."

I cross the distance that separates us. My boots gliding on smooth concrete, and my pulse sprinting in my throat. Who needs Mitch to act as witness to my stalking when we have the hospital's entire security system zooming in on the side of my face?

"Luc," she tries again, dropping her hands and lifting her gaze. "You need to find—"

"There is no one else." I stop just a single foot from where she stands, her perfume slamming into the base of my lungs and her long, brown curls whipping forward to tickle my arm when the breeze kicks up. "There is no one, Bear. There's just you and me. And there's nothing else I want outside of us."

"Luc, I don't—"

"Marcus asked me to drive you home." I lean closer and inhale her exhaled breath. Because I want it. And I knew she'd release it when I told her I'm her ride for the night. "I know he said he'd pick you up. But I was here anyway, and he has to work in the morning. So I told him I'd get you home."

She brings her thumbnail up and nervously nibbles as she looks around. "Marcus isn't coming to get me?"

"No. Because I'm here." I take that last step forward and stop only when the toes of my boots touch hers. Fuck knows what stains my shoes, and a little girl's blood marks my pants. It's why we wear dark clothes on the job. "He trusts me to get you home, Bear." I duck my head just a little lower. "He's trusting me to get you there safely."

"In his truck?" Her eyes wheel around, searching for it. Desperation radiating from her pores. "Did you bring the tr—"

I tug a set of keys from my pocket and let them dangle from my finger. And when her eyes swing back and her brain registers her new reality, her cheeks pale while my lips come up.

"No."

"We're going on the bike, Bear. Which, I recall, was something you always wanted to do."

"When I was eighteen years old! I've grown up since then, Luc. I've matured."

"Cute." I grab her hand and turn before she can run. "I haven't."

"Luc!" Her sneakers slide against the concrete. Her nails, digging into my wrist as she works to peel my fingers away. "Luc! You can't just force me onto a machine without my permission! I could fall off. Maybe I'll let go, just to teach you a lesson."

"Great lesson." I spy my battered bike, parked between a couple of cars, and steer us that way. "You're the one who'll have road rash on your ass. If you get hurt, I'm a paramedic, though. Can't say I won't jump straight to CPR."

"You're a child!" She fights my hand and, if the cops just so happened to drive by right now, her flailing would be hella incriminating. "Stop!"

"Stop making a scene." I lower my voice, but my lips split wide into a grin. Taunting her is way more fun than watching her cry. "You're gonna get me arrested if you don't stop screeching like that."

"I want you to get arrested!" She balls her fist and slams it against my shoulder, her backpack sliding along her arm because of the momentum of her swing. "Go to prison, Luc! Maybe then I'll get through a single friggin' day without seeing you."

"I'd miss you, though." I stop by my bike and release her hand. An action, I'm sure, she didn't expect. Because she stumbles back, almost dropping to her ass if not for the car to her left. "Get on the bike, Bear. Your world won't end if you give me this."

"But I think it might," she whimpers, heaving for breath and searching for someone to save her. Her cheeks are too pale. Her eyes, terrified. "Luc, if I get on that bike with you—"

"You're at risk of admitting you still love me?" I grab the helmet I made damn sure to bring today and turn to face her. "God forbid you give in to what your heart wants."

"My heart is wrong! And why the hell do you have a helmet? You never wear a helmet."

"Because *you* need a helmet." I snatch her bag and set it on the bike, then I bring the helmet up and smile when her eyes desperately swing to mine. "It's the middle of the night, Bear." I set my finger beneath her chin and tilt her head back until her gaze moves to the sky. "The stars are out."

Her throat quivers. "Luc…"

"Anything that happens in the dark, stays in the dark. We're in those magical hours before the rest of the world exists." I release her chin, but I cup the helmet between my palms and bring it up until it hovers over her head. "Give us this night. Get on my bike and stop worrying about all the bad shit that could happen. Think, instead, about all the good that could come of this."

"What good?" she trembles. "What good could possibly happen? I fall in love with you… *again*? I forgive you? I become hopelessly dependent on you, just like I used to be? What, Luc?" Her eyes dance with unshed tears. "I have nothing left to give you."

"Give me this." I lick my dry lips and swallow when her gaze drops to the movement. "Give me this ride, and I promise to make sure you get home none the worse for wear."

"Physically," she groans. "I'll be safe, physically. But what about my heart?"

"I want to heal that, too. I want to make everything better, Bear. Not worse." I examine her beautiful eyes and prepare to get on my fucking knees and beg if that's what it takes. "I'm not here to hurt you any more. I want to fix what I broke. Let me put your helmet on and take you for a ride."

She's petrified. Shaking. Her mind sprints a million miles a second, so plainly obvious in the way her eyes flicker. Her lips tremor, and her hands fuss.

But she draws a deep, shuddering breath, and nods. "Okay."

"Okay?"

"Fine." She brings her hands up and claps them over mine, yanking the helmet down and taking back her control. Her hair sits in her eyes, long brown locks puffing in every direction and annoying her as she huffs and digs her fingers into the helmet to fix the mess. But she makes quick work of it, fastening the strap beneath her chin and flipping the visor upward to meet my eyes. "If we crash, you'll probably die, you know that, right? Helmets are important when riding a bike."

"Careful, Bear." I turn to the bike and grab her bag, then handing it back, I slip my leg over the seat and wait for her to get herself organized. "If you keep that up, you might be accused of giving a shit about me."

"I'm more concerned with the walk home if we crash and you perish." She sneers, visible even with the helmet between us, then she steps back and examines what comes next.

Wrapping her legs around my bike and snuggling in tight is next. Sucker.

"If we crash and your brain is smeared on the road, don't expect me to find a bucket so you're buried with all your parts."

"Your concern is endearing." I twist and pat the seat. "Now get the fuck on my bike. You're wasting time."

"And you're an asshole," she growls. "Still. Perhaps, unbelievably, worse. Which is quite the accomplishment, really."

"Uh huh." I grab her hand and yank her in, feeling only mildly guilty when her chest clashes with my shoulder and her breath races out to bathe my chin. "This is the longest non-conversation I've ever had in my life. I'd like to get *away* from work before my next shift starts, if that's cool with you."

Snarling, she jerks her hand from mine and tightens the straps on her bag as though terrified it'll fly off during our trip. Then she approaches her section of the bike, unsure where the hell she should put her hands and still maintain her air of rage.

"On my shoulders, beautiful." I tap my shoulder and glance back to meet her fiery eyes. "You gotta touch me to make this work."

"I could touch a shovel and dig your grave. That sounds more fun."

"Your threats are oddly specific and slightly awkward." I practically fucking tremble when she throws her leg over the bike and settles in behind me. Though I'll be dead and buried before I show it.

Just as dead as I'd obviously be if I ever accepted the six inches she places between us.

She thinks she's so fucking clever, sitting so far back and holding me with the tips of her fingers. But I hook my arm around instead, cupping the small of her back before she can stop me. Then I yank her closer, swallowing down my groan when her chest crashes against my back and her legs hug my thighs. Her core is like lava and her breath is sweet on the back of my neck. "That's better." I look over my shoulder and smirk. "Now wrap your arms around my body. Kinda how you would if we were fucking."

"I think this might be my stop." Jess pushes off Kane's lap and shakes her head, circling away from the table and snickering. "You're about to tell *those* stories. And I'm not sure I need to hear them."

"I wanna hear them." Kane lounges back, opening his legs wide and grinning. "I know there are years of built-up frustration here, Lenaghan. And it's all about to blow. Bet you a million dollars shit gets violent fast."

Jess mock gags, heading toward the living room to where the twins play and giggle. "La-la-la-la-la-la-la." She plugs her ears. "I don't need to hear this stuff."

I meet Kane's eyes and chuckle. "Kari and I didn't hook up that night."

His lips flatten, disappointment like sparks in a bonfire. "Lame."

"But I got her on my bike. And I sure as shit didn't take her straight home."

At that, his eyes lighten and his lips curl once more. "Attaboy. Kidnapping them is my favorite thing to do. That line between consent and non-consent..."

"Kane!" Jess barrels back into the kitchen. "He is my brother! Can you not?"

Kane only snickers, his chest and shoulders bouncing. "I *love* that gray area between yes and no. It's a fucking thrill."

My stomach jumps with disgust. My nose, wrinkling with horror. "I don't need to know that." Then I look at Jess and point. "You're lucky you're already married and mostly happy. Because if I knew this shit years ago, I'd have put you on a cargo ship headed for Greece."

"Yeah," she rolls her eyes. "Lucky me."

27

LUC

IS IT ST PATRICK'S DAY?

I slow the bike at a truck stop, twenty or so minutes outside the little town we call home. Paddy's, which is where truckers come to rest in between Point A and Point B, to fuel up and get a meal. They come in to have somewhere quiet to stow their trucks and catch a little sleep. And when they're feeling brave, they head inside and spar with the buxom Dolly —Paddy's loud and large waitress.

Mitch and I come out here sometimes when we have time and a hunger for fried bacon.

Often, we're called out here on a job because folks cause trouble and need a band-aid or two, and they don't want to go into town for that.

"I didn't agree to this." Kari peels her chest off my back and unravels her arms from my stomach. She tried the frigid, *barely-gonna-touch-you* thing only until we hit the train tracks leaving town. After that, I figure she decided *fuck it*, when in Rome and all that, resting her helmeted cheek against my back and linking her hands in my lap. She melted into my body as though we've done this a million times before, and even as I left the town limits behind, she didn't tense up.

She doesn't mind we've gone for a detour. She minds that I parked and now she has to actually acknowledge my existence once more.

If I was smart, I'd have kept going into the next state, then to the next five after that.

It's damn near silent out here now, the roads all but empty and the

263

trucks that are out here, parked and dark. Paddy's is lit up like a Christmas tree in December, creating an air of busy-ness that doesn't quite pan out, because only a stingy few people sit inside, their heads bowed over a plate and their elbows perched on the laminate booth tables.

This is where I wanted to come, where no one knew us, and we know no one else. Where pretenses don't matter, and hopefully, Kari won't feel the sting of what I've done to her over the years quite so severely.

Slowly, she unsnaps the strap of her helmet and pushes it up to reveal bright eyes. Too wide, too awake considering the hour.

Too fucking beautiful.

"I didn't agree to come all the way out here."

Liar, liar.

"I know." I take her hand in mine, gripping when she'd rather pull away. Then I help her off the bike and onto her own two feet before I release her fingers and trade them for the helmet she places down. "Tonight was huge for you, Bear. First day on the job, and you fucking rocked it." I carefully hang the helmet off my handlebars and snag the keys from the ignition. "I'm still ramped up from my shift, so I wasn't ready to go home yet."

"I was ready." She's such a fucking liar, folding her arms and lifting her chin. "You didn't ask my permission to bring me an hour out of my way."

"And you didn't say shit when I turned right instead of left." I pocket my keys and push off the bike. My thighs are a little like jelly. My knees, embarrassingly weak. But I turn from the bike and look down into perfect green eyes. "You have a voice, Bear." I bring my hand up, steeling the tremor in my fingers, and gently run my knuckles across her jaw. "We both know you know how to use it. You've managed to make your wishes clear since your return to town. So if you had a problem with me hitting the freeway, then you could have said something."

"I—"

"You wanted this." I stroke her cheek with the pad of my thumb and thrill in the way she shudders. "You like how it feels when you're flying through the air at seventy miles an hour, your body wrapped around mine and your heart pounding against my back."

"Luc—"

"You're just really scared to admit it. You're so fucking terrified, Bear. Because I screwed us over already. I know." I slide my fingers beneath her chin and draw her up until she extends onto her toes. "I know what I did, Kari. And I'm so fucking sorry for it."

"Sorry doesn't make it go away," she whispers. "It doesn't fix it. Sorry is what people say when they don't want to feel the consequences of their actions anymore. So they say it, and the person hearing it is expected to move on. It's manipulation and guilt."

"Not from me." I slide my thumb over the bump of her chin and study the way her lips drop into a seductive pout. How they tremble and tempt. But how they're not mine. Not now, and maybe not ever. "I accept the consequences of my actions. I've been living with them for six fucking years, and ninety-nine percent of the time, I've left you alone. I'm not here to manipulate you. But maybe—"

Her eyes glisten, and yet, narrow. "But maybe, what?"

"Maybe I can help fix what I broke. I can rebuild trust. And after that, maybe you can have faith that I'm a better man. Come on." I take her hand and turn toward the front doors. "This place is open twenty-four hours. It's quiet. They make amazing scrambled eggs, and mostly criminals hang out here."

"Wait." She skids to a stop. "Why are criminals being here a good thing?"

"It's kind of like a tomcat and mouse situation. The mice are pests, and the cats keep them away. In our case, crowds are pests, and criminals keep them scarce." Chuckling, I bring her through the heavy glass door and into the diner that hasn't been updated since some point a few decades before I was born. Then I smile at the voluptuous Dolly whose boobs are always a few steps ahead of her. "We'll take a booth."

"Go for it, Handsome." She wipes the counter with long sweeps of her arm, winking when she casts a quick, discreet glance toward Kari. Then she asks, "Coffee? Or cocoa?"

I look at Kari for a beat, her head bowed low and her bravery all but gone now that other people are around us. Then I glance at the clock on the wall and note the time. It's all fun and games to be awake in the middle of the night. But soon, we have to sleep. And chugging caffeine probably isn't the choice mature, responsible, first responders would make. "Cocoa," I decide. "We'll only be here an hour, then it's time for bed."

"On it." Dolly winks and turns to get started, so I tug Kari a little closer and give a wide berth to the booth occupied by three guys. Two on one side, and the third opposite them. The two are almost a matching pair. Not identical, but the genes run strong enough to promise a brotherhood. A direct biological link. Whereas the third doesn't appear to be related at all.

"We don't look at them," I mock whisper, drawing a furious blush to Kari's cheeks. "And they won't look at us. They don't want to be noticed. And honestly, we want to be left alone."

"Are they..." She swallows and side-eyes the trio. "Are they cops? I see a gun."

"We don't see a gun," I snicker. "Trust me, we see *nothing*." I bring her to the booth furthest from anyone else, perched in a dark corner where the light reaches but the shadows are most prominent. Only half of the booth gets a window view, whereas all the others get to look out to the gas pumps no one is using right now. "We'll sit here." I keep hold of her hand. I know she wants to wrench it free. I know she wants to force me away and take back her personal space. But I'm stronger than she is, and I have a plan to just... *exist* in her space until it becomes her new normal.

"I can sit without your help." She's as predictable to me as the sun rising in the east, attempting to squeeze her hand free. "Let me go."

"I'm being a gentleman." I help her slide in and chuckle when she snarls. But then I release her since I'm not actually trying to upset her. It's a delicate balance to walk.

Normalize my presence. Beg for forgiveness and prove I'm a better person.

"How do you think your first shift went?" I slide in after her. Fuck sitting on the other side; to do so would, *one*, mean I don't get to be near her, but, *two*, it would also mean sitting with my back to the criminals we're *not* paying attention to. No thanks. "From where I was standing, all I saw was badassness."

"Badassness is not a word." She lifts her chin and looks out our partially obstructed window. "And I froze up when the girl came in. Hardly the bedrock of badassery."

"Is *badassery* a real word?" I turn in my seat, just a little, and rest my elbow on the back. "You didn't freeze. You took a second to process."

"I'm an RN who chose the emergency room. Taking a second to process could kill someone."

"She was six years old, had a busted face, two broken limbs, and was begging for her mom." I reach across and grab her jaw, dragging her around until her eyes meet mine. "She had just fled a home invasion. You didn't fuck up, Bear. You were being tested by a really cruel universe."

"A test I failed."

"Bullshit!" I make her jump with my bitten-out word and attract curious glances from the three huddled together a handful of booths away. Then I rein in my temper and repeat, "Bullshit. You took care of that girl the way she deserved. You were a guardian angel sent to her when she needed one most. Just like Mr. Turner was sent to you and Marcus. Stop downplaying something truly amazing."

"I barked orders at a doctor." Her cheeks flame bright red. "That was *so* bad!"

"That was entertaining as hell," I laugh. "Eastgate is decent enough. He can move a little slow, considering his line of work, and you knew what needed to be done. Perhaps if Cleo had landed a different nurse, she'd have been ten minutes slower. Twenty. Waiting for a doctor to order tests and a scan." I drag my bottom lip between my teeth and grin. "Your one second delay wasn't a bad thing, Bear. It was you *loading* badassery."

"You'll say anything to make me feel better." She glances across as Dolly steams milk, the hiss playing out through the tiled room and the large woman's bodacious backside bouncing as she dances to a song only she can hear. "I could have amputated her leg, and you'd say it's cool, since clearly prosthetics can be customized to pink these days."

"I mean... Yeah. Maybe. But she could totally get Barbie or My Little Pony branding on the side. A six-year-old would heal fast and learn to walk on their prosthetic within weeks. It's totally fine."

She rolls her eyes, finally playful, which is a hell of a lot better than hateful. "Your assessment of my abilities is not unbiased or trustworthy."

"So ask someone else to assess you. You could blow shaving cream up a patient's ass, and I'd still think you're the best." I lean in a little closer. Too close for strangers, and yet, not nearly close enough to assuage the want in the pit of my stomach. "What do *you* think of your first day on the job?" I grab a long lock of curly brown hair and bring it up to study the ends. "What's your self-assessment? And don't tell me you screwed up with the girl."

"I think..." She snatches her hair back and draws a deep breath. "I think I'm glad I spent my entire college career huddled up in my room, reading textbooks instead of partying like everyone else. I was able to draw on what I'd learned tonight, and I was able to do it reasonably quickly. That made me confident, when, in other emergency situations, I might've panicked."

"You're our newest nurse in town, huh?" Dolly plops two steaming mugs on the table and pushes one across to sit in front of Kari. "Luca's been talking about you for years. How you're top of your class and gonna shake things up once you got back from college."

Stunned, Kari looks at me. Her eyes wide and her lips dangerously thin.

Then of course, I look at Dolly and firm *my* lips. "A little discretion, please. What is said between the hours of midnight and one should remain confidential, no?"

"Of course." She winks and wrinkles her nose and brings her focus back to Kari. "Forget I said anything. Your man has definitely not been out here in the middle of the night before, waxing poetic about your pretty face and brilliant brain."

"He's not my man," she breathes, pale and flustered. "He's just... he's a family friend."

"Yeah, kinda like how I wanna be a *family friend* to that delicious specimen over there." She hooks a thumb toward the criminal trio, smirking when one of them glances up. Black eyes. Tattoos covering every inch of exposed skin except for the bits on his face. Then she focuses back on us and raises her hands to create finger quotes. "'*Family friends*'. The kind that share a bed." She drops her hands. "I'd like to point out that your family friend is completely and ridiculously besotted with you, Miss Cutie Face. I ain't never had a man look at me the way yours looks at you."

"I'd like to drink my cocoa in the quiet." Kari's humiliated. *Humiliated!* Because Dolly doesn't mind a scene at all. And the other guests inside this diner hang on every word the woman speaks. "Please," she pleads.

"Oh sure." Dolly huffs and does that thing women do, bouncing her head. "No one ever wants to talk to Dolly, except when they're lonely. And even then, they only wanna talk about the woman they're in love with. I never get to be the talked *about*. Just the talked *to*." She presses a hand to her chest. "Why is life so cruel?"

"I can't..." Kari drops her face into her hands and shakes. "I can't handle this."

I laugh in the back of my throat, bouncing until the movement vibrates against our chair. But I look at Dolly and find a little mercy for Kari before she combusts. "Can we get a stack of pancakes please? Just one really big stack, and two sets of silverware."

"Family friends." She blows out a *harrumph* of displeasure and spins on her heels. "My ass."

"You brought me here to torment me." Kari peeks out from behind her hands, her cheeks blazing a bright red. *"Here, Bear. I'm soooooo sorry about upsetting you all these years. Let me take you somewhere you'll hate."*

"In my defense," I grab her wrists and carefully drag her hands from her face. "Dolly has always been nice to me. And I think she's showing off for those other guys. Guess she's got a thing for dangerous red flags."

"Those were *my* red flags!" Kane preens at my kitchen table, beaming because he was seen. In my memories, in a whole other lifetime, there he was. "By the time I snagged Jessie, I was so sure you'd forgotten you ever saw me."

I shrug and look down at a sleeping Billy. "My entire life has been spent in my memories. While Kari was away at college, I was with her in my mind. And now that she's..." I swallow when a heavy ball of grief lodges in my throat and cuts off my air. But I cough the intrusion away and bring my gaze up. "My memories are a good place to be when the rest of the world sucks. So I guess it makes sense to me that I'm pretty good at recalling them."

"And your memories of that night have nothing to do with Kari finally getting on your bike," he counters with a smug grin. "You saw me there. *The criminal trio*," he chuckles. "Cap would take offence to that label."

"Cap and I are okay. And you'll handle your brother." I bring my hand up and stroke the bridge of Billy's nose. "Getting Kari on my bike was a fucking miracle. But having her back in town *and* talking to me were miracles, too. Seems I was on a roll."

"She was spitting venom," Kane snickers. "I'd hardly call those love sonnets."

"Arguing with her was better than not speaking to her for three years at a time. And I'd done that twice already. I wasn't risking a third."

"So you got her on your bike. Shared pancakes, and... what?"

"And then Brittany threw the hammer down at family dinner a little while later. Destroying what little progress I'd made and landing me in a whole lot of shit."

"Oh!" Jess' feet thunder across the living room. "Oh! Oh! I know this story. I was there for it!"

"Britt?" Kane's eyes widen. "She told Kari what you guys did?"

"She told the whole fucking family." I think back to that night, smiling now that years separate it and us. But Jesus, at the time... it was rough. "She... well... all the girls, really, were deep in their *sneaking around with guys* phase."

"We called those our hoe days." Giggling, Jess plops down onto Kane's knee and faces me. Luckily for her since murderous black eyes shoot up to the side of her face. "Laine was sneaking around with Graham."

"That fucking asshole," I snarl.

"I was sneaking around—"

"With who?" Kane squeezes and pins her to his knee. Which could seem abusive, I suppose, in most other relationships. But not for Jess. She holds no fear as far as her thug goes. "Who were you sneaking around with, Jessica Ann?"

"Not you," she sniggers. "Had I known you were already hanging around town, I might've come looking sooner. But since I didn't..."

"Britt had started dating Jack," I push on. "The fighter who would eventually become her husband. But back then, he was just a one-night stand. One she revisited a few times."

"He was big and strong and sexy," Jess adds. "And since his family owned the club we always danced at, he had keys to the office for a little one-on-one fun with Britt."

"Which was all good and fine," I sigh. "But Alex was always gonna be Alex. So by the time Britt brought Jack home to meet the family, X was losing his mind."

"Because he was a fighter that she was having casual sex with?"

"Because Jack's girlfriend before Britt, Steph," I clarify, "had died in a car accident the year before. Jack was driving."

"But it wasn't his fault," Jess interjects. Her eyes dance, from humor to hurt in a single second. "Like with you," she sighs, studying me, "drunk drivers get behind the wheel sometimes. It's what they do. And unfortunately for Jack and Steph, she didn't survive it."

"So X was losing his mind because his baby sister was dating a fighter," I fill in for Kane, "but that fighter was also the dude whose girlfriend died."

"And X just so happened to catch Britt and Jack banging in public that one time." Jess giggles again, her chest and shoulders bouncing with it. "So he was *pissed*. She brought Jack to dinner to meet the whole family, and X did what X does. He was throwing a tantrum and tossing insults at Jack. And Britt did what Britt does—"

"Tossing them straight back," I finish. "Alex was being an asshole, and Britt wasn't tolerating it. Alex mentioned something about how Britt was a good girl, and good girls don't have casual sex."

Joining the dots, Kane grits his teeth. "Oh shit."

"Yeah," I scoff. "Oh shit. In all her maturity and wisdom, Britt pointed straight at me, at the fucking dinner table, and said yes, girls like her *do* have casual sex. Because she had, in fact, fucked me."

Kane lets out a piggish snort that almost makes me smile. "Damn, Britt."

"Alex carries a gun," I snicker. "And an extremely short temper. So I hauled ass out of that house so fucking fast, I'm pretty sure I was gone before my chair hit the floor."

"Coward," Kane cackles. "The chief is a pussycat. You didn't wanna stick around to see what would happen?"

"Oh, I knew what would happen. So I removed myself before Alex ended up in prison. But of course," I sigh, sobering, "Kari was at that dinner table, too."

"But she knew about you and Britt. She doesn't get to be angry twice. And Britt didn't know about you and Kari, so her announcement was... well, not cool. But not malicious."

"I was never mad at Britt for that." I drop my hand away from Billy's nose and trace her puffy lips instead. "It happened. It was in the past. And it's not like I could ask her to censor herself. That was her life and her actions to speak about whenever she wanted. Kari's horror wasn't in the details this time."

"It was in the delivery," Jess adds, understanding a new, fresh perspective on that day. "Britt made a scene, and even if the rest of us had no clue about you and Kari, we now knew about you and Britt. That would make it hard for Kari to eventually reveal that you and her were together when the time came."

"Pretty much. It was just another blow to the heart I wanted so badly to mend."

28

LUC

HOW MUCH HURT CAN A HEART TAKE?

"Hey, Kari!?" I catch sight of her at the end of the hall, her dark blue scrubs just another in a sea of blue scrubs. But her hair is wild and beautiful, acting as a beacon amongst waves and storms. "Hey!"

She hears me, glancing my way when I lift my arm above my head and wave. But she doesn't want to be near me. She doesn't want to know me. So she continues into a room and leaves me in her dust.

Stay the fuck away, jerkoff.

"Ouch." Mitch stops on my right, his elbow touching my arm as the emergency room runs amidst a chaotic calm around us. Our latest patient has been handed off. A grown man who fell off a ladder. I'd bet my hat they'll find it's broken in more than one place once they get him up to x-ray. "Things still aren't okay between you two, huh?"

"New drama." I turn on my heels and step out of the way when a trauma team wheels a stretcher past us and into the elevator. "She was talking to me last week. Now we're back to square one."

"What did you do?" He reaches up and turns his radio down, the chatter and static, a sound I'm not sure is ever truly gone from my ears. Even when I sleep, I hear it. Even when I'm on my bike, alone, just me and the road, I hear it. "How could you have possibly tossed everything in the trash and fucked up so bad you're back to square one?"

"I didn't." And with that, I shove away from the wall and move in the

273

direction she left in. "I didn't mess anything up this time. I'm a victim to circumstance."

"Sounds like a cop out," Mitch calls at my back. "Maybe don't piss her off anymore."

"Take your thirty-minute break," I respond instead. "I'm taking mine." I quicken my steps and peek into rooms as I pass. The ED is filled to the brim with idiots after a Sunday and too much free time. Dudes who climb ladders to fix something on their roof. Kids who stack their bikes or fall out of treehouses. Mitch and I have been in and out of the hospital all shift, like yo-yos at the end of an elastic string. But union rules say we're entitled to a break, and I'm done letting Kari ice me out when, in the most basic sense, I did nothing wrong. "Kari Macchio?" I peek into a room and draw the eyes of two techs—neither of which are who I'm looking for. "Do you know where Kari is?"

Both shake their heads, so I pull out and move to the next. "Kari?"

"In the storeroom," Doctor Eastgate steps out, hooking his thumb backwards to guide me. "I was just in there."

"Great. Thanks." I shove through the heavy wooden door and find her busily scanning the shelves for supplies. So hurriedly, I examine every wall. Every corner. Then I spin and lock the door again so no one else gets to come in.

"Luca?" Kari's shaking voice hits the back of my neck. "What are you—"

"I'm done letting you run from me." I give the handle a gentle, final jiggle, to make damn sure we won't be disturbed, then I turn and press my back to the wood and look Kari up and down. Scrubs are not made to be sexy. They're boxy and awkward. Pockets galore, and with those pockets come all sorts of lumpy contents that further distort a woman's shape beneath the fabric. But I study her now, from her plain black sneakers and up to the cute little watch pinned over her chest. I spy her wild hair, tied back in a braid that would minimize volume on most other women. But not Kari. Her hair won't be tamed. I bring my focus up to her terrified eyes and thrill in the emotions dancing in them.

She knows why I'm here. Which means she can't claim ignorance.

"Luc—"

"I'm sorry about what happened at dinner." I stalk away from the door, slow, measured steps, and stare at the way she nervously swallows. "I'm sorry it went down the way it went down."

"I'm not mad at Britt." She fakes confidence and lifts her chin, gripping boxes of gloves in her hands as though they become her shield. "She didn't know about our history."

"But you're mad at me." Another step closer. "You're mad that it ever happened."

"I've had nearly four years to come to grips with the fact that it happened." Aloof, she looks straight through me. "I'm over it."

"You're not over it!" Another step, until just three feet separate us. "You're not over it, Bear. Because we were talking a few days ago. It was shaky and stilted, but it was happening. And now you leave a room when I'm in it. You stare into my fucking eyes when I call your name, and then you walk away, anyway."

"I'm working!" She thrusts the boxed gloves between us. "This isn't a vacation, Luc! We're being paid to be here."

"And now you're on your thirty-minute break." I snatch one of the boxes from her hand and lob it across the small storeroom, so it hits the shelf with a clatter. "It's time we duke it out, Bear. We can do it here, now. We still have twenty-nine minutes to work through our shit. Or we can do it later. We both get off shift at the same time, which means you'll put your ass on my bike, we'll ride somewhere no one will hear us, and then we'll argue."

"I don't wanna—"

"We'll argue until we come to an understanding. Because I'm done with this! I'm done walking on eggshells and being terrified of speaking just one wrong word, for fear you'll hate me more."

"I'm not making you—"

"I'm done feeling like the world's biggest fuck up. I've done my time, Bear!" I grab the second box and toss it, too. "You act like I killed your dog. When all I ever did, all I ever wanted, was to protect you! You were a child when you were begging me to kiss you."

"I was eighteen."

"You were three minutes past eighteen! Which means three minutes before that, you were a fucking child. Maybe the law is black and white on that stuff, but as a man who was guarding your heart, I knew you still had a world of growing up to do. Turning eighteen doesn't magically flip a switch in your brain and make you all-knowing."

"You rejected me!"

"I sent you away to college." I stalk forward until our chests clash and her body scrambles back in response. She hits the shelf with a grunt and looks around wildly in search of escape. "Your brother is my best friend,

Kari. So forgive me for putting *everyone else's* happiness and well-being ahead of my own."

"You don't get to decide what is best for everyone else!" Finally, she snaps back and starts our war. It's happening now. In this storeroom. And in twenty-eight more minutes, we'll come out with a new understanding, for better or for worse. "You don't get that kind of power, Luc!"

"If I was acting only for me," I lean into her, sneering in a way I never would have believed I was capable of. "If I was only looking out for *me*, I'd have fucked you a long time ago."

Her lips twist into a rage-filled sneer. "Pig."

"Honest. If I didn't worry about your well-being, and about Marcus' approval, then I'd have fucked you way back when you were eighteen and begging for me. I could have claimed you for myself, Bear. Kept you in town. Married you up and gotten everything I ever wanted. Instead, I sacrificed six fucking years without you. Six years!"

"Oh sure," she seethes. "And you were *sooooo* lonely during those six years. Britt wasn't the only casual encounter you had, Luca!"

"And as far as I was aware, you had a live-in, ten-inch cock filling you up on a daily basis. I thought I lost you! I thought we were done, so yeah, I dated. I went out and met other women. I'm not a fucking monster for living, Kari."

"You—"

"The alternative felt like death. I thought everything we'd ever had was dead. Not just the romance. Not just the heat. All of it." I press my hand to her chest. Not copping a feel. But pinning her. It's the best I can offer, considering my hand tingles to wrap around her throat instead. "I thought we'd lost a lifetime of friendship, too. A lifetime of growing up together. I thought it was all gone, and you were out there shacking up with a dude. So don't come for me just because I casually dated for those years you didn't exist in my life."

"You could have had me." Her jaw trembles. Her lips quiver to the same beat as the tears in her eyes. "Six years ago, you could have had me. I would have loved you forever, and I would have experienced my college years *with* you. You chose *for* us, Luca! And that wasn't fair."

"I chose because you weren't capable of making sound decisions!"

"An opinion," she growls. "That's *your* opinion, and it is not rooted in fact. Now, because of you, we'll never truly know what we could have been."

"We will know!" I duck my head low, but stop with an inch between her lips and mine. Her frantic breath on my tongue. "We will know, Kari.

Because I'm not walking away while you ride your self-righteous pony into the sunset. You're holding on to all that mad because I said no six years ago. Six fucking years, you've held on to a grudge, and every time I stepped even an inch out of line, you added that infraction to your list of justifications and continued on with your mission to hate me. All because I said no."

"You fucked my best friend!"

"And you fucked Ten, daily, in the apartment I helped pay for."

"I never fucked him! We were never in a relationship. You've taken one tiny scrap of information and…" Her words trail off, her eyes widening when my lips curl into a victorious smile. "You asshole."

"You admit to being single." I slide my hand a little higher on her chest. Up, until I feel her pulse under my palm. "That's one. Now admit to being head over heels fucked up and in love with me."

She clamps her lips shut and glares straight into my eyes, defiant and stubborn. "No."

"Because I'm in love with you." I stroke the hollow at the base of her neck and lean a little closer. "I'm sorry we've both suffered these last six years. And I'm sorry we'll continue to suffer once Marc finds out about us. He says these decisions are yours to make, but I know he won't understand us. He won't accept it easily. But I'm done putting him ahead of us. And I'm done using your age and life experience as an excuse."

"So you admit your reasoning was a load of shit?"

"No. I admit to doing the very fucking best I could within the circumstances we were in. Back then, you were practically a child who needed protection. Now…" I press my forehead to hers and suck down every breath she exhales, "you're a grown woman. Whatever your choices are now, they're yours to own. If we end up together and you regret it, then that's a choice you will have made with both eyes open."

"And if we *don't* end up together? If that's what I choose?"

"Then I guess you fuck things up for both of us. But," I trace the bridge of her nose with the tip of mine, "I'm done tiptoeing around you and your feelings. Bad shit happened. We were both hurt by it. I get it," I groan. "We were *both* hurt. Now I'm just a man, Bear, begging you to step down off your soapbox and give us a try. If we attempt this and it all fizzles out, then we can do that together, as mature grown-ups who can still be friends afterwards. But not even trying…" I roll my forehead over hers. "Not even trying will be the biggest mistake either of us ever make."

"So we just…" Her voice crackles; pain, or passion? Fear, or perhaps, curiosity. "We decide to ignore the bad, like it never happened?"

"We grow from it. We take those lessons and make damn sure not to repeat them. I'm done apologizing for loving you, Kari. And I'm done letting you be too afraid to even try."

"We could be celebrating six years together by now." Her eyes dance with unshed tears, flickering between mine. "We could have been together this whole time."

"And if we had, maybe we'd have fucked things up worse. Or maybe not," I accept. "Maybe we could have been happy. We'll never know." I look down to her trembling lips and wonder: do I? Don't I? "You asked me to kiss you once before, Bear. You begged me. Just one kiss."

Her heart thunders under my hand. Her body sizzles with warmth, pressed against mine. "Yeah? So?"

"So ask me again." I hover my lips just a fraction of an inch above hers. "Beg me. Then have me."

"And if I don't? What if I still don't want this?"

"Then I'll beg you." I draw my hand up and cup her jaw, sliding the tips of my fingers into her hair and bringing her closer. Closer. "I'll beg you every day from now until I'm a hundred and ten. And after that, I'll follow you into the afterlife. Because I'll still love you there."

"Kiss me." Her breath comes out on a gusty exhale, as though her words are a bravery she works so hard to cling to. "Fine," she gulps. "I'm asking you to kiss me."

"My fucking pleasure." I slam my lips to hers and swallow down her cry of desperation. The gasp of air that bursts from her lungs. Then the flavor explosion of her tongue on mine. And because I've waited six years for this, I drop my hands and cup her thighs. I pick her up and inhale her squeal of delight, then I slam her back against the shelf until its contents rattle and her legs wrap around my hips. "Finally." I bite her lips and suckle on her tongue. My cock roaring to life in my pants, though I'm grown enough to know we're not going there here.

Not today.

Not at work.

"Fuck," I break our kiss, only to run my lips along her neck. Biting. Tasting. I nip at her flesh and growl when she lets out a whimper of need. "So much better than I remember."

"More handsy than I remember." She drops her head back, a goofy grin plastered on her lips as she makes room for me to taste. To touch. "Last time, you wouldn't have dared slam me against the wall."

"Last time, I was being the moral fucking hero." I pin her up with my hips, carrying her weight easily, and run my hands over her thighs. Her hips. Under her shirt and up to trace her ribs. "This time, I'm gonna please myself. Fuck everyone else and their wants."

"Except mine, right?" She looks down into my eyes. "Fuck everyone else... except me?"

"No. I fully aim to fuck you, too."

Her cheeks flame bright red. *Scandalized.* "Luc!"

"Sorry. I meant, I love you so much, I hope to someday make sweet, sweet love to you." I move my hand around to trace her back, my fingers itching to unsnap the catch on her bra. Though I don't dare. "It's not that I'm wanting you for the sex, Bear. But I sure as shit hope to enjoy it. Eventually."

"I'm still a virgin."

Like a fucking grenade tossed into a foxhole, she drops her words and freezes in my arms. Or maybe it's me that freezes. Tenses. Stops breathing as I carefully, so fucking cautiously, extract my hands from her shirt and pull back to meet her eyes.

My heart thunders out of control. Sprinting, although my lungs stopped working.

"Hmm?"

"I haven't... I didn't..." She gulps, a heavy lump of nervousness rolling visibly along her throat. "I wanted you. And then all that stuff happened. And then I was dating Blake, except we weren't actually dating. He comes from a super religious family who doesn't support who he is, so he asked me to help him out. And all the while, I was still pining after you and—"

"Virgin?" I search her eyes and scrub my soul clear of memories I thought I had to carry. Memories that didn't actually exist. "You've never...?"

She shakes her head. "I wanted you."

"You're twenty-five years old. And you've lived with your girlfriends, off campus, for five years. Not once in all that time did you—"

She rests her arms on my shoulders and licks her dry lips. But then she cinches her legs around my hips and shakes her head again. "Don't make it weird. I wanted someone I couldn't have, and I was fake-dating someone I wasn't compatible with. I got busy with school, and then time just..." She draws a long breath, releasing it on a noisy exhale. "Time got away on me. Now we're here..." She glances to her left. Then to her right. "In the storage room at the hospital. Oh god." Her face pales when that realization hits her.

"Oh god. We're in the storage room. And the ED is full. And people know we came in here. People know what we're doing!"

"We're not doing anything." And yet, to prove myself a liar, I duck in and take her lips with mine. "I mean, we're not fucking. We're reuniting."

"We're making a scene!"

"*You're* making a scene. I'm mentally planning how to fuck you without, like, hurting your feelings *and* without making you bleed."

"Luca!" She slams her fist to my collarbone and wriggles until I release her legs and allow her to slide down. Then she fixes her shirt with a huff of indignation. "I'm gonna get fired."

"You won't get fired." I crush her between my body and the shelf at her back. "No one actually knows anything about us except Mitch."

Her eyes flare wide. "Mitch?"

"Well... yeah. He's my partner, and he's watched me sulk about you for years. But everyone else..." I wave a hand toward the door, absentminded and unenthusiastic. "They will have seen us come in here, but as far as they're concerned, you're my best friend's baby sister and that's..." I shrug. "It. People see what they're told to see."

"So you're saying I can walk out of here and no one will know we were... we were..."

"We were what?" Teasing, I drop a kiss on her plump lips. "No one can see us, Bear. No one can hear us. So those on the other side of that door will know only what we tell them."

"And we can tell them..." She glances to the left and looks down at the box of gloves I tossed. "That I came in here looking for supplies."

"Sure." I drag her bottom lip between my teeth and grin. "You can tell them that."

"And you won't say anything different?"

"I'm not here just so I have something to tell everyone else." I comb my fingers into her hair and tilt her head to the side. To make room along her deliciously scented neck. "I'm here because I'm gonna love you for the next hundred years. If it's possible, I'd like to do it by your side. It's way better than doing it from afar."

"And you'll just... You won't tell anyone?"

"Not a soul until you're ready. Though I suggest we mention it, even if casually, before we send out the wedding invitations."

"Oh my god." She blows out a frustrated breath. "You're moving a million miles a second."

"I'm catching up on the moves we missed over the last six years." I drag her face across and feather my lips over hers. "I've made my move, Bear. I'm in love with you. Stupidly, painfully, irreversibly in love with you. Now I'm waiting for you to catch up. And while I wait, I kinda hope you let me kiss you some more."

"And what about..." She gulps, noisily and visibly. "What about sex? You're gonna want to do that, too."

"I assure you," I glide my tongue along her lip and grin when she groans. "When you're ready, you're gonna want to do it, too."

"What if it takes me another six years to be ready? Ya know, to make sure you're really committed to this?"

"Then I'll do what I've been doing for years already." I pull back and smile when our eyes meet. "I'll reach into my pants and tug my cock, and I'll think of you." I drop a fast, sneaky kiss to the center of her lips. "It works a treat. Trust me."

"Luc?" Mitch's voice echoes from the other side of the door. A heavy *knock, knock, knock* that makes Kari jump a full foot into the air. "We gotta go, bud."

"Just getting supplies!" Kari practically squeaks, scrambling out of my arms and bending to collect the tossed boxes. "Luc was helping me reach the gloves."

"Good luck, Bear." I grab another box down and plop it onto the pile she's already creating. "You lie so well. This is gonna be a blast."

"Shut up." She shoulder checks me and charges toward the door. "I'm still gonna be mad at you. It's become part of my personality at this point."

"That's cool. I'm gonna continue to love you. We'll counteract each other until something shakes free. Now unlock the door, babe." But her arms are full, so I wander from the shelf and come up behind her to do it myself. I smack her ass and lean around to press a kiss to her cheek, then I flip the lock and open the door to reveal a smirking Mitch. "Not a word."

He raises his hands in faux surrender. "I said nothing. But we gotta go. They've got a situation brewing just outside town. They're about to call for extra buses."

"Alright." I look down at Bear and flash a fast wink. "Guess my break is over. Thanks for your time, Ms. Macchio. It was fun."

"You squeak when you lie, by the way." Mitch leans in, poking his head past the threshold and grinning for Kari. "You squeaked when you mentioned the gloves."

"Shut up!" She charges past him and storms into the hall. She wants to make a grand exit. All queenly and shit. But she skids to a stop and stalks back until he's forced to tilt away or risk a headbutt. "Not a word, Mitchell Rosa! This isn't to be discussed with anyone outside of us three."

"No problem, *Pipsqueak*. My lips are sealed because as an older brother of a young lady too pure to be with a man, I sure as fuck wouldn't want to hear about her getting hot and heavy with my best friend in the storage closet."

"Shush!" She flexes her hands and flattens her lips. Then she shoots an angry glare my way before spinning on her heels and rejoining the rest of her shift-mates.

"You're a dead man," Mitch sighs, setting his hands on his hips and shaking his head. "Dead. Fucking. Meat."

"I'm a man in love. And love conquers all, doesn't it? Someone famous once said that."

"Yeah. But now that person is dead."

29

LUC

THE BEGINNING OF THE BEGINNING

"And thus," Jess sighs. "The start of a secret love affair that went on for, what? A whole year before Marc found out? Two?"

"Thereabouts." I push up from my seat at the table, holding Billy in just one arm, and circle around to slide my chair back in. "A year or two of sneaking around. A year or two, where Britt was dating Jack, and Laine was dating Graham."

Kane snarls. "Fucking prick."

"Marc was with Meg, and Scotch had Sammy back. Alex was readying to marry Jules, and Oz was finally settling down with Lindsi and the kids. Everyone was pairing off. But Marcus, even with Meg and the baby on the way, was still watching over Kari like his life depended on it. She and I were still figuring out who we were and what we could be as a couple, and Marcus was living what was probably the most stressful year of his life. So instead of adding to that, Kari wanted to sneak around instead."

"She didn't even tell us," Jess murmurs with a small, soft smile. "We knew she was with *someone*, considering she wasn't always at the apartment. She was spending the night *somewhere*, and she wasn't denying it when we suggested she was with a man. But no one could have guessed who the hell she was with." She perches on Kane's knee and watches as I prepare one last bottle for Billy before we head back to the hospital.

We have people to see. Arrangements to make. A life together to plan.

"Not once, in all my wildest guesses, did I consider she was banging my brother."

"Which is how they got away with it," Kane concludes. "A whole emergency room sees them sneak into a storage closet together, yet everyone believed they were actually getting supplies."

"Because that's who we were," I finish. "Back in school, when Marc wasn't watching her back, I was. When he couldn't give her a ride, I did. When she needed an escort and he was working, I was next up to bat. He trusted me to take care of her. To treat her like a sister. Seeing us together was as normal as seeing the big old tree in the park in the middle of town. It just... *was*. The fact that I was working, essentially, at the same place she was, only made it easier to sneak. A guy turning up to her workplace and offering her a ride at the end of shift? People are gonna ask questions. *Me* being there at the end of shift? Totally normal."

"A whole year?" Jess sighs. "That's a long time."

"I mean, I reckon it was closer to two," I shrug. "But sneaking around can be kinda fun, too." Then I look past Jess and sneer at Kane. "You two would know."

"My sneaking around was *not* fun!" Jess inserts. "It was the most stressful time of my life. I was dating a criminal," she mock-whispers. "A wanted felon. Alex wanted to toss him into prison, and Jules was riding my desk daily, checking in on my progress at the office. I learned how to shoot a friggin' gun. I met some really scary people. *I stopped a home invasion!*"

"You shot at Cap," Kane chuckles.

"I shot at you, actually." She twists to meet his eyes. "Eric just happened to be in the wrong place at the wrong time. That was his own fault."

"So while you were sneaking around with criminals and learning to defend your life," I mutter, "Kari was sneaking around with me, learning how to ride a motorcycle and finally, how to do a 360 ollie heelflip without Marcus nagging her to be careful."

"Practically the same life experiences," Kane sniggers. "And from what I hear, you ended up way worse for wear than I ever did."

"Marcus damn near killed me when he found out." I drop powder into water one-handed, then place the nipple onto the bottle and carefully twist to fasten it. "But you're skipping ahead. I don't get my ass kicked for a little while yet."

"And he hurt you so bad," Jess mumbles. "So friggin' bad."

"Luckily I had my own nurse by that point." I flash a playful grin and turn back with Billy's bottle while Luna and Rose dash through the kitchen.

"So I got her to kiss me inside that storeroom that one time. That was the beginning."

"Should I leave now?" Jess pushes off Kane's knee and drops her hand to the top of his head. It's a gentle massage. A scratch of his scalp that instantly turns the man to jelly. "I suspect we're heading toward the, *Kari is no longer a virgin,* portion of this story. And while I'm here to celebrate her, I'm not really interested in hearing about my brother's role in all that."

"I won't tell that part of the story," I snicker. "It would be disrespectful to the woman who craves privacy."

"Dammit, Jessica!" Kane turns to his wife and play-snarls. "I wanted to hear the sex, too! Why the hell would I stick around for the romance if I don't get to see the rest?"

"You're still a pig." She drops a kiss to the top of his head and gives the side of his face a little tap... I swear it verges on a slap. "Never change, babe. Girls?" She turns on her heels and starts in the direction her twins went. "Mommy wants to play with you now. She's done talking to Uncle Luc."

Kane watches her leave, grinning like he thinks he's the luckiest mother-fucker on the planet. Then when she's gone, he swings back around and meets my eyes. "Tell me the sex stuff."

30

LUC

THE SEX STUFF

idnight rolls around, and the end of another shift sneaks closer. I've been on the job a hell of a lot longer than Kari has, and my shifts are always with Mitch, which means we know each other now, we know how the other works and the strengths each of us bring to the job. That means we have a system that has me out of the bus on time, except in the case of an emergency.

Tonight is not one of those nights.

I sit in the ambulance dock, hidden in the shadows, and watch the doors as they whir open and the afternoon shift wander out. Nurses. Doctors. Administration. It's a hard change once midnight hits, which means any patient inside, if they're in pain at midnight, will have to wait a second for the handover to occur and the new staff to familiarize themselves with what's going on.

It's not a perfect system, I know. But this is a small town, and it's rare that anyone is left for more than a minute or two for the personnel change over.

"I can give you a ride." Bernadette—a nurse—moves through the doors with a to-go cup of coffee in her hand and a purse dangling off the other arm. But her companion, Kari, is who holds my interest. "It's not safe for you to walk home alone, Kar. And we don't live all that far from one another, so I don't mind—"

I step out of the shadows, casual as fuck, and grin when the duo glances across at the movement. Bernadette's shoulders slump, relief, while Kari's come up.

"Hey." I swagger closer and swing my keys around my finger. "Marc is working at the club tonight and asked me to come get you."

"Oh well, that's easy then!" Bernadette winks at me and continues on. "Thank god Marcus is organized, huh? I was getting worried."

"Thank god for Marcus," I agree as Kari's eyes narrow. "Come on." I move in closer until only a foot separates us and sling her backpack out of her hands. Slipping my arm through the strap, I turn to walk by her side. "I'm taking you home tonight."

"You're being insanely obvious," she growls. Her body is taut and her lips barely move. "Luca…"

"Sneaking isn't always about not being seen." I wrap my hand around her bicep and steer her into the shadows. "Sometimes, it's about ensuring you're seen in all the places you're expected to be." I look down and smirk. "It's math."

"It's stupid." The moment we're out of the light, she yanks her arm from my hand and snatches back her bag. "You're stupid."

"You're cranky." I lead her to my bike, which just so happens to be two feet from the hospital exterior wall. Then I shove her against the bricks and inhale her gasped breath. "You're cranky when you want me. You're cranky when you've got me. What do I need to do to make you smile?"

"I'm just a cranky person in general." Her perfect, emerald eyes search mine. But fuck, her hands come to my hips, too. Her throat rolls as she swallows the lump clogging the middle. "It's who I am now after years of being angry. I'm sorry."

"Don't be sorry." I lean in and feather a kiss along her jaw. Nibbling. Biting. Beaming when she gasps. "Be here with me. We only get to experience this time in our lives once." I take her bottom lip between my teeth. "Be present, and stop looking for a reason to hate me."

I cup her jaw and force her head back. Her hair catches in the brickwork, tugging and tangling as I move her. But she doesn't complain. She doesn't push me away. If anything, she pulls me closer, her chest lifting and falling as she searches for air.

"Come for a ride with me, Bear." I dive in and savor the flavor of her neck on my tongue. Her sweet, floral scent. Her warm, heady intoxication. "We can take an hour before you have to be back. No one will even notice you were gone."

"I'm actually really tired." Blushing, she forces her eyes open and searches mine. "That's not a cop out, though. I'm on my fifth, consecutive twelve-hour shift, and my eyes feel like they might spontaneously combust."

"Take you home?" My heart stutters. Her rejection, so gentle, and yet... right there. "You want me to just drop you home?"

She swallows, gulping noisily. "But you could come in with me."

My heart comes to a dead standstill. "What?"

"Britt's staying at the house with X, Laine's staying with Graham, and Jess has been working a bunch, so she'll be asleep. If anyone saw your bike out front, they'd assume you were visiting your sisters. You could come in..." She hesitates. "We could just hang out. No... ya know."

"No sex?" My face hurts with how wickedly fast my smile curls up. "You're asking me in, but you're laying down a boundary."

"I just... I want to spend time with you. But I'm not even sure I'd have the strength to hold on if we go for a long ride. I thought this was a decent compromise, but if you—"

"I accept your terms." I shoot forward and slam my lips to hers, bashing the back of her skull against the bricks again. But guilt fails to fill my veins. Instead, I feel something else entirely. Love. Want. Mostly anticipation. To spend time in her home, in her room... just her and me...

What am I? Seventeen fucking years old?

"I'll stay as long as you want me to." I slide my fingers along her ribs and smirk when she trembles. "I'll hide in the fucking closet if you need me to. If the twins were to ever become suspicious, they'd be cool anyway. I don't give them trouble about their dating lives, they don't give me trouble about mine."

"Perhaps you should get more involved. Laine's dating a complete jack-ass. None of us like him."

"Laine's a big girl. If she wants my help, I'm here for her. But if she wants to date a guy, I'm gonna trust her judgement."

"Negligent," she teases.

"Respectful. Marc should try it sometime. Now come on." I grab her ass and drop one last kiss to her lips. Then I pull away and snag my helmet from the bike's handlebars. Because whenever *she's* on the bike, the helmet comes with us. "Put this on." And yet, I do it for her, raising the helmet and plopping it over her head so her hair becomes a curtain covering her eyes.

It's cute, really, the way she practically inhales her own locks and frantically brushes them aside to clear her vision.

"Climb on after me." I let her fix the straps on her own and throw my leg over the bike instead, scooting forward to ensure she sits closer and swinging her backpack around to wear it on my front. I set the key in the ignition and start the purring engine. Then I grin, because she slides her leg over the seat and nestles onto the bike with her chest practically plastered to my body. Her breath touches the back of my neck, even with the helmet in the way, and her arms come around to crush my ribs. "You ready to go for a ride, Bear?"

"You ready to stop announcing everything we do? You make it weird, and then I get shy."

"Ohhh, so like… you *want* to go for a ride, but you don't want me to ask if you want to go for a ride?"

"Right. It's weird."

"Kinda like you want to go to bed with me. But you don't want me to ask you if you want to go to bed with me? Because then you're forced to reject me out of habit, or admit you want me."

"Luca—"

"You want me." Pleased, I balance the bike and kick the stand up. Then I slip the gear out of neutral and into first. "I understand now, Bear. You want all the things. You just don't want to say them out loud."

"I want you to stop talking," she grumbles. "I'm quite happy to tell you so."

"See, now you're being cranky again." Chuckling, I use my feet to steer the bike out of the shadows and away from the wall. Then, when I have a little space, I gently release the clutch until the gear catches and we're moving ahead. "You're too shy for your own good." I use just one hand to steer, since we're still in the hospital loading dock, and I use the other to reach down and stroke her leg. "Don't worry," I speak a little louder. "I'll speak enough for us both."

"She wanted all the things," Kane sniggers. "She just wanted you to be forward enough to take them. She considered asking for them a weakness on your part."

"I mean…" I slip the bottle's nipple between Billy's lips and shrug. "I'm no shrink, but I guess that's how it was. She was too timid to say the words out loud. I basically had carte blanche to do as I pleased."

"So you took her home and went to bed with her." Kane is way too fucking comfortable digging towards the details of intimacy I shared with Kari. All those nights secreted away. All the times we snuck out to be alone. All the family events we attended together, but not *together*. "All yours for the taking?" he prompts, eager.

"You have a serious boundary problem." I stare down at my daughter and shake my head. And instead of speaking my words out loud, I hold them within myself. More memories I get to visit. More love, just for me and Kari.

31

LUC

FIRSTS

I cut the bike's engine about three buildings before Kari's, using the momentum to roll the rest of the way, and the silence to sneak closer. Because even if my sisters are gonna be cool about all this, Kari still wants privacy, and I'm not ready to have my ass handed to me by Kari's older, larger, dangerously protective big brother.

I bring the bike into the driveway out front, gravel and rocks crunching under my wheels, then I squeeze the brakes gently, slowing us to a stop and using the streetlights overhead to guide my way.

"That was smooth," Kari whispers, reaching up already to unsnap her helmet and pull it off to reveal wild hair made curlier from the ride. "I never considered rolling it into the driveway."

"I'm too smart for my own good." I accept the helmet when she offers and dangle it off the handlebar, then I do the same with her bag, using the straps to hang it. I thrill under her touch when she places her hand on my shoulder and her feet on the ground. She uses me for balance. For strength.

All for naught, because the moment she's off, I hook my arm around her hip and yank her in until she perches, off balance, across the bike in front of me. Looking down into her eyes, exhausted, and yet, dancing, I smile when her lips twitch with a ghost of the same. "I feel like I'm dreaming." I lick my dry lips and study the million tiny freckles smattered over her cheeks. I visually trace her long lashes, and the locks of hair draped over one side of

295

her face. "I know we're still figuring us out. And fuck, Bear, I know we're scared. There's so much at risk—"

She searches my gaze. "But...?"

"But I feel like it's all a cruel dream and you're still away in the city pretending I don't exist. I'm scared I'm gonna wake up soon with the biggest fucking heartache ever."

"That's kinda how I feel too." She nibbles the inside of her cheek and allows her eyes to flicker between mine. "You said no for so long, and now you're all in, shouting yes. I'm still catching up."

"So we're both kinda shell-shocked." I lean in and press a kiss to her sweet lips. "And now you're inviting me inside. To your bed."

"Don't make it weird." She slaps my shoulder and shoves up from the bike, snagging her bag as she goes. But she doesn't throw my hand off when I grab on. She doesn't fuss or snarl when I link our fingers and tug her back so we can walk side by side. "You and I aren't compatible on the way we discuss these things. You seem to thrill in making me uncomfortable."

"I mean..." I press my lips to her temple and chuckle as we start up the steps. "I do. Kinda. It's the asshole in me. But it's for the greater good," I add when she shoves her elbow back and nails me in the gut. "I swear. If neither of us say anything, then we're never gonna get anywhere. But if I continue to nudge you out of your comfort zone and into the outside world with me, then eventually, maybe, we'll be able to get married and live our lives together forever."

"Jesus." Exhaling, she slides her hand into the front pocket of her backpack for her keys. "You're never afraid to say the craziest things. I'm blushing over the word sex, and you're out here spouting off about marriage."

"That's because I know where I'm going." I snatch her keys and do the honors. "I've known, Bear, all along, where my life was heading. I just had the unfortunate luck of having to wait for you to live yours in the meantime."

"Making decisions for us both," she whispers, lowering her voice when I open the door and cross the threshold. "You think you get to dictate my life."

"An argument we've already hashed and beaten to death. I'm not interested in fighting over that anymore." I pull the key from the lock and turn to close the door at our backs. But I don't miss the sneer on her lips. The lingering rage she continues to work through. "Come on," I take her hand and duck my head. It's weird, and Pink Panther-y, but I lead her through the living room and down the hall. I've been in this apartment countless times, despite the fact that the main occupant wanted nothing to do with me for the longest time. Which means, luckily for me, I know which room is hers. I don't have to slow us down and explore an unfamiliar place. "Has Blake ever slept in your room?"

"Oh, shut up." She thumps my shoulder, silent and painful, and takes the lead past my sister's closed bedroom door. She hovers by hers for a beat. Hesitant and shaking. But when I lean into her space and raise a single, challenging brow, she rolls her eyes and pushes through. "Fine," she hisses, holding the door just long enough for me to cross the threshold. Then she pushes it shut again, careful not to make a single sound with the latch.

"So this is your bedroom, huh?" I glance around the spacious room. The bed that'll easily—with a little extra snuggling to compensate—hold two. I peek at the dream catcher hung on the wall and the fairy lights dangling from the ceiling. When the main light is out and the fairy lights are on, I imagine it's almost as though she's sleeping under the stars. "It smells like flowers in here." I turn from the back wall and find her waiting by the door. Shy. Hesitant. Terrified. "I'm not judging you, ya know?"

"I don't..." She searches my eyes, desperation making her voice quiver. "What?"

"You think if you say something—like, asking me to kiss you, or asking me to love you—is reason to be embarrassed. But I'm not judging you."

"I know. You're—"

"You could ask me to wear devil's horns and fuck a horse in public, and I still wouldn't judge you."

"A horse?" Her lips wrinkle in disgust. "You would fuck a horse? What the hell is wrong with you?"

Chuckling, I drop my hands by my sides and wander in her direction. "No, I wouldn't fuck a horse. But you could ask me for anything, Kari." I stop in front of her, our toes almost touching and her choppy breath hitting my chin, "And I'll go to the ends of the earth to be what you need me to be."

"But you won't assault a horse?"

"Not unless you really, really begged. And then you'd have to write a five-page essay outlining your very specific reasons as to why you think I should do that to the poor beast. He doesn't have a voice, after all, and sexually assaulting an animal is a crime in forty-nine US states."

"Pretty sure it's all fifty," she sniggers. "Or, it should be."

I bring my hand up and place it under her chin, gently tilting her head back until it rests against the door. "Should I tell you when I'm gonna kiss you? Or will I just do my thing?"

"Telling me makes it formal and odd," she gulps. "That makes me feel weird."

"So I'll just do me then." I pinch her chin between my thumb and finger and draw her to the tips of her toes. "And you'll tell me when I've done something you don't like."

She licks her lips and nods, barely, considering the grip I have on her face. "Yes."

"And you'll speak up, clearly, and loudly, if I'm approaching a boundary you don't want crossed?"

She swallows and nods again. "Yes."

"Are there any boundaries you'd like to voice right now? Since we're talking and things are already weird, you may as well use the moment to say what you need to say."

She shakes her head, wordless and yet, a million thoughts flitter in her eyes.

"Can I pick you up?" I release her chin and gently peel her bag away, allowing it to slide to the floor with a too-loud scrape of the zipper against the door. "Can I put you to bed?"

Her cheeks burn a horrified red. But she closes her eyes and nods. So fucking brave. So trusting. "Yes. To both."

"Thank fuck." I slip my hands down her ribs and around to her backside. Then I lift, slamming my lips to hers when she opens her mouth to squeal. I turn on my heels, suckling her tongue into my mouth and groaning when she wraps her arms around my neck. She's terrified. But she wants this. Fuckin' A, she wants it, and I've waited for what seems like a million years. "You're so fucking beautiful." Instead of tossing her to the mattress, I turn and sit instead, holding her on my lap and grunting when she grinds down over my hardened cock. "So delicious, Bear."

"Take control of this," she pants, rolling her hips and teasing me with what could be. "Be bossy and stuff, so I don't have to be in charge."

I slip my hand beneath her shirt and trace the long lines of her back. Over her ribs and along the valley of her spine. "You want to be passive in this." I break our kiss and dive in to taste her neck instead. I bite, but I don't suck. I nibble, but I don't leave a single fucking mark for someone else to witness tomorrow. "That's not the Kari I remember, demanding I kiss her on the halfpipe."

"That Kari was younger and braver." She reaches down to the hem of her shirt and lifts it until the fabric catches on her chin. She surprises us both, staring into my eyes when, for the first time in my life, I don't help a woman undress. "And she wasn't asking for sex back then. Just a kiss."

"You want to fuck tonight?" My lips curl higher, playful and verging on goofy. "You move fast, Bear. From *I hate your guts,* to *split me open,* in the space of a single shift at work."

"Split me open?" She rolls her eyes, mocking. But at least she's back to her normal, challenging self. "You think quite a lot of yourself, don't you?"

"I don't think. I know." I shrug. "You don't dive straight into the deep end on your first day at the pool, Bear. You gotta wade in slowly. Bring a big, strong man along to keep you safe."

She pitches her shirt and looks to her left. Then she half climbs off my lap, so the only reason she doesn't splat to the floor are my hands gripping her hips. She yanks her bedside drawer open and pushes random notebooks and bits of paper aside. Then she takes out a dildo that has my eyes popping wide and my heart skipping a beat. "Six years, I've wanted you." She straightens on my lap once more, holding the bright pink *tool* between us so I get to see. "Six years, Luc. I'm *technically* a virgin, in that no man has penetrated my body. But…"

"You're a naughty girl." I snatch the dildo and hit the button on the end, starting the vibration until it rolls along my arm and leaves the woman trembling in my lap. "How often did you think of me while you did this, huh?" I bring it up and let the vibrating end touch, feather soft, her plump lips. "How many times did you explode and think of me?"

"Too many." Sighing, she drags her lip between her teeth and groans. "So many times."

"Even when you hated me?"

She exhales a choppy, stilted breath when I drag the vibrator over her clavicle and down to rest between her breasts. "Maybe even more then." She rolls her hips and buys me a one-way ticket to hell. "I wanted you, even when I wished I'd never met you."

"Angry sex is the best kind." I lower the dildo and place it between her legs on the outside of her pants, pressing the hard length against her core and sending myself closer to the edge because the vibration rockets along my cock, too. "You can stay mad at me a little longer if you want." I bite her lip, eliciting a groan of desperation that arrows straight for my heart. "Just for this one time. Now that I know you're not some inexperienced, damsel virgin." I hold her hip and push mine up. I can't help myself. I couldn't stop the movement even if I wanted to. "Now I know I don't have to be careful…"

"I mean…" She backs up a little, allowing her shy side to win in a battle against bravery. For a moment, at least. "Be a little careful…"

Snickering, I toss the vibrator aside and spin on the bed, dropping a squeaking Kari onto her back and following until I can kneel between her legs. Her chest lifts and falls, her heart racing and stressing her bra on every inhalation.

"Let me taste." I dip my fingers into the waistband of her pants and give a gentle tug. Just enough to let her know what I'm doing, but not so much to expose her. I want to give her time to say no. "I can fuck you tonight if that's what you want. Or I can just lie here and chat since you're so tired."

"Luc—"

"But I wanna taste you first." Carefully, I drag the blue fabric down, pinching the drawstrings of her pants and freeing them from the knot she created at the start of her shift. "Dildos can't tongue fuck, Bear. That's for me only."

"Oh god." She sets her feet on the bed and presses her palms to her eyes. But she lifts her hips and allows me room to maneuver the fabric. "Don't ask me for permission for these things." Her cheeks flame beneath her hands. "I'm begging you, don't ask. It makes me feel awkward."

"But you're not too shy to show me a fuckin' dildo." I drag the pants along her creamy thighs and grin when I find her legs smattered in freckles too. From her time spent at the lake, swimming in the sun and *not* inviting me in. *Blasphemy.* "*I'm too shy to say I like you, Luc. But I'm not too shy to show you my sex toy collection.*"

"That's not my whole collection." She smirks when my gaze snaps back up to meet hers. "Just my current favorite."

"Fuck me." I drag her pants down and tangle the fabric in her shoes. Desperate, I tug her laces undone and toss her sneakers aside, one, then the other. Kari giggles, her lithe body vibrating just like the bright pink dick buzzing on the bed. Then I unsnap my pants just to allow myself a little extra room to breathe. My cock roars in my boxers, seeping and pulsing with a feral need that is far more violent than she deserves. More violent than she could handle. "Please, Bear, for the love of everything holy, please let me taste you."

"Stop ask—"

"I'm gonna taste you," I cut in. Not asking. Not making it weird. "I'm gonna take everything I've been dreaming of for six long fucking years." I kneel on the bed, my knee between her legs, and scoop my free arm beneath her back to half lift, half drag her along the mattress. My touch is rough. Bruising. My desperation, palpable. "I'm gonna make us both really fucking happy."

She crushes her hands to her eyes and shudders. "Oh god."

"And your only job is to tell me *no* if something bothers you."

Her breath hitches on the way out. "Okay."

Lying her down, her head on the pillow, I bring my arm back and slide my fingertips over her flesh. Goosebumps sprinkle to the surface, nerves a physical, visible thing. But she circles her legs around my hips, demanding I stay close and sending shots of adrenaline firing through my veins. "Fuck, Kari." Breathless, I lean over her and take her pebbled nipple between my lips. She still wears her bra, a simple, black, lace-less T-shirt bra that becomes the most beautiful fucking scrap of material I've ever seen in my life. "You're gonna kill me, Bear."

"Don't die yet." She cups my face and pulls me closer, latching her lips onto mine and taking my very soul with her kiss. "I've waited too long for this. You don't get to check out yet."

I snort and drop my lips to her neck. Her collarbones. The underside of her jaw. "I swear, however long you've waited," I pull back and search her eyes. "I've waited longer."

Her eyes glitter with emotion. Such a familiar look I've long ago grew accustomed to. But there are no tears this time. There's no sadness.

"I love you," she whispers. "Even when I hate you."

"Fuck." I dive in and take her lips with mine, my heart thundering in my chest and my cock pulsing against her core. Could this be real? Is it possible, after all these years, we've come out the other side of all the hurt and heartache, and finally, this gets to be our *reality*? Fuck knows. But on the off chance it's real, I dig my fingers into her underwear and find her soaked and waiting.

"Oh god!" She cries out, too loud. Way too loud, considering she shares an apartment. She slams her own hand to her face and latches her teeth into the heel of her palm. "Luc!"

"I love you too." I slip my fingers into her pussy. Since we're not asking. *Not making it weird.* Just one finger at first, then two until I feel the stretch. "I've loved you for as long as I've known how to love." I pepper my lips over her forearm. Her jaw. Her chest. And when she mewls, I pump my fingers and grin when she explodes. Wet and demanding, her tight pussy clamps down and begs for more. "You're so needy."

"I want to fuck." She lifts her hips, chasing my hand and panting when I make her work for it. "Luca."

"I wanna taste, first." I steal my hand from her underwear and take the fabric as I go, exposing the short, curly thatch of hair that guards her entrance. My mouth waters at the promise of what's to come. My stomach topples at the idea of coming with her.

In her.

"Go." She drops her hand to the top of my head and pushes. Demanding and bossy enough to make me chuckle. She releases her legs from around my hips and lets them drop wide, then she tangles her fingers in my hair and continues to guide me down. "God, Luc." Her breath comes out fast. Harsh. Fragmented. "Please."

I study her sweet pussy. The swollen lips and throbbing clit just waiting for me to touch. Her creamy release already makes her glisten. The wet patch on her bed, like a beacon calling me closer. Fuck savoring. Fuck delayed gratification. I bury my nose against her clit and slide my tongue along her slit until she cries out. She bites her own hand and lets out a muffled groan. And when she attempts to snap her legs closed again, I press my palm to her thigh and nudge it away. "You taste like heaven."

"Luc—"

"Like heaven if they were serving cocaine and candy." I slip my fingers in and hook them back to glance across that bundle of nerves. Instantly, she detonates, filling my mouth and drenching her bed. "That's my girl," I pant, pressing the pad of my thumb to her clit. "Such a good girl."

"Luca!"

"More." I spread my fingers apart and tickle her asshole with the tip of my pinkie. Her body freezes. Every muscle turns taut, and her breath comes to a dead standstill. A boundary creeps closer, so I glance up and study her eyes, grinning when they scream a million thoughts a minute. "You can say no." I kiss her thundering clit. "Or you can let me touch. Neither are wrong. And if you choose the second, that doesn't mean you can't stop me in a few minutes."

"Okay…" Her word comes out on a crackling, almost-painful gasp. She licks her dry lips and nods, just a single drop of her chin. "Alright."

"Such a brave girl." I circle her clit with my lips and suckle until her eyes roll into the back of her head. Then I slip my digit into her ass and hum with pleasure when she groans. "Surprised you never tried this with your toy collection." I lap at her slit and swallow down her delicious release. "A whole fleet of dildos and you never thought to grab a plug and shove it in your ass?"

"Oh god." She bites her palm again and whimpers. "Stop talking about it. You're making it weird."

I snort and nibble along the very top of her thigh. "I'd like to talk about your asshole, Bear."

"Luc—"

"It's so tight," I growl. "So pink and welcoming."

"I'm gonna kill you."

I chuckle and reach across for her dildo. Taking it in my hand, I close my eyes for a second as the vibration ricochets along my arm and into the depths of my chest. But when I open them again, I meet her stare and smirk. Her perfect green gaze watches my hand. Her teeth come out to play with her bottom lip. She might be a virgin, but she knows how this feels. "You're telling me you've *never* put this in your ass?" I look down between her legs. The glistening sheen and the hungry pulse of her cunt. Then I lean back just a little more and spy her ass. "Never once accidentally tickled it and thought, let me try that?"

"Stop." She covers her flaming face with her palms. But fuck it because she's smiling. "I'm never doing this with you again if you insist on making it awkward."

"Hell you aren't." I turn the vibration high and bring the tool down to glide between her folds. To slick it with her own release before I stop with the tip at her opening. "This is one of those medium-sized kinds, huh?" I nudge the head in, just a half inch until her breath catches and her eyes spring wide. "It's not small, like a bullet. But it's not large, like a real cock."

My hips jut forward, like it's me entering her body and not an inanimate fucking toy.

"You got the starter size, huh?"

"It's respectable." She whimpers when I slide it an inch in, clamping her lips shut and angling her head back so I see the strain of her neck. I see her pulse beneath delicate skin, and the blue veins that swim just below the surface. "Luc…"

"*I'm* not respectable." I drag the dildo out, only to slide it in again. But this time, she gets two inches. "And I'm not as small as this thing."

"You can't be nearly as big as your ego."

I snort and give her another inch. "That's what you think." I bring my free hand away from her ass, eliciting a cry of despair when she realizes her loss, then I slip it into my pants instead, circling my cock and groaning when that touch alone has my release sprinting to the surface. "You can tell me to stop, okay?"

I fight my zipper and shove it down, desperate to free my dick from its constraints. "First time is still the first time, Bear. And a dildo was something you controlled. This is gonna be different."

"I trust you." Panting, she sets her feet on the bed and tilts her hips to take more. Her eyes glitter with need. With want. With desperation. Then she comes apart around the dildo and melts into the mattress. "Luc..."

"So responsive." I draw the dildo out and set it on the blankets, then I reach up, one-handed, and draw my shirt up. "So fucking responsive, Kari. You're gonna kill me."

She worries her bottom lip and shakes her head side to side. "It's gonna be fine. I promise."

"I don't have any condoms." I lean in and kiss her. I force her to taste herself on my tongue. Her release on my lips. "I haven't carried a condom around with me for a long time, Bear. So unless you have some, we can't—"

"I don't have any." But she rears up and wraps her hand around the back of my neck, holding me closer when I start to move away instead. "I trust you."

"Babe..." My heart shudders in my chest. Her blind faith, far more powerful than any other words she could toss my way. "It's not—"

"I'm on birth control. And you're claiming forever."

I choke out a desperate laugh. "Yeah, well—"

"We're both clean. You love me and I love you."

"You're a virgin, Kari. And you're not even demanding protection." I release my cock and fold over her until my forehead rests against her chest. "You're giving too much away."

"Luc?"

I swallow the lump lodged in my throat and close my eyes. "Yeah?"

"Six years. And you're gonna make it weird if you force me to convince you." She slides her fingers into my hair and grabs on tight enough to make it sting. Dragging my head up, she waits for our eyes to meet. "If you make me ask, then we may as well stop. I can't feel good about myself if I have to beg you to—"

"To take advantage of you?" I lean closer and press a kiss to the center of her lips. "You don't want to have to beg me to take your body and soul and lock them away for the rest of our lives?"

"I want you to want me," she whispers. "So much, that you can't even stop and think. I want you to have me. And then I want you to keep me."

"Fuck." I drop my face to the middle of her chest and reach down to circle my cock. "Just say stop when you need me to stop." I kiss her warm flesh and bring my tip to her fiery opening. She's like lava, and I'm not sure I can take the heat. "Tell me to stop, okay? I'm begging you to—"

"I trust you." She cups my face and drags me up. Her eyes glisten with moisture. But they don't spill over. They don't break my heart like they have so many times over the years. "I trust you, Luc. It's gonna be okay."

"Fuck. Okay." I lick my painfully dry lips and reach down to grab her leg. I hitch it higher to make room for my thighs, then I nudge, so fucking carefully, the head of my cock into her warmth.

Instantly, she realizes this isn't the same as her dildo. Immediately, her breath comes to a stop and her eyes widen.

"It's gonna hurt, Bear." I roll my hips and give her just a little more. "The stretch will sting. Are you sure—"

"Don't ask." She drops her head back and slams her eyes closed. But I see the way they roll in pleasure first. The way they express desire. "Be bossy. It's easier for me."

"Fine." *Fuck.* "Fine." I rock a little closer and grit my teeth when her vise-like grip is enough to destroy me. "You're so fucking tight. So tight and perfect."

"Luc..." She swallows, so the movement is visible in her neck.

"You're doing so good." I give her more and feel like an asshole when she hisses. But I slide my tongue over the line of her collarbone. "You can take all of me, Bear." A little more. "You can do it."

"Oh god." She abuses her lip between her teeth and bites down until her skin turns white. "Luc—"

"You're so perfect." I take her lips with mine, saving hers from her teeth and a scar she won't like. Then I nudge a little more in and choke out a breath of desperation. My balls tighten and beg for release. Already. So easily. Because she's so tight. "You're so wet. So needy."

"You can push in a little more." Opening her legs wider, she draws a long breath and forces herself to relax. "You're really not as large as you think you are."

I bark out a laugh that I know would get me in trouble if my sister wakes in the next room. But I bring my focus back to Kari. To her playful expression and smart mouth. Her cheeks flame and her eyes dance. She wants to be sassy, so I give her what she asks and slide in until she's taken me all and her breath hitches painfully. She draws a long, fast gasp, but to stop the sound escaping, I slap my hand over her mouth and accept her biting teeth as punishment.

"I hope you like what I've got, Bear." I rock a little faster now to lubricate myself with her previous release. "Because this is the only cock you'll ever know." I groan as she tilts her hips and mewls. "I'm not leaving now that I've finally got you back."

She wraps her arms around my shoulders and whimpers when I speed up, digging her nails into my back and marking my skin. "Oh god. That feels so... Ah." She whimpers, part pleasure, part pain. "So good."

"Filled you right up." I hook my hands under her back and around to her shoulders. Then I slam forward and hold her to me so she can't escape along the bed. "You're doing so good, baby." I close my eyes and pray, I fucking *hope*, not to come too soon. "So fucking good."

"It doesn't hurt so much anymore." She lifts her legs and wraps them around my hips. "Go a little faster."

"And you said you couldn't be bossy." I crash my lips over hers and suckle on her tongue, groaning when she cries into my mouth and breathes all the way down into my lungs. "You're doing amazing." I move faster. Faster, until it's a piston that draws me perilously close to the edge. "So fucking amazing, Bear."

She crushes her eyes closed and scrapes her nails along my back. "I'm gonna..." She moans. "Luc, I'm gonna—"

"Jump." I move faster and hold my fucking breath. Anything, to keep myself on this side of the line. "You can jump, Bear. I'll be right here, ready to catch you."

32

LUC

THE SOUND OF SILENCE

"You frigid motherfucker." Kane shoves up from the table and catches Rose when she dashes through the kitchen. He swings her into his arms and crushes her to his chest. But he points a finger right in my face and sneers. "I know you just cheated me out of some of the story. I did my time, Luca. I deserved the payout."

"Visit Sonia's office recently?" I press a noisy kiss to Rose's cheek and step away with a grin when she cackles. "Daddy probably should go talk to the good doctor sometime soon, huh?"

"Don't be passive aggressive through my baby." He sets her on his hip furthest from me and glares. "You made me sit through the *woe is me* shit, but you won't share the *apple pie* stuff."

"There's something legitimately wrong with you." I turn on my heels and head through the doorway. "I'm taking Billy upstairs for a fresh diaper and clothes. Then I probably should head out to the hospital."

"Tell me the good stuff!" He stalks to the doorway. "Luca Limpdick Lenaghan! At least tell me what happened after."

I look down into Billy's sweet, sleeping face and shake my head. "He's sick. And I'm not sharing Mommy's private life with him. Because I *am* respectable. Mostly."

"**K**ari! I'm heading to the bakery in a second to get pastries and coffee."

I wake to Jess' voice echoing along the hall. My eyes shooting wide and my heart stammering to a painful stop. Then I jerk up in bed and find Kari lying on her back, innocent and sweet. Her long hair fans across her pillow, tickling my arms, and her eyes are completely fucking relaxed.

It's a role reversal.

"You finished your last night shift last night," Jess continues. I twist and look toward the door, my neck aching from the quick movement and my stomach jumping at the thought of being caught in here. "You're off for the next two days, so I figure you deserve a nice coffee after all your hard work."

"So much hard work," Kari whispers, snickering when I swing back around to meet her teasing gaze. She slides the tip of her finger over the ball of my shoulder and giggles when I think I might expire from stress.

"Kari?"

"No thanks," she calls back. Her voice is a little hoarse. A little croaky until she coughs to clear it. "I'm gonna sleep another hour or so. Not getting up yet."

"You got a man in there?"

I drop back to the mattress and sling the blankets up to cover my face. Like a child, I hide under the covers and hope to not be seen.

"I heard you last night," Jess snickers. "Just a little bit."

"Um..." Kari's blush carries under the sheets too, spreading onto her chest and out to the tips of her breasts. "I uh..."

Jess claps. Loud, slow, obnoxious clapping that brings a pit of nausea to the base of my stomach. "I put my headphones in the second I heard the first peep. But we're gonna talk about this later, okay?"

"Er..." Kari chokes on that single syllable. "Okay."

"Whoever you are," Jess calls out to the mystery man in her best friend's bed. "I'm fluent in karate, kickassery, and judo. I'm immune to gaslighting and skilled at un-isolating isolated women. I'm also a highly paid, largely respected practicing lawyer, and your girl will have full, free representation all the way to the Supreme Court."

Kari ducks under the sheets too and giggles. "She hasn't sat the bar yet."

"I know! She's my sister, Bear. I know she hasn't sat the bar."

"So I'm gonna give you guys privacy," she adds. "Because Kari is too tightly wound for her own good, and getting dick sometimes is healthy for repressed women."

"Oh god." I gag as beads of sweat ball on my forehead. "For fuck's sake."

"But be aware," she continues, "just as soon as you're gone, she's gonna tell me *everything*. We compare all dicks to fruit, so if you want to be spoken of fondly, behave in such a way as to inspire her to say nice things. Also, be a giant eggplant! Anything less will be laughed at."

"Please go away." Kari's eyes water, tears forming in the corners and her shoulders bouncing with laughter. "I'm begging you to please go away. By the time you get back with coffee, he'll be gone."

"*Then* we'll talk," Jess declares. No room for argument in her words. No fucking way around. "Eggplants or string beans, Kar. I wanna know about it."

"I'm gonna puke." I throw our covers off when footsteps echo along the hall and the front door swings open and closed. Then I turn and stare down at a humored Kari. "She heard me fucking you!"

"She heard me *being* fucked. There's a slight difference."

"She wants you to describe my string bean!"

She cackles, curling in on herself and holding her belly. She was the one who was afraid last night. Today, she's back to being a pain in my ass. "Your sister wants me to draw your dick on a napkin and compare it to a string bean. Which, by the way, isn't a fruit."

"She's gonna see my bike outside!" My stomach lurches as I bound out of bed and stride across to the window. The sun is already up. Already glaring through the curtains. But Jess wanders into the street, walking the block or two to Main Street instead of sliding into her beat-up car. Which just so happens to be parked in front of my bike. "Fuck, Bear!" I drop the curtains again and turn. "My sister is a deviant. And you're out here making a game of comparing dicks."

"In my defense," she sniggers, "I haven't been able to contribute to the game except way back when we were calling Blake '*Ten*'."

My eyes narrow to dangerous slits.

"I didn't see it! Swear. He's tall, so we just assumed. I didn't want to look like a total loser, so I called it a papaya, and *your sisters* ran with it. It's *their* fault."

"My entire life is filled with filth." I stalk back to the bed. To the beautiful, decadent, buck-ass-naked woman who does nothing to cover herself up.

Then I crawl onto the mattress and place one hand on the side of her knee. I push it to the side and open her legs, instantly making her laughter stop and her breath hitch. "Sneaking around with you is stressful." I crawl into the gap between and take her pebbled nipple between my lips. "I'm gonna die of a heart attack long before I die for banging you in private."

"Maybe you should not bang me then." She squirms beneath my touch, wriggling when my cock brushes against her pussy. "Maybe we should quit and forget this ever happened?"

"Maybe you should stop talking crazy and instead tell me you love me again." I reach between her legs and glide the tips of my fingers through her soaked slit. Already, she's ready for me. She's responsive. Needy. Perfect. "Let's fuck again," I groan. "We have lots of time to make up for. Then we gotta act normal when other people are around."

She snorts, but that turns to a groan when I slide in and stop only when my cock is sheathed to the base.

"Shit," she whimpers. "Dammit, String Bean. You gotta go easy on me. I'm still new."

33

LUC

WE'RE HEADING TO THE FARMER'S MARKET

"Alright." Kane stomps up the stairs, following me and Billy into the nursery. "Fine. You won't tell me *the stuff*. But what happened after that?"

"After?"

"Yeah, like," he flicks his hand in my direction, "you clearly hook up at some point, considering that cute little booger you're carting around like a new handbag. There had to have been a first time. And since you were sneaking, there was clearly a first morning after. A first *nearly got caught*. I want those details."

"Your wife was largely involved in all that." I lay Billy on the changing table. Already, I smell the stench of a massive, milky load dropped in her diaper. So I unzip her onesie and work on tugging her tiny legs out. "She tried to threaten me. Though, she didn't know *I* was the one hiding in Bear's bedroom."

"Oh my gosh." Jess wanders up the stairs and stops in the doorway beside Kane. Changing a shitty diaper is an entire family adventure, I suppose. "You were in her room, and I didn't know it?"

"A million times. But that particular time, you mentioned judo, ass-kicking, the Supreme Court, and string beans." I place Billy's leg on the plastic mat and reach into her romper for the other. "Then you went off to buy coffee and breakfast."

"I remember this!" She claps a hand to her mouth and gasps. "*You!?*"

"You don't have to leave," Kari giggles, climbing out of the shower and grabbing my hand as she rushes back into the hall. She drips on the floor and snatches out a pair of men's jeans from the basket as we pass. Charging into her room, she yanks me in and slams the door, then she tosses the jeans at my chest and drops her towel. "You can be here when she gets back. You've been in this apartment a million times during weird, annoying hours. She'll assume you've come to see her."

"And these men's jeans?" I pull them away from my chest and sneer. "There a reason you're dressing me in another man's clothes?"

She rolls her eyes and snags a fresh pair of panties from her closet. "They're Marc's jeans, goober. Relax. You're practically the same size, and you have to get changed, because sitting at our table in your uniform eight hours after end of shift will look sus. But if you look fresh, and you act normal, she'll assume you arrived while she was out for coffee."

"But I..." I lose my train of thought and tilt my head to the side when her tits are just... they're there. "I..."

She looks down at her mostly naked body, then glances up again and snarls. "Grow up, String Bean. Get changed. Leave your uniform in my room and I'll get it washed and back to you. In the meantime, you can still hang out, you'll see Jess, and no one has any clue what the hell you did to me last night."

"What *I* did to *you*?" I push my cargo pants back down and hobble on one foot to get them off. Then I step into my *best friend's* pants and hope to god no one ever finds out about it. "Excuse me, Ms. Please Fuck Me."

She lobs her towel across the room, so it smacks my face and hangs off my head until I grab it.

"You were on such a roll, Luca. Sweet, for approximately seven hours. And six of them, you were sleeping."

"And now you're stuck with me anyway. No return policy." I drop the towel and hitch the jeans up, over my hips, and fix the zipper. "What the hell do we do next? How do I look Marcus in the eye again, knowing what I know?"

She slides into a bra and reaches back to fix the clasp. "What exactly do you think you know?"

"That your pussy tastes like candy and you have a teeny tiny smattering of freckles right next to your clit." I firm my lips when her eyes swing up to meet mine, then I raise a brow when she huffs. "Only people who *know* things will know that about you."

"Good thing my brother doesn't know that about me," she sneers. Charging past me, she opens the bedroom door and hesitantly peeks into the hall. The coast is still clear, so she darts out in just her underwear, then back in again in under a second. She flings a plain black shirt at my chest and slams the door shut until it rattles in the frame. "They're just plain jeans. Plain shirt. No one has to know who they belong to. And you don't have to tell people about the vagina freckles." She stalks to her closet and snags a pair of itty-bitty shorts that have no business being outer wear. "I feel like it's common courtesy *not* to bring up such delicate matters in everyday discussion."

"But they're my *favorite* freckles now." I shrug into the shirt and scowl, knowing I'm not wearing *my* shirt. I'm wearing another man's. Even knowing who that man is, it still gives me the ick to be given another dude's clothes by the woman I'm gonna keep for myself. "What are you doing today, anyway? We have forty-eight off before our next shift."

"Well, if you stay, then I'm probably gonna eat a pastry with Jess and *not* discuss eggplants, since she won't wanna bring that up in front of you. If you leave, then I'm going back to bed and hoping by the time I wake from my ten-year coma, she'll have forgotten about all the stuff she may or may not have heard last night."

"She's tenacious." I pull the shirt down over my torso and fix it at my hips. "Even if you escape her today, you're gonna have to deal with it tomorrow."

"Like I said," she reaches back into her closet for a shirt, "ten-year coma. I have a plan, and it's wrapped up entirely in complete and total avoidance. I'm just thrilled it's your sister who knows stuff, and not my brother. That's a whole other bag of hell."

Footsteps echo on the stairs outside. Extra noisy. Extra heavy, almost as though the owner is generously signaling their approach.

The fact that these girls—my sisters—have a *guy-system* makes my stomach roll uncomfortably.

"Shit!" Kari sprints forward and shoves me toward the door, smashing my shoulder against the frame and opening it before I'm truly out of the way. The wood bounces off my foot and crashes shut again. So she pushes me to the side, opens it wider, and deposits me in the hall. "Go to the kitchen! Make a coffee. Act as annoying and entitled as you always do when you come over here."

"Entitled? Bear, I—"

"Go eat the last of something out of the fridge! Spill sugar on the counter. Be obnoxious!" She closes the door in my face and presses her back against the wood—I hear the muffled thump—meanwhile, keys jingle in the front door.

"Go!" she snaps.

With my heart in my throat and adrenaline zinging in my veins, I dart along the hall, my feet skidding on the rug in the living room and nervous nausea slinging through my gut as I glide past the front door. Then I crash into the kitchen, smacking my hip on the counter when I overshoot the landing. I grab a mug from the sink and toss it beneath the coffee machine spout just as the apartment door opens, and the sound of crinkling paper packaging echoes through. "Luca?"

Jess' curious voice carries in the air. The sound of her keys, then the muffle-thump of her shoes as she kicks them off. "Are you here? I saw your bike out front."

"Hmm?" Calm as a fucking cucumber, I wander to the fridge to get creamer and gulp when my sister emerges in the doorway, beaming when our eyes meet. "Hey." *Cool. Cucumber.* "What did you say?"

"I saw your bike." She sets a tray of coffees on the counter and strolls across to slide into my side for a fast hug. "Did you seriously *just* get here and you're already in our fridge?"

"Those are *not* pants," Marcus' angry baritone makes my heart come to a dead standstill. I extract myself from Jess' hug and step to the left to find not only my best friend standing at the front door, but Kari waltzing into the room as well, wearing teeny tiny shorts and rolling her eyes.

"Good to see you too." She's better at this than I am because she strides through the room and kicks the rug back into place before heading to her brother. "It would be nice to see you sometime and you *weren't* trying to control what I wear."

"Funny," he grumbles, dropping a tender kiss to the top of her head. "It would be nice someday to visit my baby sister and not see her ass."

"Except... this is my private apartment." She extracts herself from his hold and smiles the smile of a fucking angel. "My private, personal, *can dress how I like*, apartment. Do you see me fussing over the things you wear at your place?"

"Do you see my best friend over there?" He shoves a hand in my direction, growling when I sling my eyes away from Kari's long, bare legs. "He's a grown ass man, Kar. And he has a reputation for liking the ladies. Do you think it's appropriate for him to see your ass at this time of the morning?"

"Your reasoning is absolutely laughable. And toxic. But sure, I'll cater my outfits in my own home on the off chance you and your friends drop by uninvited." She drifts by me, too fucking close, too tempting, and brushes her shoulder over mine. "Morning, Luca. You look rested despite your late night."

"My late…" I swallow, noisily and nervous. "My late night?"

"Finished up work at midnight, same as me." She moves to the coffee machine and snags the coffee I started. Then she looks at Jess and grins. "What pastries did you get?"

"**Y**ou were him!" Jess snarls. "You were that guy hiding in Kari's room that morning? Luca!"

I peel Billy's overflowing diaper open and attempt to breathe as little as humanly possible. "I sure as hell hope she didn't have any other dudes hiding in her room." Wrinkling my nose, I reach across for wet wipes and begin cleaning up the greenish-brown mess. "Then, of course, Marcus had to walk in with you that morning, too."

"I asked about your…" Jess heaves. It might be fake, or she might really be ready to blow chunks. But the fact she does it while Billy's poo-stench fills my lungs makes all this so much worse. "A hundred times over the next few weeks, Luc! I asked about your *thing* so many times!"

"Your family is toxic and weird," Kane grumbles. "What the hell is wrong with you, Blondie?"

"Oh, shut up!" She smacks his arm. "You're literally begging him for the sordid details. I was asking, but that was only because I thought she was banging someone *not* related to me. But you—*you!*—are completely aware, and yet, continue to ask for every description. Don't talk to me about weird."

W eeks after my first night with Kari, I sit on Marc's back porch and drink a beer with everyone else. Marcus. Scotch. Ang. The twins, Britt, and of course, Kari.

The grill has been fired up, and the laughter rolls.

Marcus, after all, is happiest when he has his little sister safe and within his sights.

"Apple?" Jess tosses one into Kari's lap, uncaring that it smacks her friend's stomach first, bouncing off and almost tumbling to the ground if not for Kari's fast hands. "That's a reasonably sized apple, right? Kinda thick. But if we're just talking, like... length size..."

Kari flattens her lips, unimpressed as she sets the fruit on the table in the middle of our group. "No, thank you."

"A banana, then?" Laine joins in, grinning as she places the long, yellow fruit on the table next. "It's on the smaller side, I guess. And not crazy thick. So it's just, like..." she shrugs, earning a curious tilt of Ang's head. "A snack."

"I don't want a banana either." Kari smiles, angelic and yet, intolerant. "Not hungry."

"Is an eggplant a fruit?"

"They are, actually." Marcus, that dumb motherfucker, tips his beer back and takes a sip. "They're often considered a vegetable," he rumbles, clueless to the fact that he's participating in a game of, *'how big was Kari's secret dick?'* "But they technically grow from a flowering plant and contain seeds, which makes them a fruit."

Britt beams, glancing back toward the house at the fruit bowl overflowing on Marcus' counter. "Would you like an eggplant, Kari?"

"No." Furiously playing with the label on her beer, she picks at the paper instead of looking up. Instead of looking at me. "No eggplants for me, please. I'm saving my appetite for dinner."

"Oh come on!" Jess scowls. "Giant carrots, then? Not those pesky little snack kinds. But the big fat, farmers had a good year, kind?"

"What the fuck is with the food discussion?" Marcus peers across to me. Like I can somehow be his backup. "Did they have a stroke?"

"One of us did," Britt snickers, losing her cool and bouncing off her chair before she ruins all their fun. Her eyes glitter with unreleased laughter as she trudges into the house. "There's a whole watermelon in here! It's like, the size of a basketball. Surely that's too much for any one person to consume."

"I'm gonna cook the steaks." Shaking his head, Scotch stands and follows his sister into the house. "They're being weird, and I don't recall inviting them here with us anyway."

"I invited them," Marcus declares. "I don't see my sister enough these days."

"Could be because of the farmer's fruit markets she keeps going to," Britt cackles, throwing her head back and holding on to the kitchen counter for support. "She's busy working and fruitin'."

Kari looks at me, her face stony and hard. "She's strange."

"Yep." I bring my beer up and sip. "She sure fuckin' is."

34

LUC

CLUB NIGHTS

"We're going to Club 188 tonight." Kari wanders into her room, grinning when she closes the door and I'm laid out on her bed. A single sheet affords me modesty, while my clothes lie on the floor, rumpled into a ball. She carries a coffee mug in one hand, and a metric smile on her face. "This band is playing; you might've heard of them?"

I steal the coffee from her hand the moment she's within reach, then I set it on the bedside table and hook my arm around her hips instead. Her yelp of surprise rings out, echoing from wall to wall. But we're here all alone. Which means I could walk through the apartment naked as the day I was born, and that would be okay.

I mean... I wouldn't. Because fuck knows the pain I'd be in if someone dropped by unexpectedly. But still. The opportunity is there. Sort of.

"I heard the drummer is the sexiest of them all."

She snickers, rolling to her back and holding on so I practically rest on top of her. Her long hair fans out, covering her pillow and tickling my arm. "Considering that band is made up of my foster brother, actual brother, dude I grew up with, and you..." She purses her lips, though her eyes dance. "Yeah. I'd say, aesthetically, of course, you're my favorite."

"Aesthetically." I lean in and nip at her bottom lip. "What are you wearing to the club?"

"Why? You want to control my choices?"

"No." I slide my tongue along her lip and grin. "Wear whatever the fuck you want. But if you show bunches of skin, I'm gonna have to listen to Marcus whine about it. Which is cool and all," I press the tip of my nose to hers. "I've listened to him complain for decades already. But a heads up would be nice. His mood matters to the set we play."

She snorts, turning her head and presenting her neck for me to taste. "I'll wear jeans, probably. A cute, little top."

"Wear a skirt," I hum, "and I'll fuck you in the hall, and no one will even notice."

Her skin flushes, hot and pink, as her breath comes a little faster. "Luca—"

"You're so used to being told to dress down. To not attract attention." I bite her neck and groan when her nails dig into my shoulder. "It flusters you when I tell you to slut up."

"When are we supposed to tell everyone else what we're doing?" She pulls back, just far enough to search my eyes. Her cheeks switch from blushing intensity to terrified white in the span of a single second. "The girls know I'm seeing someone. And Marcus has nearly caught us a hundred times. You're ready to screw around in the hall at the club, which means you're hardly even trying anymore. And I'm—"

"Too scared to admit to Marcus you're a grownup now?" I take her lips with mine. Calm her thoughts. Be her smooth seas when storms brew on the horizon. "I'm gonna follow your lead on this, Bear. When you're ready to tell, I'm ready to tell."

"That easy?" Her heart thunders, pulsing against my chest so I feel it. "You know Marcus is gonna *lose his mind*. Like… *really* lose it. This isn't just admitting I'm grown now. It's admitting I've been sharing a bed with his best friend for the last two years. He's gonna go nuts, and you're just… *whenever you're ready, Bear.*"

"I'll stand up when you tell me to and say what I've gotta say."

"Your friendship won't survive that!" She digs the heels of her palms into my chest and pushes me back. "Do you understand what's gonna happen when he finds out, Luc? Your friendship will be over."

"It won't. He knows you date. He's not thrilled about it, but he knows it happens. You went away to college for years, so he knows you have a life outside of him. He's gonna be pissed when he finds out I'm involved, but again, he knows I'm a good fuckin' dude. He'll be angry at first, and then we'll move past it."

"A lifetime of friendship," she trembles. "He's gonna snap, and you're gonna catch the horrible end of that deal."

"You underestimate his ability to see reason. I can feel your heart sprinting, Bear. You're worried about this, but I think you're taking on way too much stress when it's not necessary."

"His entire life has been wrapped up in protecting me!"

"And now his life is wrapped up in Meg. He's having a blast with her in his bed. So let's not pretend his every thought is about you anymore." I chuckle when her eyes flash. Hurt. Pride. A little pain to the latter. "He still loves you, Kari. And he'll forever want to protect you. But he's also a grown ass man with a sex life and a relationship he's trying to figure out. His every thought does *not* revolve around you."

"Hey, Kari, do you—"

Britt strides through the bedroom door without knocking, skidding to a stop, and startling when I swing my gaze around. Instantly, I grab the sheets and pull them up to make sure my ass is covered, then I shoot a look back down at Kari as panic lances through my veins.

"Um—"

"Oh my god!" Britt turns, then turns again. She walks straight into the doorframe and bounces off. Then she spins back in our direction but slaps her palms over her eyes and gulps. "Kari!"

"Close the door!" Kari slips out from between me and the mattress, smoother than a fucking snake in long grass, then she rushes her friend and grabs her wrists. Holding her hands there or pulling them away? I'm not sure. "You can't say anything!"

"You and Luc?" she squeaks. *Squeaks!* "You and Luc?!"

"Shhhhh!" Kari kicks the door closed and presses her friend against the wall. "Not a word."

"You and Luc," she whimpers. "How long? Since when? Why!?" Then she drops her hands and stares straight across at me. "Marcus is gonna *kill* you!"

"Ya think?" Kari grabs Britt's jaw and forces their eyes to meet. "Not a word!"

"But fruit," she moans. "And all that talk at dinner. And *fruit*." She looks across to me, desperation in her stare. "Dude!"

"We're gonna tell him soon." I sit up on the bed and make sure the sheet covers all of me. Lifting my knees, I set my elbows on top and groan. "We've been working on it, Brat."

"But you have to shut your trap in the meantime!" Kari snarls. "Not a word."

"But how long?" She stares at the side of my face, bright blue Turner eyes both dancing and filled with dread. "How long has… and when did…" She claps her hands to her cheeks and exhales. "Holy shit. I've gotta tell Jack." She looks at Kari. "I wanna tell Jack!"

"You tell anyone and you're dead meat." Kari releases her friend and groans all the way into the depths of her stomach. "You can't say anything, Britt. Marcus is not gonna take this well."

"I think he'll be fine," I rumble. "I mean… sure, he'll be enraged at first. But I'll tell him I love you and that I intend to marry you. And that'll—"

"Marry?" Britt gasps. "Marry! Luca, you don't marry chicks."

"Thanks, Brat." I look at the back of Kari's head and shake mine side to side. "I've been in a committed, monogamous relationship with your best friend for two years now, jerkoff. Can I get a little faith, please?"

"Two years!" She booms, loud enough to rattle the walls. "Are you insane?" She glares at Kari. "Are you even my friend? Two years, and you said nothing?"

"Marcus." She looks to me, widening her eyes impossibly round, then back at Britt. "That's all I need to say on the matter. *Marcus*! He's going to prison once he finds out. And Luc is permanently relocating to the cemetery. Excuse me for not wanting to rush the process!"

"I say she's being dramatic." I scratch a hand through my hair and sigh. "He's gonna be pissed. He's not gonna end up in prison."

"No," Britt quips, so fucking easily. "You're wrong. He's gonna claim temporary insanity and end up in the whacky cell block. Either way, you should probably pick out your headstone now if you want any say in what it looks like."

"Kari?" Marcus' voice echoes from the front of the apartment. Instantly, Britt and Kari freeze up and pale. "You home, Kar?"

"Oh shit!" Britt yanks the bedroom door open and swings it wide, then she grabs Kari's hand and looks her up and down. *Dressed? Yes. Decent? Sure.* She tugs Kari into the hall, then pokes her head back into the room and snarls, "Get dressed, stupid. Climb out the chimney or some shit. You're so dead if he finds out."

"He's not gonna kill me!" But do I keep my voice low? *Fuck yes, I do.* The second the door closes, and the girls are out of my sight, I bound out of bed and focus only on finding my boxer shorts. My pants. I don't cling to every word the girls say outside of this room—I mean, I would if I could, but the walls are too thick.

I trip into my pants and tug the fabric up to sit on my hips, then I step into my boots and risk my neck when I leave them untied. I snatch up my shirt from the floor, and when I'm close to the door, I catch the murmurs of Marcus fucking Macchio in the living room. Settling in for a little visit with his baby sister, since I guess he's done screwing Meg for today.

They're hot and heavy when they're together, but when they're not, he's back to obsessing about his sister.

"We're playing a set at the club tonight," he declares. "Just coming to see what you were doing, since it's the weekend."

"We're going to the club too," Britt announces. *Seriously fucking loudly.* "Kari and I were just thinking about getting breakfast at the diner, then we were gonna decide what to wear."

"Jeans." Marcus comes closer to the hall. His voice carries louder. So I shrug on my shirt and prepare to have my ass kicked. "You can wear jeans and a winter coat. It's cold out."

"Oh geez," Kari rolls her eyes. I mean, I don't know for sure that her eyes move. But the tone of her voice sure as shit indicates they do. "It is not cold out. And I'll wear whatever I want." She pauses for a beat, allowing the tension to build, before she adds, "Probably even a cute little skirt."

"You were hiding in her room!" Kane giggles. Giggles! *Who knew tattooed thugs giggle?* "Dude. You just walk out of that room and say hey, I'm here, I'm banging her, get used to it."

"He nearly killed Luc." Eyes deathly serious, Jess looks up at her husband and shakes her head. "Like, we love Marc. Really, we do. And god knows, his reactions are based in trauma. His entire life was built around protecting Kari, and none of that makes what he did right, but it provides a little context, at least. The day he *did* find out?"

"He nearly killed me." I bring my hand up and touch my jaw. Pretty sure he splintered the bone that day. Busted my eyes. Trashed my nose and ribs. "He wouldn't be reasoned with. Couldn't be reasoned with."

"He did so much damage," Jess whispers. "We were so worried."

35

LUC

PAY THE PIPER

The girls know.

I swear, I think damn near every single person in this town knows at this point.

But Marc doesn't. He remains blissfully unaware of the things his sister does in private, and no one else is rushing to share the news.

So we just... we continue on with our lives.

With a vague, loosely made plan to *eventually* tell him when the time is right.

But until that point...

"We could go into the city or something." I lounge back on the couch in the middle of Kari's apartment, groaning when she sidles onto my lap and grinds just a little closer. "Go out on a real date," I moan. "We could hit a fancy restaurant and sit there until closing. Get a little tipsy on good food and nice wine, then stay in a hotel for the night." I drag her top up, gentle as I draw the fabric over her head. I've pulled her hair too many times to count. Tangled it in her earrings more times than we can recollect. It's the price we pay, I think, for me to be able to sneak around with a beautiful woman.

The moment the fabric clears her face and our eyes meet, I grin. "Will you come out to dinner with me, Bear?" I drop the shirt and slide my hands over her delicate ribs. "I miss you so fucking much when we're in this town."

329

"You miss me when we're in town?" Her cheeks warm. "How is that possible? We practically work together, and we sleep in the same bed five nights out of seven."

"Yeah. But we can't be open about who we are." I slide my hand up and around to cup the back of her neck. "I want to tell the entire world who we are."

"Luc—"

"I know." I draw her in and press a gentle, barely-there kiss to her plump lips. "Marc's going through some stuff with Meg and the baby, and you don't want me to die." I brush the threat of a beat down aside and chuckle instead. "The time isn't right. I'm ready when you are, but it's your call."

"Soon." She trembles on my lap, rolling her hips and studying my eyes. "Swear. But not while all the Meg stuff is going down. In the meantime," she leans closer, her long hair draping around our faces to create a curtain we both get to hide within. "I don't want to talk about them while I'm grinding on your lap."

"Thank fuck." I dig my fingers into the waistband of her pants. "I don't wanna talk about them while my cock is hard. It's… off putting."

She snickers, her breath hitting my tongue and her breasts pressing to my chest. "We have work in a few hours."

"All the more reason to get on my bike, right now. Head to the city. Call in sick."

She rolls her eyes, though her smile is small and delicious. "That won't look suspicious at all. People could die if we're not at work."

"Sounds like a *them* problem." I massage the round globes of her ass and grin when she smacks my shoulder. "Tomorrow night, then?" I draw my hands along her back and trace the valley of her spine. "No work tomorrow. No dead people on our conscience. Besides, how am I supposed to ask you to marry me for real if we're never openly a couple?"

"Marry?" She freezes in my lap. Stiffens and widens her eyes. "Luc, you—"

"Did you forget this was where we were heading?" I lean in and take the warm column of her neck between my lips. "Did you think I was bullshitting when I said I loved you?"

"Well…" She gulps so I hear the sound through her delicate skin. "No. But we're—"

"Endgame." I cup her jaw and tilt her head to the side to make more room. "We're forever, Bear. We have time, since forever never ends. But my intentions have been clear from day one."

The apartment door opens without warning. No knock. No keys in the lock. No boots stomping on the steps outside. I lean to the right, expecting to find my sisters on the threshold. Not ideal, considering Kari is half naked, but not nearly as bad as what I actually find.

"Marc?" My stomach heaves. Painful, horrified, sickening nausea sprinting through my gut as Kari swings around on my lap. "Dude, we can explain—"

"Marc!" Kari bounds up off my lap at the same moment her brother charges from the front door. Red in his eyes and fists already balled and coming for my face. "No!"

He slams his fist down on my jaw, a sickening crack echoing through to the back of my skull. Then blood spurts across the floor and bells ring in my ears, clanging and deafening, so I don't even hear Kari's screams.

"I'll kill you, motherfucker!" Marc swings again, tossing me off the couch and raining hands down over my face. It's all I can do to bring my arms up and shield myself. Guard. Don't fucking die. "She's mine!" he snarls, spittle hitting my skin alongside my own blood. "Mine!"

He's a man possessed. Owned by his own fear and pain. Devastated by the circumstances of his life. And still, I let him. Bones crumble beneath his fists. Muscles ache because of his strength. But I don't dare fight back. I let him take out a lifetime of anger and fear on my face and hope I'll live tomorrow to still see Kari.

It could be an hour. Or it could be a single second. Fuck knows, my vision turns dark, and my arms scream for relief. But Marc continues to rain enraged fists down on my body. Kari screams for him to stop. He screams for me to undo what I've done. My brain screams for the pain to stop.

Then he's gone. Reeling backwards when a pair of hands grab on and drag him away. He kicks out wildly, his feet arcing through the air and slamming my chin until stars float in my vision and exhaustion tries to drag me under.

Then he's gone... and so am I.

"Luc!" Kari skids down by my side, her hands fluttering over my swollen face. "Oh my gosh!" She cries out. "Luc!"

"Cool it!" Jack Reilly's voice booms throughout the apartment. "Dude! Fucking cool it, or I'll call X."

"Luc!" Kari uses her shirt and presses it to my cheek. *Am I cut? Is it bad?* "Holy shit. I can't believe he just—"

"He touched my baby sister!" Marcus roars. Kicking and fighting from somewhere else in the apartment. "I'll kill him. I'll kill that motherfucker!"

"I think you already did, you fuckin' idiot. X," Jack adds... *on the phone?* "You need to come to Kari's place. Now. It's Luc. He might need an ambulance or something."

I search for Kari. For her beautiful green eyes, but all I find are tears. She's crying again. Because of me.

"Don't cry." My jaw hurts. My words. My whole fucking head. "No crying."

"Marc. Beat the piss outta him," Jack rumbles.

"He beat the *piss* out of me?" Dizzy, I bring my arm down and feel the crotch of my jeans. *Just in case.* "Nah."

Sobbing, Kari lays her face over my chest and shakes. "You need an ambulance."

"No." I push her off. I swear, I don't mean to shove her off. I never, ever, in my entire fucking life want to send her away. But I clear her off me and roll to the side. My body aches, and my ribs sing. Maybe they're broken. Maybe they're just really fucking sore. Coughing, I get my knees beneath my body, then my hands to the floor.

I ignore the blood spatter patterns the local coroner might study if this day goes worse. But then I stumble to my feet, swaying left when my brain rejects the notion of *upwardness.*

"Luc!" Kari scrambles to her feet and slides under my arm, holding me up when my knees prefer to tremble. "You need to sit down."

"I need to see Marc." My words slur, rolling the way they have in the past when I've consumed too much alcohol.

In fact, my tilting steps are kinda the same too.

"Let me go." I unlink Kari's arm from around my body and stumble out of her hold. Then I close one eye and search for the direction Marcus went.

I need to talk to him.

To clear shit up.

To tell him I love her.

This isn't one of those one-night fuckeries he's accustomed to associating me with.

"Marc..." I weave toward the kitchen, toward Jack's rumbled words, and catch sight of Marcus for just a second. A single moment in time. Then he dives my way and swings his fist out.

I close my eyes to prepare for the pain, but Jack grabs him before he can get to me. "Cool it, man!"

"I thought we were brothers!" I crack one eye open and watch the duo wrestle. One, for freedom, and the other, for submission. Kari sidles up beside me, squeezing my arm just tight enough to remind me I'm hurting. But Marcus only burns hotter. "I thought I could trust you!"

"Kari and I..." I swallow the nausea that has sweat rolling along my back. "It's not as bad as it looks, brother, I swear."

"Don't call me brother! You're no brother to me." He scrambles to escape Jack's grip. While my heart, my whole fucking soul, shrivels at his words. "I thought we were family, Luca! I thought you had my back, but you do this?"

"It's not like—"

"She's not like Sassy!" he roars. "She's not like those girls."

"I swear," I groan. "It's not like that. If you'd just listen to us—"

"Us? *Us!*" He looks from me to Kari, sneering the longer we remain standing side by side. "There's no *us* for you two. You're her brother. Not her fuck buddy!"

"Marc." Kari steps forward to challenge him, but I shoot my arm out to stop her. It's muscle memory. It's my protective instincts, stupid as they may be. Because that one, simple move has Marc fighting against Jack's hold.

"You don't stop her from coming to me, you motherfucker!"

Kari slips around my arm and stands in front of her brother, looking up into his eyes with tears pouring from her own. "It's not so bad," she pleads. "I promise. We're in love. If you take a breath, I can explain it."

"In love? He's a fucking whore, and you're my baby sister."

"I'm not a damn baby anymore!" Angrily, she shoves him back and charges forward to get in his face. If not for the puke rolling along my throat, I'd like to think I might stop her. "You need to get it through your thick head. I'm grown now! I don't have to ask your permission to date someone."

"You don't get to date *him!* You need to put a fucking shirt on, then he's leaving and never coming back. You'll never see him again, Kari!"

"Oh, for fuck's sake. You don't get to make that call! I'm in love with him. Do you hear me?" She taps her fingers to the side of his head. "We've been seeing each other for a *long* time, but you don't know that because you refuse to see me as a woman instead of a scared seven-year-old girl."

"Seems he has no problem seeing you as a woman!" He slips free of Jack's distracted hold, and swinging out, faster than my body can even think to react, he slams his fist down on my tender jaw until I'm flying.

It's kinda like I'm on my bike. And yet, as my head goes one way and my body goes the other, it's not like being on my bike at all. I trip on my own feet, my brain too fucking damaged to even consider bringing my hands up in protection. Then the side of my face collides with the cabinet and that's… that.

Sleep.

36

LUC

BEAT. DOWN.

I turn at the changing table with a fresh Billy in a clean diaper and new clothes, only to stop on an eternally familiar set of emerald eyes as they watch me over Jess' shoulder.

Marcus drops his gaze, shame still pulsing through his blood despite all the years that've passed since that day inside the girls' apartment.

And because things are better now, I smile to help ease the self-loathing he forces upon himself every time he remembers back.

"Aww. How about that, Bill? Uncle Marcus is here."

Stunned, Jess peers over her shoulder and looks up at the man she's known essentially as a brother her whole life and smiles. She watches him with adoration in her gaze. For a second, anyway. But then she balls her fist, winds her arm back, and smacks his shoulder with as much strength as she can muster. "You didn't have to hit him that last time and smash his head on the counter, ya know?"

"Ow." Marc brings his hand up and rubs his arm. But his lips curl up. He's hurting because of her fist, which to him, means he's being punished. Punishment, in his eyes, is atonement. And atonement, as far as he's concerned, is something he can live with. "And just for the record, I've apologized for all that."

I scoff and bring Billy up to rest in the crook of my arm. "Tell that to the arthritis in my jaw." Smirking, I stalk forward and deposit the baby in his arms. Because he needs to hold her almost as much as I do. There's only one other person on this planet hurting as much as I am today, and that person is him.

"Too bad you didn't get here five minutes earlier, Uncle Anger Issues. You could've changed her loaded diaper."

"I've done my time with diapers." He brings Billy up and presses a gentle kiss to her temple. "Everyone sleep okay last night?"

"Dipshit over here has kept me awake since two," Kane grumbles. "But Billy's been out all night."

"Why the fuck would you be up at two if the baby was sleeping?" He rolls his eyes—exactly the way his sister does—and turns on his heels to head toward the stairs. "I always knew your daddy was a bit funny in the head, Bill." He peppers tiny, repetitive kisses on her forehead. "He always just thought he was funny, like, haha. But Uncle Marc knew better."

"Don't talk shit about me to my daughter." I pack up the dirty diaper, rolling it into itself and fixing the sticky tabs. Then I place it in a little bag, and the little bag inside the genie to stop the smell from leeching into our furniture. "You had free rein to say things to your sister. You don't get to do the same with Bill."

"But you remind me of your mommy," Marcus chatters playfully. "Not *exactly* the same. Because you got the Lenaghan blonde, but you have your mommy's chin." Kiss. "And her cute little jaw." Kiss.

"He wanna kiss my kid, too?" Kane drawls. "She got the Lenaghan blonde as well."

"He doesn't want just any baby to obsess over." I move into the hallway, then cut left to the bathroom to wash my hands. "He wants the mini-Kari to fuss over since that's his thing."

"Shut up." Marcus grumbles from the stairs. "I've grown and evolved since back then. And besides, she's my baby sister. A dude's allowed to get a little rowdy when he finds out his best friend and his baby sister have been sneaking around in private."

I pump soap into my hands and flip the tap on, but I look up in the mirror and purse my lips when Kane's eyes meet mine. "Grown and evolved. I'll believe it when I see it."

"It's too late now." Kane glances back into the hall and shakes his head. "He already scarred your skull, and Kari already spit out the mini-sis for him to freak out over. We've come too far."

"He's too old to throw hands like he did back then." I rinse the soap from my hands and turn the tap off, then I dry them and wander into the hall, only to peer across to the stairs and find an overly worried, sick-with-it big brother loving on the only connection he has to his sister right now.

I can talk shit and bag on him all I like, but none of that takes away from the fact he's hurting today, too.

Sighing, I head his way and tap his shoulder as I pass. "Coffee? We're gonna head up to the hospital in a little bit."

37

LUC

HEART PAIN. HEAD PAIN. NOT REALLY SAME SAME.

"No broken bones that I can find. Ya know, like with my hands, and not an x-ray which we totally have access to down at the hospital." Mitch firms his lips and runs his fingertips along my arm. My head thuds with an ache so fucking deep, I'm not sure if there's a drum line somewhere in the back, or if a train is using my skull for a set of tracks.

He sits on the edge of Kari's bed—first and last time—and examines my tender body. "I can't find anything while probing your bones, Lenaghan. But you could have a million hairline fractures, and we won't know until you get the damn scan."

"Not getting a scan." My words are slurred. Heavy. And my eyes don't open all the way. But I spy a quietly crying Kari in my peripherals. Her eyes are swollen too. Red and puffy, albeit for a different reason. "Hey, Bear." Weak, I reach across and tap her hip to draw her attention. "You okay over there, beautiful?"

"He's going to prison," she chokes out, twisting to look me up and down. "And you're going to the hospital."

I shake my head, slowing the movement when it feels like my brain rattles inside my skull. "Neither of those things are happening."

"They should be," Mitchell snarls. "You need to have your head scanned, at the very least. And he needs a little time in a cage to cool off. Ten to twenty-five oughta do it."

"Oh god." Kari sobs into her hands, her back bouncing from the tears wracking her frame. "He was so mad. So mad!"

"We knew he would be. Hey?" I pinch the fabric of her shirt between my stiff, aching fingers, and tug it to get her attention. "Bear? Look at me."

"I can't. I'm so ashamed."

A long, silent growl reverberates in the back of my throat. Then I bark out a non-playful, "Look at me!"

Dragging her face from her hands, she glances across and blinks fresh tears onto her cheeks.

"It's gonna be okay. I've known Marcus most of my life, Bear. He flashes hot, then he cools down. It's gonna be fine."

"He *deserves* to go to jail for what he did," Mitchell growls. "I get the big brother thing, Luc. I really do. But this is next-fucking-level unhinged."

"He's not going to jail on my account." Swallowing the acid creeping along my throat, I set my least-painful arm on the bed and use it to hitch myself up to sitting. A long moan rolls through my throbbing chest and erupts with a side of a whimper, and when I try to force my eyes open, the whole world swims.

It's momentary and dizzying.

But then things slow. The nausea bubbling in my belly settles. The universe calms the fuck down. Then my lips curl into a small, teeny tiny *so the splits don't split more*, smile that still sends shards of glass through my veins. "See?" I swallow the lump in my throat and ignore the pain radiating along my forearm. "Everything is okay."

"Luca!"

"I'm not going to the hospital. I'm not making a statement with the cops. And I'm not—"

"The cops already know!" Mitchell sneers. "The chief of fucking police is the same dude you eat Sunday dinner with, stupid. He knows!"

"And he won't press charges if I don't ask for them. He knows Marcus, too." I bring my hand up and gently probe my swollen jaw. "That's his foster brother, Mitch. He knows Marcus just as well as I do."

"Which means he knows he has a fuckin' danger on his streets. What happens next time someone pisses Marcus off, and a world champ fighter isn't there to pull him away?"

"Dude…"

"He would have killed you," he grits. "He wasn't thinking with his brain in that moment, Luc. He was just… doing. He couldn't control it. So what happens next time his temper is triggered, and he can't switch it off?? Do you wanna explain to that person's family you could have prevented someone's death, but you didn't, because you wanna protect your friend?"

"The only person on this planet at risk of a beat down from him is me." I run the pads of my fingers over my cheekbone, examining my damn self, since Mitch is more concerned with arguing than he is with his off-the-books patient. "His only trigger is Kari. He's not a risk to anyone else, so calm the fuck down and stop talking." I massage my temple. "You're hurting my head."

"You probably have a concussion, stupid. You'll go to sleep in a few hours and never wake up again." He claps my shoulder and grumbles when a long hiss ricochets along my throat. "Once you die, the cops will pursue charges. And I guess I'll have to get used to having a new partner on the bus with me. Which fuckin' sucks, by the way. It took me easily ten years to get used to the way you hum along to the radio."

"You're so fucking dramatic." I slump, too tired to sit up straight, but I reach across and grab Kari's shirt. "You need to chill out, Bear. It's gonna be okay."

"It's not gonna be okay!" Her eyes spill over, drenching her cheeks and dribbling off the ledge of her jaw. "He hates us, Luc. He's pissed at me for lying. And he's gonna try to hurt you again. Every single time you're in the same room, he's gonna hurt you, because we snuck around and broke his heart."

"I have strong bones." I hook my hand in the back of her hair, twisting until her tears stop and her eyes widen, then I pull her back and lie down so we land together, her head resting on my tender shoulder. Instantly, like she knows how she fits, her thigh comes up to rest on mine and her arm slings across to cover my throbbing ribs. "Give me today to rest. Give him today to cool down. He can go back to Meg, and she'll talk him off the ledge, then tomorrow, we'll figure it out."

"Next week," Mitchell snarls. "Tomorrow, you're gonna hurt even more than you're hurting today. Next week, you'll probably stop pissing blood."

"Is that your professional medical opinion?" I close my eyes—I would roll them if I had the energy—and slide my fingertips over the ball of Kari's shoulder. "Everything's gonna be fine."

"You promise?" Kari's voice trembles, her heart tumbling down, down, down into the pits of despair. "Do you swear, Luca? You'll make it right between you and my brother?"

"I swear on everything we are. You're my forever, Bear, and he's my best friend. Beneath his rage is just a terrified man who wants to protect you." I turn my face and drop a kiss on her brow. "We have that in common."

"**W**as it better the next week?" Kane leans against the wall and folds his arms. But he looks down at Marcus and Billy and grins. "Was it all over after a good heart to heart sesh with your bestie?"

Marc chuckles, shaking his head and staring down at Billy's pert nose. "Took about six more months, a lot of bitching and awkward family get-togethers, then almost losing my baby." He glances up and swallows, his Adam's apple bobbing with the action. "I felt, amidst my grief, that Luc was part of the reason I was losing my son, too. In my eyes, he was the reason my whole fucking life sucked."

"Mostly, I was just trying to do the right thing," I murmur. "I was standing in the middle of a whole bunch of people I loved, and all of those people had a different idea of what the world should look like. If I chose Meg or Kari, then I was hurting Marcus. If I chose Marcus, then I was neglecting the woman I loved, and I would have been on the wrong side of right and wrong."

"He was breaking my heart, every single day for most of a year."

"And then?"

Marc snorts, slipping his finger into Billy's hand and smiling when she closes her fist around the digit. "Then, Meg was nine months pregnant, and I thought I was gonna lose her, too. Luc and I did what Luc and I had grown used to doing—we were arguing over Kari. Months had passed since that day inside the apartment, and she was still with him. I was bleeding and hurting because I'd made it an ultimatum: him or me. And as far as my brain stretched, the fact that she didn't dump him, meant she chose him. I know differently now," he amends, leaning in and kissing Billy's forehead. "I get it all now, but back then, we were all hurting. So Luc and I were bickering, like always, and Kari was putting herself between us. Telling us to knock it off."

"Next thing we know, Meg is in labor," I finish. "She's laid out on the garage floor, screaming for help, and so fucking sure she was gonna die. And Kari and I were... well..."

"A paramedic and a nurse," Kane nods, firming his lips in thought. "Handy."

"So we're calling for an ambulance, and I'm shouting at her *not* to push. Filthy garage floor. Loads of nasty germs. Keep it in and just wait things out. But of course—"

"Babies are gonna come whenever they're gonna come. And my son..." Marc chuckles. "He's made a name for himself of moving at whatever the fuck speed *he* wants to move at. Fast or slow, he sets the pace, and the rest of us are scrambling behind to make sure he survives his latest crazy shit."

"Either way," I shrug, a small smile rolling across my lips when Marcus looks over, "Meg was screaming, and his baby was crowning. Marcus was still pretty fucking pissed at me, and then I was gonna have to ask his girl to take down her pants in front of me."

Kane snickers, his shoulders bouncing as he looks at Marcus. "Salt in a wound."

"He didn't make it weird though." Grumbling, Marcus rocks the baby. It's unnecessary. She might be *the most* content infant I've ever known. But it's what adults do: they rock the baby. It's self-soothing just as much, if not more, than it's infant-soothing. "The baby was coming faster than the ambulance, and I had a paramedic and a nurse right there. So..." He shrugs. "I let him do his thing."

"He said if I delivered and kept mom and baby safe, he would forgive me forever. It was a deal made during crisis," I smirk, "and such deals probably shouldn't be enforced—"

"Hell they shouldn't," Kane declares. "That's the point of striking while the iron is hot."

"I genuinely thought I was gonna lose them both," Marcus adds. "I kept telling Meg she would be fine, but in the back of my panicked mind, I thought that was it for me. The culmination of the worst year of my life, and I was about to lose the woman I loved, *and* my baby."

"He swore forgiveness if I helped him," I finish. "Which worked for me. I was gonna help no matter what, but he made the deal, and I had a chance to get my family back together. So I accepted the terms, kept Meg breathing, delivered Marcus' son, and then I made damn sure he kept his side of the bargain."

"Then I asked him to be godfather to my child," Marcus sighs, gazing down at my daughter much the same way he gazed down at his son years ago. "I told him I'd be cool with him and my sister, since he'd proven he did, in fact, love her. It wasn't a one-night thing. It was forever. So I said fine.

Everything would be cool between us, so long as he and Kari never, ever, *ever* kissed in front of me or made things weird."

Grinning, Kane glances over to me. "You sucked her tongue into the back of your throat right then and there, didn't you?"

Marcus' nose and lips wrinkle with disgust.

But I laugh and shake my head. "No, though at this point in the story, we were at the hospital, formally meeting Chance *Luca* Macchio and hearing about the godparent stuff. Kari was feeling sassy after months and months of family drama, so I guess she was going all in. She sat on my lap and kissed me, and though Marc was grinding away at the enamel on his teeth, she was done dealing with the bullshit. We were together and we weren't hiding anymore."

Kane presses a hand to his chest and mocks, "The greatest love story of all time."

"Shut up, Bish." I roll my eyes and push away from the wall. We're just three grown ass men, loitering at the top of a staircase when there are better, comfier places in the house to be. So I move past Kane and head onto the stairs. "It was *our* love story. And even with all the shit we had to go through, even after all the years where we couldn't be together, it was the greatest love story I would ever know. She was my forever, and I wasn't stepping aside or quitting her for anyone."

"Which just so happens to be okay with me." Marcus follows me down. "Once I moved past the anger, I was okay with how things had turned out. Because if a dude *must* see his sister with a man, then I suppose that man being his best friend is a decent solution. Twenty years of character assessments. Loyalty. Kindness. Honesty. There are absolute fucking monsters out there, preying on women with the sole intention to isolate her away from her family and fuck shit up."

"Like with Laine," Kane snarls. "That prick who fucked her up."

I drop my chin in acknowledgement and turn off the stairs and head toward the kitchen. "Like Laine. But we dealt with him and got her out of that situation."

"Who dealt with him?" Kane speeds his steps, brushing past a lazier, slower Marcus, and grabs my shoulder, spinning me back until we're eye to eye. He stares into my fucking soul and rumbles, "What did you do about Graham?"

I flash a pleased smile and keep walking. "Nothing." *Everything.* "I was just there for my sister as much as I could be. As much as she would allow. Though mostly you and Jess owned all that real estate."

"The twink needed her sister," he grumbles. "And I wasn't going anywhere without Jess. So..."

"And then Ang made his move. Now both of my sisters are hitched and safe. Babies are dropping all across town—Chance, the twins, Laine's baby, Jay and Soph's. Spence and Abby, Cap and Katrina. Everyone has made babies in the last ten years, while Kari and I were a little slower off the mark."

"Probably lingering trauma," Kane snickers. "Kiss the girl, and Marcus belts you black and blue. Make a baby with her..."

"And we're hit by a fucking drunk." I come to a stop in the middle of the kitchen, turning with fresh grief pulsing in my heart. We were joking. Having fun. Reminiscing. And now reality has come crashing down over my head once more. Just another fucking reminder that me and Kari... we have to work for us. All those years of lost time. Then all the years of hiding. Then losing Marc. And now, losing everything.

The universe refuses to give us a clear run. And that... that's not fair.

"I hurt Graham," I admit on an almost whisper, "for what he did to my sister. And I'll hurt that drunk for what he did to my family. Later, when I have time to think and to plan it out. I'm gonna take care of business."

Kane balls his fist and extends it in offer. "Welcome aboard, son. Uncle Kane will be glad to walk alongside you when you're getting shit done."

I look down at his fist, hovering in the air between us, and think of a man who came before the prick in the pickup truck. I think of the life I've lived and the pain I'm forced to feel because of someone else's poor choices. Billy shouldn't be here without her mom and brother, and I sure as fuck shouldn't have had to leave the hospital without the other half of my family.

Resolute, I swallow and tap his fist with mine. "When I have time."

He sets his hands on his hips and chuckles. "Some things are worth making time for. But I'll be patient. So you were openly banging your girl after that other baby was born? Public exhibitionism and shit?"

"Dude!" Marcus shoulder checks Kane and passes through to me. "No."

Fuck me. But Marc is a brave man for hitting a Bishop and giving him his back. But that's who he is, I suppose. Way too fucking reactive when it comes to his baby sister. I tilt to the right and stop on Kane's eyes, damn near midnight black with revenge. "Down, boy. You just heard how I nearly died because of his reactivity as far as Kari was concerned."

"He's lucky he's holding a baby." He backs up to lean against the door-frame, smirking and folding his arms as Jess wanders through with one of the girls. "Men have died for less." He looks at me. "So you and Kari are together. It's open. Big brother Marcus is accepting... grudgingly, but it's happening. Now he has a new baby to obsess over."

"Timing was serendipitous," I chuckle. "He was focused on Meg and Chance, and so Kari and I had a free run for the next little while. From that point on, we could be completely and totally open about who we were. Seems dumb," I clarify. "But walking into the diner and sitting together, holding hands, even kissing... all in public. It was a new experience for us."

"No, it's not dumb." Kane's eyes follow Jess as she stops by the fridge and helps herself. His lips curl into a small, secretive smile. "We had to hide at first, too. So I get it. Having that freedom to be open with the world about who we are..." he shrugs and brings his eyes back to me. "It feels good."

38

LUC

NOT SNEAKING AROUND

At some point over the last couple of years, after Jess moved out to live with Kane, Laine moved out to live with Ang, and when Britt shacked up across town with the world champ, Kari's apartment was essentially left mostly empty.

The rent was still paid, and the sparse furniture remained behind.

The place was, technically, somewhere any of the girls could go to get a little alone time when they needed it, but as the years passed on and memories fill the rooms they left behind, everyone just… stopped going there.

It simply stopped being somewhere anyone went to find comfort.

Now Kari's things are in my apartment. Her clothes are in my closet. Her shoes, littering my floor. Her dream catcher, the one she hangs above her bed, now hangs above *our* bed. And if I'm being completely and totally honest, I'm not sure I could even pinpoint when exactly we started living together.

It was never a discussion we had. We never sat down and decided where we would live or who would pay which bill. No one wrote out a chore chart, assigning dishes to one person and the laundry to the other.

We just stopped sleeping apart. And now here we are, her tampons are under the sink, and her hair litters the shower floor.

And there's not a single fucking thing I would do to change it.

"Let's go, Bear!" I button my shirt and stare into the mirror, a grin on my face and trembling giddiness bubbling in the depths of my stomach. "Swear to Christ, if you make us late again, I'm gonna be pissed."

"I'm doing my best." She slides along the hall and collides with the clothes rack at the end, sending hangers flying, and grunting as the metal pokes her arm. This apartment is tiny. Smaller, even, than the one she left. Which means our closet just isn't big enough for us both. "Ouch." Hissing, she rubs her arm and scowls under the mess that is her wild, brown curls. "Have I told you lately how much I *hate* that thing being there?"

I shrug and watch her in the reflection of the mirror. "There's not enough room to put it elsewhere. Let's go. We have reservations for seven. And it's currently..." I glance across at the clock on the over-filled bedside table. We're not messy, dirty people. We're just two busy human beings, cramming two lives inside an apartment the size of a shoe box. "Six fifty-nine. Dammit, Bear!"

"Don't come at me." She tears a dress off the rack, pinging yet another hanger to the floor. Then, stepping into the fabric, she yanks it up and tucks herself away from my hungry eyes. "You didn't get out of the shower until five minutes ago. The fact that I can shower after that and still be mostly dressed by now is a miracle. You don't get that kind of hustle with Jess and Laine."

"Yes, but I'm not in a relationship with Jess and Laine." I turn from the mirror and walk the five steps from one side of the room to the other. Then I spin her around and grin when her hands come up automatically to push her hair out of the way. I grab the zipper of her dress and gently bring it up. "I'm in a relationship with you. And you, my beautiful little pain in my ass, are gonna be the reason we're fuckin' late. Again."

"Oh please." She peeks over her shoulder, eyes narrowed in dangerous slits. "You make it sound like I'm *one of those girls* who can't get their shit together. I've been late once in my life, and you think you get to make it my whole personality."

"Says the chick whose alarm clock now reads seven." I release her zipper and slap her ass, forcing her forward with a squeak and a growl. "Shoes on. If we're not sitting at our table by seven fifteen, we lose it. Then we'll have to get burgers and eat in the car."

"Which is a perfectly valid date, just so you know." She wanders all three feet to the bed and sits down with a grunt. Then opening her legs, she drags the blankets up and searches for her shoes beneath the bed frame.

We're classy like that.

"Heels?" she ponders. "Flats?"

"You can go barefoot for all I care." I drop down on the bed beside her and snag my boots from beneath the bed. "But you have thirty seconds to get your ass out the door before I smack it."

"If we didn't have so much shit scattered across six hundred square feet, maybe I could find a hairbrush easier. Or shoes. Or a whole outfit. Or!" She decides on a pair of pumps and slips her feet inside. "If your shower was larger than a port-a-potty, maybe we could shower together. Save time and money."

"You mention saving money, but you ask for a luxury bathroom big enough to fuck in." I grab her face and smack a noisy kiss to her lips. "You're high maintenance and needy."

"And you're an asshole." She shoves me off and pushes up from the bed, then she snags her phone and a tiny purse from the top of our drawers. "You're being a jerk. In fact, you've been a jerk for the last few weeks." She stalks through the door and makes a beeline for the living room. "Stress is a cute excuse, Lenaghan, but we both work demanding jobs. You only get that pass for so long."

I follow her out and head to the front door, holding it wide so she can move through. "Or maybe you're being overly sensitive and critical?"

She swings around with no care for the fact that she could overbalance and topple down the stairs. No care because she intends to tear my heart out and stab it with the heel of her shoe. "Excuse me? Overly sensitive?"

"What?" I slide my arm around hers and lead her downstairs. A fight is a fight, and that's all good and well, but we've got somewhere to be. So we'll call this a *drive-thru domestic*. "We've been together a while now, Bear. So I know when you cycle."

"Cycle?" Her eyes widen, feral and ready to rumble. "Did you slip in the shower and hit your head? What the hell, Luc?"

"What?" I move to the car—it's safer than a bike, *allegedly*—and open the door. Then I practically toss her in and skip around to my side. "Women cycle, babe. It's okay. It's completely normal."

"And sane, smart men know not to blame natural monthly cycles for how women express their feelings. I mentioned our small apartment, and now, according to you, I'm hormonal?"

"*You* mentioned hormones, not me." I fix my seatbelt and kiss the tips of my fingers. Before she has a chance to argue, I slap them to her lips and clamp down on my own when she growls. "Love you, Care Bear. All the way to the stars."

"Let me out!" She makes a grab for her door, but I switch the car on and slam it into reverse before she gets the chance. Then speeding onto the street, I chuckle, almost completely silently, and reach across one-handed to snag her seatbelt and buckle it up.

"Luca!"

"You're so pretty."

"You're a jackass! What the hell changed between, *'I'm going to have a shower; we have a date,'* and this?"

"You changed." I slow at the end of the block, glancing to my right so I catch her fiery eyes. But I only smile and continue around the corner. "You shouted from the shower because you hit your elbow."

Scowling, she cups her elbow in her palm and rubs. "It hurt."

"The shower has been the same size since its date inside a manufacturing warehouse. Nothing changed, Bear. Except you became less tolerant of the small space we have."

"So instead of agreeing with me, you thought picking a fight and invalidating my feelings was the smarter choice?"

"I think being with you every single day is all I need to be happy." I take her hand, prying her fingers apart and sliding mine between instead. "I don't care that my back rests against the wall when we're in bed. And I don't care that my elbows hit the taps in the shower. I don't care that your hair tangles in my toes because you don't clean it out of the drain. And I sure as fuck don't care that we keep clothes on a rack in the hallway."

Her entire face wrinkles. Her chin, nose, lips, and brow. Like a little kid who was told 'no' to dessert, she scowls and says nothing.

"I care that I wake up beside you." I bring her hand to my lips and kiss the top. "I care that I get to have you, openly and for the world to know. I care that that douchebag Roy at the hospital is afraid of me, so he doesn't openly flirt with you anymore."

She coughs out a small, almost silent giggle.

"I care that you want to be with me. And that, even though we live together and practically work together, you still say yes when I ask you out to dinner."

She firms her lips and scowls deeper. "You're being romantic and sweet when I thought we were having a fight."

"Hormonal cycles. It happens."

She swings her hand out of my grip and slaps my stomach until my lungs evacuate and the car swerves. "Bear!"

"Don't mention hormonal cycles if you wish to live, jackass. I'm allowed to have feelings about things and them *not* be because of the time of the month."

"Are you sure, though?" I snag her hand and force her to hold mine. "Because I'm noticing a certain pattern, that's all."

"Where are we going?" She squeezes my hand and growls when I turn another corner and snicker. "Pinocchio's Restaurant is the other way, dummy. And we're already hitting ten past seven. We don't have time to—"

Her words come to a sharp stop as I bring us over the train tracks and out to the edges of town. I turn into an overgrown driveway, amidst tall trees and a raggedy For Sale sign with a shiny new SOLD sticker slapped across the realtor's face. Then she spins, her eyes alight and her cheeks bright red. "Luc!"

"What?" Parking the car and cutting the engine, I lean over and unsnap her seatbelt. "You were saying some shit about needing extra space?"

"Luc!" She pushes out of the car when I pull back and do the same, slamming the door and stepping back to study the sign out front. "Are you serious right now?"

"What?" I wander her way and take her hand in mine. Then I reach into my pocket with the other, drawing out an extra set of keys from the depths. "Why are you *still* shouting at me?"

"Did you buy a house?" Her voice breaks. It literally crackles and squeaks as we meander across gravel and an overgrown front yard. This place has been deserted for too many years. Renters lived here before, and the landlords lived here before that. This place belonged to a couple who are damn near a hundred at this point.

Now... it belongs to us.

"You can't buy a whole house without talking to me about it!"

"Can't I?" I draw her up the stairs and stop by the rickety wooden door. The sun is still out despite the hour, summer holding on once more, but inside the house, darkness prevails. I'd know—I've been here each night for a fucking week, sneaking around, preparing, and probably, now that I think about it, planting the seeds of the fight Kari thought we were gonna have tonight. "Do you tell me when I can or can't buy a burger for lunch?"

She growls again. "Don't be ridiculous. I'm not controlling your money."

"And you don't tell me when I can buy shoes, or jeans, or hell, a new guitar."

"Trick question. You never buy jeans or shoes. I buy them for you. And you have seven trillion guitars already, which is ironic considering you prefer the drums."

"Drums are for playing in the band. Guitars are for sitting on the couch and writing songs about you. Come on." I slide the key into the door and turn the lock, then I push it open and reveal... well, not a lot of anything. Dirty floors. Dusty walls. A staircase straight out of a really rich mother-fucker's house. And massive picture windows that'll someday, after a bunch of cleaning, become the focal point of our forever home. "Buying homes," I finish with a grin, "is for proving to you that we're forever."

"You bought a whole friggin' house!" With tears in her eyes, she charges ahead of me, stalking across hardwood floors so her heels clip-clip-clip and echo from wall to wall. "Luca! It's a house. For us?"

"It'll take a few months to fix," I admit. "Bunches of hard work. The upstairs bedrooms have carpet we'll have to pull out eventually. And there are a few walls with body-shaped holes in them."

"Oh god." Snickering, she turns and starts toward the kitchen. "I don't even want to speculate about those holes."

"The kitchen is original." I follow her through the house and stop in the doorway to lean against the frame. "Like, Scottish Highlands original. So good luck with that when you're relegated to housewife duties and I'm too busy to help."

She snorts and runs her fingertips along the laminate countertop. "Jackass."

"But Marc said he'll help."

Stunned, she yanks her hand away like she thinks the laminate will bite, then she looks at me with wide eyes. "Marcus?"

"Yeah. I mean..." I fold my arms and shrug. "He inspected the place with me a couple of times. We walked through and drew up some floor plans."

"Marcus?" she breathes. "My brother?"

"He wants to be in charge of refinishing the stairs. In fact, his exact words were, *'if you touch these fucking stairs and ruin them for me, I'm gonna slit your intestines out and feed them to the cow.'* Which is such a random and inaccurate threat, considering cows are herbivores. But when I went ahead and pointed that out, he assured me he would buy pigs if he must."

"You talked to Marcus about this place?" Her eyes dance with unshed tears. Just like I knew they would. "He knows?"

"He gave his blessing. He likes homes with good bones, and he thinks this one is gonna be good for another two hundred years. According to him, it's safe enough and, once we patch those holes in the walls, classy enough, for his baby sister."

"You asked my brother if you could buy a house with me?"

I lift a single, nonchalant shoulder. "I'm buying it *for* you. Not with you."

"But I—"

"A symbol of my love for you." I move away from the door frame and across the kitchen, taking her shaking hand and tugging her in till her body melts against mine. "I'm not here for a good time, Bear. I'm here for a lifetime."

"Luc..."

"Come upstairs. I have some stuff I wanna show you."

"Marc's not here, like..." She gulps and looks around. "He's not here right now, is he?"

I bark out a laugh and lead her back the way we came. "Fuck no. I love the dude, but I'm not in a relationship with him. He doesn't need to be a part of everything we do."

"And he just..." Her head swivels around as though on a stick. She notices the stair treads. The sconces on the walls. The light fixture. The yellowing wallpaper in some sections. "He knows buying a house with me, or for me, is officially, like... moving in with me?"

"We've been sharing a bed for years already."

"Right. But that was an informal arrangement. No one discussed it, and no one labeled it. Buying a house... that's..." she exhales a noisy breath. "That's super official. And he was cool with it?"

"You are damn near thirty years old." Chuckling, I crest the top step and hold her hand to bring her up beside me. Our future bedroom is to the left, and our child's future nursery is to the right. It's so easy to see. So easy to plan a lifetime ahead with the woman who simply makes life worth living.

"You realize he doesn't get to boss you around anymore, right?" I tug her around and press a smiling kiss to her lips. "He's married and a dad now. He's busy with the farm and the cow and the life he's living where he's not controlling your every move."

"You say that, and yet, you sought his opinion on the house." She drags her bottom lip between her teeth and studies my eyes. "Admit it, Luc, his word still matters."

"It matters to me because it matters to you." I kiss her again and savor, tugging her bottom lip from her worrying teeth. "Anything important to you is important to me."

"I can't believe how utterly annoying you are. Picking fights and poking me into an argument just for fun. Then you bring me here and remind me exactly how romantic and sweet you are."

"What can I say?" I slide my hand up and stroke the long column of her neck. "I enjoy seeing you get angry. Turns me on."

"And then you go ahead and ruin a moment by saying shit like that." Laughing, she turns on her heels and starts toward the main bedroom door.

So I let her go. I allow her to explore.

Then I hold my breath and wait as she opens the door. Startling with a cry when she finds the ceiling aglow with fairy lights. A thousand tiny bulbs strung up to create the illusion of a night sky.

Tulips fill a hundred vases, creating a rainbow of colors and a smell almost as sweet as the woman who stumbles into the room with her hands over her mouth.

I follow her to the doorway, my eyes on her back while hers are everywhere, all at once. She spies the picture window, filled to the brim with out-of-season flowers that Mitch's florist sister helped me procure. A massive, brand-new bed sits in the middle, overflowing with luxurious blankets and cloud-like pillows.

While the rest of the house is in complete disrepair, this room has been refinished already. New walls. Plaster. Paint. The carpet was pulled up in the moments I could steal away from Kari's notice, and the brand-new bed was delivered just this morning.

Because fuck it, we deserve the best.

And we'll hand wash our dishes for the next few years, since we can't afford a dishwasher.

"Luc…" Her voice cracks, emotion clogging in her throat and drawing tears to her eyes. But she runs her fingertips along the sheets I've already made the bed with. The blanket rolled to the end of the mattress. The tulips laid on top, just two of them, waiting for her.

Then she glances at the bookshelf Marcus built for her by hand.

"Oh my gosh." Her entire body trembles, her dress moving because of it. "Luc, I don't…"

She turns my way, so I lower to one knee and dig a hand into my pocket for the ring I've held on to for… fuck. A long time.

"Oh my gosh!" she repeats, though this time, it comes on a cry of surprise. "Luc!"

"I'm only gonna say his name once, since this is *our* moment, and I don't wanna think about him too much."

Her eyes spill over as she moves closer.

"I asked Marcus for his blessing in this, too. So now that's out of the way, I don't want you to bring him back into this conversation."

She chokes out a teary laugh and nods. "Okay."

"I've thought about everything we are, Bear." I bring the ring up, pinching it between my fingers and staring past the diamond into her eyes. *So much prettier.* "I've thought about who we were way back when we met, and then who we became over the years that followed." I drop my gaze for a beat and chuckle. "I've reflected on who I was in high school. And who you were. The demons you fought and the secrets you kept, all to save everyone else from pain."

Swallowing, I reach out and take her hand. Her entire arm, shaking. Her fingers, quivering. But I don't slide the ring on. "I look at who we are now, and I know that there is nothing in the world I can't live without... Except you."

Tears track over her cheeks and dangle from the edge of her jaw.

"I could live in a tiny apartment for the rest of my life, so long as you're in it with me. I could live here in this giant house with holes in the walls, but only if I have you. I've come to the conclusion that it doesn't matter where I am, Bear. Nothing matters to me, except that I have you. That's why I couldn't move on when we were younger, and it's why I couldn't choose the brotherhood I had with Marcus over you."

"I thought we weren't bringing him back into this?" she snickers. It's snotty and tear-filled, which is honestly so fucking cute, I wanna puke. "*You* did that."

"Shush." I tug her closer and stop only when her leg touches my knee. "I can't choose anything else over you. I've tried," I groan. "I swear, I've tried. But there's no me without you, Kari. And so, if you say no, then there's no life for me beyond you."

"Emotional manipulation?" she giggles. "That's where we're taking this?"

"You're being an argumentative pain in my ass." But hell if my eyes don't itch. My heart thunders out of control, and yet, there isn't a single shred of doubt in my soul. "I'm telling you that we don't exist outside of us. We're two halves of one whole, Bear. It's always been that way for us, which is why we're so fucking willing to set the world on fire for each other. We don't mean to harm anyone else. But we..." I shake my head. "We belong together. There are no other options."

"Yes."

"Hush. Don't interrupt my proposal."

"But I'm already saying yes."

"Shush!" I drag her closer, not a single shred of guilt in my heart when I force her to kneel, too. "I will prove to you, every day for the rest of my life, that being my wife is the right choice."

"I already said yes."

"I want to marry you, Kari. I want to spend my life coming home to you. I want to see you at work, and I fucking thrill watching you do it."

"Did you hear my yes?"

"I want to have a giant, stupid, romantic wedding, where you walk the aisle in front of everyone we know and love, and I want you to kiss me in a church until God blushes. I want to swear my life to you in front of our friends and family. I want your brother to see me—"

"*You* brought him up again. And I already said yes."

"Shut up!" I grab her lips and pinch them shut. But her chest still bounces with laughter. Her eyes, spill over with tears. "I want to make babies with you, Kari. I want to make a whole fucking family tree with you, starting in this house and enduring into forever. And so..."

Releasing her face, I guide her up again, helping her to her feet and grinning when she looks down over me.

"If you would say yes, Bear. If you would promise to love me forever, then I swear to cherish every single moment we have. I promise to come home to you, every single night. To make you happy, and to bake those chocolate lava cakes you love so much. I promise to kiss you so often, Marcus will want to stab me."

"That's four."

"I want you to be Mrs. Lenaghan. And when the time comes, I want you to be the mother of my babies. But more than anything else, I want you to be happy. With me."

"Yes." She slides her finger closer, hooking it in the ring I hold and pausing only when it grows tighter at her knuckle. "I choose you, Luc. Even when you pick fights with me for the sake of fighting."

I chuckle. Or at least, I think I do. I try to. My heart pounds so heavy, I'm not sure what the fuck I'm doing.

"I choose you, even when you annoy me," she tremors. "Especially because you do it so well."

"Decades of practice." Slowly, I slide the ring to the base of her finger. "It took us till now to make sure I'd perfected it."

"I choose you." She lowers into a crouch, pushing me back until I drop to my ass, then she straddles my lap and presses her knees to the floor. "And you choose me," she whispers. Settling over my cock, she smiles and looks down into my eyes, like the fucking vixen she is as her hair drapes around us like a curtain. "You created a room for us where I get to sleep under the stars every single night."

"And tulips," I add. "Even though they're out of season."

"And books." She looks at her sparkling ring and beams. "I see the books. And the chocolate. You remembered a conversation we had a lifetime ago, and you made it happen here, tonight, in the forever home you bought for me."

"You deserve all the stars." I cup the side of her neck. "You especially deserve a man who listens when you list off all your favorite things."

"Even though that night was the beginning of six years apart?"

"Most painful years of my life." I pull her closer and stop only when our lips are a hair's breadth apart. "Six really fucking lonely years where my brain reminded me, over and over and over again, the things that would make you happy. I locked that list down and burned it to the back of my consciousness so I would never forget. Because on the off chance you came back to me, I wanted to know how to be the man you deserve."

"I love you so much." She dives in and takes my lips with hers. They're wet from her tears. Trembling for the same reason. But she grinds down over my cock and turns a sweet moment into something else entirely. "I love you, Luca. I always loved you, which is why it all hurt so friggin' much when we weren't together."

"Never again." I pull her bottom lip between my teeth and glance across to the bed I made up for us already. "Wanna get up off the damn floor yet?"

She barks out an evil, seductress laugh that has my blood running warmer and adrenaline skittering in my veins. "We could spend time right here on the floor. Then we can go over there and try it again. Then we can try out the kitchen. And the hallway. And the bathroom since we have forever."

39

LUC

FOREVER ISN'T SUPPOSED TO HAVE AN EXPIRATION DATE

"I know you're gonna stop that story right there," Marcus snarls. He cradles Billy against his chest and breathes like a wounded bull. "I don't wanna hear what happened next."

"Fuck off, farmer." Kane turns and glowers at my best friend. "*I* want to know what happens next."

Frustrated, Marcus widens his eyes and looks at me. So I chuckle, though the sound is less *real* now that we're getting to this part of our life. That time we swore forever. That night we promised to never be apart again.

It's hardly even clever irony that I'm here in that house now. With Billy. With the guys. But without my son, and without the one person on this planet I *need* to exist.

"She promised to never leave," I rasp out, ignoring Kane and Marcus' issues and turning toward my kitchen instead. My voice turns thick with dread. The pain in my heart, seemingly heavier today than it was yesterday. "We made promises inside this home. To always be here together. And now I have to go back to the hospital and I..." I look at Jess, who lingers, wringing her hands together. "It wasn't supposed to happen like this."

"We just have to give it time," she whispers. Her voice breaks, aching and sad as she swallows. "I just..." she shrugs. "We have to be patient."

"Tell us about the wedding," Kane rumbles. "That's the next step, right? Tell us that stuff."

"You were there." I chew on the inside of my cheek and spin to go to the fridge. Anything to avoid looking into their eyes right now. "All of you were there that day. So I don't need—"

"Tell it to us anyway," Jess inserts. "We only saw what we saw. The gown. The church. The *I dos*. But we weren't in your head. We weren't in the moments between you and her."

"Probably best," Marcus grumbles. "Some things are best left private."

"Can you do me a favor, Marcus?" Swallowing, I grab a can of soda from the fridge and turn back to search his eyes. "Can you take Billy up and get her ready to go see her mommy?" I look down at the onesie I had dressed her in. Plain and practical. Zippers instead of press studs to make a diaper change easier. But Kari deserves better. She deserves the frilly, pretty-in-pink doll she always dreamed about through eight hard months of pregnancy. "Put her in a dress or something. A bow on her head. Make a whole thing of it."

"Sure." He frowns and remains still. Hesitant. But he angles back toward the hall. "I'll…" Then he nods. "Sure. Okay. You alright?"

"Yeah. I just figure it's an important day for us all. So get her in a dress or something. Kari picked out a million of them before the babies arrived, so I thought—"

"I got it." He rocks Billy, though she's already asleep, and turns on his heels cautiously. "I'll just be upstairs, alright? I won't be long."

I take my drink to the table and pull out a chair to sit down. Then I look at Jess and nod at Marcus' back. "Wanna help him? You have practice dressing girls."

"Sure." She comes around behind me and wraps her arm across my chest. Resting her cheek on mine—it's a hug, but also, a chance to communicate with her husband whose eyes narrow—then she plops a kiss on my cheek and pulls away. "I'll be back soon. Promise."

Nerves swarm the church, palpable as though they're actual waves in the air we can all see and feel. My stomach bounces with anxious energy and my heart thunders as the clock ticks closer to two and still, the girls aren't here.

Marcus stands on my left, and beside him, Angelo, Scotch, and then

Kane. The other side of our platform, where bridesmaids should stand, is empty. Jess, Laine, and Britt, are off somewhere else, fucking around and becoming a direct threat to my mental well-being.

Sammy sits in the front row, holding the sweet girl she and Scotch adopted. And beside her, Jules cradles her and Alex's daughter. Kane and Jess made daughters. Jay and Soph: daughters. Ang and Laine: a daughter. Seems our town has had a baby boom of the female variety. Except Marcus and the little baby boy I helped deliver. And Britt and Jack, who went ahead and made sons too. Loads of them. Big, strong, black-haired future fighters who came into this world with Brittany friggin' Turner and Jack 'The Jack-hammer' Reilly as their parents. It's a potent mix, really. Boisterous and dangerous. And still, Britt shows no signs of slowing.

"Why are they taking so long?" I look at Marcus, my jaw clenching as anxiety grows too strong in my blood and my palms turn sweaty. "She's not like my sisters, Marc. She's not the diva who wants a grand entrance."

"No," he smirks, "but she's *with* your sisters. So even if she was ready early and wanted to get in the car, what do you reckon the twins said about that?"

"Stop talking shit about my wife," Kane grumbles. "I can hear you moth-erfuckers."

"Don't say motherfucker in church," Ang snarls, pressing his arm to Kane's chest and nudging him back. "Be better, Bish."

"They're fine," Marcus rumbles. We have an entire church filled to the brim, hundreds of people watching us. Waiting. Bored, because the bride isn't here yet. So we're forced to keep our words low. Our lips, barely moving. "Meg is planning this thing, and she's with the girls. She already texted me that everything is fine."

"*Everything?*" Ang questions. "Laine is good?"

"Last I heard, they all did a shot of tequila to calm their nerves."

"Fuck." Me, Ang, and Kane all drop back onto our heels. Because tequila means trouble. And trouble on my wedding day... I look at Scotch and scowl. "This is gonna be like that time you got your new nickname, dickhead."

"Me?" He grabs the lapels of his suit and chuckles. "What the hell did I do?"

"Don't say hell in church," Kane growls. "Have some class, man."

"*I'm* right here," Scotch presses on. "Sammy's over there." He lifts his chin in her direction. "We have nothing to do with this mess."

"Your sister is the ringleader of messy," I snap. "Britt is the bad influence and you know it."

"Says Queen Messy himself," Jack rumbles from his seat. "My wife is an angel. So you better mind your manners, Luca. Besides, everyone knows the Lenaghan twins are the fuckin' issue."

"Don't say fuck in church!" Kit—his older sister—slaps his chest. "Dammit, Jack."

"I'm hearing a lot of negativity rolling around about my wife," Kane sneers. "I'm obligated, as her man, to throw hands on her behalf." He looks at Jack and raises a brow. "I can fight, bro. Don't test me."

"You gonna bring a gun to a fistfight?" Jack chuckles. "Or will you roll like a man?"

"Define *like a man*." Kane steps off our platform and casually fixes his tie. "You say fighting with your fists is noble. I say ending a fight with expediency is smart."

"We could give it a try," Jack taunts. So fucking casual, tucked up beside his big sister. He's a grown ass man, married to Britt, and a world champ a few times over. But he smiles now because he has two fighter women sitting on each side of his chair. His sister. And his sister-in-law. Both know how to choke a dude out without breaking a nail. "You know where my gym is. I'll have security let you pass."

"Security," Kane snorts. "Bitch, I am your security."

"Don't say bitch in church!" Kit explodes. "What is wrong with you people?"

"You gotta calm down," her husband sniggers. "You're overreacting a bit, babe."

"Overreacting?" She spins on him, exorcist style. "You think I should calm down, Bobby?"

The organs begin playing, loud enough to drown out Bobby's plea and apology. Then Kane laughs when Jack blows an air kiss. My entire life, everyone I know in it, is fucking crazy. But Kane, at least, backs up to stand in line beside Ang, and the doors at the rear of the church open with a loud creak and heated anticipation.

Sunlight spills in, bathing the wooden floors and illuminating dust that floats in the air. Then a wildly pregnant Britt steps in first, her skin glowing and her smile large enough to almost suggest she, too, was downing tequila shots.

She wasn't, of course. But I have no doubt she was the one who supplied the liquor.

"See?" Marcus rumbles in my ear, grabbing my sleeve and pulling me back so I'm in line once more. I didn't even realize I'd stepped out of it. "They're here."

"And they're not stumbling." I lean to the left and search for the rest of them. Jess. Laine. Most importantly, Kari. But the sunlight is blinding, and Britt is taking up all focus. "Bear's gonna be with them, right? She's not in a separate car?"

"Shush." Jack sneers from the front row. "It's Britt's turn to shine."

"This is *my* wedding! You shush."

Jack only snickers like a kid in a candy store, hopped up on sugar and ready to set shit on fire. "You're super tense, bro. You okay?"

"Shush!" Kit snarls. "Have some respect."

The organs continue to play Pachelbel's Canon in D. The music is slow and sweet, which is the very opposite of everything we, collectively, are. But Britt wears a beaming grin, swaying her hips and radiant in a strapless gown of midnight black that goes all the way to the floor. Her usually straight hair is done half up, half down, with expertly ironed curls that give her extra height. Her lips glisten bright red, and her eyes sparkle a blinding blue. She's stunning in her happiness. Playful in the way she almost dances along the aisle. Then she turns right instead of left, sneaking a kiss with her husband before she goes the way she's supposed to and takes up her position on my right.

Pachelbel continues and Laine steps into the doorway, and right beside her, Jess follows, slipping her arm in our sister's and creating a united front.

They could have walked separately. They could have each had their moment, gliding along the aisle and drawing my torture out as long as possible. But they choose togetherness. Ever since Laine's run in with her ex, they now choose unity.

And for that, I'm both relieved and thankful.

Nothing good ever comes when they're apart.

Kane and Ang practically vibrate. Their eyes hanging out of their heads and their smiles giddy and, frankly, gross. But while the girls walk and the guys ogle, I take a moment to prepare myself. To take a deep breath and fill my lungs. To clear my eyes and firm my jaw.

Because fuck me, it quivers a little bit.

Finally, the twins reach our end of the aisle and go to their men first. Completely against protocol, and yet, there isn't a single part of me that begrudges them for their happiness. They exchange kisses and sweet words, then the girls step away, passing me with smirky grins and trouble in their eyes.

The organs stop, suddenly, shockingly, almost like the power has been cut. But then a recording plays over the speakers instead. The strum of a guitar I would recognize anywhere. The soft melody of a piano. And then Scotch's deep, gritty singer's voice.

They've taken Cyndi Lauper's *Time After Time* and slowed it right down, until emotion clogs in my throat and my heart gives a final, painful splat that could be the end of me if not for the beautiful woman who steps through the doors and glows hotter than the sun itself.

"Oh shit." I press a hand to my thundering heart and groan. "Fuck, Bear."

"Don't say fuck in church," Marc chuckles. Then he claps my shoulder and breaks away from his place on my left. He dashes along the aisle, literally runs, and makes an entire fucking scene I expect to draw a vicious blush to Kari's cheeks. But when he takes her arm in his instead, she just... she allows it.

"We lied to you about a few shifts at work," Scotch murmurs, nudging closer now that Marc is missing. "Kari wanted this song, and she wanted us to play it for her."

I lick my dry lips and watch as the brother-sister duo make their way along the aisle.

"We could have set up our gear and played the set while she walked, but she didn't want you to be alone up here either. She wanted this day to be as special for you as you want it to be for her, so she had us practice this song and record it for today. So we could still be with you, and so Marc could give her away."

"She asked Marc to give her away?" I turn my head, breaking my view of her smiling face for just a beat, and meet Scotch's eyes. "She wanted that?"

"She asked him to give her to you," Ang inserts. "This isn't about ownership or giving her up to any random dude. She wanted him to give her to *you*. No one else will do."

I bring my hand up and wipe it over my mouth, scratching along the stubble I never truly get rid of, and pray I don't cry like a bitch on my wedding day. "Wow. That's..." I draw a heady breath and look back at Kari. Finally, she's close enough I can actually see her eyes. The pink swelling that says she's been crying, and the wide grin that assures me she's okay. "That's a big deal," I finish. "I thought she was gonna walk alone."

"She's a proud woman," Kane finishes. "But she's not so proud as to give all of herself to you."

"Stop talking," Marcus snarls from six feet away. "Focus!"

Kari giggles. It's watery and silly. But it's happy, and that's all I ever ask of her.

To be happy.

"You asked for this song?" I step forward, though I'm not sure I'm supposed to, and extend my hand in expectation. "Bear? You wanted them to play this for us?"

"Because I choose you." She drags her lip between her teeth and releases Marcus' hand. Taking mine instead, she steps in and stops only when her chest touches mine and my free hand comes up to cup her neck. "I will always choose you. Time after time."

"Alright!" Jay Bishop clears his throat and increases the volume of his voice until everyone can hear him. Even the fucking cow sitting out at Marc's house right now. He lifts his arms, like Moses himself parting the red seas, and wears a robe I'm certain he stole from a real priest. Then he looks at me and smirks. "We are all gathered here today to sign some lifetime binding contracts."

40

LUC

THE AFTERPARTY IS ALWAYS WAY MORE FUN THAN THE ACTUAL WEDDING

"We drank one shot!" Jess bellows, sitting on Kane's lap and shooting... well, another shot. "It was to calm her nerves!"

"It made you late," Angelo growls. "A grown man is apt to worry if the people he loves are supposed to be somewhere at a certain time and they're *not*."

"You're insane if you think I didn't have eyes on them," Kane chuckles. "My whole fucking army had them in their sights the whole time."

"We got there at like, ten minutes past," Laine rolls her eyes. "You need to chill. We were safe. *And* the entire police force escorted us from the house to the church steps."

"Did they?" I look across the dining room to Alex, who sits with his wife and daughter and smiles wide while Oz says some shit I guess is funny. "No one mentioned they were gonna do that."

"Because you don't always have to be in charge of everything." Kari grabs my jaw between her fingers, her eyes alight with playfulness and her lipstick none the worse for wear despite the number of times I've attempted to suck it off today. She looks me up and down, challenging as her brow quirks. "You think you're always in control, Luca. Telling me no. Then telling me yes. You think you get to decide when we get together. And then you decided on our house. You decide what side of the bed you get to sleep on."

"I sleep closest to the door! I'm protecting you."

"You think you can choose the movie we watch on Friday nights."

371

"Because you only ever want to watch romcoms from the 90s. Literally, that's it, for the rest of your life. I know them all *word for word* at this point."

"So?" She leans in and rests her forehead on mine. "I like the guarantee of a happy ending. I want my entertainment to be entertaining, not stressful. I don't care for action movies and annoying espionage stuff."

"And as always," I pinch her chin between my fingers, "I oblige you anyway. Despite the fact that I know Hugh Grant's lines better than Hugh Grant knows them himself. Stop whining."

"I chose the songs today," she grins. "And I chose to make you wait ten more minutes. I chose to have my brother give me to you. And now I'm choosing to keep you forever. Isn't that what you wanted all along?"

"Well…"

"Well?" she challenges. "Did you, or did you not, ask for forever?"

"Yes. I did."

"So what are you complaining about again? I seem to have misplaced your point way back when I was eighteen years old, and you sent me away."

"You're feeling pretty fucking sassy tonight, huh?" I drag her closer and groan when she gives herself to me. Lips. Tongue. Body and soul. "You wanna fight, Bear? Or are you trying to ensure I smack your ass later tonight?"

She glances up, red-cheeked and mildly panicked as she looks around at those who share our table. But Marcus is busy with Meg, and Jess is making out with Kane. Laine and Ang have eyes for only each other, and Jack is busy running circles over Britt's swollen belly.

"No one is paying attention to us," I whisper into her ear. Then for good measure, I bite the lobe and grin when she gasps. "No one can save you."

Slowly, seductively, she draws her gaze around again and stops. "Don't even think about it."

"Think about what?" I slide my hand beneath the tablecloth, dragging the white linen closer until it sits over our laps. Then I flash a wide smile when Kari's eyes widen. "You can't tell me what to do, Bear. I'm untouchable."

She snarls when I slip my hand beneath her gown and slide it up to her knee. She sweats from the multiple layers of fabric. Or maybe she's just hot for me. "Try and stop me."

"Luca!" She slaps her hand down over mine, but hers is outside the gown and mine is in. "Stop it."

"No." I press a fast, almost chaste kiss to her lips and grin when she vibrates. Anger. Humiliation. Heat. "What are you gonna do about it, huh?"

"I'll scream so everyone looks at us."

I scoff and slide my hand just a little higher. "You're just gonna lie to my face like that? On our wedding day?"

"I'll break your fingers."

"For touching my wife?" A long, baritone growl rolls along my throat when I say those words out loud. "*My wife.*"

"I'll let you touch me. At home, in private."

"Or maybe I should touch you right here," I snicker, crawling my fingers just a little higher along her thigh. "Teach you how to be quiet when the need arises."

"Luc," she breathes. Her cheeks burn hot enough to let everyone know, if only they were to turn and look. "You can't..." she shakes her head. "We can't..."

"Because you don't want to? Or because you're afraid of being caught?"

"The second." Her voice crackles, desire and need, pulsing from her flesh to mine. "Definitely the second."

"So you're not morally against me touching you." I walk my fingers closer and grin when she parts her legs. Just a little. Just an inch or two. "You're just pre-embarrassed on the off chance we get caught. Which," I swallow down my groan when I find her wet. Waiting.

That's not sweat. It's need.

"We won't be caught. Anyone looking this closely is being inappropriate. And we're completely covered. Any person who thinks we're doing something wrong has a filthy mind and probably should see a shrink."

"You're being ridiculous." But she releases a soft, beautiful breath of surprise when I find her fiery slit and discover: *no panties.*

"Really, Bear?" My cock roars to life, crushed between her backside and my own fucking leg. "No underwear? You're naughty."

"I'm told the wedding night is supposed to be... ya know, fun."

"So you thought you'd save me the step of removing them?" I slip two fingers deep into her pussy and take her lips with mine when she releases a cry that would get us both busted. I steal her every sound. Every breath. Every moan. And I secret them away in the base of my lungs. Her wedding gift to me. "Shhhh," I whisper against her lips, sliding my fingers out, then back in again. "You have to be discreet or we're both getting in trouble."

"This is wildly inappropriate." And yet, she wraps her arm over my shoulder—it looks like a hug, I'm sure—and crushes herself close. "Luc..."

"Quietly, beautiful." I find her clit with the pad of my thumb and swallow to lubricate my throat that has gone suddenly dry. "You want more? You want faster?"

She closes her eyes and simply concentrates on breathing.

I extend my pinky and slide it into her ass, earning a whimper of surprise and delight, and the first wash of pleasure filling my palm.

"Shit," I groan, wishing for nothing else in this moment but a bed. Privacy. A chance to push her dress up to her belly so I can lap at her with my tongue. "I love you so much."

"Don't stop now." She squeezes me closer like that'll somehow ensure my compliance. "Please don't stop."

"Open your eyes." I hold her hip with my free hand, anchoring her sweet body to my lap, and sliding my tongue along her bottom lip. "Open them, Bear. I wanna see you."

She flickers them open, gifting me with two beautiful, glassy green eyes that literally reflect myself back. Then hesitantly, she turns and looks out at our crowd. None are really paying attention to us. We're all family here, and the social bubbles were set long ago. But they're here anyway, in this room. So close. "You're such a naughty girl." I bite the ball of her shoulder and fill her tight pussy. "So naughty, getting off with an audience."

"Luca..." She brings her gaze back around, her lips dropped wide and pouty and her eyes, hooded. "You should stop."

I smile, victorious when she explodes in my hand anyway, soaking my palm and making a mess of us both. "You need to let go," I tease. "Enjoy new experiences."

I catch her when she slumps against my chest, pressing my lips to her forehead when she hums with pleasure, and when she continues to crush my fingers, I simply... leave them there. Touching her clit every now and again until she vibrates. "Such a good girl, Mrs. Lenaghan."

41

LUC

ALL THE DETAILS

"I didn't catch the last bit of your story." Kane sets his elbows on the table and his chin in his hands, and grinning like the Cheshire Cat, he bounces his brows. "You said Jess and I were making out, then you stopped talking out loud, bro. Finish it."

"I did finish it." I crack the seal on my Coke and turn the can so the lip faces me. "I just didn't feel you were entitled to hear it out loud. Anyway, you know what happened that day. Got married. Danced. Drank. We were gone before midnight and the rest of you partied on. I'm not asking you what you did, and you don't ask me what I did."

"You're lucky my wife is your sister." He points a finger, like a gun, straight between my eyes. Then scowling so a long line marks the middle of his forehead, he grumbles, "Damn lucky. I know you hid some of the good details from me, Lenaghan. I've hurt men for less."

"Uh huh." I pick up my soda and take a long sip. "That night was two years ago. And now here we are. The house has been mostly finished. The yard is like... a little bit landscaped. The nursery was set up, but only because of Kari since I was clearly too fucking busy to help."

"You were working extra shifts and making money for your family. Don't spiral down that hole and fuck your mental health up. You were setting up your family's future."

"We needed time together! We have money, Bish."

"And hindsight is always gonna kick a man when he's down. You wanted to set things up so you could stay home for a bit with Kari and the babies. That's not something to be ashamed of."

"Coveting money when we were already comfortable is shameful." I turn my Coke on the table and hold my temper before it explodes. Before Jess comes running, on a mission to save the fucking day. "We're still selling music, Bish. We have passive income. The hospital is not the only injection we have into our bank accounts, but still, I chose to work. When she asked me to help set up the nursery, it was always, 'next weekend'. Always, 'when I get a second'."

"Dude—"

"It was never, 'sure, babe! Let me fulfill those promises I made to you on our wedding day!' Why was I so fucking busy when all I've ever wanted was more time with her? We'd lost so much of it already, and here I was, staring down the barrel of two kids and the very life I always wanted. And what? I was too busy to be around?"

"You were future proofing your life." He leans onto the table and stares into my eyes. "You know me, Luc. You know I'm the last guy on this earth who will blow hot air up another's ass just to save his feelings. I'm not the ass patting, *there there* kind. But I'm sitting here now anyway, telling you that you did what you thought was right. You do not deserve more punishment than you're already suffering."

"We argued that day in the car." I choke out a sobbing breath and lock it all down. I still my lungs and firm my jaw. I think back to twelve days ago, the sun beating down on us and reflecting off the car's windows. Kari was almost full term and ready to pop. In pain every fucking step she took because she's so small, and she had *two* of my babies in her belly. "She only wanted time with me, Bish. She wanted to enjoy our last couple of weeks where it was just us, because although we both fought for those babies, although we both wanted them, we still wanted us, too. I actually *like* spending time with my wife, man. But the currency she wanted to trade in was time, and I was dealing only in money."

"That asshole shouldn't have been on the road." Kane sneers, his lip curling into a dangerous curve. "If *he* didn't make those choices that day, then *he* wouldn't have run that red and hit you. *He* is the reason your car was totaled, and *he's* the reason Kari's pregnancy ended the way it did. Fuck, Luc. *He* did this. Not you."

"And yet, here I am, broiling in the consequences of getting into the car that day." I sniffle and look up to meet his almost black eyes. "She wanted to stay home, ya know? She wanted to stay in our room where the ceiling was made of stars and watch a movie. Lay on the bed and just... be. Us. She wanted to close the windows and lock the doors. Shut the world out. Her request was so fucking simple. So pure and sweet. And I chose, instead, to head out. Drag her along somewhere she didn't even wanna go." I pull my bottom lip between my teeth and bite down just hard enough to distract my brain from the ache in my heart. "So don't sit there and tell me I'm innocent in all this. Don't pat my back and make me out to be some hero, all because I chose work over her. I chose comfort over love."

"You chose those things *for* love," he snarls. "You weren't saving up for a singles trip to Bali, stupid. You weren't putting that cash in the slot machines or drinking your way to oblivion. You wanted to make a good life for your family, so stop with the *woe is me* and harden the fuck up. I will die on this hill and defend you until my last breath. Because you sure as hell seem to have given up on defending yourself. And you still have a family to take care of. Quit the shit and get back to work."

42

LUC

THE CHOICES WE MAKE

"Can't we just stay home?" Kari is stunning, her eight-month belly exiting the house a whole step before the woman herself. An inch of her stomach shows because even her maternity clothes struggle to cover her bulging bump. And her feet, already, are red and swollen despite being on them for only minutes. She sweats because it's warm out, and her hair seems to have grown during pregnancy.

But fuck, she's beautiful.

They say pregnant women glow. It's a cliché, after all.

But I'll be damned if it isn't fact in Kari's case. Her skin is clear, her freckles, like stars. Her eyes glitter with something playful. Something fun, even though she's tired and begging to stay home.

"We could watch *any* of the movies you want to watch," she pleads. "Even *Top Gun*, I suppose. If you feel really strongly about it."

"I just wanna go to the hardware store real quick." I beep the car unlocked but drop the keys into my pockets and head back to the front door. Taking her hands, I help her down the steps and onto the path I long ago transformed from overgrown weeds and cement leftovers, into something a little more functional. Steppingstones. Pebbles. And on either side, luscious grass. "I wanna check out the fencing options so we can get the yard taken care of."

"We don't need a fence," she grumbles. But she walks. She clutches to my arms and allows me to lead her. "Our property backs into the trees, Luc. Let *them* be the fence."

"Cute. Until a fuckin' bear takes one of the babies while we're not watching." I shuffle her toward the car and around to the passenger door. Then helping her in, I crouch and lift her legs, smiling when she huffs and looks across, fatigued as though she's just run a marathon. "You're beautiful, by the way."

"You're a pain in my ass. I'm sweating like a pig, my feet hurt, I'm really hungry, but I don't want to eat anything, and Twin A is about to get her ass grounded." Hissing, she reaches down and presses her palm to her belly when a leg—or foot, maybe. Perhaps a knee or shoulder—distorts the skin and brings pain to the woman I swore to always protect. "She's feeling fussy and it's making it hard to breathe."

"We really should come up with better names than Twin A and Twin B, huh?" I dive in and press a kiss to her forehead. Then I snag the seatbelt and hand it over so she can fix the latch. Closing the door, I skip around to my side and slide in. Far quicker than Kari. Way less puffing and wheezing.

Yeah. I owe her for life. I know.

"We'll be quick, I promise." I insert the key into the ignition and quickly start the car before she manages to escape. I want to go to the store. But I want to be with her too. Which means she has to come. She has to be here with me. "We'll be an hour, tops. I'll take you to lunch after. Then we can come home and watch something Hugh Grant starred in." I glance over and smile. "Deal?"

She rolls her eyes and looks at the road as I pull out of our driveway and onto the street. "I like the name Billy, but for a girl."

"After your dad?" I settle back as we cruise along the road. Not too fast. Not too slow. We're in no particular rush, except to get back and watch movies. "Your dad was Bill."

"William," she sighs. "Which turned to Bill. I feel like, since this baby is bigger than her brother already, and my dad was a really tall guy, she could be Billy too. A kind of homage." Insecure, she peeks from the corner of her eyes and studies me. "Does that sound okay? Do you have other suggestions?"

"Billy works just fine for me." I reach across and set my hand on her thigh. So tiny compared to the size of her belly. "Billy is a cute name I can totally get on board with for a girl. What about our son?"

"Do you have a preference?" She nibbles on her bottom lip and studies me. "I named one, so maybe you can name the other."

"Your mom's name was Rose."

"Yeah, but Jess and Kane already have Rosalie. No need to have cousins with the same name. What about your parents? Hugh and Sadie."

"We're *not* naming our son after Hugh Grant, no matter how sideways you try to slide in on it," I chuckle. "And we already have our girl's name. Sadie's a cute name though, so maybe next time."

She scoffs, rubbing circles over her swollen belly and attempting to hide the grimace Billy's knee elicits. "You're dreaming if you think I'm risking twins a second time. We'll adopt," she hisses. "Or find them in the street and keep them."

"Felony charges. But you do you, babe. What if we name the boy Marcus?" I peek across and wait for her reaction. Good. Bad. Otherwise. "He named his son for me. He honored me with that, and he's the second most important guy in your world."

"Second." She snickers, her lips curling up and her cheeks filling with a sweet pink. "You've always thought quite highly of yourself, haven't you?"

"What about Dominic?" Nerves flutter in my belly, though it's odd. Unexplainable, really. "If we're not using family names, and you're not jumping at using *Marcus* for a first name, I've always thought Dominic was cool. Dom. He's a badass. There's a famous skateboarder named Dominic, *and* a famous drummer as well. Dom sounds like a motorcycle rider."

"My son is never getting a motorcycle," she drawls. "Ever."

"Dominic is a good, strong name," I grin. "Dominic sounds like he can fight. He'll catch up and overtake his sister's growth once he's no longer stuck in a tiny womb with no leg room. Then he'll protect her later. They'll take over the school, kicking ass and slamming people with skateboards when they act stupid."

"You're just planning out their entire futures based on a name?" She purses her lips. Though I see the smile hidden in the twitch. "What if Dom wants to play piano, or become a nurse, or can't stand up on a skateboard?"

"He can do all of those things." I twine our fingers together and bring them to my lips. "He and Billy can be whatever the fuck they want to be. Because you and I, and all their uncles and aunties, will have their backs and clear the way for success. It's why we struggle, Bear. So our kids don't have to."

"What happens if our son falls in love with someone he can't be with?" Her eyes flicker over my face. "What if he sends her away and breaks her heart? Risking a happy future because he was afraid of things going wrong."

"Then we'll tell our kids our story." I press a kiss to her knuckles and pull into town, puttering along residential streets and making my way toward Main. "We'll tell them how we met, and how we hurt. We'll tell them the things we went through that were probably completely unnecessary, and then we'll guide them, hopefully better than we guided ourselves."

"How *you* guided us. All that shit was your fault, Luca. I was just being pushed around and told where to go."

"Yeah." I place our joined hands in my lap and drop my chin, hitting the indicator as we come upon Main Street. "I was young. Stupid. Impulsive. Hindsight never fails to make me feel like a moron."

"Just as long as you're aware." Her phone rings, buried somewhere in the depths of her pockets, so she steals her hand from mine and tilts to the side to free the device. Pulling it out, then checking the screen, she casts a look my way while answering and placing the call on speaker. "Hello, Jessica. Obsessed with me, or what?"

"Just checking if you've popped yet. You're about ready to go, Big Mama, and I wanna be at the hospital when you do."

"You're not invited into the birthing suite," I grumble. "That's my wife. You're my sister. It's called boundaries."

She scoffs. "If you respected boundaries, then there wouldn't be any twins coming any day now. Where are you guys?" She pauses for a beat and listens. "You driving?"

"We're heading to the hardware store," Kari drawls, firming her lips. "Luc thought today was a great day to build a fence in the backyard."

"I'm not building the fence today. I'm sourcing supplies for the fence today. It's called planning ahead, ladies. You ought to try it sometime."

Though of course, just as the words leave my mouth, guilt trips along my veins and my eyes shoot to Kari's. Of the two of us, it was her who styled the nursery. It was her who chose clothes for the babies, shopped for outfits and diapers. She was the one who built the changing table, because I chose shifts in the bus instead. She was the one who sourced formula samples, knowing despite her wishes to exclusively breastfeed, plans are often usurped by reality, and having twins will make breastfeeding more difficult. It was Kari who coordinated the meal trains our friends insisted upon, and Kari whose career will ultimately suffer after taking maternity leave.

"I'm sorry." Guilt is like a thick, black sludge pumping through my veins. But I grab her hand again, draw it up, and press her palm to my cheek. I make her hold me because I'm weak and an asshole. "I was kidding. I didn't mean it."

"Are you dilated yet?" Jess inserts her nose back into our reality, adding a fresh layer of fun to wash away the tension. "How many centimeters?"

"Not really an appropriate question to ask your sister-in-law," Kari drolls. "You want to know the size of my vagina?"

"I was your friend before he was your husband. So stop being shy and describe your poon to me."

"For fucks sake." I release her hand and bring the car to a creeping roll as we approach an intersection. "Please never ask her that question again in front of me. It creeps me out."

"I'm three centimeters," Kari answers. "But I've been three centimeters for weeks. So that's not new."

"Contractions?"

"Nada. Things tighten a little now and then when I'm exerting myself. That's pregnancy, not labor."

"Have you picked a baby girl name yet?" Jess pauses for a beat. "Jess is available."

"We *have* picked names," I insert. "Jess isn't one of them."

"He's cranky today, huh?" She verbally rolls her eyes as I bring the car to a stop and wait while the lights allow traffic to go. "Luc used to be fun. He was good entertainment. Now he's a dad and such a drag."

"I just wanna buy some shit for a fence," I groan. "Then I want to go home and spend time with my wife. Remind me again why you're calling and sucking my energy away?"

The lights turn yellow as two remaining cars cross, then red, though there's no one on that side to pull up to the line. Finally, our light turns green, so I take my foot off the brake and place it on the gas instead.

"I'm just checking in on my best friend," Jess grumbles. "I feel we've already covered the fact that she was mine before she was yours. My best friend, right now, is practically crowning with a couple of Lenaghan babies. I'm entitled to ask about it."

"One of the babies is breech anyway." Kari rubs her belly again. "I won't be pushing, no matter when this all goes down. We're getting as close to forty weeks as we can, and then the theater is waiting for me when we get there."

"What if you—"

I look to my right for reasons I can't truly explain. No noise called me that way. No apparent movement. Nothing but Kari and her two hands, one holding the phone, and the other stroking her belly. This town is tiny. It's rare for a trip from one side to the other to take more than ten minutes. Traffic jams don't exist, and car accidents are few and far between.

There are simply not enough of them on the road at one time.

But the universe decided today would be that day. A rusty, old, piece of shit truck doesn't even glint in the sunlight. The paint is too peeled. The hood, too rusty and dented. The front light is already busted, and the bumper hangs on only with duct tape and hopes and dreams.

I guess maybe I expect the driver to stop. We're in the intersection. We have the right of way. So my heart doesn't completely register panic until the massive front grille crosses the solid white lines. Instantly, with my heart in my throat and the air caught in my lungs, I slam my foot on the gas to floor it out of the way as the truck barrels closer.

Kari hisses at my sudden speed. Her phone flies out of her hand and her eyes swing to me. The world moves in slow motion, her perfect, wild curls flying in the air, then it moves again as she follows my gaze and looks out the window on her right.

She releases a peeling scream.

But it's too fucking late.

The world is moving slow, but the truck is defying the laws of speed. His bumper slams into Kari's door, T-boning our car and sending us skidding across the intersection until we slam into another. A truck on either side, both larger, harder steel than our little sedan.

"Fuck!" My head raps against the side window, my vision blurring as we come to a sudden stop, the stench of burning rubber filling the car and Kari's scream... silenced.

"Hello?" Jess's frantic cry pulses throughout the car. "Luc!"

"Shit." Stars float in my vision as the car continues to rock. As horns bleat and already, sirens squeal. "Kari?"

"Luc!" Jess shouts out from somewhere far away. The phone. Dropped. "Luc! Are you okay?"

I peel my eyes open and drag them to my right. My head throbs and my jaw aches. But I don't know hurt until I find Kari, dazed and bleeding. Blinking and groaning. "Kari! Oh shit." I startle in my seat and try to jump toward her, catching myself on my seatbelt and crying out in frustration. "Kari! Babe."

"Luc?" Jess calls. "What the hell happened?"

"Call an ambulance!" I unsnap my seatbelt and lunge over the seats. "Kari! Wake up, baby. Wake up."

"The babies." Her words are slurred, her face, covered in blood and nicks from glass I hadn't even noticed shattered. "Luc, the babies—"

"They're okay. Just relax for a second and let me check you over." I press my fingers to her neck, but my eyes go down. It's an automatic response. I don't even think about it. So when I catch bright red blood smeared over the seat and soaking through her pants, my heart fucking stops. "Oh no. Oh god. Oh no." I shove out of the car and sprint around to Kari's side, thankful the truck skidded off to the right and isn't blocking her door. My head swims, and if not for holding on to my car, I might stumble too far to the right and miss my landing.

But I find her door, yanking the handle and opening it wide. People scream, somewhere far, far away. Others cry. Others, still, run out of shops and into the street with their hands to their mouths and tears in their eyes.

These are scenes I've witnessed a million times over the years. But never, in the history of ever, was I the one in the middle.

"Somebody call an ambulance!" I unsnap Kari's seatbelt and catch her when she slumps. All of my training says not to move her. Spinal injuries could mean she never walks again. But leaving her inside the car, bleeding and barely responsive, typically fucking equals dead. "Come on. Come on. Come on. Come on." Tears blur my vision and burn my eyes, but I hook my arms under hers and drag her out, damn near falling to my knees when I find not just blood stains on the seats. But a fucking *puddle*. "Don't you dare leave me like this."

Rage burns in my veins as I pull her out and still, people just fucking watch. The driver of the truck stumbles out of his cab. The driver of the other truck, the one we hit, tries to open his door. But he's trapped inside, the steel crumpled on one side and folded against the traffic light pole on the other.

"Luc!" A familiar voice roars in my peripherals. A panicked gasp. Then Alex sprints to where I try to pull Kari out carefully. He instantly grabs her legs, his face pale as a ghost, but he's a first responder too. He's been to tragic situations a million times. "What the fuck happened?"

"Red truck hit us." I gently place Kari on the road and look up, appreciative as a wad of towels slap my shoulder and land on the road. Katrina, a local waitress down at the diner, gulps as I bundle the fabric and place it under Kari's head. Then I skid around to her other end and pull her shorts down. "I need something." My stomach heaves. Anxiety swirls and makes me sick. My head thuds and still, my eyes blur as I desperately look to Alex.

Older. Protective. Authoritative.

"My..." My brain isn't connecting. The neural pathways, broken. "Something."

"What?" He grabs another towel and places it on the road beneath Kari's backside. "What do you need?"

"First aid kit?" *Why the fuck do I say it like a question?* "I think..."

"Luc!" Katrina pushes into our space and grabs my face. "She's bleeding, Luc. Like, a lot."

"Placental abruption?" Questions. So many fucking questions. "I think... maybe..."

"Which means you have to get them out." She tears Kari's underwear down and cries out at the blood already pooling on the ground. "Oh god, Luc. You have to get them out."

"I can't get them out! Dom is upside down."

"You have to try!" She grabs my hands and holds them firm. "Maybe it's not abruption. Maybe it's just ruptured membranes."

"They're scheduled for theater."

"They're here right now!" she snarls. Shoving me around, she forces me to see them. My family. My whole fucking world. "Stop thinking this is Kari," she orders. "It's just work. Motor vehicle accident. Thirty-four-week pregnant female carrying twins. What do you do, Luc?"

"I get her to the hospital." My hands shake. My entire soul quivers. "I minimize the bleeding and I get her into the bus."

"No," she commands. "Look! Push that blood aside, Luca, and you see a head. They're ready to come out."

"I need to stabilize the mother!"

"You need to stabilize all three of them. One is already in the birth canal, so what do you do?"

"Fuck. Fuck. Fuck. Fuck. Okay." I look to my left when Alex tosses a first aid kit at my leg, but then I glance at Kari. Because that isn't gonna help shit all. "Dammit! Okay. If it's abruption, we have five minutes to get them wired up."

"Ambulance is on the way." Alex goes to Kari's head and drags the hair out of her face. "Two minutes out. So you've gotta handle it till then."

"Are you awake, Bear?" I slide my fingers around the baby's head, testing for the elasticity of Kari's skin and knowing she's about to be torn the fuck up. "Bear? Can you hear me?"

"I'm 'ere," she drones, sluggish and sleepy. "Hurts."

"I know, babe. I know it hurts." Tears ball in my eyes and drop from my cheeks. This whole fucking scene is dirty. Glass litters the road and dirt is already on her legs. On her thighs. "I'm gonna need your help to get the first one out, okay?"

"Tired."

"I know, honey." I shrug and swipe my cheek on my shoulder. "The accident has pushed you into pre-term labor, and I'm really worried you're bleeding inside. I need you to help me get this one out. Then the bus is on the way to finish up."

"Wonder if I'll die," she drawls. Curious. And completely... content. "Least I didn't get shot in the belly, huh?"

"You're not fucking dying." I snatch up the first aid kid and tear the zippers open. This isn't a hospital. There are no proper tools here. But I grab the scissors from the pack and bring them between her legs, shaking and sick with what I have to do. "This isn't strictly by the book, Bear. And it's gonna hurt. But I have to cut you."

"S'okay." She drops her head to the side. Sleeping. Yet, awake. Here, but not. "S'fine. My stomach hurts."

"Don't let her sleep," I order Alex. Then to Katrina, "I need water. Like, bottled, spring water or something. We'll need more towels. And probably find me some gloves or some shit."

"I've got it." She bounds to her feet and sprints away.

So I bring my focus back to Kari's laboring stomach. She's not here, but her body is doing the work anyway. Labor has begun, whether we're ready for it or not. "Don't go to sleep, Bear."

"Hey?" Alex taps her cheek. "Wake up, sweet girl. You need to stay awake."

"Can you push for me, Bear?" I snip her skin, heaving when the tiny cut turns to a third-degree tear when the baby's head presses against it. "Fuck," I groan, sick to my stomach at the thought of hurting her. "I'm so sorry, Kari. I'm so fucking sorry."

"Push," Alex coaches. He reaches down and takes her hand in his. "Your baby is already crowning, Kar. Which means they probably can't breathe right now. You gotta get it out."

Kari's eyes snap open in panic. "What?"

"You don't tell the fucking patient their baby is dying!" I slip my fingers in beside the head, twisting and adjusting her angle to help her move easier with the contraction. "Your job is to keep her calm, dickhead. You don't freak her out."

"Is she okay?" Kari shoves, dizzily, to her elbows and turns green from the movement. "Luc?"

"Just push, Bear. Lay down and push. Let Alex help you."

Alex's radio crackles to life. Ambulances are on the way. A minute out. Blah blah blah. All things I've heard countless times. But a minute is too long. Kari's body is pushing, forcing the baby out, first her head, then down to her shoulders. "Oh god. Oh god. Oh god."

"Get them out," Kari cries. She yelps from pain when we get to the shoulders and her tear grows wider. Ah!" She screams. "Luc!"

"Nearly there, Bear. Hold on." I slide my hand in and adjust Billy's shoulders, inching one out, then the other, while a block away, ambulances scream around the corner, their tires skidding on the tar. "One more, okay?" I grit my teeth and hiss when I pop Billy's shoulder free. "One more push, then the ambos are gonna be here with the good drugs. They're gonna help us, Bear."

"Hey. Whoa!" Alex catches Kari when she droops into his arms and her eyes slam closed. "Kari?" He taps her face and leans over to be all she could see—if only her eyes were open. "Kari!"

"What happened?" I guide Billy out. It's easy after the shoulders, so I catch her in one hand and snag a towel with the other. But my heart pounds in my ears, drowning out the thump of my aching brain. "X! What happened?"

"She's unconscious. I don't..." He taps her face and presses his fingers to her neck. "Luc, I don't know."

"Is she breathing?" Panic lances through my blood, my words coming out louder. Frenzied. "Alex! Is she breathing?"

I look down at Billy, almost hurling, because her skin glows dark purple and her first, sweet screams are yet to come. "Oh Jesus." I cry out and place the baby on the ground, then I open her towel and start resuscitation. "Breathe for her, X!" I carefully place my mouth over Billy's lips and nostrils, exhaling a deep breath and watching her lungs fill.

"We're here!" *Other* paramedics, the kind I don't work a shift with, slam their doors open and go to work yanking a stretcher out. One grabs a kit, while the other sprints our way. "What's happened?"

"MV accident." Dizziness washes through my brain and turns my vision spotty. "Direct hit on her door. She's thirty-four weeks. Reasonably healthy pregnancy. Twins. Twin A just arrived." I lean in and repeat my actions, closing my lips around Billy's and filling her lungs. "Twin B was breech at last scan. Twin B is failure to thrive in the womb, so already medically fragile."

"Mother isn't breathing," Alex announces, shuffling out of the way when the second paramedic darts closer to help. "She dropped about twenty seconds ago."

"Infant isn't breathing," I shout. "It's been about forty-five seconds since delivery."

"We have a thready pulse," one of the paramedics announces of Kari. "It's weak."

"Significant blood loss inside and out of the car." I snarl when the second paramedic steals Billy away and slaps a mask over her face. Already, her coloring is coming back. But still... I don't hear her cries. I don't see her little fists clenching. "Suspected placental abruption, but I'm not sure. I can't..." I shake my head. "I dunno."

"Let's get them up and in the bus." The duo help themselves to Kari, no concern for her body or possible spinal injuries. They load her up and pop the stretcher back to its full height, then they lay Billy, whose cord is still attached to her mother, in the gap between Kari's hip and the bed rail.

Then they go.

Whisking my family away.

"Another ambo is on the way," they shout back. It takes me a moment to realize they're talking to Alex. The chief. "We'll call a third and get everyone seen to. Mother and babies are priority right now."

"I don't..." I look down at my hands, smeared in blood. My knees, torn from the road. I spy the towels laid on the tar, smattered in dirt and crimson. Then I look at Alex, my body overtaken by violent tremors. "X..."

"It's okay." He pushes up to stand and yanks me up beside him, then he claps his hand to the back of my head and pulls me in until I break. Until I burst out with grief and attempt to turn, searching for my family when the EMTs slam the doors closed. "I'll get you to the hospital," he soothes, murmuring as the sirens come to life. "I'll get you to them, I promise."

43

LUC

RECKONING

"It's time to go." Marcus steps back into my kitchen, his arms overflowing with a pretty baby-pink gown that drapes across Billy's small body and hides her legs completely. Her head is dwarfed by an oversized bow, and her eyes shine bright, searching for me in one of the rare moments she's awake.

A large lump forms in my throat, cutting off my air and damn near dropping me to my knees. Because Kane's face is pale. He already knows what happened in the middle of that intersection in town. He caught the reports. But he wasn't there, breathing for a baby. He wasn't there, holding his dying wife and hoping, praying for a miracle.

Marc takes another step closer, hesitant as he looks from me to Kane. "What's wrong? What happened?"

"Nothing." I push away from the table and head across the room, scooping Billy out of his arms because I can't bear for us to be apart. I nearly lost her. And now, I need her. "I'm ready to go," I rasp. "But I still don't have a car, so—"

"You can go in ours," Jess murmurs, stopping in the door and softening her eyes. "You and Bill can ride with Kane, and I'll drive our girls up."

Contemplative, I look at Kane, as though to ask, *that okay?* But already, he nods and starts my way. Clapping me on the shoulder, he nudges me through the door and in the direction of the front entry. "I already have the car seat in the back, and Jess will get the baby bag in case you need things while we're there."

"Laine and Ang are already at the hospital," Jess adds, turning and ushering her girls through the house. "And Britt and Jack, too. They left their kids at the estate with Jack's sister, so no extra noise."

"I'll swing by and grab Meg and meet you there," Marcus continues. "Chance wants to see Billy anyway, so…"

"Scotch and Sammy are also gonna meet us there," Jess concludes. "Alex and Oz are on shift, but you know they'll make it work."

"That's a lot of people." I emerge through the front door and into the sunlight outside. Immediately, Billy's eyes snap shut and her lips pale as she wrinkles them together. "Are we sure we wanna have that many—"

"Kari and Dom are loved," Marc rumbles. "And so are you and Bill. Everyone wants to be there today."

"Is there much we have to do?" I look at Kane, though fuck knows why. He's not a lawyer. Or a hospital administrator. "Like, stuff we have to sign, or…?"

"I think just a couple of forms." He leads me to his truck, bigger even than the one that created this fucking domino effect in my life. Then opening the back door, he steps out of the way instead of taking Billy from my arms. "Most of it's been taken care of, I think. So it shouldn't take long."

"And then we just…" Carefully, I place Billy in her car seat and shuffle her dress around so I can secure the five-point straps. "Then we can take her? No more delays?"

"As far as I'm aware." He waits for me to finish buckling, smiling, albeit small, when I glance back and meet his eyes. "Last I heard, everything is pretty much good to go. And if not, then one call to Soph, and it'll be dealt with, no questions asked." He nods toward Billy when I pull away. "Wanna ride with her, or up front with me?"

I consider for only a beat, before climbing into the back and settling in so I can see my sweet baby. Her eyes already droop, sleepiness taking over after a fresh outfit change and a bottle of milk.

Shutting the door, Kane walks to Jess and presses a kiss on her cheek. They talk for only a second before he nods and turns away, then he comes back and slides into the driver's seat and shuts the door. "Laine just texted and said Meg and Britt already arrived. So we're not waiting for anyone except us."

"Guess that makes you the guest of honor, Bill." I reach into the carrier and take her hand in mine, sliding my finger into her fist and swallowing when she squeezes hers shut. "You ready to go see your mommy?"

Kane pulls out of the driveway, but only after Jess and Marcus go first, then he settles onto the street as cars come along and match our speed in the back.

"We got an armored escort?" I peer back for just long enough to catch the rumble of a Hummer. "Was it necessary?"

"Drunk driver pussy was let out on bail." He catches my eyes in the rearview mirror. "Tells me the roads aren't safe. I'm just waiting on you to give me the thumbs up on that, then we can head on over to the trailer park and pay him a visit, Bishop style."

"What are you gonna do?" I gulp the choking lump from the middle of my throat. "Beat him to a pulp? Alex already hit him that day at the scene."

Kane scoffs. "Alex had to stop at one or risk his entire career." He grins, wide and wild. "We won't be using our fists." But then he shrugs. "Unless you wanna. You can hit him as much as you want, until you get that rage out of your belly. Then we'll slit his fuckin' throat and be done with it."

I glance up again, meeting his eyes, and know, he's not joking.

Bishop's do not make idle threats.

"Blood in, Lenaghan. I'll take care of it, or I'll help you take care of it. Either way, he won't be driving for much longer."

"You could go to prison for saying that stuff."

He laughs, hitting the turn signal when the convoy ahead of us does the same. "I'm never going to prison. Don't worry about it."

"How do you get rid of the rage?" I chew on the inside of my cheek or risk accidentally squeezing Billy's hand and hurting the tiny, fragile bones inside. "He hurt my family, Bish. What he did was..." I shake my head. "It was unforgivable. Maybe, if it was his first offence, it wouldn't be so bad. One mistake is just, ya know, a mistake. But the same mistakes repeated..."

"That's malice," he finishes. "Or negligence, at best. We know he wasn't aiming for you guys that day. So it wasn't personal."

"It feels fucking personal to me! I was the one tearing Kari open, like a savage, trying to save them all."

"It wasn't personal," he repeats, slower, gentler, "but he made that choice to drink and drive. He's made the same, fateful decision in the past which ended someone else's life. Wayne Hart has hurt too many, even some we know personally." He checks the mirror and meets my eyes. "I'm done letting the legal system handle it. Now it's our turn. That's how *I* deal with the rage." His lips twitch. "I do what the law can't. I did it for Laine when

Graham hurt her, and I'll do it for Kari for the same reasons. Word on the street is that his son is asking around to see who's gonna deal with him. He wants him to pay after a childhood of abuse. Eliminating the issue is usually pretty fucking productive in calming my desire to burn the entire town down. Seems we get to help more than a couple of people dealing with this one."

"What did you do to Graham for Laine?" I sit forward, resting my elbow on the seat ahead of me. "What happened?"

He scoffs, peering over his shoulder to meet my eyes. "What did *you* do to Graham?"

I sit back again, startled when his stare sparks something dangerous. A memory I'd long ago set aside in favor of my own sanity. A rage I worked through… in seemingly the same way Bish is suggesting.

"I saw some pretty interesting scars on Graham's torso this one time," he explains. "Got me thinking."

"Why would you possibly have reason to see Graham's torso?"

He grins again, shaking his head and bringing us around another corner. "No comment, Officer. Just let me know when you're ready to purge the poison. Until then, I've got eyes on the dude." Coming around one last corner and bringing the truck into the ambulance driveway where he's sure to get a ticket, he pulls up a few yards from the emergency doors and cuts the engine. "Tell them not to tow me," he chuckles, unsnapping his seatbelt and turning to meet my eyes. "If they do, I'll have to get Soph to deal with it, and she gets kinda pissy about that stuff."

My door opens, drawing my eyes to Marcus' as he steps back to make room. "I wanna see my sister, Lenaghan, but I feel like it would be disrespectful to go in there before you and Bill. So…"

He waits as I unbuckle my daughter and turn to slide out, then he stands over her and strokes her brow.

"I'm gonna need you to hurry up and get in there."

"What if I don't wanna go in?" My voice thickens, shame and grief coalescing until it hurts the very center of my throat. My heart pounds, and beneath all the fabric that is my daughter, my hands shake. "What if I can't see her? What if I can't be brave enough to do it?"

"Then I guess I'll help you." He claps his hand to my shoulder and turns me until we're heading toward the doors. Jess walks ahead of us, clearing the way and carrying a little shoulder bag overflowing with baby paraphernalia. Kane comes up on my left and Marcus walks on my right, then we emerge through the doors and Mitch steps into our path, his eyes soft and compassionate.

He carries a ball cap, the one I've seen him wear a thousand times, in one hand. And a bouquet of tulips he would have gotten from his sister in the other.

He's not in uniform, which means he made his way here anyway, having heard that we'd be by.

"Mitch."

He offers the flowers and tips his chin, studying a sleeping Billy and forcing a small smile. "Lenaghan. Baby Lenaghan."

I choke out a soft, tear-filled chuckle and slip the bouquet between my arm and ribs to free up my hand. Then we're moving again, Marcus' grip on my arm and Mitchell stepping out of the way.

"I messed everything up," I tell my escorts. "Breaking her heart when she was eighteen, then breaking it again every day for the following six years."

"You're lucky you said no at eighteen," Marcus rumbles. Semi-joking. "Dating my sister in her twenties was bad enough. I might've legitimately killed you if you swooped during her teens."

"I hurt her heart so many fucking times." I allow them to lead me into the elevator, then out again on the third floor. "We fought the day of the accident, all because of a fucking fence."

"Fighting is better than not talking at all." Marcus clears his throat as we make our way through the halls, coming around one corner, then turning another. No hesitation. He knows where we're going. "Fighting means you both still care. That's important."

"Shit." My eyes burn as we come around our last corner and my family crowds the space. Britt steps forward first, her eyes red and swollen and her bottom lip gently, almost invisibly, trembling.

"Brat…"

"Luca." She steps in and wraps her arms around my shoulders, careful not to squish Billy between us. "How was your first night at home?"

"Shit," Kane answers as she pulls back. "We've been awake since two."

"It's hard to sleep with her not home," I rasp, stepping out of her reach and grimacing when Jack taps my shoulder. That's his hug, I suppose. His affection. "It's impossible to sleep under those stars when she's not there with me."

"Hey, Luc." Laine steps in next, squeezing against my side. She presses a kiss to the ball of my shoulder and pulls back to meet my eyes. "You look really, really tired."

I cough out a laugh and lock down on the emotion clawing along my throat. "'Cause I am."

"Come on," Marc gently pushes me along. "Let's not keep her waiting."

I extend my hand, fist closed, as we pass Ang and Scotch. Then I swallow the ache in my throat as we approach Alex, who stands by the door. He's on duty, in full Chief mode. But he allows his lips to curl into a small smile that somehow eases a little of the dread in my belly.

"She's pretty as hell, huh?" He runs his fingers over the dress covered in pink tulips and brings his gaze back up to mine. "Takes after her momma."

"She sure does. Have you been..." I tip my chin toward the closed door. "Have you been in there today?"

He nods. One short, sharp movement of his head that neither brings me comfort, nor does it erase the dread settled in my belly. "Yeah, I've been in. A couple of times, actually."

Marcus scowls. "You were supposed to wait."

Alex only chuckles, lifting his shoulders in a shrug. "According to the department shrink, I sometimes lack impulse control, especially when emotions are high. But hey, at least I didn't beat my best friend almost to death."

"Right," Marcus drawls. "But I'm pretty sure I saw you pull your gun at dinner that time, so..."

"Let's go," Kane admonishes. "We're not here for a hallway party. We came for one reason."

Fuck. Fuck. Fuck. Fuck. Nerves swim in my veins and lance across my belly until I feel like I want to puke. But even if I could turn my feet around and run away, Kane opens the door and guides me in with a hand on my shoulder.

"Time to suck it up," he murmurs, low and serious. "It's gonna be okay."

"But what if it's not? What if she—" I lose my words when he tears the curtain aside and reveals not only a friendly face, Blake, checking Kari's files and grinning when our eyes meet, but I'm awarded the perfect view of Kari in her bed, half inclined, and little baby Dom suckling at her breast.

She glances up, surprised at our arrival, then thrilled, beaming when our eyes meet. "Hey, handsome." Her eyes drop to the sleeping Billy and well up with thick tears. "And my baby girl, too. Hey."

"How are you feeling?" I break away from Kane and make a beeline for Kari's bed, coming up on her left and looking down at Dom, who is almost half the size of his sister.

It won't be forever.

And it won't hurt him long term.

But for right now, for the next few months, he just needs a little extra time.

"You look so fucking beautiful, Bear." I lean in and press a kiss to her brow, before pulling back and setting the bouquet in a vase on the bedside table. "How was your night?"

"Tiring," she sighs, reaching out one-handed for Billy. So I maneuver the baby and settle her in the gap between her hip and the rails. Just like on the ambulance stretcher. "Dom's cluster feeding," she mumbles lazily, stroking Billy's puffy cheeks and sniffling as her hormones continue to wrack through her body. "And the doctors check my incision a million times a day. They keep waking me up."

"Are you glad to be coming home today?" Hesitantly, I lower into the chair beside her bed and rest my elbows on the sides. "Excited to be back in your own bed?"

"With you?" She drags her eyes away from Billy and meets mine instead. "After nearly two weeks in hell and a couple of really crappy surgeries?"

"You had to have a hysterectomy, Bear." I swallow to lubricate my painfully dry throat. "That's not a small deal. And it could have been avoided if I wasn't such a dick."

She shakes her head. Softly. Sweetly. Side to side. "I've told you already, you were not a dick. And I'm not mad at you."

"You *should* be." My eyes burn, itching to spill over and make me look more a fool. "You should be furious."

"Because we went for a drive that day? That's hardly something you should be sorry for."

"Yeah, but—"

She reaches across, grimacing at the movement, and yet, places her fingertips over my lips. "I will forever and always choose you, Luca. Now, can you please take me home? I wanna sleep under the stars with my family."

The End

399

ACKNOWLEDGEMENTS

6 years.

And 65 books.

That's how long it took for us to get here. To the book I intended all those years ago, directly after finishing Finding Hope.

Luc and Kari were chatting to me, all the way back then, but the story they wanted to tell, the one they deserved, wasn't ready to unfold.

I didn't have the tools yet to give them justice.

I didn't have the cast and town where it's at now.

And we needed all of them to fill out the whole, rich picture needed.

So although I started this book years ago—stopping, starting, stopping again—it took until now for everything to come together and for the story that needed to be told, to work.

6 years and 65 books.

What a freakin' ride.

A lot has changed since back then. My plans for Luc and Kari (and Jess and Laine and Britt, etc) have evolved since I wrote the Rollin On series.

Yes. I know the timeline isn't perfect in this one. And I'm aware there is a plot hole that has emerged since Finding Hope. I know in Hope, Luc was with that blonde in the ice cream shop. Because 60 books ago, that's where his character arc was at. But so much has changed since then. The characters have grown and matured, and for me to include that plot thread in this book would mean to hurt Kari more than she already was.

She deserved better, so I made the decision to move on.

While writing this book, I had 130,000 words to work through 20 odd years, 60 books, and 9 or so series.

I sincerely feel I did my best. I poured my heart and soul into this story.

I hope it is received with the same love it was written.

I want to throw a very special shout out and thank you to Suzanne, one third of my Fact Checker Trio, for going above and beyond, researching all the facts for me to keep this story accurate.

Every time I had to confirm a detail (something I'd written years ago) she was on it, racing back through all that history and ensuring I had my facts straight.

Thank you, Suzanne! You made writing Tulips exponentially easier, because of your memory and speed reading abilities.

Thank you to the rest of my Fact Checker Trio, Steph and Jill, for following behind us and keeping things straight. I appreciate you both.

And thanks for the laughs, too.

Thank you to my editor, Britt, for your hard work.

My proofreader, Lindsi, for always making my books shine.

Thank you to my team, always, for having my back and ensuring I publish the very best version of every story floating around in my mind.

Perhaps, most importantly, thank you to my readers. For those of you who support me in silence. Those who post about my books. To those who traveled to Cleveland to come see me in person so recently. To those who follow my socials and comment, no matter how dumb my post is.

Thank you all. Because if I didn't have readers to share my words with, I wouldn't continue writing.

I want to share these characters with people who will love them as much as I do.

Thank you for being that person.

For the first time ever, I don't have a 'continue this series with (insert book title here.) Because this is it. Tulips and Lost Time.

It's just one book, that ties in to every single other book I've written. But it doesn't lead into a book 2.

I hope all of these years waiting was worth it.

If you're new here and you want to catch up with all the crazy characters on the side, visit:

Kane and Jess in Pawns

Ang and Laine in Till The Sun Dies

Marc in Always You
Jay in Rise Of The King
Mitch in Redeeming The Rose
Alex in Because of You
Scotch and Sammy in Surviving You
Jack and Britt in Finding Hope
Bobby and Kit in Finding Home
Jon Hart in Finding Redemption

Thank you for being here.
Emilia
xx

ALSO BY EMILIA FINN

(in reading order)

The Rollin On Series

Finding Home

Finding Victory

Finding Forever

Finding Peace

Finding Redemption

Finding Hope

The Survivor Series

Because of You

Surviving You

Without You

Rewriting You

Always You

Take A Chance On Me

The Checkmate Series

Pawns In The Bishop's Game

Till The Sun Dies

Castling The Rook

Playing For Keeps

Rise Of The King

Sacrifice The Knight

Winner Takes All

Checkmate

Stacked Deck - Rollin On Next Gen

Wildcard

Reshuffle

Game of Hearts

Full House

No Limits

Bluff

Seven Card Stud

Crazy Eights

Eleusis

Dynamite

Busted

Gilded Knights (Rosa Brothers)

Redeeming The Rose

Chasing Fire

Animal Instincts

Pure Chemistry

Battle Scars

Safe Haven

Inamorata

The Fiera Princess

The Fiera Ruins

The Fiera Reign

Mayet Justice

Sinful Justice

Sinful Deed

Sinful Truth

Sinful Desire

Sinful Deceit

Sinful Chaos

Sinful Promise

Sinful Surrender

Sinful Fantasy

Sinful Memory

Sinful Obsession

Sinful Summer

Sinful Sorrow

Sinful Corruption

Lost Boys

MISTAKE

REGRET

Crash & Burn

JUMP

JINXED

Underbelly Enchanted

The Tallest Tower

Diamond In The Rough

Lost Kingdom

Luc and Kari

Tulips and Lost Time

Rollin On Novellas

(Do not read before finishing the Rollin On Series)

Begin Again – A Short Story

Written in the Stars – A Short Story

Full Circle – A Short Story

Worth Fighting For – A Bobby & Kit Novella

Printed in Great Britain
by Amazon

52541655R00238